RAVE REVIEWS FOR RONDA THOMPSON!

PRICKLY PEAR

"A sure bet. High-tension desire and quick tempers between Wade and Cam make for an exciting, delicious read. Especially fun and engaging, this one is an unexpected surprise!"

—*Romantic Times*

"Ronda Thompson's *Prickly Pear* holds the flavor of a true western historical romance skillfully seasoned with sexual tension."

—Jodi Thomas, two-time RITA award-winning author of *To Kiss A Texan*

"Wow! From the very first page, you'll feel like you've been strapped onto the back of a wild mustang. Hang on. You're in for the ride of your life!"

—*Under the Covers Book Reviews*

COUGAR'S WOMAN

"*Cougar's Woman* has an energy that, once you begin reading, makes you want to read on to find out what's going to happen in this tale of the wild and woolly West. Enjoy the synergy between the feisty heroine and the mule-headed hero as they discover romance."

—*Affaire de Coeur*

"Ronda Thompson has a gem here. When I turned to page one, I leapt in and was a goner. I loved the characters and the mischief created in the bumptious trail to romance."

—*Romance Communications*

"*Cougar's Woman* is a book filled with compassion, understanding and wisdom. The plot twists and turns, evolves, carries the reader along on a floodtide of action, reaction, emotional involvement and surprises. Ms. Thompson has proven herself to be a writer of distinction and power."

—*Under the Covers Book Reviews*

AN EASY MISTAKE

"You'd better go inside," he said.

She glanced around, fumbling with her night dress nervously, but she made no move to follow his suggestion. "I'm wide-awake. Maybe we could talk some more."

"Talk about what?"

Her gaze wouldn't meet his. "Mistakes," she answered, chewing her bottom lip in a manner he'd come to recognize. She wrestled with something, but whatever it was, his own struggle was worse. The longer she stood before him, the harder it was to refrain from touching her.

"We can talk about mistakes," he answered. "And the one you're making right now."

She lifted her gaze abruptly. "What mistake?" she whispered, and her lips looked so petal soft, so tempting, he had to turn away from her.

"I want to kiss you," he answered bluntly. "And if you don't go, I am going to, whether you ask me to or not."

Other *Leisure* books by Ronda Thompson:
PRICKLY PEAR
COUGAR'S WOMAN

In Trouble's Arms

Ronda Thompson

LEISURE BOOKS   NEW YORK CITY

A LEISURE BOOK®

May 2000

Published by

Dorchester Publishing Co., Inc.
276 Fifth Avenue
New York, NY 10001

ISBN 0-8439-4716-0

To my great-aunts, Cloye, June and Myrtle. Thank you for the love and support you have given to me over the years, and for the wonderful childhood memories I will always cherish.

In Trouble's Arms

Chapter One

Loreen Matland had never envisioned her wedding day this way. In what seemed a lifetime ago, her innocent youth, she had seen herself wearing a white lace gown, standing inside a church. The morning should have been that of a cool spring day, when the promise of summer kissed the air but couldn't fully thaw the remains of winter. There should have been friends and family. There should have been love. And at the very least, there should have been a choice.

As the hot sun beat down upon her, Loreen lifted the limp folds of her soiled work dress and wiped the moisture from her face. She glanced down at her hands. They were red and chapped from a morning spent behind a plow. She doubted a wedding ring would be slipped upon her finger today, and wondered how differently her life might have turned out had she been given one five years ago, as should have been her right.

What might have been no longer mattered. Loreen tried to remind herself of all that did. Survival, the children, a chance to escape the destruction she had single-handedly brought down upon her family. Dreams of white wedding gowns and sins without consequence were just that . . . dreams.

"Reckon that's him?" Toby, her younger brother, asked.

Shading her eyes from the sun, Loreen squinted at the hazy images of two men riding toward them. "I don't suppose anyone else would be venturing out this way with Preacher White. Go to the house and see what Wren's gotten into. Make sure she stays inside. And fetch the rifle down from over the door."

"Heck, Loreen, we ain't gonna shoot him, are we?"

"Depends," she answered. "If he's as ugly as a mud fence, put the rifle back. If he's not, fill his hide full of buckshot and send him packing."

"That don't make sense, Lori" Toby argued. "Why would you want to marry an ugly feller?"

"Never you mind. Just do as you're told."

The boy nodded and moved toward the house. Loreen watched until he made it inside, waiting to see his shadowy figure at the window. Toby was a good boy. He didn't give her as much trouble as the feisty Wren. Unfortunately, he couldn't shoot a gun worth spit.

As the men drew nearer, the tempo of Loreen's heartbeat increased. Self-consciously, she straightened her clothing and tried to calm herself. She recognized Mr. White, a traveling preacher, by the mule he rode. The other man, the one she intended to marry, she had never seen before.

Tears threatened her eyes, but Loreen blinked them

back. She was a Matland, and nothing short of cholera or murderers got the best of her clan. Life had left her few choices since the death of her parents. To survive, she would do what was necessary.

Preacher White stopped a short distance away, pulling a handkerchief over the lower half of his face. He'd obviously heard of the sickness that plagued her family. That was just as well. Loreen wanted a measure of privacy. She and Jake Winslow had a few things to discuss before she did any "I do"ing.

With the sun directly behind him, her husband-to-be's features were hard to discern. She doubted Toby would be able see him clearly from the house. He wouldn't know whether to fill him full of buckshot, or put the gun back over the door. That was just as well, too.

She hadn't been thinking straight when she'd given her younger brother the instructions. Tired to the teeth, she hadn't realized that Preacher White would find it odd if she ran off her intended the minute he came within shooting distance.

The fabrication she'd come up with was that their families had known each other back east. At least that was the story she'd told Jake Winslow to tell the preacher once he found him. The two of them had exchanged one letter apiece since Winslow had answered her advertisement for a husband. The letters had sealed a bargain but they'd given her little insight to the man approaching her.

She supposed all that mattered was that he'd agreed to her terms, and that the small town of Miller's Passing would soon know she had a husband—a protector. A shadow fell across her. She glanced up, her breath catching in her throat. If her brother could see what she saw, buckshot would be flying.

The man sat tall in the saddle, broad in the shoulders, lean everywhere else. His face, with a coating of dark stubble along his cheeks, was the type that would make a woman look twice at him. He stared at her from deep-set eyes fringed by dark, thick lashes.

Like quilt squares, separately, his features were nothing out of the ordinary, but arranged all together, along with his strong jawline and slightly cleft chin, they made up something special. Which immediately put her on the alert. One of the hardest lessons she'd learned had been never to trust a good-looking man.

"I'd like to speak to the lady of the house," he said.

The man had the kind of voice rightfully belonging to his handsome face: smooth as aged whiskey and just as satisfying if one were trying to warm up inside.

"Did you hear me, child?"

Suspecting that the children had come creeping from the house, she cast a warning glance behind her, but they'd done what they were told and stayed inside. Her gaze snapped back to Jake Winslow, if indeed this was the man she intended to marry.

"Who are you?" Loreen demanded.

"She's expecting me. Tell her Jake Winslow's here."

"*She's* not expecting you. I am. I'm the lady of the house."

The man laughed outright. "I expected a widow woman, not an orphaned child."

Their meeting had already turned sour and they weren't yet properly introduced. Loreen drew herself up to her full height. "If you've done any living at all, you should know people don't always get what they expect. I turned twenty-one a week ago. I'm well past marrying age."

"Twenty-one?" He looked her up and down, then

glanced at the surrounding area. "The place isn't much."

"I never said otherwise. It isn't much, but it's yours if you keep your end of the bargain."

"You're sure you want to go through with this?" he asked, shoving his hat up from his forehead.

With his hat pushed back, she noticed the inky blackness of his hair. He had blue eyes, as did she, only his were the dark color of the sky before a thunderstorm. Something was wrong. No man who looked like this had to marry a woman who'd advertised for a husband.

"Depends. What's wrong with you, mister? Why'd you agree to marry a woman you've never set eyes on before?"

His smile faded. "I'm here, and I'll keep my end of the bargain. Do my reasons matter?"

Loreen tried to decide. This wouldn't be a real marriage. She wouldn't be his wife for more than a few months. Just long enough to raise a decent crop, sell it, then take the children back east. She didn't have a choice, or she wouldn't have stooped to such desperate measures in the first place. So what if the man wanted to keep secrets. She'd kept a few from him, as well.

"Are you ready, then?" she asked.

"Mind if I climb down from my horse?"

"I suppose you should," she agreed. "It might be wise to give me a hug and a peck on the cheek. You did tell Preacher White we've known each other for some time, didn't you?"

"I told him," he answered, dismounting. "But I don't know if he believed me."

"Then you'd better be convincing."

When he stood before her, she had to look up.

15

Despite his unshaven face and the dust on his clothes, he was regrettably handsome. He also appeared as if he had the muscle to push a plow and lift a bale or two.

"Will I do?"

She realized she'd been staring and felt a blush rise in her cheeks. "We'd better commence with the hugging and kissing so we can get married and have done with it."

A slow smile crossed his lips. "You don't beat around the bush, do you . . . ?"

"Loreen," she quickly reminded him. "And no, Mr. Winslow, I don't believe in wasting time. There's chores left to finish."

"Get rid of that braid."

Her hand went automatically to her hair. "I-I beg your pardon?"

"Let down your hair," he repeated. "The braid makes you look younger than you are. Remove that loose apron tied around you, too. Bargain or no bargain, I'm not taking a child to wife."

"You won't be *taking* anything, Mr. Winslow," she reminded him, her voice sharp. "This marriage is in name only. I'll have your word you'll honor that part of the bargain, as well."

His gaze roamed her from head to toe again. "No need to worry on that count."

He'd insulted her. Yet Loreen wasn't offended by his lack of interest in her, just relieved. With a sigh, she undid her braid and shook her hair loose around her shoulders. She removed the baggy apron from around her neck. Winslow suddenly appeared less cocky than he'd been a moment earlier.

His eyes widened a fraction, then narrowed, running

over her as if he were appraising a horse up for sale. Her skin began to tingle everywhere his gaze landed. She broke into a full-blown blush when he stared too long at her bodice.

The dress was old, a tight fit and threadbare. If she had the gun from over the door, she'd fill him full of buckshot herself for his impropriety.

"If you've looked your fill, we should get on with the wedding."

His response was slow in coming. It took a while for his eyes to make their way back up to her face. Loreen tilted her chin defiantly, refusing to allow him to fluster her.

"First we have another matter to attend to. I'll try to be convincing."

Before Loreen understood his intentions, he took her in his arms. His mouth settled firmly over hers, drowning out her gasp of surprise. She'd been kissed before—long ago by an eighteen-year-old boy and recently by Billy Waylan, a disgusting exchange forced upon her. But Jake Winslow's kiss was different from any she had experienced. His lips were warm and teasing against hers, not clumsy or rough. Gentle persuasion lowered her guard, and in that instant Loreen felt an unfamiliar flutter deep within.

She tried to pull back, startled by her reaction, but the stranger held her tight. Heat snaked a path up her body. Her knees felt weak. Afraid they might buckle, she clung to him for support. That was when she became aware of the hard feel of him pressed intimately against her.

With as much strength as she could muster, she pushed him away. To his credit, he released her. His eyes were as dark as midnight when he looked down at her.

"Reckon that convinced him?"

"I should slap your face," she said, embarrassed by the huskiness of her voice.

"Yes, probably." His gaze swung toward the preacher. "But the good reverend might find your actions suspicious."

He'd made a valid point. There wasn't a darn thing she could do about his familiarity with her. Not if she wanted to carry out her plan. Not if she wanted protection from Billy Waylan. Loreen swallowed her pride and tried to slow her racing heart.

"I suspect Preacher White is anxious to get to town. We've wasted too much time already."

"You're still willing to go through with the wedding?"

Willing wasn't what she felt—*desperate* described her feelings better. Her mind screamed no, but her lips said yes. It occurred to her he might be having second thoughts. "And you? Are you still willing?"

His gaze slid over her. "You're a woman grown, and although the place isn't much, it's more than I have. I'm willing."

A lump formed in her throat, and she couldn't call to the preacher. Instead she motioned him forward. He didn't venture too close before he opened the worn Bible he held. In a daze, she heard him say a few words about marriage; then he asked questions. She answered yes to all of them, although she didn't really hear what he asked, but knew to respond only when he stopped and looked at her.

Jake Winslow answered the same, and, with a loud whack that startled her out of her stupor, the reverend closed his Bible.

"Is your pa any better?" he called.

Loreen shook her head sadly. "He's gone. Died two days ago."

A curious glance from her new husband sent heat rushing to her face.

The preacher frowned. "Sorry about your troubles. Billy isn't gonna like this, you marrying up with another man."

Although her heart lurched against her chest, she tried to school her features into a cool expression. "I'm sure he'll accept matters, since he can no longer control them."

Preacher White shook his head. His gaze settled on Jake Winslow. "You'd best watch your back, mister. Good luck; you'll both need it," he muttered in parting.

She watched him turn his horse toward town, her spirits sinking. Her new husband lifted a brow.

"What was that all about?"

"You'll want to put your horse in the barn."

His hand closed around her arm. "Your letter said your menfolk were already gone. And who is Billy?"

The lump finally made it down her throat with a loud gulp. She had hoped she would have more time to explain the situation fully to him, time to ease him into the horrible mistake he had just made. Supposing there was no time like the present, she turned to him.

"My pa's been gone for two months. I couldn't let anyone know I'm here alone—defenseless."

"Defenseless against what?"

Loreen began plucking at the limp folds of her skirt. "More of a who than a what. Billy Waylan. He has a mind to marry me and have this land."

Winslow blinked. "You had a man willing to marry

19

you and you went and advertised for a husband? Are you daft?"

She straightened and glared at him. "I can read, write, and do figures. I'm not daft, Mr. Winslow, but I am certain any fate would be better than marrying Billy Waylan."

He gathered the reins of his horse. "What's wrong with the fellow?"

"Besides being meaner than a snake and about as principled, besides being the town bully, a drinker, and a womanizer, he's a murderer. He killed my older brother in cold blood. He killed him because of me."

Her explanation was as good as a horse kick in the gut. Jake knew trouble when he saw it, and Loreen Matland had it scribbled all over her. He'd known the minute she took down her hair and stripped away the baggy apron: she wasn't the child he'd first mistaken her for—not by a far stretch.

The woman's long hair shimmered in the sunlight, a mixture of red, gold, and brown—not one color, but an enticing blend of several. Her eyes were the purest shade of blue, and her mouth . . . she had a pouty rosebud mouth that begged for a man's kisses without saying a word.

As she took the reins from him and moved toward a ramshackle barn, the sway of her hips drew his attention. Her dress had seen better days, but the ripe breasts straining against the fabric, the smallness of her waist, and the flare of her hips all added up to one thing: she was the kind of woman men killed for— died for—the kind a man should avoid at all cost.

He'd ridden away from trouble only to run smack-dab into its arms again. He'd hoped she would be a plain woman. He'd hoped the farm would be more than an eyesore against a barren backdrop. He'd hoped to make a new life for himself to go along with his new name. But as she had said, *People don't always get what they expect.*

Although his instincts told him to grab his horse, mount up, and ride hell-for-leather away from Loreen Matland, he found himself following along behind her. Jake considered his situation. All he had to do was keep his hands off of her and raise a decent crop. They would split the money. She would move on and he'd take over the farm. It had sounded easy. Too easy, he should have realized.

Remaining unmoved by this woman's beauty wouldn't be easy. Raising a crop in this rain-starved, godforsaken Texas territory could be next to impossible. Now he had to contend with a man who might hold it against him that he'd married the woman he considered his future bride—a man who had killed her brother.

"Damn," Jake swore softly, his gaze still glued to the hypnotic sway of her hips. What other surprises had Loreen Matland failed to mention in her letter?

Chapter Two

There were two of them: a boy Jake suspected was about twelve and a girl no older than five. They came creeping into the barn while he unsaddled his horse, hiding in the shadows as if he wouldn't notice them. Jake had developed a sixth sense during the past year. He noticed.

"You need a cat," he said to the woman silently watching him. "I think I hear a couple of mice scurrying around in here."

Loreen shuddered delicately, a complete contradiction to the strong-willed, no-nonsense persona she'd presented earlier.

"We have a cat, but he's good for nothing. He'd rather eat scraps from the table than catch a mouse. I keep hoping he'll run off."

A small gasp sounded. The girl stepped from the shadows, a mop of red curls bouncing with her walk.

She stopped a few feet away and planted her hands on her waist.

"Midnight ain't going nowhere," she said. "He's my kitty."

His gaze settled on Loreen. Her composure slipped for a moment, her face paling before she wheeled around to confront the girl.

"Don't say 'ain't,' Wren. Midnight *isn't* going anywhere."

"That's what I said," the girl insisted.

"Jake Winslow, this is Wren. Wren, this is Mr. Winslow."

Midnight's fate obviously forgotten, Wren came closer. The child looked him up and down. "You need your face shaved."

Jake ran a hand across his whiskered cheeks. "And you need yours washed."

The child drew herself up indignantly. "Do not. I washed it yesterday."

"Toby, I told you to make her wash this morning," Loreen scolded.

As if that were an invitation to exit his hiding place, the boy stepped forward. "I told her to," he defended.

"You know telling her doesn't do any good. You have to stand over her and make sure she does it."

"I'm tired of being the nanny," the boy declared.

"I ain't no goat," Wren piped up.

Jake cleared his throat. All three of them snapped to attention. "Are there any more surprises lurking in the shadows?" he asked Loreen.

She blushed. "No."

"You didn't tell me about these two, among other things," he added.

"I didn't think Toby and Wren were any of your

business." She'd regained her cool composure, staring haughtily down her perfect nose at him.

He removed his hat and ran a hand through his hair. "I thought I had two mouths to feed; now I have four. I'd say that was my business."

"I don't eat much," the boy said quietly. "And Lori, she doesn't eat hardly anything."

The urge to saddle up again overtook Jake. He'd gotten more than he bargained for by marrying Loreen Matland. He wasn't going to take on a man possibly set on killing him and two kids to boot. As far as he knew, he didn't even like children. A small hand curled into his. He glanced down to see Wren staring up at him.

"My brother and sister don't eat much because they give what little we have to me. I'm trying hard not to be hungry, but I am."

His heart did a funny little lurch. He stared down into her big blue eyes and, just as he had earlier, felt as if he'd been kicked in the gut. Hell, the least he could do was give this family a decent meal. Jake set his jaw and replaced his hat. He nodded toward the rifle clutched in the boy's hand.

"Know how use that?"

He wouldn't met his gaze. "If I knew very good, we wouldn't be hungry."

Jake threw his saddle over a board and walked forward, taking the rifle from the boy. "I'll get supper."

A satisfied smile settled over Loreen Matland's tempting mouth. Jake frowned. Later, he'd tell her he wouldn't stay. He had enough troubles without stirring hers into his pot. A man couldn't very well lie low and escape notice with a woman who looked like Loreen trailing along behind him.

"You ain't gonna kill any rabbits or such, are you?" Wren had blocked his escape. Her tiny hands were on her waist again.

"Figured I might," he answered. "Do you have a problem with that?"

Her red curls bounced when she nodded.

"Wren loves animals," Loreen said. "All animals."

Jake sighed. "What does Wren eat?"

"I like berries," the little girl supplied. "And candy."

"I'll see if I can't scrounge up a few berries, but candy doesn't grow wild. You'll eat whatever I bring home."

He thought the little hellion would argue, but the girl's sister snatched Wren's hand and pulled her from his path.

"Let Mr. Winslow pass," Loreen said. "We have things to do."

The child groaned. "Please don't make me do chores, Loreen. I'm too tired."

"You're never too tired to play. Come along. You can start the wash."

Her eyes full of rebellion, Wren followed her older sister from the barn. Jake started after them, noticed the boy, and motioned him forward.

"Come along. It's time you learned to shoot."

Loreen wilted beneath the afternoon sun. Her hands were raw and blistered from pushing the plow through rock-hard ground. She thought by now she would have developed calluses, but her delicate hands refused to toughen up.

"Come on, Ben," she called, urging the old plow horse forward with a flick of the reins. She glanced nervously toward the house, worried about leaving Wren unattended.

It was bad enough that she and Toby were burdened with so many responsibilities since their parents' deaths, but Wren was just a little girl, too young to be worried about where her next meal would come from or faced with days of drudgery instead of play.

Still, they all had to pull their weight. A little laundry wouldn't hurt Wren. The child had been spoiled all of her life. Even today, Loreen hadn't allowed the wash water to boil, fearful Wren would scorch herself. Their clothes wouldn't be as clean as she'd like, but then, all they seemed to do daily was get them filthy again.

A glance at her dress verified the fact. She was coated with dust. It was everywhere—in her nose, in her teeth when she gritted them. She ran a hand over her stinging eyes, wishing she could summon tears to soothe them.

She hadn't had time to grieve the loss of her mother. She'd been too busy trying to save her father. Her older brother wasn't even cold in his grave when the sickness had struck. There had been no time to deal with the injustice of his death. Nor had her father been well enough to demand restitution.

In the space of two months, Loreen had gone from being the eldest daughter to the head of the household. Her brother Toby held his feelings inside, trying to be a man when he was still a twelve-year-old boy. Wren woke her often during the night, screaming in her sleep, crying out for the comfort of a mother's arms.

The responsibilities of mother, father, provider, and protector were wearing on Loreen. She'd been too afraid to go into town for supplies, too frightened to let Toby go without her. She was drowning in despair, and her only saving grace rested in the hard, cracked ground beneath her feet and a man she'd never set eyes on until today. A man, she suspected, who was already planning to abandon her to her own sorry fate.

Loreen couldn't blame Jake Winslow if he rode out and never looked back. Her letter had been misleading. She'd made her proposition sound simple. Of course, if she'd told the entire truth, no man in his right mind would have agreed to marry her. Maybe his leaving would be just as well.

He wasn't at all what she'd expected. The remembered feel of his lips against hers made her shiver in the afternoon heat. Jake Winslow was trouble. And trouble, the Matlands already had plenty of. It wouldn't be the first time a man ran out on her, but it would be the last time one took advantage of her naivete.

A shrill scream jerked her from her thoughts. Loreen's heart started to pound. *Wren.* She threw down the reins and ran for the house, cursing the plowed ground that slowed her progress. Had Wren scorched herself? Had Billy Waylan finally found the nerve to encroach on the Matlands' sickness-stricken territory?

Any number of horrors might befall an innocent left alone in the yard. Loreen grabbed a heavy stick on her way. If danger threatened Wren, whatever or whomever it was would have to go through her.

It was a whom. Two of them: her brother and the stranger she'd married a short time earlier. Loreen stopped short at the sight of them, placing a hand against her pounding heart.

"What's wrong?" she managed to gasp.

Wren screamed again and ran toward her, burying her little face in the folds of Loreen's dirty dress. Toby grinned and raised two hairless animals for her inspection.

"Rabbits, Loreen. I shot one of them."

Trying to soothe the distraught Wren, Loreen couldn't help but notice the loud grumble of her stomach. Despite the gruesome sight, her mouth watered. She hadn't had a decent meal in weeks.

"You shouldn't have shown them to Wren," she scolded her brother. "You've upset her."

"Heck, we've got to eat. She's old enough to understand it was them or us."

Although his argument had merit, Loreen pulled the girl to her side and walked toward the house, careful to keep herself between Wren and the rabbits. The child's aversion to meat, or rather to killing anything living, had come on the heels of her parents' passing. Loreen suspected Wren was just now understanding the finality of death.

"Put them on the porch," she instructed Toby. "I'll tend to them after I've finished plowing."

Jake stepped forward. "The children are hungry, and you look like you're about to drop. Start the meal; I'll work the field."

Telling him to go on and ride out rested on the tip of her tongue. He'd at least provided them with a decent meal. Loreen glanced tiredly at the waiting field. Toby tried to help with the plowing, but the past two months were starting to show on his reed-thin body. He couldn't muster the strength to do any better than her. Plain and simple, she needed Jake Winslow, for however long he would stay.

"Fetch me some firewood for the stove, Toby." She

bent to look at Wren. "Why don't you find Midnight? He's probably curled up asleep in the barn."

The child blinked back tears. She sniffed. "You mean I don't have to finish the laundry?"

From the looks of things, Wren had barely started the chore. Loreen couldn't find it in her heart to be angry. "I'll do the washing while dinner is cooking. Run along."

Wren didn't have to be told twice. The child had an aversion to more than just eating meat; she also had one to work. Toby placed the rabbits and the shotgun on the porch, then walked toward their dwindling woodpile. Loreen was left standing alone with Jake.

"I found a few blackberries." He extended a small pouch. "But berries aren't going to put meat on that little girl's bones. If you have the supplies, I'd make a stew out of the rabbits. It'll last longer."

She wasn't in need of his instruction. Loreen knew a stew would last longer, but she wasn't certain there were enough vegetables left in the root cellar to prepare one.

"We're short on supplies," she admitted. "I haven't gone into town for a while."

"Short on money, too?"

"I have a little. Maybe enough for flour and sugar but little else."

Jake reached inside his pocket and withdrew a few coins. "Take this and get what you need tomorrow morning."

Accepting money from a stranger felt wrong. Loreen's suspicion that the man planned to abandon her grew. It was as if he were trying to pay her off. She didn't reach for the money, but glanced into his eyes. He was leaving, all right, probably tonight—sneaking away under the cover of darkness.

"You're not staying, are you?"

A guilty blush crept into his handsome face, but he didn't glance away from her. "No."

Rather than slump in defeat, she lifted her chin. "At least you're honest. I can't accept your money. Since there is no longer a bargain between us, it would be the same as accepting charity. Good-bye, Mr. Winslow."

Loreen gathered her dirty skirts in one hand and marched toward the house. She didn't get far before Jake blocked her exit.

"Stop being stubborn. I won't leave a couple of kids here to starve because of your pride."

Well, he obviously had a conscience; Loreen had to give him that much. But he'd also belittled her efforts to care for her family, suggesting she'd actually allow them to starve.

"Toby and Wren are not going to starve. I don't care what I have to do; I'll make sure of that!"

His gaze lowered to her lips. "Those words may come back to haunt you. You're too hardheaded to swallow your pride and accept my money. I hope you're not forced to swallow it later and accept money from a man who'll expect far more for a few dollars than I do."

It took a moment for Loreen to understand his warning. She might not have understood it at all had he not kept running his gaze over her in an appraising manner. Did he think for one second she'd stoop to . . . ? The urge to slap his arrogant face surfaced. Loreen squelched the temptation. She would not resort to violence.

"I'd rather die," she ground out through her teeth.

"Then Toby and Wren would starve for sure." He stuffed the coins down the front of her bodice and turned away. "I'll plow for a while and have a bowl of stew before I go."

Her skin tingled where his hand had brushed her flesh. Her head pounded from the rush of anger his bold actions caused. If she were to be totally honest, she was almost as angry at herself. Winslow was right: her pride should not compete with Toby and Wren's welfare. She should have accepted the money before he had an opportunity to force it upon her. Despite the realization, she couldn't bring herself to thank him.

Jake wouldn't save her from the nightmare her life had become. But he had put off starvation for a while longer. Tomorrow she must go into town for supplies—must face a possible confrontation with Billy Waylan. Loreen choked down panic. She wouldn't think about the future. Her grumbling stomach allowed her to think only about the moment. Tomorrow would come soon enough.

Forced to make the best of a bad situation, Loreen went into the house and added the money to her small supply. When Toby entered, she instructed him to stoke the fire in the stove and put a large pan of water on to boil. He grumbled about women's work but went about attending the task. The root cellar didn't hold many treasures. She did manage to scrounge up a few potatoes and an onion.

Preparing the stew took longer than she anticipated. Loreen used the blackberries and what was left of the sugar and flour to make a pie. It had been so long since the children had had a treat. Maybe if she used the rest of the supplies she wouldn't be able to talk herself out of going into town the next morning.

The smell of food cooking made her stomach growl louder. Loreen summoned her strength, intent on finishing the laundry. She heard Wren singing in the barn. Toby had joined Jake in the field, walking ahead of Ben to throw the biggest rocks from his path. Her savior for a day handled the plow well—at least, much better than she herself did. He'd have the field plowed in half the time it would take her.

Maybe she shouldn't be in such an all-fired hurry to see him go. So what if he'd turned out to be more handsome than she'd anticipated? So what if he was mannerless and arrogant? And what difference did it make that his kiss had shaken her to the core?

He wouldn't be kissing her again. She could look past his raven hair and stormy blue eyes, see beyond his cocky smile. Loreen could view him for what he was—a means to an end, nothing more and nothing less. She'd learned her lessons of the past all too well.

Thoughtfully, she let her gaze stray toward the field. Jake had ceased his plowing. She frowned. Was he stopping already? His lack of stamina disappointed her. A moment later, she realized he meant only to remove his shirt. Loreen sucked in her breath sharply at the sight of him half-naked. If she thought Jake Winslow had looked sturdy with clothes, he looked better without them.

His skin was darkened by the sun, smooth slopes and valleys of polished copper. The muscles in his arms were well defined, his stomach flat and corded like the old scrub board she used for washing clothes.

A smattering of ebony hair covered his chest—not too thick, but not too sparse, either. The sun overhead suddenly felt hotter, the air around her thick. Loreen knew she was staring. She couldn't help herself.

"My lord," she whispered. "He has to go. And the sooner the better."

Chapter Three

Jake Winslow couldn't be gone fast enough in Loreen's opinion, but she felt honor-bound to feed him supper. If not for him, there wouldn't be a thick rabbit stew bubbling on the stove or a freshly baked blackberry pie cooling on the porch. Contrary to her earlier suspicions, the man had plenty of stamina. He'd done a good day's work in the space of one afternoon. She owed him something for his trouble.

"Toby, find Wren. I imagine she's fallen asleep in the barn. Then both of you take some soap and water to your hands and face before you come in for supper."

Loreen plucked more laundry from the line and tried to keep from staring at Jake. She'd brought a couple of buckets of water, and at that moment he was in the process of washing the dirt from his face and upper body. It wasn't decent, his lack of modesty—even if she saw nothing he should be embarrassed about. Still, a man ought to keep his clothes on around a woman he hardly knew.

"Could I trouble you for something to dry off with?" he asked.

She'd been so flustered by the sight of him strolling into the yard without his shirt, she'd forgotten to set a towel beside the buckets. Loreen plucked a threadbare cloth from her basket, keeping her eyes downcast as she approached him.

"The stew smells good."

He had a nice scent, also. A combination of soap, dust, and honest labor. "I suppose I should thank you for all you've done today."

"Since you can't seem to look me in the eye, it'd be hard to tell if you were sincere."

Her gaze lifted. He had slicked his dark hair back, showing his handsome face to full advantage. There was *something* wrong with Jake Winslow, all right. With his looks, she imagined he could have women lined up to marry him. The fact that he'd settled for a woman he didn't know confirmed what she already knew about handsome men: they couldn't be trusted.

She took note of his broad shoulders. Droplets of water clung to the coarse hairs sprinkled across his chest. She followed one drop's journey down his corded abdomen to the waistband of his pants.

"The towel."

Realizing he'd caught her gawking, Loreen snapped her gaze back to his face. She flung the towel at his chest, jerking her hand away when her fingers met with warm skin.

He said nothing, just stared into her eyes as he dried himself. Loreen refused to glance away, determined to pretend his nakedness didn't affect her one way or the other. The longer their gazes remained locked, the hotter her cheeks grew. He wasn't looking through or around her, but seemed to be staring into her very soul.

"You're a beautiful woman, Loreen. You shouldn't have any trouble finding a man to take you to wife. And in truth."

"I don't want a husband in truth," she countered, cursing the rush of pleasure his compliment delivered. "Even if I did, there isn't a man around these parts brave enough to court me. Not after what happened to my older brother. Billy Waylan has his brand on me, and the whole town in his pocket. No one has the nerve to go up against him."

"No one but you," he said, a smidgen of respect creeping into his voice.

"So it would seem."

He smiled. "Do you think I'm a coward?"

"I don't know you well enough to make judgments, Mr. Winslow."

His laugh startled her. "I know you well enough to know that's a bold-faced lie. You've been judging my muster since I stepped foot on this sorry excuse for a farm."

Loreen stiffened. "I assure you, you're mistaken."

"You've been watching me—or should I say, trying not to watch me—all day."

"I've paid you scant attention," Loreen persisted. "And now I can add conceit to the rest of your unappealing qualities."

"There," he said in triumph. "You just admitted you've been sizing me up."

"I did no such thing." Loreen's cheeks were starting to burn again, but with anger rather than embarrassment. She thought she'd done a good job of watching Jake without his noticing.

"I've been watching you, too," he admitted. "Sometimes it just happens that way between a man and a woman. They both like what they see and there's no use denying it."

There was more than one reason to ignore the attraction he claimed stood between them. Loreen knew where it could lead. She wouldn't be made a fool of by a man again. Besides needing Jake Winslow to help with the crop and to protect her family, she had no use for him. Another life waited for her and the children back east. Nothing would compromise her plans to escape this godforsaken, brutal country.

"I'm glad you're leaving," she snapped. "The more I know about you, the less I like."

He handed her the towel and reached for his dusty shirt. "And the last thing I need is to be strapped with a couple of kids and a woman with trouble breathing down her neck. At least we both agree that my going is for the best."

When he shrugged into his shirt, Loreen noticed the way his muscles rippled. The fact that she couldn't seem to be around Jake without noticing his masculinity irked her. She had thought the man who would answer her ad would be older, maybe down on his luck, ideally a man who reminded her of a father, or a kindly uncle. Someone who could help with the workload and protect her family without stirring up her female emotions. Someone who could finally make her feel safe again. Winslow was not that someone.

Uncomfortable with the silence that had settled between them, Loreen cupped her hands to her mouth and called Toby and Wren in for supper. The children came running from the barn. She walked up the steps, pausing to turn to him.

"Are you coming in for supper?"

Jake had been watching her hips again. He quickly glanced up, and although he said he'd eat, his decision to leave almost had him refusing. The sooner he left the better. The way he'd been staring at Loreen Matland all day was even more reason to leave.

"You should eat before you go," she said, as if sensing a battle taking place within him.

He nodded and followed her, thinking Loreen was the type of woman a man might follow to hell and back. Well, he'd already been to hell and back during the past year. His dreams of finding a peaceful place to settle and put down roots had crumbled the minute Loreen had began explaining her situation. No one would blame him for abandoning her. No one but his conscience.

The small log cabin's interior was cozy and clean. There was one room at the rear and a loft above, where he suspected the children slept. Toby helped his older sister put wooden bowls on the table, and Wren sat in a rocker, still pouting, he supposed, over the rabbits.

"Can I help?" he asked Loreen.

She nodded toward a bench at the table. "Sit down. There isn't much, so it won't take long to put out."

He glanced at the little girl. "Are you coming to supper, Wren?"

A mop of furiously shaking red curls was his answer.

"She said she wouldn't eat the stew because of the

rabbits," Loreen explained quietly. "I'm at my wits' end with her. She has to eat more than berries and sweets."

Jake walked to the rocker, hefted Wren up, and seated himself. He settled the stiff, skinny girl on his lap.

"Sometimes we can't choose what goes into our bellies, Wren. We have to eat what's been provided for us. If you don't eat, you'll get skinny and sick. You don't want that, do you?"

"I don't want to get sick," she whispered. Her big blue eyes widened. "My mama and papa got sick. Was it because they didn't eat rabbit stew?"

He could be such an idiot at times. Jake had already forgotten the Matlands' circumstances. He didn't know about the mother passing on from the sickness as well.

"No," he answered, unconsciously smoothing a red curl from her face. "They couldn't help but get sick, but you can. I want you to come over to the table and have some stew. Don't think about what's in the bowl; just think about how it will help Loreen and Toby if you stay well for them. Think about how it will help you do your chores."

The child frowned. "I don't like chores."

"No one does," he assured her. "But they have to get done. And if you're feeling strong and healthy, you can do them twice as fast so you'll have plenty of time to play."

She seemed to consider his words. "You mean, if I eat a rabbit, I'll be as fast as one?"

He drew a blank. Jake wasn't used to being around children, didn't know they could come up with such ridiculous notions. He glanced toward Loreen. She wore a slight smile that suggested he was on his own.

"There's only one way to find out." Jake lifted Wren from his lap and rose. He steered her toward the supper table.

Although the vegetables were a bit on the skimpy side, the meal was one of the best he'd had in a long time. Wren picked at her stew at first; then hunger obviously got the best of her. The child ate two heaping bowlsful. Jake discovered Loreen knew her way around a kitchen when he tasted her berry pie. He pushed back from the table feeling as if he'd pop.

"I don't know when I've had a better meal," he complimented the cook.

Her cheeks turned a becoming shade of pink. "Thank you, Mr. Winslow." Loreen rose from the table. "I'd better get this mess cleaned up."

She looked bone-weary to Jake. Her shoulders were too slim to carry the burdens left on her by her deceased parents. As if Toby understood his next chore, he began stoking the fireplace next to the old rocker.

"It's hotter than heck during the day around here, but the nights still get chilly," Loreen explained. She stretched her back and began gathering the dishes.

Jake turned to Wren. "Now would be a good time to see if the stew worked. I wonder if you can get these dishes to the dry sink by the time I fetch a bucket of water?"

The girl cast him a wary look. He thought she wouldn't be tricked into doing chores for a moment; then she was out of her seat. Her older sister's mouth fell open when the child began gathering the dishes. Jake rose and started for the door.

"I'll empty the buckets and refill them."

"Maybe we can hunt again tomorrow, Mr. Winslow," Toby called, his voice hopeful.

"I'll help you with the buckets," Loreen said. Once outside, she wheeled around to face him. "It's not getting any earlier. You should go."

"Guess I've worn out my welcome."

She lowered her gaze. "Toby and Wren like you. You have a way with children, did you know that?"

Jake frowned. "I don't know how I could. I don't know much about kids. I don't think I even like them."

"Well, they like you . . . and that's why the sooner you leave the better." She walked over and emptied the buckets they'd used to wash. "Good luck, Mr. Winslow."

Glancing toward the barn, then at her retreating figure, Jake admitted she was right. He should saddle up and go before it grew darker. His feet wouldn't cooperate. Jake swore softly and went after her. He took the buckets from her hands as he drew up beside her.

"I have time to fetch water for you. Go on back to the house."

"I've fetched those buckets back and forth from the watering hole plenty, Mr. Winslow. Just leave and be done with it."

"I'll go when I'm damn good and ready!"

Jake wouldn't be bossed around by a woman. He set off toward the watering hole in the distance. When had he developed a conscience? He'd been on the run for over a year and hadn't given anyone else a second thought. He had no family of his own, hadn't had one for a long time. Loreen Matland was trouble, all right. She actually had him feeling guilty about leaving her. The marriage wasn't supposed to be one in truth. He owed her nothing. She didn't even know his real name!

Angry both at himself and at her, he filled the water buckets. Jake was in the process of stomping his way

41

back to the cabin when a sound drifted to him on the night. He stopped to listen. There it was again, the soft sound of a woman weeping. He set the buckets down.

In a clearing where three crosses rose from the cracked ground, he found her. Loreen was on her knees, her face hidden in her hands. Sobs racked her thin shoulders. She looked so small, so helpless and defeated. Jake didn't remember going to her, but suddenly he was touching her shoulder. She glanced up, tears streaming down her cheeks.

"I haven't even had time to mourn them," she whispered, as if in apology. "It all happened so fast. First my older brother. Then Mama took to her bed. I thought she was grieving, but I noticed the sweat on her brow and the dull look in her eyes. She was gone in less than a week. Pa collapsed after he put her in the ground, and I knew the sickness had come to claim him, too. He tried to hold on, and I know it was for us he fought, but after two months, he finally gave up."

His fingers tightened on her shoulder. He had never loved, never experienced her particular pain. At least not in years. It surprised him when she came to her feet and fell into his arms, sobbing. Jake held her. He didn't know what else to do—didn't know what to say. After a moment he realized he didn't have to say anything. All she wanted was for him to hold her. She needed his strength because hers had run dry.

At some point he began to register the feel of her against him. The way she fit perfectly into the shape of him. The softness of breasts pressed flush against his chest. He smoothed damp curls from her temple, trying not to pay attention to his body's silent longing.

"It'll be all right," he said softly, and his lips grazed her temple as he spoke. Without thinking, he trailed a path of kisses across her wet cheek, his mouth poised too closely to hers. When she turned her head, the softness of her lips brushing his, he did what felt natural.

She tasted as sweet as the blackberry pie he'd eaten at supper. Loreen didn't pull away or slap his face, which led Jake to believe she needed this kind of comforting, as well. He kissed her slowly and tenderly, the shyness of her response a surefire clue to her innocence. And it was that innocence that made him regain his senses.

He glanced down at her beautiful face. Her eyes were still closed, her lips parted as if she didn't know the kiss had ended. Abruptly her eyes opened. They widened. Even in the moonlight he saw red creep into her cheeks.

"You took advantage of me," she accused.

After he opened his mouth to argue, he closed it again. Maybe her lips had accidentally grazed his. Maybe he'd just been wanting to kiss her so badly he had misinterpreted her actions.

"I guess I did," he agreed. "My mistake. I'll sleep in the barn tonight and leave at first light."

With a tip of his hat Jake walked away. Loreen watched him go. She'd expected him to argue with her, expected that he would say that she had as good as invited him to kiss her . . . and he'd be right. In a moment of weakness, she had let herself need the arms of a stranger. A moment of weakness was the reason her parents were dead, the reason her older brother was dead. If not for Loreen's sins, they would never have journeyed to Miller's Passing to start another life.

Guilt came close to consuming her. It was just as

well if he went . . . and even as he did, she felt something dying inside of her: hope.

Regardless of her sinking spirits, Loreen straightened her spine and headed back to the house. She found two buckets of water he'd left behind. With a weary sigh, she hefted them into her work-raw hands and hurried onward. Wren had the dishes piled in the washbasin and had fallen asleep in the old rocker.

"What took you so long?" Toby asked.

"I had to tell Mr. Winslow good-bye."

Toby's face fell. "He's leaving? But he can't. He married you and all."

"You knew it wasn't going to be a real marriage," she reminded him. "And his leaving is just as well. We don't need him. We'll do just fine on our own."

Her voice rang of false enthusiasm, and she knew it—Toby knew it, too. Loreen toted the buckets to the dry sink.

"Take Wren up to the loft for me. I don't have the strength to carry her. You'd best get on to bed yourself."

"You ran him off, didn't you?"

The anger in her brother's tone startled her. She turned to look at him. "He's going because he wants to, Toby. He won't be strapped with our troubles. He . . . he's a coward."

"Didn't figure him for one," Toby argued.

"Well, now you can. Please go to bed. I'm too tired to argue with you."

A usually obedient boy, Toby surprised her by bolting for the door. "Maybe he'll take me with him. I don't want to stay here with you. Our troubles are all your fault!"

"Toby," Loreen whispered, but he'd already rushed

out. She placed a hand against her pounding heart. Did Toby know she was to blame for their predicament? He'd been only seven when—too young to understand . . .

Wren moaned, drawing her attention. Loreen stared down at her features, so much like her own. Gently she pushed a stray curl from the child's forehead. When Wren began to cry in her sleep, she gathered the child up. She moved toward the loft, her strength nearly giving way before she made it upstairs and settled Wren into bed. Again, the child cried out for her mama. Loreen kissed her cheek.

"It's all right," she whispered. "I'm here."

And it wasn't only a way to pacify the child. She could tell Wren the truth while the little girl slept, though come morning, the lie would continue—the same lie she'd been living for the past five years. Loreen's soul cried out because of the injustice of life, and her heart ached with the need, for once, to simply tell Wren the truth. To hold her as she'd wanted to do for so long. To admit she was the girl's mother—had always been her mother in her heart, even if society dictated that she continue to hide it. For Wren's sake, the truth had to stay hidden.

Once Wren had drifted back into peaceful slumber, Loreen kissed her softly again and went downstairs. Toby came back inside. Without a word, he climbed the ladder to the loft. She was tempted to follow him, confront him, but Loreen didn't have the strength.

She glanced at the neatly stacked dishes and rubbed her aching back. Loreen had never left the chore unattended, but tonight she'd make an exception. She was worn out, cried out, and would seek the comfort of her bed. Tomorrow, Jake Winslow would be gone, and she'd do her best to forget she'd ever set eyes on him.

After entering the room her parents once slept in, she stripped and climbed into bed. Visions of Jake half-naked kept her from falling asleep. The remembered feel of his kisses made her toss and turn. That and worry about the children's future had her mind whirling with thoughts until well past midnight. It seemed as if she'd only closed her eyes when the dim rays of dawn crept past the opening in her curtains.

Loreen opened her eyes, feeling worse than before she'd gone to bed. Her lids felt puffy from crying, her lips swollen from . . . In an instant, she was up. She grabbed her robe and shrugged into it as she hurried through the house. He was gone. She knew it in her heart but had to make certain. Loreen was out of the house and poised before the barn in seconds. She swung the door open and gasped.

Jake glanced up from hitching Ben to the Matlands' buckboard. "Morning, Loreen."

"What are you doing?" she said in a croak.

When his gaze ran the length of her in an appreciative manner, Loreen clutched her robe closed.

"I may be five kinds of a fool, Loreen Matland, but I'm no coward. Get the children. We're going into town."

Chapter Four

Deep ruts in the road to Miller's Passing nearly shook the old buckboard apart. Loreen gritted her teeth and wondered why she had allowed Jake to stay. No, he wasn't staying, she quickly corrected. He meant only to see that she and the children had a few supplies— that was all.

He looked more handsome this morning. He'd shaved yesterday's stubble from his cheeks and wore clean clothes. Loreen glanced down at her blue calico, wondering why she'd chosen to wear her best dress. She'd tied her hair back with a silk ribbon, too.

"You look mighty fetching this morning, Loreen."

Wren giggled, Toby frowned, and Loreen felt a blush rising in her cheeks. Surely Winslow didn't believe she'd gussied up for him?

"It's an old dress," she mumbled, which wasn't a lie. It just happened to be her prettiest old dress.

"Loreen only wears it on Sunday-go-to-meeting day," Wren said. "And she hardly ever wears a ribbon in her hair. She says ribbons are for special—"

"Wren," Loreen interrupted. "It isn't polite to talk too much."

The little girl's lips formed a pout, but she quieted. A few minutes later, the silence grew uncomfortable. The countryside wasn't much to talk about. They passed an occasional homestead, but a good number of the outlying farms had been abandoned.

"Not many neighbors," Jake commented.

"There used to be more," Loreen said. "Most folks have been bought out or run out. Billy Waylan owns nearly all of the land surrounding Miller's Passing."

Jake flicked the reins and frowned, staring at the untilled fields. "What's he doing with it?"

She shrugged. "Nothing. He runs a few herds of cattle, but mostly he just likes owning things."

"He has more money than anyone in town," Toby piped up. "His pa was rich, and when he died a few years back, he left everything to Billy. Anyone who needs to borrow money, they have to go to him."

"And that's why he has the whole town in his pocket," Jake reasoned. "Everyone owes him money."

"Everyone but us," Loreen said proudly.

The streets looked deserted as they creaked into Miller's Passing. There was a mercantile, a livery stable, an eating establishment, and one saloon. A few houses were scattered around, mostly those belonging to the few who worked in those establishments. Loreen tried to control the sudden pounding of her heart. If she was lucky, her family might not even cross paths with Billy Waylan today.

Jake pulled up alongside the mercantile. When he

jumped down and tied the old horse to the hitching post, Loreen took a moment to study him. His sturdy build and impressive height were more than adequate to command respect from other men. She admitted she felt safer with him by her side.

"Is there any law in Miller's Passing?" he asked casually, glancing around.

"None save Billy Waylan and his gang of no-goods," she answered. "If there were, Billy would be behind bars, where he belongs."

She couldn't swear to it, but she thought an expression close to relief settled over his features. He lifted his arms to assist her down from the wagon. "What do we tell the merchant?"

"I imagine Preacher White already spread the news when he passed through yesterday," Loreen answered, accepting his assistance. He lifted her down from the bench seat as if she weighed next to nothing. His hands, she noted, rested too long on her waist.

"That will look odd to everyone, won't it? You having a husband one day and not having one the next?"

Loreen had already thought about that last night. "I'll pretend you're still around, tending the farm, for as long as I can get away with it. After that, I'll think of something else."

He arched a dark brow. "A lie is usually quick to catch up with a person."

She lifted her chin. "Are you speaking from experience, Mr. Winslow?"

A smile stole over his mouth. " 'Mr. Winslow' is a little formal, isn't it? All things considered."

When his gaze settled on her lips, Loreen felt another blush rising in her cheeks. How ungentle-manly of him to remind her of the kiss they'd shared last night! A kiss she'd tried hard to forget. She suddenly realized she hadn't answered him, and that she was staring at his mouth, as well.

"Wren, Toby, come along," she said curtly, stepping away from Jake. "Let's go inside."

The children climbed from the back of the buckboard and raced ahead of them. When Jake extended his arm in a polite gesture, Loreen had little choice but to accept it. She felt curious eyes on them, and although the streets were deserted, she suspected the two of them were being watched.

Wren had already reached the candy counter by the time they stepped inside the mercantile. Toby was eyeing a new rifle with obvious admiration.

"Good morning, Loreen," Andrew Johnson called. He hurried from behind the counter, regarding her solemnly. "Sorry to hear about your pa. Preacher White passed through yesterday and told me the news." The man's gaze moved to Jake. "Said you'd gotten yourself married, too."

Her new husband extended his hand. "Jake Winslow."

"Andrew Johnson." The man pumped Jake's hand while giving him a good once-over. "So you knew Loreen from back east?"

"Our families were as thick as thieves," he lied smoothly.

Too smoothly, in Loreen's opinion. "Jake and I have been betrothed for a number of years," she quickly supplied. "I swear, I thought he intended to make me a spinster before he finally showed up to honor his pledge."

"Seems as if he showed up just in time," Andrew remarked. "Your folks and all," he added.

Loreen lowered her gaze, having no difficulty summoning tears. She felt Jake's arm settle across her shoulders.

"Loreen knew I was in Fort Worth running cattle," he said. "She sent me a letter saying I'd best hurry to Miller's Passing."

Andrew lifted a brow. "I sent that letter for her. If I remember correctly, it was addressed to the newspaper there."

"That's because I didn't know what outfit Jake was working for," Loreen explained. "I thought if I posted an advertisement asking him to come, he might see it. It was the second letter that I addressed to him, after he sent me one. Remember?"

"Oh, yeah, I do recall," Andrew said. He eyed them suspiciously for a moment, then shrugged. "Well, I bet you were sure happy to see him ride up with the preacher, Loreen. What with your troubles and all."

"No happier than I was to see her." Jake squeezed Loreen's shoulder, pulling her close. "I'd forgotten what a pretty thing she is. I'm surprised she waited for me all these years."

Loreen forced a fake smile to her lips, and tried to regard him lovingly. For a man who was leaving her, he was pouring it on way too thick—and his hand dangled dangerously close to her breast. With more than a slight nudge to his ribs, she stepped away from him.

"Wren, keep your fingers off of those licorice sticks," she called.

His ribs stinging, Jake watched her walk away. What had he done, to deserve that jab? He hadn't done anything. Well, maybe he'd thought about the kiss they shared last night. He'd thought about that a lot. But that was no reason to—

"What can I get you folks today?"

Jake dragged his gaze from Loreen, turning his attention to the mercantile owner. "What do you have in the way of seed?"

Andrew's brow shot up again. "You aren't figuring to plant, are you? I assumed you'd take Loreen and the children away from here. Maybe back east, where you both came from."

At Andrew Johnson's uneasy expression, Jake felt a prickly sensation at the back of his neck. The man looked as if he'd just gotten a good whiff of trouble.

"I plan to take over the farm," Jake said. "And a man can't grow a crop without seed. Do you have any or not?"

Andrew scratched his head. "I have some crook-nose maize. Good for feed, and it might grow around these parts—although if you stay, you'll soon learn nothing much does. It's tough to irrigate, and in this clime—"

"Maize?" Jake mulled to himself. He couldn't remember much about farming from when he was a boy, so he couldn't see what difference it made as to what he tried to grow. "I'll take whatever you have."

The merchant nodded. "Anything else?"

"Loreen has a list of supplies." He glanced at her, noting the longing on her face as she studied a bolt of pretty cloth. "Throw in enough of that fabric she's eyeing to make her and the little one a dress, and a bag of candy, and that rifle the boy can't stop slobbering over."

An excited flush spread up Andrew's neck. It was obvious he didn't sell much but necessities. Suddenly the man's eyes narrowed. "You ain't hoping to put this on credit, are you?"

Jake reached inside his pocket and withdrew a gold double eagle. "Afraid I'll change my mind about the farm and run out on the debt?"

Andrew sighed. "No. I was afraid you wouldn't live long enough for me to collect. I'll start getting your order together."

The man walked toward the counter. Jake stood there for a moment, the feeling of unrest settling over him again. He shook it off, then moved toward Loreen. He didn't want her to know about the fabric, the candy, and certainly not the rifle. Her pride wouldn't let her accept the extra items, and his conscience couldn't let her refuse them.

"Give the merchant your list and let's take a walk."

She jerked her fingers away from the gingham. Loreen fumbled through her reticule and gave him the scrap of paper. He moved to the counter and left it for Mr. Johnson, who'd already disappeared into the back room. "Wren, Toby, come with us. We'll walk while Mr. Johnson fills the order."

Both children glanced toward Loreen. Her face had paled. "I don't think we should leave the mercantile," she said.

He sighed. "You can't hide from the town forever, Loreen. You can't hide from *him.* I didn't figure you for a coward, either."

"I'm not a coward," she huffed. "I just don't think we should go looking for trouble."

"It's been my experience that trouble will usually find a person whether they're looking for it or not. I say we go out there and meet it head-on." He held his hand out to her. Loreen didn't accept his offer, but Wren did.

"I'll go with you," she said bravely, squeezing his

fingers. "I know because of those rabbits I can run real fast if I have to."

Jake smiled. Loreen refused to smile back.

"I'll go," Toby said. "I ain't afraid of nothin'. Plus, I haven't seen my friend Pete in a good long while. His pa owns the livery."

Since Wren held one of his hands, he offered Loreen his arm. She took it, but he could tell by the tight line of her mouth that she didn't want to. Jake wasn't looking for trouble, but Loreen needed to overcome her fears about walking the streets of Miller's Passing. If she couldn't bring herself to ride into town for supplies when she needed them, how could he bring himself to leave?

Together, the four of them left the mercantile and proceeded down the street. The place looked almost like a ghost town.

"Where is everyone?" Jake asked.

"It's a weekday. Most everyone comes into town on Saturday."

"Does that include Billy Waylan?"

Loreen nearly tripped. She began glancing around frantically. "Why? Do you see him?"

Jake steadied her. "No," he said with a laugh. "I don't see a soul. Besides, I wouldn't know him if I did see him. Does he live in town?"

She shook her head. "He has a ranch just outside of it. The opposite end from ours," she added.

"Then why don't you relax? You might even accidentally enjoy yourself."

"She never does that," Wren said. "She's too busy worrying."

"Wren," Loreen warned. "Watch your tongue."

The girl stuck out her tongue and tried to look at it. Toby laughed, Jake came close, and Loreen almost cracked a smile.

"Incorrigible child," she muttered.

"Hey, there's Pete," Toby said excitedly. He took off in a dead run toward the livery. Wren quickly followed.

"Toby! Wren!" Loreen called.

"Settle down." Jake took hold of her arm, because she looked as if she meant to run after them. "Let them be children for a while."

"But what if something happens to them?"

"Nothing is going to happen," he assured her. "Not today."

Loreen took a deep breath. "I'm sorry. You must think I'm a frightened little mouse."

Jake knew what it was like to live life looking over his shoulder. He'd done it for the past year. But he had a reason, and Loreen hadn't done anything wrong. Maybe this Billy character just had a good bluff on her.

"Tell me about your older brother."

Her pure blue eyes filled with tears. "It's my fault Joseph is dead."

"You said Billy killed him."

She nodded, a tear slipping down her cheek. "Joseph and I came to town alone that day. My ma was feeling poorly, and we needed some supplies. Joseph went to the livery to have new shoes made for Ben, and I left the list of supplies with Mr. Johnson. Then I decided to walk to the livery to meet my brother. Billy stopped me next to this alley."

Her gaze darted fearfully toward the alley. She shivered in the afternoon heat. "He said he was tired of me turning up my nose at him. He said I acted like I was

55

too good for him. Then he shoved me against a building and tried to kiss me. H-He tore my dress."

When she started to shake, Jake squeezed her arm in a comforting gesture. Loreen continued, "I kicked him in the shin and got away. I ran to the livery. Joseph took one look at me and stormed away, ordering me to stay put. The next thing I knew, some men were loading my brother's body into our wagon. Everyone said they didn't see who did it, but I know Billy killed him."

"Maybe it was an accident," Jake said quietly.

When her gaze snapped up, the tears were gone, replaced by fiery outrage. "Billy doesn't make mistakes. My brother was the only man brave enough to stand up to him, and he got killed for it."

So much for getting her to relax, Jake thought. He still hadn't dismissed the possibility that Billy Waylan was simply a small-town bully—all bark, no bite. The shooting could have been accidental. Billy still would have covered it up.

"I'm going to get Toby and Wren," Loreen said, pulling away from him. "Please return to the mercantile and help Mr. Johnson load the supplies. We'll meet you there."

He glanced up and down the deserted streets. "Maybe I'd better come with you."

"I know what you're trying to do," she said softly. "You're trying to prove to me I can walk the streets of Miller's Passing without a man by my side. You're right. I need to do this alone."

Jake watched her walk away, her head held high, facing her fears because he'd goaded her into it. He was a fine one to talk—a man who'd been on the run for the past year. He waited until she made it inside the livery, then turned toward the mercantile.

The saloon caught his eye. Maybe a bottle of whiskey would soothe his conscience when he left the Matlands to their troubles later today. He had every intention of riding out once they returned to the farm with the supplies.

After crossing the street, Jake walked into the dim interior of the saloon. Except for the man shining the bar, it was empty.

"What can I get you?"

"A bottle of whiskey," Jake answered.

"Guess you're Loreen's new husband," he said, extending his hand. "I'm Gus Sims."

He shook it. "Jake Winslow."

"Preacher White stopped in yesterday, told me you'd met up with him in the next town. Good thing you found him. He's a traveling preacher, you know."

Jake knew. Loreen had given him the preacher's schedule in her letter. He'd missed him twice. "Luck, I guess," he commented, reaching for his money when the barkeep slammed a bottle of whiskey down on the counter.

"Hope it holds out," Gus said. "The Matlands could sure use some. Of course, Loreen's pa never did much with that sorry scrap of land. Still, he was good man. Her brother, too. We all hoped Joseph would turn this town around. He wasn't too lucky, either."

While the exchange of money for liquor took place, Jake tried to puzzle through the barkeep's words. It sounded as if the town was counting on someone to take care of their problems. Or perhaps one problem in particular.

"Loreen says a fellow named Billy Waylan killed her brother."

Gus suddenly had trouble meeting his stare. "No one saw nothin'."

Waylan obviously had his bluff on more than Loreen. She'd said he had the whole town in his pocket. She hadn't been exaggerating.

"It doesn't appear as if spine grows too well around here, either." Jake took the bottle from the counter. "Good day, Mr. Sims."

Once back in the sunlight, Jake noticed the merchant hefting a heavy sack of seed into the wagon. He crossed the street, placing the liquor between a wrapped package and a sack of flour.

"I thinks that does it," Andrew huffed. "Come on in and we'll settle up."

"Has Loreen returned?"

Andrew shook his head. "Haven't seen her . . . Oh, there comes little Wren." The man smiled slightly. "I ain't never seen that girl move so fast."

Jake turned, smiling as well when he saw Wren running toward them. She rushed into his arms, gasping for breath.

"I guess that rabbit stew *can* make you run fast."

Wren shook her red curls. "Not rabbit stew," she said, still gasping. She lifted terror-filled eyes. "Billy."

Chapter Five

Loreen choked down her fear and stared Billy Waylan in the eye. He had blocked her exit from the livery, along with his good-for-nothing friends.

"Please let me pass," she said sternly. "Toby, let's go."

Her brother stepped forward, only to be grabbed by one of Billy's gang.

"Not so fast." Billy grinned at her. "We need to have a little talk first."

"I have nothing to say to you." Loreen tried to control her fear, but the fact that Toby was involved made the task twice as difficult. Thank goodness Wren was nowhere in sight. She hoped the child had the sense to stay hidden.

"Loreen, Loreen, Loreen," Billy said, shaking his head. "You know how much it upsets me when you act all uppity. Now, to add insult to injury, I hear you've gone and gotten yourself married. Tell me that ain't true."

"It's true!" Toby shouted, struggling to free himself. "And if you hurt Loreen, Jake will kill you!"

Billy frowned at the boy, then turned his gaze back on Loreen. "I really hoped you weren't fool enough to marry another man, Loreen."

When he reached out to touch her cheek, she jerked away from him. "Keep your murdering hands off of me. Do you think after what you did to Joseph, I'd have anything to do with you?"

He summoned a hurt expression. "I'm deeply offended you think I'd do such a thing. No one saw who shot your brother. But it don't bother me none he's gone." Billy stepped forward and grabbed her shoulders. "He didn't think I was good enough for you, either. For poor farmers, your whole family liked to put on airs." Billy pulled her closer.

"Let her go," Toby said in a growl, struggling harder, but to no avail.

"Shut up, kid," Billy said, then turned back to Loreen. "That boy has too much of his older brother in him. He thinks he can stop me from taking what I want. Maybe someone ought to put a bullet between his eyes, too."

Loreen's knees nearly buckled at the threat, and Billy must have seen her terror. The smile that stole across his lips didn't reach his cold eyes. "You don't want anyone to hurt him, eh? You're not so uppity now, are you? What will you give me to leave your brother be?" His gaze lowered to her lips. "How about a kiss? That's not so much to ask, is it?"

"Don't give him nothing, Loreen!" Toby shouted.

Billy sighed. "That kid is starting to annoy me. Maybe I should just have Horace shut him up permanently."

Bile rose in Loreen's throat. She wanted to spit in Billy's face. But she couldn't, not with Toby being threatened. She swallowed down the bile along with her pride.

"I'll kiss you. But first let my brother leave."

"Can't." Billy shook his head. "Then you might not honor your part of the bargain. I just want one kiss I don't have to steal from you. Well, that's what I want for starters," he amended. "I'll have the rest after I make you a widow."

Horace, the man holding Toby, snickered and clapped a dirty paw over her brother's mouth. Loreen thought she'd lose the battle against her nausea.

"I'm waiting, Loreen," Billy reminded her.

She took a shuddering breath, then closed her eyes. It seemed as if an eternity ticked past in the silence.

"You don't understand," Billy finally said. "I want you to kiss me, not the other way around."

Humiliation washed over her. She opened her eyes.

Billy grinned. "Openmouthed. Tongues and all."

"Why can't you just leave us alone?" she asked, hating that he'd reduced her to pleading.

The man shrugged. "I just can't. You're in my blood, Loreen. And the only way I can get something out of my blood is to have it."

She took a step back. "You're crazy."

He pulled her close again. "I'm crazy about you. And I'm running out of patience. Maybe we should slap your brother around a little. Break his legs or something."

Loreen mustered all of her strength. She bent forward, already smelling the liquor on Billy's breath, the sweat on his body.

"That's it," Billy crooned, his hands tightening on her shoulders. "A little closer."

"Damn it!"

Loreen jerked back. Her gaze snapped toward Toby. Horace was hopping around holding his shin.

"Run, Toby!" she shouted.

Her brother looked indecisive. She knew he was torn between protecting her and escaping. "Run!" she shouted again, trying to twist free from Billy's hold. She knew he wouldn't just leave her, so she shouted the only thing she could think of: "Find Jake!"

Rather than try to escape through the open doorway, which was guarded, Toby scrambled up the ladder to the hayloft. To Loreen's horror, she saw him jump from the upstairs window. She tried to rush outside, but Billy pulled her roughly against him.

"See if the damn fool broke his neck," he ordered his friends. "You're not going anywhere, Loreen. Not until I've had my kiss."

"Go to hell," she spit, frantic over the fate of her brother.

Billy's fingers dug painfully into her upper arms. He yanked her close and tried to cover her mouth with his. Loreen fought him, twisting her head to the side, scratching and kicking. Her scalp stung when he grabbed a handful of her hair, his lips looming ever closer.

"Get your hands off of my wife."

It was as if time froze with Loreen and Billy trapped in some grotesque dance, their lips nearly touching.

"I said, let go of her."

Her breath rushed out in a relieved sigh when Billy shoved her away. Loreen ran toward the open doorway.

"Toby," she said in a croak.

"I'm here."

She glanced up. Toby stood atop the hayloft. How had he gotten back up there? He was obviously no worse for wear for his daring leap out the window. Jake walked past her toward Billy.

"I don't know who taught you your manners, but where I come from, when a woman tells a man no, that's what she means."

Although temporarily surprised by Jake's intrusion, Billy quickly regained his cockiness. "You must be the bridegroom. Maybe you'd better go on back to wherever you came from, stranger. Otherwise, you're gonna be a dead one. Around these parts, it's legal to shoot a man for trespassing." His gaze strayed to Loreen meaningfully.

She stiffened in outrage. "You might own everyone else in this town, but you'll never own me."

Billy smiled. "That's what I like about her," he said to Jake. "She's feisty." He waggled his eyebrows suggestively. "Probably that way in bed, too."

Jake's jaw muscle clenched. "Loreen, take Toby and wait for me at the mercantile. Wren is there with Mr. Johnson."

"I'm not leaving," Toby argued. "He has others with him, Jake. I grabbed a rope me and Pete tied to the window up there and climbed back up, but the others are looking for me. They'll be back soon."

"The boy's right," a voice said behind them.

Loreen turned. Four men blocked the doorway— Billy's gang of hoodlums. What little confidence she'd

63

managed to regain fled on the heels of inevitability. They were outnumbered, outgunned. Someone was going to get hurt, and she felt relatively certain it wouldn't be Billy Waylan.

The situation quickly went from bad to worse. Jake had realized in the instant he saw Loreen struggling with Billy Waylan that the man represented a true threat, not an imagined one. The fact he'd obviously gotten away with manhandling the town for too long made him twice as dangerous. Billy probably considered himself above the law, beyond consequence of any crime he wanted to commit, whether it be murder or rape.

"This is Loreen's new husband," Billy drawled to his friends. "I think we should make him welcome. You wanna shoot him or hang him?"

Horace snickered, then paled. "But Billy, remember what happened when we—when her brother . . . ? If this don't look like self-defense, the townsfolk—"

"Shut up, Horace," Billy snapped, but Jake hardly heard. His blood had run cold. Billy cocked his head as if considering the matter, then shrugged. "I guess we'll have to rile him a little." He moved his jacket behind the holster strapped to his thigh. "If you want me to keep my hands off of your wife, you're gonna have to make it understood."

Jake flexed his fingers. His hand moved unconsciously toward his hip. Then he remembered: he wasn't packing a gun. He'd vowed never to wear one again.

"I don't believe in fighting," he said. "Or killing for sport."

Billy threw back his head and laughed. He rubbed a

hand over his face and chuckled again. "Then how the hell do you settle your differences?"

Jake looked him square in the eye. "With words."

Another burst of laughter erupted from Billy. "Words?" he repeated, then sobered. "Words ain't gonna do you no good around here."

"What should we do, Billy?" Horace asked. "He won't fight. How—"

"Nothing," Billy interrupted. "We're gonna do nothing." He walked forward and slapped Jake on the shoulder. "Me and . . . Jake? Is that what the boy called you?"

"Jake Winslow," he provided, his gaze never wavering from Billy's.

"Me and Jake Winslow are gonna get along fine. He won't give us any trouble. If I want to sneak over for a late-night visit with Loreen, I'll just tap him on the shoulder and ask him to move over. And if he's got a problem, well . . . we can talk about it afterward."

A chorus of guffaws sounded from Billy's friends. Jake fought to keep his hands from forming into fists. If the meek inherited the earth, it would be because they never crossed paths with Billy Waylan. He wanted to punch the man's face so bad, he could taste it. But he wouldn't, because that was what Billy wanted—to force him into violence.

"Loreen, Toby, let's go," Jake said. He waited until the boy had scrambled down from the loft before taking Loreen's arm. She looked pale and rightfully shaken by the encounter. Billy stepped aside and bowed as they passed.

"I'll be seeing you real soon, Loreen," he called. "And if your new husband's manly parts are as weak as his backbone, you'll be looking forward to my visit."

Toby glanced up at Jake. The boy's face turned dark red. "Do something," he ground out.

Jake grabbed him by the collar and shoved him forward. "Keep walking," he instructed. "Billy's just looking for a reason to shoot one of us. We're not going to give him one."

The boy's eyes filled with tears of rage. When another burst of laughter sounded behind them, Toby raced ahead down the street. Jake's jaw was clenched so tight he was surprised he didn't break a tooth. But he hadn't broken Billy's head, and they were all still alive. He'd stood by his vow—still relatively sure violence only begot violence—but not feeling much like a man in spite of it, especially not with Toby. Turning the other cheek left a bad taste in his mouth.

When he reached the mercantile, Andrew Johnson looked more than surprised he'd returned without a bullet hole between his eyes. Jake withdrew a few coins, settled for the supplies, and lifted Loreen up onto the bench seat. Toby had already scrambled into the back. Jake swung a wide-eyed Wren in beside the boy, then climbed up beside Loreen. With a snap of the reins, Ben plodded forward.

Even Wren was uncharacteristically quiet on the ride home. Jake was too busy grappling with his temper to notice for a while. Then the silence became stifling. He glanced at Loreen. Her gaze met his and slid away. She suddenly found the bland countryside of interest. A glance into the back found Wren chewing her bottom lip and Toby glaring at him.

The boy didn't try to hide his feelings. Jake turned back, his eyes trained on the ruts leading to the Matlands' farm. He'd thought being a wanted man was the lowest he could sink. But being labeled a coward was worse.

Loreen watched Jake unload the last of the supplies. Toby and Wren were in the house, putting away the cooking staples. The day's events overwhelmed her—made her feel a jumble of emotions, some understandable, others not so easily understood. She was angry at Jake, and she wasn't sure if she had the right to be. What little faith she'd placed in him had been shattered today.

"If it gets any chillier in here, the horses are going to grow winter hair," he said, stacking a burlap sack against the barn wall. He straightened, turning to regard her.

She shrugged. "Then maybe you'd better go ahead and saddle up yours and ride away."

"I was planning on it."

The hard glint in his eyes dared her to say something. Loreen was spoiling for a fight, and he looked as if he would give her one.

"You might as well leave," she said. "It doesn't look as if you'll be much use to us."

"If you wanted a hired gun, you should have advertised for one," he countered.

"I advertised for a *man*." Loreen placed her hands on her hips. "Billy insulted me today, and you just walked away!"

He moved to where she stood, staring down at her. "Sorry you didn't have to bring me back stretched out in the wagon, like you did your brother."

His words brought an ache to her heart. "You're right." She said. "I did not want another man's death on my conscience." She looked up at him, hoping he would just leave. But Jake pressed the attack.

"Yes, you did," he countered. "Or you wouldn't have placed that misleading advertisement. You wanted some fool to ride in here and take care of all of your problems for you, the biggest one being Billy Waylan. You didn't want a husband. You wanted a killer."

Her temper returned, her gaze lifting abruptly. "That isn't true. I thought my having a husband would keep Billy at a distance—at least long enough for us to acquire the funds to move away and start over. I didn't want a showdown—but I at least expected a man who'd have the nerve to stand up to him."

"We don't always get what we expect, do we?" Jake walked away and lifted the bridle from his saddle, which was draped over a board. He opened the rickety gate on a stall, slipping the bridle over his horse's head. Loreen watched him in silence. She knew he meant to go, had even wanted him gone, but something inside her told her that letting him leave might be a bigger mistake than begging him to stay.

Still, Loreen didn't try to stop him. If he stayed, and refused to defend not only himself, but her and the children, Billy would eventually just kill him for sport. And if she would end up at the murder's mercy anyway, what purpose would asking him to stay serve?

"Loreen?"

She swung around to see Toby silhouetted against the opening of the barn door. He stepped inside, holding a shiny new rifle. "I think Mr. Johnson made a mistake. I found this among our supplies—this rifle, ammunition, a bag of candy, and some pretty cloth I saw you looking at."

"Wrap them back up," she said. "We'll have to return the items."

Toby's disappointment was obvious. "Wren found the candy first. She's gobbled down half the bag."

Loreen groaned. Candy wasn't a necessity, and they didn't have the money to pay Mr. Johnson. "Go back to the house and take the sweets away from her before—"

"Let her be," Jake interrupted, leading his saddled horse from the stall. "There was no mistake. I meant for Wren to have that candy. And that old rifle of yours pulls to the right. It's no wonder Toby can't hit anything." His gaze turned to Loreen. "And pretty as that dress is, you've about worn it thin. There should be enough cloth to make yourself and Wren new ones."

It had been a while since Loreen had had a new dress. And he was right about the rifle. Her father had complained about it pulling to the right often enough, but she couldn't accept his gifts.

"Toby, wrap the rifle up. Fetch the cloth, too. I imagine Wren's already made fast work of the candy, but Mr. Winslow can get most of his money back."

Her brother refused to look at either her or Jake. "But we could use this rifle, Loreen. If Billy comes sniffing around here, I'll fill him full of holes."

Jake stepped forward, a frown on his face. "I didn't get it for you to fill anyone full of holes. I got it for you to hunt with. Maybe you're not old enough for the responsibility of owning your own rifle."

The boy puffed up. "I'm more of a man than you are. You didn't even try to fight Billy today!"

Fidgeting with his saddle, Jake said, "Fighting isn't the way to solve problems. And killing isn't, either. Any fool can learn to use his fists or a gun. A man who learns to use his head will live longer."

"A coward who runs from trouble most likely will, too." Toby placed the rifle on the open end of the buckboard, and walked toward the barn door. "I'm *glad* you're leaving," he said, then raced toward the house.

As Loreen watched her brother, she made a mental note to speak with him later about his temper. Hers had fizzled somewhat at Jake's words of wisdom. She hated violence, and yet she'd judged his worth as a man and found him lacking for his refusal to fight. Had she unconsciously been hoping for someone who would more than help her with a crop? Deep down, had she wanted a killer?

No, Loreen assured herself. All she'd hoped was that a man on the farm would dissuade Billy and buy her the time she needed to escape Miller's Passing. But it had been foolish of her to believe Billy would leave her alone just because she'd married someone else. She hadn't solved her problems, but only added to them. It was best if Jake left before she had his death on her conscience, too.

"I want to thank you for all you've done," she said.

He paused while tightening the cinch on his saddle. Judging from the set of his jaw, he seemed to be bracing himself for another attack. Loreen walked to where he stood.

"I'm being sincere. You did more than you had to do for us. More than another man might have done. You've used most of your money to feed us, and I can't in good conscience keep the gifts. You'll need the money—"

"I can find work easy enough," he interrupted, turning to face her. "That's why I came to Texas. There are plenty of ranches looking for hands. Lots of territory to drift from one outfit to another. Wide-open spaces that can swallow a man whole, make him disappear."

Although she couldn't fault his explanation, Loreen wondered about his last statement, and the haunted expression that had entered his eyes. "Why would you want to disappear?" she asked, gently touching his arm.

He shook his head, as if shaking off his thoughts. "I didn't say me; I said a man. My gender being very much in question since this morning," he added sarcastically.

The brief moment of vulnerability she had sensed in him slipped away. The muscles beneath her fingers flexed. Loreen released him. "You feel like a man," she replied. "I-I mean, hard." Her cheeks stung with embarrassment. "Strong is what I meant to say."

"As opposed to weak?" he asked, a hint of mischief entering his stormy blue eyes.

Somehow she'd managed to wedge herself between Jake's horse and him, a position made more intimate when he placed his hands on either side of her. Loreen suddenly felt trapped. Jake must have sensed it, though, because he lifted her chin, forcing her to look at him.

"You don't have to be afraid of me, Loreen. Not all men are like Billy."

She knew that not all men tried to force themselves on women. Some used empty promises and their appealing looks to get what they wanted. And it wasn't that she was afraid of Jake, but of what he made her feel. Breathless. Tingly all over. These wanton sensations she felt were novel, and she didn't know how to respond.

Loreen lowered her gaze, acutely aware of his scent: leather, horse, and something unidentifiable that marked him as male. Something that attracted her.

71

"You smell like a man, too," she commented, slipping beneath his arm. She walked to the end of the buckboard and studied the rifle Toby had left behind. "Take this with you. As hotheaded as Toby has suddenly become, I'm not sure he should be trusted with a weapon."

When she glanced up, Jake was sniffing himself. "Was it a good smell or a bad smell?"

She came close to laughing. "I didn't mean to imply you needed a bath."

"I washed myself off this morning." He approached her. "Didn't think I'd worked up enough of a sweat unloading the wagon to stink."

A giggle escaped her, followed by a soft snort. Loreen covered her mouth.

"I was about to say you should do that more often." Jake stopped beside her. "But . . ."

If he hadn't been grinning, she might have taken offense. Instead she burst out laughing. It felt wonderful to laugh again. When Jake's gaze settled on her lips, his grin fading away, she sobered.

"You have an incredible mouth." He gently traced the outline of her upper lip. "When I kissed you last night, you tasted like blackberry pie." He bent closer. "I'd like to know if you taste as sweet as I remember."

"You want some sweets, Jake? I saved some for you."

Chapter Six

Jake decided then and there that children had a way of cropping up at the most inopportune times. Loreen jerked back, her tempting mouth no longer within sampling distance. A becoming blush rose in her porcelain cheeks.

"Want some?"

A bag of half-eaten candy was lifted to him. On the other end of the bag was a sticky hand attached to a redheaded girl. Wren had a sticky ring around her mouth.

"No, thank you, Wren. But's its nice of you to offer. I hoped you'd share the candy."

"I stuck some of the pieces in my mouth, then put them back in the sack," she confessed. "Toby said he didn't want any." Her eyebrows drew together, as if she'd just recalled something important. "Toby says you're leaving. That ain't so, is it?"

With those big blue eyes staring expectantly up at him, Jake had a hard time telling her the truth. He lifted Wren and sat her on the buckboard.

"Your sister and I have decided it would be best if I go." When tears filled her eyes, he panicked. "Isn't that so, Loreen?"

The older sister nodded, and Jake breathed a sigh of relief, thinking she'd handle the situation. He was wrong.

"And I'll let Mr. Winslow explain why." Loreen fixed him with a frosty stare. "Good-bye . . . Jake. Thank you for all you've done."

Annoyed, he watched her walk away. He didn't know what to say to this woman's little sister. She was too young to understand. "Wren," he began, then sighed again.

She reached out a sticky hand and placed it in his. "You're going because Toby said you was a coward, ain't you? He hurt your feelings."

He smiled, then shook his head. "I'm not going because of Toby. I think you, Toby, and your sister would be better off without me. Sometimes people have troubles, and they meet up with other people who have troubles, and the trouble just grows. That's what I'm trying to keep from happening."

"Our troubles were worse before you came. We didn't have nothing to eat. Not even a little piece of candy."

That tightening sensation in his chest started again. Damn the Matlands: Toby and his heroic expectations, Loreen and her stubborn spirit, and Wren. Damn her for trusting in him with all the innocence of youth. Jake had never been responsible for another soul in his life—no one but himself. He liked it that way.

"You have plenty to eat now," he said, anxious to end the conversation. "And if you go slower with that candy, it'll last longer." He bent to lift her from the back of the wagon, but she reached up and clasped his face.

"What about when it's gone?" she whispered. "What do we do then?"

Jake went to his knees, meeting the child on her eye level. He reached into his pocket. "This isn't much, but it's all I have." After placing the coins in the bandanna he removed from around his neck, Jake tied the corners together.

"I know your sister won't accept anything more from me, so I'm trusting you to take care of the money. Hide it away, and if you see that your sister is running short on supplies, then give it to her."

Wren eyed the makeshift pouch warily. "Lori says I can't be trusted with important things. She says I'd lose my head if it wasn't stuck on."

"Then you prove she's wrong."

The thought of doing so obviously appealed to Wren. Her little face brightened. "Loreen is hardly ever wrong."

"Then we have a deal, right?"

With a bounce of her red curls, another bargain was struck. Jake felt a measure of comfort knowing he wouldn't leave Loreen completely destitute. The money wouldn't last long, and it wasn't enough to get her and the children out of Miller's Passing, but it was all he could do.

"You'd better go back to the house."

Wren clutched the bandanna in her sticky fist and jumped from the wagon. She skipped from the barn, her mind most likely focused on where to hide the money, her earlier concern that he was leaving forgotten. Jake took advantage of her distraction. He didn't know if he could ride away with the Matlands watching him.

His conscience would give him trouble, but he'd let the bottle purchased earlier in town soothe it tonight. Normally he didn't hold with drinking. Jake had seen too many men climb inside a bottle and never find their way out again. Before, he'd always believed liquor was a coward's cure. Maybe the Matlands were right about him.

Loreen lay awake in the darkness, listening. Wren had long ago cried herself to sleep, not bereaved by the loss of family members this time, but by the absence of a stranger. Toby had sulked the evening away, whether upset by Jake's departure or the rifle he thought went with him, Loreen wasn't certain. She'd hidden the weapon in the barn, but now wished she'd brought it into the house.

This wasn't the first night she'd slept without the protection of her parents, but now the whole town knew her father had passed on—Billy Waylan included. Jake hadn't done much to intimidate the murderer, and she wondered if the noises she kept hearing outside were imagined, or if Billy and his gang of no-goods had come calling.

If so, bed was the worst possible place they could catch her unawares. Loreen sat, her hands searching the darkness for her threadbare robe. Once properly covered, she crept through the house. Her weight made the old boards beneath her feet squeak in protest, and she silently cursed them, afraid she'd wake the children. By the time she reached the door, her heart was racing.

She questioned the wisdom of leaving the house as she reached for the old rifle. Loreen doubted she could shoot anyone if confronted, but an intruder wouldn't know she had any reservations.

The night air felt cool against her flushed skin. A full moon allowed her to clearly see the area surrounding the cabin. Nothing looked out of place. Loreen breathed a small sigh of relief, then almost screamed when a horse nickered, breaking the silence. It was just old Ben, she told herself. Animals had excellent hearing, and he must have heard her walking around outside. The horse probably wanted to be fed.

It occurred to her that Toby might have forgotten the chore. He'd been so busy stewing about the rifle, tending the animal had most likely slipped his mind. No wonder she'd been hearing noises. Old Ben was known to stomp around in his stall and raise a ruckus if he didn't get his daily ration of hay. Loreen moved toward the barn. She drew up short when she noticed the door standing slightly ajar.

Hadn't she closed it earlier? Coyotes and wolves were a danger to livestock not securely locked up at night, and she was nearly certain she'd latched the door after hiding the rifle. Nearly certain, but not positive.

The barn's interior was black as pitch. She wished she'd brought a candle with her as she carefully picked her way toward Ben's rickety stall. She bumped her knee on the corner of the buckboard, wanting for all the world to cuss. Realizing that the rifle she clutched slowed her progress, Loreen laid it aside. She needed her hands to feel her way around.

She used her feet, too, gently prodding the ground before taking a step. Her caution paid off. Something lumpy blocked her path. After trying to gently nudge the lump aside, Loreen gave up and kicked it. The lump groaned. A hand suddenly encircled her ankle.

Terror engulfed her. Loreen kicked out with her free foot, but with the other one trapped, she lost her balance and fell. She landed smack on top of the lump. Another groan sounded. Her ankle was released. Before Loreen could scramble away, the lump came to life. She found herself tossed on her back, pinned beneath a body much stronger and larger than her own.

Terrifying minutes ticked past. She wanted to scream, but fear the children might awaken and leave the safety of the house kept her silent. She couldn't see her attacker in the darkness, but the brush of stubble against her cheek made her gasp. It was obviously a man who held her pinned beneath him. But what man? His breath tickled her ear before he inhaled deeply.

"Loreen," he whispered, not a question, but as if he had simply identified her.

"J-Jake?" she stuttered.

"Mmm, you smell good." He nuzzled her ear with his mouth.

"You smell good, too. Good and drunk!" Loreen tried to push him away, but his tall, muscular frame proved too heavy to budge. "You scared me half to death!"

"At least I didn't kick you. Or sit on you. I knew you'd haunt my dreams no matter how much whiskey I swallowed, but I thought you'd be gentler about it."

Now that Loreen had realized she had nothing to fear, she was furious. "You are not dreaming, Jake Winslow. Get off of me!"

He made no attempt to follow her order. Instead he nuzzled her ear again. "I must be dreaming. Otherwise you wouldn't be here."

The top of her head felt as though it would burst. "You're in my barn! And I'd like to know what the heck you're doing here!"

"Your barn?" Although she couldn't see him, she felt him pull back. "Can't be. I camped a good two hours' ride from here."

She sighed, losing patience with him. Jake had gotten himself so liquored up he didn't even know where he was, or what he was doing. Or she assumed he didn't realize his hands were starting to stray—and to territory where he had no business roaming.

"Stop that." She swatted the fingers inching toward the front of her wrapper. "You didn't tell me why you're here."

It was his turn to sigh. "I must be dreaming I'm in your barn because that's where we were the last time I wanted to kiss you. And I think you wanted me to." The dark shape of his head moved closer.

He was talking about earlier, when Wren had interrupted them. She *had* wanted him to; she felt something every time this man looked at her. But she'd made this mistake before, and Jake Winslow was not a man who would stick around. When his lips brushed hers, she not-so-patiently waited for him to hurry up and get it over with.

Although Loreen couldn't fault the way his mouth gently teased hers—increasing the tempo of her heart, building the anticipation for the moment when he would completely claim her lips—she was not in the mood to be wooed. A rock dug into her back, it was well past midnight, and she knew a good night's rest was a necessity to see her through tomorrow's endless chores. She had neither the patience nor the time to humor Jake.

It made perfect sense for her to take matters into her own hands. She placed her arms around his neck, slanted her mouth beneath his, and forced him to kiss her soundly. He did so with a skill that surprised her, considering his condition. He tasted of whiskey, but it wasn't a flavor she found unpleasant. The feel of him spread out flush against her could also be easily tolerated.

Physically, there wasn't a single aspect of Jake that didn't appeal to Loreen: not his tall, muscular body, his thick, ebony hair, his stormy blue eyes, and most definitely not the way he kissed. She felt intoxicated herself, drugged by his kiss. And since Jake suffered the delusion that he was dreaming, she saw no reason to keep a tight rein on her emotions. She doubted that he would even remember come morning.

The possibility intrigued her. Could she kiss him with wild abandon? Make his heart race and his blood tingle? Make him feel all the wanton emotions he made her feel? Shyly, she touched his tongue with hers. Jake made a low sound deep in his throat. Loreen tasted him as he had tasted her, reveling in the heat of his mouth, and in the warmth she felt rising from beneath his clothes. He let her have her way with him for a while, lulling her into the false belief that she was in control; then the kiss changed.

Desire, white-hot, exploded between them. Jake's lips were no longer teasing or passive, but possessive and demanding. His urgency frightened her; it was both alarming and exciting. She had never felt more alive than in that moment, part of her wanting to push him away, but most of her wanting to pull him closer. Most of her won out. Loreen entwined her fingers in his thick hair, meeting the hot urgency of his lips with a passion she thought she'd only reserved for hatred— or fear.

But her fear had been consumed by something stronger. His lips chased away her ghosts, her worries, and allowed her simply to feel. She yearned for forgetfulness, wanting to delay for as long as she dared the moment when she must surrender him to the cruel reality her life had become.

Only when Loreen felt him gathering her nightgown higher above her knees with one hand, and with the other unfastening the buttons of her high-necked gown, did she realize how far she'd strayed from the path of propriety. Jake was obviously lucid enough to want more than kisses, and her behavior had led him to believe she was not only willing, but wanton.

Panic quickly replaced passion. She twisted her head to the side, abruptly ending the kiss. "Don't," she said in a gasp, her breathing ragged and uneven. "Stop this instant!"

He seemed to freeze in place, one hand at the buttons of her nightgown, the other clutching the material gathered just below her hips. His breathing sounded harsh in the silence. He bent his head toward hers, not to kiss her as she thought he might, but to rest his forehead against hers.

"Now I know I'm not dreaming. If I were, you would never have said that."

Humiliation washed over her. Had she lost her mind? What had she been thinking to kiss him the way she had, to encourage him to take liberties with her? Loreen felt shame and embarrassment. She'd allowed her physical attraction to a man who was nothing more than a stranger passing through her life—a drunkard and a coward to boot—to compromise her. How could she ever look him in the eye again? Simple. She wouldn't.

"I want you to get on your horse and ride out. Don't ever come near me again. Understand?"

When he didn't answer, she splayed her hands against his broad chest and tried to shake him. "Understand, Winslow?"

His head slid to the side. He snored loudly in her ear. Loreen wanted to cry. "Don't you dare pass out," she ordered. "At least get off of me first!"

His response was a soft snort, followed by another loud snore. Unconscious, he felt like deadweight on top of her. Loreen tried to scoot from beneath him, or to shove him to the side, but neither worked. She couldn't just lie there beneath him all night.

What if Wren or Toby saw them together this way? Mustering her strength, she tried harder to disentangle herself. Her pushing and prodding stirred the unconscious man.

"I must be dreaming again, or you'd already be gone."

"You are not dreaming!" Loreen shouted. "Get up, you big oaf, before you suffocate me!"

Jake seemed to rouse himself. He started to rise; then she heard a thud and he dropped back down, forcing the air from her lungs with a loud whoosh. She gasped for a few seconds, then groaned. Jake might think he was dreaming, but Loreen felt as if she were trapped in a nightmare.

"Now what am I going to do?" she said in a moan.

"Loreen? Are you all right?"

She froze. "Toby?"

"I heard noises. I went to your room, and when you were missing, I hurried out here. Who is that, and what was he trying to do to you?"

Loreen thanked heaven it was pitch-black in the barn. Otherwise, her brother would see the guilty flush she felt settle in her cheeks. "It's Jake. H-He's drunk."

"That don't explain what he's doing here and why the two of you were scuffling around in the dirt."

He had a good point. "Can you help me move him?" she asked, avoiding the subject. "He passed out."

A few seconds later, to Loreen's relief, Toby helped her shove Jake's body from on top of her. With a soft groan, he rolled to his side and took up his snoring again. Loreen quickly adjusted her clothing. She had to tell her brother something.

"I mistook Jake for an intruder. He'd been drinking, and when I kicked him, well, we scuffled."

"Did he hurt you?"

Another burst of heat exploded in Loreen's cheeks. "No."

Toby sighed. "At least he's still breathing. He must have a thick skull. I hit him over the head with that heavy frying pan you keep on the stove."

Loreen froze again. "You did what?"

Jake's head was pounding. He tried to open his eyes, but the light had him quickly squeezing them shut. A rock jabbed into his back, so he assumed he was sleeping on the ground. Something rested on his chest, and he heard a strange vibrating noise in his ears.

Last night seemed fuzzy. He remembered riding

away from the Matland farm, and not getting far before he reached for the whiskey in an attempt to keep from turning back. He'd made camp, drunk himself into a stupor, then . . .

His eyes flew open. The rafter beams above him were Jake's first clue he might not have been just dreaming that he'd returned to the Matland farm. The furry black ball resting on his chest, purring contentedly, was the second. The little red-haired girl standing at his feet, staring down expectantly at him, was the third.

"Midnight likes you," Wren said. "He's glad you came back, and so am I."

The action of lifting his head to stare into the cat's big, yellow eyes made him groan. "Get him off of me," he rasped, thinking he sounded as if he'd swallowed a throat full of rocks. "I don't like cats."

Wren looked properly outraged. "How come?" she demanded.

Her sharp little voice made him wince. "I just don't," he snapped. "Run along, Wren. And take the cat with you."

She made no move to obey him. Jake swore the cat's purring had become louder. He tried to brush the animal aside, but it dug in its claws. The rock beneath him dug deeper into Jake's back. His head felt as if it would explode. When the cat rose, turning so that its tail swiped him in the face, Jake lost all patience. He pushed Midnight off of him and sat up, immediately clutching his pounding head in his hands.

"Don't you have something else to do?" he asked Wren. "Chores to tend or something?"

"You're my chore," she informed him. "Loreen told

me to see about you. She said to make sure you were still breathing. She's cooking breakfast."

Mention of food made Jake's stomach roll. He fought down the bile and lumbered to his feet. His muscles were stiff from sleeping on the ground, and his head began to spin. "Go on back to the house, Wren. I need to wash off in the watering hole."

"You don't smell very good," Wren agreed. "And you look bad, too. Loreen said if you were a funny color and all stiff, to come tell her."

"Then maybe you'd better do what you've been told."

To his relief, Wren shook her mop of curls and raced away. He'd never been much of a drinker. Truth be known, he couldn't tolerate the stuff, but he'd never woken up from a good drunk feeling this bad. He stumbled from the barn, cursing the bright morning sunshine. The smell of Loreen's cooking filled the air.

Under normal circumstances, his mouth would have watered. Instead he almost gagged. Jake hurried toward the large watering hole behind the cabin. A dip in the chilly water would clear his head. Then he'd have to examine all the reasons he couldn't seem to leave the Matlands to fend for themselves, and all the consequences of staying.

After stripping, Jake waded into the watering hole. The frigid temperature made him gasp. He used sand from the bottom to scrub himself, then dunked his head in an effort to clear the cobwebs from his brain. The night's events returned to him in snatches. He moved toward the bank, a hazy recollection of being kicked in the ribs surfacing.

Had he scuffled with someone? Jake bent to retrieve

his clothes; then he remembered. *Loreen*. The smell and taste of her. The feel of her beneath him. He shook his head, wondering if he'd been dreaming. But he'd never had a dream he recalled so vividly, one that seemed so real.

He closed his eyes and let the memories wash over him: Loreen's passion and his, his hand brushing the smooth skin of her legs as he gathered her nightgown higher. He couldn't remember what had happened after that—no, he did remember.

She'd told him to stop. He recalled thinking he couldn't be dreaming, because in a dream Loreen wouldn't have regained her senses. Jake rubbed a hand across his forehead. Had he been dreaming? And if he hadn't been, had he stopped when she asked him to? Or had too much whiskey and his attraction to Loreen pushed him past decency?

With a heavy sigh, he opened his eyes. The object of his worry stood not three feet away, her hand clutched to her chest, her blue eyes wide. For a moment her shocked expression was all the proof he needed that he'd crossed the boundaries of decency the previous night, but then her gaze lowered and Jake became uncomfortably aware of the morning chill. He stood before her naked as the day he was born.

Chapter Seven

Loreen knew she should look—no, run—away. But she couldn't seem to make herself do either. Judging by Wren's description of Jake—*stiff, smells bad and is a funny color*—she'd half expected to find him in the barn dead. When he wasn't there, she'd gone back to the house to question Wren. The child remembered he'd said he was going to wash up.

After a short time had passed, Loreen had become worried. She'd feared that the knock Toby had delivered to Jake's head might have made him pass out. There were parts of the watering hole that were very deep. She didn't want to find Jake floating facedown in the water.

Not for a moment had she considered that she'd catch him in his present state. She finally managed to look away, but not before she saw too much—and there was a lot to see.

"I became worried you might have drowned," she said, staring at her feet.

"You were worried, or hopeful?"

She thought the last part of his question odd, and stole a peek at him from beneath her lashes. He'd slipped into his pants. His bare chest glistened with drops of water, and his dark hair had been slicked back from his face. He stared at her in a way that made her self-conscious, as if he were assessing her for damage.

"Worried," she answered. "Toby hit you over the head with my heavy frying pan last night."

He winced and brought a hand to the back of his head. "I thought I must have run into more than too much whiskey. Any particular reason why your brother walloped me?"

Loreen refused to look at him. "Toby mistook you for an intruder. We took turns checking on you throughout the night. I'm sorry he hit you."

Although she didn't hear his approach, she knew by the sudden stirring of her senses when he stood before her. He lifted her chin.

"I think I should be the one apologizing. I'm just not sure what all I should be sorry about."

Embarrassment flooded her. Jake remembered. Loreen wanted to die of shame. She pulled away from him, presenting her back so he wouldn't see the guilt she knew was stamped on her face.

"You should be sorry you didn't leave, like you were supposed to do. You can't keep riding in and out of our lives. It confuses Wren. . . . It confuses me."

His touch startled her. He turned her around. "I'm still a little confused, as well. What happened last night?"

The man could be so blunt. Her cheeks stung with shame. "You showed up drunk, that's what happened."

He rolled his gaze upward. "I know that much." His thumb brushed her swollen lips. "Did I hurt you, Loreen? Did I force you?"

Was that what he thought? That in his drunkenness he hadn't stopped when she'd told him to? That he'd forced himself on her? "Can't you remember?" She was curious as to exactly how much he did recall of last night. Judging by the heat that entered his eyes, and the lowering of his gaze to her lips, Loreen figured he remembered enough.

"I thought the whiskey might have distorted my memory as to what I think happened and what might have really happened. I thought you were willing. . . ."

When his voice trailed away, Loreen realized he was waiting for her to confirm the fact, to confess to being a wanton. She also realized that if she wanted, she could lie and place all of the blame for what happened between them on him. But she wouldn't, because Jake looked so genuinely distraught about the possibility that he'd taken liberties without her permission.

"I was willing," she said softly. "And you did stop when I told you to. Toby hit you over the head shortly after that, but I believe you intended to honor my wishes. Now I'll ask you to honor them again and leave me and my family alone."

She started past him, only to have him stop her.

"I've done some thinking. I wouldn't be much of a man if I left you and the children here alone to take on the crop and Billy Waylan."

Loreen arched a brow. "I thought you didn't believe in fighting."

"I don't."

"Then what will you do when Billy comes after you?"

"Wait and see if he does, then decide."

She sighed, exasperated. "I don't need another grave to dig. Leave, Jake. Forget about us."

"That's the problem," he said. "I can't forget. If I don't stay and see our bargain through, the Matlands will haunt me for the rest of my days."

"If you stay, you won't have many days left," she pointed out. "Besides, after, well . . . you can't stay."

Jake pulled her closer. "It was just a kiss. You don't have to look at me as if I'm some kind of monster. I won't apologize for what happened between us, because I'm not sorry it happened. But I will take responsibility. It wasn't your fault. You can stop beating both of us up over it."

She frowned up at him. "What do you mean, you'll take responsibility?"

"I mean, I've been around." He walked away, bending to pull on his boots. "I'm not the innocent you are. The way I see it, I took unfair advantage."

Loreen narrowed her eyes at him. "Are you saying that because you've acquired certain skills, I was helpless to resist your charms?"

He straightened, shrugged into his shirt, then flashed her a cocky grin. "If you say so."

Loreen stormed to his side. "Of all the arrogant assumptions!" She stuck a slender finger in his face. "Let me set you straight, Jake Winslow: I didn't do anything last night I didn't want to do! You were drunk. If anyone took unfair advantage, it was me!"

He lifted a brow, a slight smile spreading over his disturbing mouth. "Feel free to indulge yourself at my expense anytime you choose."

Damn him. She felt herself blushing again. "Why don't we both take responsibility for our actions and drop the matter. Forget it ever happened."

If she became any stiffer, Jake thought she'd snap. He didn't think either of them was going to forget last night or the desire that flared between them. Not for a very long time. If she wanted to fool herself, who was he to tell her otherwise? So she'd kissed him passionately? Nothing more had happened, and he, for one, was thankful she obviously had more sense than he did.

He supposed that, had she been willing to go further, he'd have happily obliged her and been sorry about it this morning. Loreen wasn't like the women he usually associated with; she was decent, and he had about as much business seducing a virgin as he did deciding to stay with the Matlands. But he had decided to stay, so he'd better get busy doing what he should be doing instead of mooning over something too good for a man like himself.

"I'd better get to work."

Her hands went to her hips. "You're *not* staying."

He stood his ground. "Yes, I am. We had an agreement. I aim to honor it."

When she moistened her lips, Jake was reminded of how sweet they tasted. "Then you'll honor my wishes, too. If I agree to let you stay, you will not touch me again. You will not kiss me. There will be nothing between us but a common goal. In exchange for your participation, you get the farm—and only the farm. I receive the required funds to leave Miller's Passing and start over somewhere else. I want your word on it."

And he wanted to touch her, to kiss her. But she was right. He hadn't bargained for a family, couldn't be that selfish when he had trouble of his own to deal with.

"You have my word I won't do anything where you and I are concerned, unless you ask me to. I'm not someone you should fear, Loreen, but I'm not a saint."

"I won't ask you to," she assured him.

He smiled. "Then there's no problem, is there?"

She bit her lower lip for a few moments, obviously trying to decide whether she could trust him. "No, there's no problem," she finally said. "Now, come eat your breakfast. Like you said, you have work to do."

His stomach roiled at the mention of food. He watched her hurry up the incline. She paused at the top, brushing a wisp of hair from her face, the action pulling her dress tight against her breasts. Despite his talk with himself, he stared at her womanly attributes, and fully appreciated them.

She set off toward the cabin. Jake still couldn't stomach the thought of food. He had something to do before he started in the fields—something he'd put off for too long. He went up the path the back way to the barn. Once inside, he dug in his saddle pack and removed a carefully wrapped item. Peeling the canvas back, he stared down at the gun. It was the root of all of his problems.

He'd sworn to leave his past behind, to become a new man. He was a farmer now, it seemed. Taking the gun outside, he slipped behind the barn and dug a hole. There he buried his past, said good-bye to what he'd been. He was Jake Winslow now. And he had a family to look after.

Feeling better, Jake walked out into the field.

Morning slipped into afternoon. The moldboard was old; the shovel attached was duller than the steady throb in the back of Jake's head. Sweat poured off of him, nature's way of cleansing his body. His mouth was drier than the clotted ground beneath his dusty boots. He continued to plow most of the day, stopping only to eat a quick lunch, then return to work.

Loreen had baked fresh bread all morning, and although he couldn't fault her talents in the kitchen, the baking made the cabin hotter than blue blazes. Still, it had been more tolerable than the field. He wiped an arm across his brow and decided hell must be cooler than the Matland farm.

"Whoa, Ben," he called, pulling up on the reins.

The old horse was covered in sweat, too. Jake unhitched the animal, and with a swat to the rump, sent him plodding toward the water trough. He walked across the half-plowed field and grabbed up a bucket filled with water. He dipped up a ladleful and drank it down, wincing at the water's lukewarm temperature.

Toby, he noted, looked as if he might drop where he stood. His face was bright red beneath his hat. The boy had spent the day walking ahead of him, throwing the biggest rocks from his path so Jake wouldn't break the plow's shovel.

Loreen's brother had hardly said two words to him, still stewing, Jake supposed, over yesterday's trip to town. He motioned him over. Grudgingly the boy obeyed. Jake handed him the dipper.

"Get a drink and catch your breath. You won't be much good to me passed out."

A set of pale blue eyes narrowed on him over the top of the dipper. Toby swallowed a sip, then wiped his mouth with the dusty sleeve of his shirt. "About as much good as you'll do us if trouble comes sniffing around here."

Jake sighed. Damn, but it was hot. "We had this conversation yesterday. It won't end any differently today. A man has to stand up for what he believes in."

"I figure I have the right to believe different than you," Toby said. "The only way to save us all from being killed by Billy Waylan is to kill him first."

It was a sad thing for a boy as young as Toby to have already drawn such a deadly conclusion about life. "I don't think Billy aims to kill you or your sisters."

"Maybe." Toby replaced the dipper. "Loreen is the problem. If it wasn't for her, Billy would leave us alone. He just wants to . . . well, you know what he wants."

Jake lifted a brow, curious as to how much Toby understood about matters between men and women. "No, I'm not sure what he wants. Why don't you tell me?"

The boy's face grew redder. "The same thing *you* want," he bit out. "You ain't staying because you care about what happens to me and Wren. You're staying because of her. Maybe I shouldn't have bashed you over the head last night. . . . You'd already have gotten what you want and been gone."

His own temper flared over Toby's lack of respect for his sister. Without thought, Jake grabbed the boy's shirt collar. "I don't want to hear you talk about Loreen that way again. What happened to your brother wasn't her fault. There might have been a scuffle and the shooting was accidental. No one has any proof Billy was even involved."

Toby glanced down at the hand clutching his collar. "You should take over the farm. You'll fit right in with the rest of the cowards in Miller's Passing."

Abruptly Jake released the boy. He'd let his temper get the best of him, which was not a good example to set for the already hotheaded boy. Something in Toby's voice when he'd said Jake should take over the farm struck him as suspicious.

"You don't want to give up the farm, do you?"

"She didn't even ask me," he said. "I'm the oldest son now. By right, it's mine when I come of age. But Loreen doesn't care about anything but what *she* wants."

"That's not true," Jake defended. "She's trying to look out for you and Wren. Trying to provide for your future. Doing what she thinks is best."

Resentment festered in Toby's eyes. "What would be best for us is if she just went ahead and became a whore, gave you and Billy what you both want so you'd leave us be. Then I could work the farm and we wouldn't have to run away again—run because of her."

Damn, but the kid had a smart mouth. Jake was tempted to wallop him. But he remembered being twelve, and he'd been no saint either. He and Toby both needed to get their tempers under control. Jake grabbed the boy's collar again, marching him away from the field.

"Come on. We both need to cool down."

Toby wasn't of a mind to go peacefully. Jake dragged him kicking past the house, where Loreen, in the process of hanging clothes on the line, stopped to stare wide-eyed at them. Little Wren was digging in the dirt. She jumped to her feet, running along behind.

"What are you doing to Toby?" she demanded, her little legs having trouble keeping up with them.

"Go back to the house," he ordered.

He managed to get Toby to an incline above the

deepest end of the watering hole. Jake had spotted the area earlier, thinking it'd be good for swimming. With one good shove, Toby went over the incline and landed in the water.

"What do you think you're doing?" Loreen appeared beside him, gasping for breath.

Jake smiled at her. "Toby needed to be cooled off."

She didn't return his smile. Her face paled. "He can't swim," she whispered.

Before her words could register with Jake, Loreen went sailing over the incline and into the water. She came up coughing water. Wren whimpered, drawing his gaze.

"Damn it," Jake swore. "I didn't know he couldn't swim."

Wren's big blue eyes filled with tears. "Loreen can't either," she said in a moan. The little girl took a deep breath and jumped off the incline. "And neither can I," she shrieked on her way down.

Jake dived in. He surfaced next to a flailing Wren. Without much effort, he steered her toward the shallows and a muddy patch of bank beneath the incline. When she could touch bottom, he said, "Climb up on the bank and stay there!"

His heart pumping at an alarming rate, he glanced around the area. Loreen clutched the branches of a dead tree rising up from the water, her gaze frantically searching the surface.

"I can't find him!" she shouted.

The first thought that entered Jake's mind was that Toby was probably also tangled in the tree, but below the water. He started toward her, but the boy surfaced directly ahead of him, gasping for breath before he disappeared again. Jake lunged forward.

He went beneath the water where it deepened, spotting Toby directly ahead. The boy sank deeper and Jake's lungs felt as if they would burst. He thought he'd have to resurface, but his fingers brushed the top of Toby's head. He grabbed a handful of hair and pulled him up.

They both surfaced gasping for air. Panicked, Toby fought him. "Calm down," Jake instructed him. "You'll drown us both. Relax and I'll get you to the bank."

Toby went limp. Jake put an arm around his neck and swam toward the bank. He hauled the boy out, plopping down beside him. He glanced toward Loreen, expecting to see relief etched on her face. She wasn't there.

Chapter Eight

"She's gone," Wren cried. "She saw Toby and let go of the tree, but she went under and she didn't come back up!"

Since Toby appeared to be recovering, Jake hit the water again. He remembered thinking before that to make the area a safe swimming place, he'd have to haul out the dead trees. A person could easily get his clothes tangled up in the branches. He figured that was what had happened to Loreen.

Finding her wasn't a problem. It was just as he had suspected: her dress was caught in the branches below the surface. The problem was, she didn't appear to be breathing. Jake tugged at the hem of her dress, unable to free her. He didn't have much air left, but he knew that what little he had, he had to give to Loreen.

He clasped her head in his hands, her long hair floating around them like the tentacles of a sea creature.

Jake placed his mouth over hers, prying her lips apart before he breathed life into her.

She struggled, wanting more, needing more. Jake didn't have his knife or he would have cut her free. There was only one way to save her. With a sharp tug, he tore her apron away. His fingers fumbled with the buttons on her dress, and, gentleness be damned, he began ripping. She struggled, he supposed purely by instinct, then seemed to realize his intent. She helped him, frantically clawing at her clothes. Once he pushed the dress down over her hips, she was free. Jake took her beneath the arms and kicked toward the surface.

Sounds of Wren's shrill screaming filled his ears; then the sweet relief of air filled his mouth. He breathed deeply, then noticed that Loreen felt limp in his arms, lifeless. Jake pulled her close, placing an ear against her lips.

She was breathing, but barely. The screaming had stopped. He glanced toward the bank. Wren stood shivering, Toby's hand on her shoulder. They were both as pale as a December day.

"Get Wren to the house!" he called to the boy. "Find me some blankets!"

"Is Lori . . . is she hurt?" Toby shouted anxiously, his anger forgotten.

"She's going to be fine," he answered. "Now do what I asked! I'll be there in a minute."

As the children scrambled up the rocky incline, Jake swam toward the bank with Loreen. He hefted her into his arms and climbed the bluff. He hardly remembered the trek to the house, but he managed to get them there. Wren was still crying, shivering uncontrollably. Toby had a stack of blankets in his arms. Jake nodded toward Wren.

"Wrap one of those around her and bring me the rest."

He moved to the back room he thought had once belonged to Loreen's parents and gently laid her on the feather bed. Her skin felt cold.

He began to rub her arms. Since her breathing still sounded shallow, and blowing air into her had seemed to help beneath the water, he tried it again.

"What are you doing?"

At the angry tone of Toby's voice, he glanced up. "Bring me those blankets," he instructed.

Toby entered the room, but he didn't do as instructed. "Get your hands off of her."

Jake ignored him, still trying to rub heat into Loreen's chilled limbs. "Leave the blankets and tend to Wren. Make sure you keep her warm and calm. Tell her Loreen will be all right."

The blankets landed in a heap on the bed. "I'm not leaving you here alone with my sister. Not with you touching her all over and trying to kiss her. Do you think I'm stupid?"

Patience was a virtue, but Jake was all out of it. "I am not trying to take advantage of your sister. I'm trying to save her life. Now get the hell out of here and take care of Wren!" He sighed when the boy bristled. "You're going to have to trust me, Toby."

Suddenly Toby's shoulders slumped. His eyes filled with tears. "I didn't mean what I said earlier. I was just mad. Mad about everything. I don't want her to die."

Realizing that Toby was still just a kid, and a frightened one, Jake softened. "She's not going to die," he assured him. "I just need some time to warm her up, to get her blood pumping again. I could do that a lot easier if I knew you were seeing to Wren. She's had a bad scare."

The boy nodded. "I'll take care of her." He turned to leave. "Loreen will be all right, won't she?"

"You have my word on it," Jake said. "I know the word of a man you consider a coward doesn't count for much, but that's all I have to give you."

"You weren't a coward today," Toby said quietly. "You saved us all."

Jake started to say he wouldn't have had to rescue them had he known Toby couldn't swim before he pitched him into the water, but the door closed softly before he had the chance. He refocused his attention on Loreen. A little color had returned to her flaxen skin, but she hadn't opened her eyes, and her breathing still sounded shallow.

He set to work, rubbing her arms vigorously. When he accidentally pushed against her ribs, she coughed up water. He turned her head to the side and pushed again. She coughed up more, turned over, and proceeded to expel what appeared to be half of the watering hole. Jake helped her settle back against the sheets, relieved by the sound of her deep gasps for air. She opened her eyes. They widened.

"Toby and Wren," she whispered.

"They're both fine," he assured her. "How do you feel?"

Her teeth started clicking together. "I-I feel half-f-frozen."

"That's because you're still soaking wet." Jake began to peel her damp underclothes away. He did so without a thought of impropriety, stripping her totally naked before he grabbed a heavy wool blanket and

101

wrapped it around her. Her eyes were closed again, her teeth chattering.

"Loreen." He clasped her head between his hands. "Look at me."

"So cold," she whispered, her head lolling to the side.

"Damn it, Loreen," Jake swore. He felt helpless and frightened, as well. Neither the blankets nor rubbing heat into her chilled flesh was going to do the job. She needed a lot of heat, and she needed it fast. Only one solution came to mind. "You want to be warmed up, all right," he said. "This should wake you up."

He rose, removed his soggy boots, and stripped from his wet clothing. Jake crawled into bed beside her. He wasn't cold. In for a penny, in for a pound, he decided, pulling her closer. Loreen didn't respond, and she seemed oblivious to the fact that she had a naked man in bed with her.

At least, she did until she sensed his warmth. Jake knew it was his heat that drew her to him. Her body's need for it had her snuggling up next to him. Nevertheless, when she threw one leg over him and slid her upper body on top of his, he had to question his decision to climb into bed with her. He tried to ignore the feel of her breasts pressed against him, the long, slender length of her leg resting over his thighs.

Jake told himself he couldn't think of her as a woman, not under the current circumstances. She had no idea of what she was doing—or what she was doing to him. He willed himself to feel nothing as she snuggled closer: not the smooth, silky texture of her skin nor the warmth of her breath against his neck. His teeth ground together when she shifted, sliding the rest of her body on top of him.

They were almost as close as a man and a woman

could get, all parts in complete alignment. And with the soft female part of her pressed against the male part of him, he could no longer remain indifferent. He cursed himself for his weakness, there amid the tangle of legs and the heat she'd stolen from him, and he realized Toby was right: he wasn't any different from Billy Waylan.

But he wanted to be different, so Jake altered their positions, studying Loreen to make certain that sharing his warmth with her had sufficiently roused her from death's door. Her face held more color—a lot more. A healthy rose hue stained her cheeks, and she looked so innocent lying beneath him.

Her lashes fluttered; then she opened her eyes. They locked with his, dazed for a moment, as if she were trying to comprehend where she was, and why. A second later, her eyes widened. She glanced down.

"What are you doing?" she rasped, starting to struggle.

"Settle down." Jake captured her wrists because whether she realized it or not, her nails had curled into claws. "This is completely innocent."

He realized how ridiculous his words sounded. She could feel him against her, and, naive or not, she probably knew enough to know that his body's traitorous response to her wasn't at all innocent.

"How could this be innocent?" Her voice held a hysterical edge. "What have you done to me? What—"

"Loreen," Jake said with authority, because he had a feeling that if he didn't get the situation under control quickly, she might become hysterical. "I had to share my body heat with you. You almost drowned, remember? You were cold, freezing."

Her struggles ended abruptly. The color he'd

brought to her cheeks fled. "Toby and Wren. You did tell me they were safe, didn't you?"

"They're fine," he assured her again. "Your brother and sister are in the other room, worried about you. How do you feel?"

It was another ridiculous question. She felt fine, more than fine. Her eyes narrowed on him, and if they were loaded weapons, he'd be dead. She had returned from death's door, all right. And she still had spirit. What had he been thinking?

"If you don't get off of me this instant, I'll start screaming. I'll tell Toby to get that old rifle from over the door, shoot first, and ask questions later!"

He didn't think for a second she was bluffing. Jake released her wrist and rolled away from her. Since she snatched the blanket and covered herself, modesty wasn't an option for him. *No matter.*

She'd already seen him naked once that day. As Jake struggled into his soggy clothes, he felt her gaze boring into his back. He wasn't certain, but he thought he felt it boring into other parts of him, as well. One thing he was sure of: Loreen Matland would have questions for him later. Plenty of them.

Wren had been tucked in upstairs, and Toby sat in the old rocker, whittling. Loreen had spent most of the rest of the day resting, surprised to find supper on the table when she rose. Jake had made the children help him. He didn't share the meal with them, but said he'd eat outside and watch the sunset.

She knew Jake had finished his meal—she also knew he still sat on the porch, watching the day turn to dusk. Loreen battled a jumble of emotions: embarrassment, anger, gratitude, and more anger. Throughout the afternoon, visions had kept plaguing her.

The cold, murky depths of the watering hole, then hot, forbidden flashes of Jake in bed with her. Jake without so much as a stitch on, and her just as naked, their bodies pressed together, legs entwined. Loreen paused to fan her cheeks before she stepped out on the porch.

His head turned. Their eyes met and locked. "I've come for your supper dishes."

He lifted a dark brow. "I don't imagine that's all you've come for."

When he rose, turning to face her, Loreen took a step backward. She silently cursed the reaction and stepped forward again.

"You're right. We need to talk about this afternoon."

"I owe you an apology for what I did to Toby. I didn't know he couldn't swim. The thought never crossed my mind."

Loreen had already questioned Toby on the matter. "He told me the two of you exchanged words and that he'd said some things he shouldn't have. I know you meant only to cool his temper."

"Then nearly drowning your whole family isn't what you want to discuss?"

She had a feeling he already knew what she wanted to discuss, had known since she stepped outside. Loreen walked past him, staring out across the half-plowed field. "No," she said simply, not certain where to go from there.

"Nothing happened," he began. "I told you—"

"I know what you told me." She turned around. "Am I just supposed to take your word? How do I know—"

"If I had taken advantage of you, believe me, Loreen, you'd know." He joined her. "I assumed you were innocent, but surely you know what happens the first time a woman is with a man. About—"

"I don't care to discuss this with you," Loreen interrupted. Her face burned with more than embarrassment. She knew about lost virginity: the pain, the blood. What she didn't know was if a woman could tell if she'd been with a man once her virginity had been stolen away from her. She, of course, would not pose the question to Jake. Her fears had been laid to rest; otherwise he wouldn't still be ignorant about her innocence, or, rather, her lack of it.

"Then what are we discussing?"

"Nothing," she said in a clipped tone. "The conversation is over."

He didn't step away and let her pass. "Not quite. We need to get a few things straight. I'm not so desperate to have a woman that I'd take advantage of you while you were unconscious. What I did today, I did to save your life. I know I've been, well, forward with you, Loreen, but . . . I had no intentions other than to keep you warm."

Obviously having said all he intended to say, Jake walked past her and down the steps of the porch. Loreen watched him move toward the barn. He made it sound as if she trusted no man. As if she thought any and all of them wanted one thing and one thing only from her. Loreen didn't consider herself vain, merely cautious when it came to the opposite gender. Especially good-looking, smooth-talking ones.

Had she let the past jade her? Did she believe in her heart that, if given half a chance, most men would only use and humiliate her? It was a harsh reality to admit. She'd loved her father and her older brother. She certainly loved Toby. But then, that was different. The only other two examples she'd been given of men of no relation were not good ones.

But that wasn't Jake's fault. Loreen ignored the dishes she'd meant to gather and followed him. She found Jake brushing down Ben. His pretty mare stood in the stall next to the workhorse, and Loreen patted her soft muzzle.

"It seems as if I owe you an apology."

He lifted a dark brow, but kept brushing Ben's sweat-matted coat.

"And a thank-you for saving all of our lives today."

Sliding under the animal's neck, Jake said, "There have been too many 'sorrys' exchanged between us. You've said yours and I've said mine. Let's forgive and forget it."

In the short time they'd been acquainted, Loreen realized there was already a great deal to forgive and forget. She didn't know what else to say, so she turned to leave.

"When Toby and I went back to plowing today, I told him I'd teach him to swim. You and Wren are welcome to join us for lessons."

"Perhaps we will," she responded, taking a step toward the door.

"I also told him I'd teach him to shoot his new rifle."

That stopped her in her tracks. "I thought we were in agreement that Toby is too hot-tempered to handle a weapon."

"We were. But Toby and I made a bargain: he won't shoot it unless we're hunting, and he's promised to let me handle any situation that should arise with Billy Waylan."

Loreen almost started another argument with him, but besides being sorry, arguing was all they seemed to do with one another. Not all, she quickly corrected, but she didn't want to think about last night, or of finding him in her bed this afternoon. As a show of good faith, she walked to where she'd hidden the rifle and retrieved the weapon.

"I guess I'll have to trust you on this one," she said, handing him the gun.

"That's not easy for you, is it?"

"What? Trusting you?"

He took the rifle, leaning it against a board in Ben's stall. "Trusting anyone."

She had trouble meeting his gaze. "I learned a long time ago that people aren't always what they appear to be. Not much has happened since to change my mind."

"Why did your folks decide to settle here?" He snatched up the rifle and opened the gate to Ben's stall.

The question made her nervous. She didn't want Jake prying too far into her life. There were things about her she'd just as soon he not know.

"My father worked in a mercantile. He didn't own the store, but he ran it for a man rich enough to hire others to make his living. From the time I was a little girl, my father talked of having his own land, being his own boss. When . . . well, when he heard that land was dirt cheap in Texas, he loaded us all up and moved out here."

"He had a noble dream," Jake said. "Some people are oxen, and others are the whips that drive them. Most of us would rather be the whips."

She laughed at his comparison. "And because you would rather be a whip, you answered my advertisement. You're like my father: you think you can make something out of nothing."

"I had hoped there would be more to the farm," he admitted, pitching Ben some hay. When his mare whinnied, he fed her as well. He turned to Loreen. "Why don't you have any livestock? A cow for milking and at least a few chickens?"

"We used to. Over the years my father had to sell off livestock in order to survive. He spent a good portion of money on the cabin. My mother was horrified by the sight of so many sod houses in Texas. She thought they were ugly and uncivilized-looking. Since lumber is scarce in these parts, he had logs brought in."

"In other words, he started out in the hole."

"He was a good man," Loreen defended passionately.

"I didn't mean to say he wasn't," Jake quickly assured her.

As he walked away to replace the pitchfork, Loreen wondered about his parents. "What of your folks?"

Jake stared thoughtfully at the pitchfork he'd just replaced, snatched it up, and shoveled a pile of hay onto the dirty floor. "Dead," he answered. "My mother died when I was around ten. My father followed her a few years later."

He paused to survey his handiwork, then spread a blanket over the hay before he continued, "We had a farm, too. A nice, fertile stretch of land. After my mother passed away, my father began to work himself to death. I didn't understand that that was his way of dealing with grief until I became older. But at the time I resented him, and I vowed I wouldn't stay around

109

and watch him die, too. I left. A couple of years later, I heard his heart gave out—maybe it was just too broken to mend."

Loreen placed a hand against her chest, moved by his story. "Your father must have loved your mother very deeply."

"The way I saw it, he cared only about himself. He didn't think about me, or that I was hurting, too. All he cared about was working from sunup until sundown. He never talked to me about her death. He hardly spoke to me at all."

Despite his matter-of-fact tone, Loreen sensed that Jake had been deeply hurt by his father's indifference toward him. "It takes some people longer than others to deal with grief. Maybe if you had stayed—"

Jake closed the distance between them. "Are you saying it's my fault he died? My fault he worked himself to death?"

She took a step back. "No. I'm not implying that your father's death was your fault. I—"

"I'm tired," he interrupted, turning away from her. "I didn't mean to snap at you. Besides, that's all history. There's nothing I can do to change it, so there's no point in dwelling on it. Some people can't move past the mistakes they've made, or concentrate on anything but how their lives might have turned out different had they acted more responsibly. I don't aim to be one of them."

For a moment Loreen thought he was referring to her, that he'd somehow discovered her secret. But, of course, he couldn't have found out, because she was the only one who knew. "Some mistakes can't be forgotten. Not when they hurt innocent people."

Jake wheeled around, his expression startled. Quickly his mask of control settled back into place, but not before she'd seen a hint of panic reflected in his eyes.

"I already apologized about today," he said.

Loreen had trouble believing he thought either of them had been referring to the accident that afternoon; nevertheless, she nodded and turned to leave.

"Loreen," he called. "In town yesterday, you thought I believed you were a frightened little mouse. You have plenty of courage. Your family all risked your lives for one another today. Stupidly, maybe." He laughed. "But you all did it."

She turned to look at him. "You risked yours, too."

Jake shook his head. "I knew how to swim. What I did can't be counted as an act of bravery. Besides, I didn't have much to lose."

He lied. She'd seen his face when he realized Toby couldn't swim. He already cared for the children; he just didn't know it yet. She turned and left the barn. A distant rumble caused her to glance up. There wasn't a cloud in the sky. Curious, she walked into the field.

Dusk was upon the land, and she had trouble seeing. As she stood there, the rumbling grew louder. A few minutes later, her eyes registered the outline of dark shapes: devils with horns racing straight toward her.

For a moment Loreen felt as if her feet were rooted to the ground. She knew that if she didn't run, she'd be trampled to death. Finally her legs moved. She took off across the field. The recent plowing greatly hampered her progress. The thundering of hooves shifted the dirt and pounded in her head. She tripped on the hem of her dress and nearly fell, but a strong hand curled around her arm.

"Run, Loreen!"

It was Jake. Loreen snatched up the skirt of her dress, half running, half being dragged behind him as he pulled her from harm's way. Their breath came in gasps as the cattle raced by, their sharp hooves destroying three days of hard labor in the field. There were other noises: the whoops of the men driving the cattle, and the sounds of their laughter. Loreen knew who they were. Billy's boys, there to remind them their boss hadn't forgotten the Matlands.

When the dirt started to choke her, Jake guided her to the porch. Loreen collapsed onto a step. Jake did likewise. They sat there long after the cattle were gone, the air still thick with dust. It was the second brush with death Loreen had experienced that day. She felt too numb to cry, or even to be afraid. Surprisingly, she almost felt calm.

"How are you going to handle that?"

Loreen looked over her shoulder. Toby had posed the question. He stood behind them, had probably been standing there throughout the entire stampede. She glanced at Jake, certain that because of his and Toby's agreement, the question had been aimed at him. Although she sensed the tension in him, like a tightly stretched bowstring ready to snap, he shrugged in a casual manner.

"Simple. We'll build a fence."

Chapter Nine

There was nothing simple about building a fence on land shy of timber. After three days of watching Jake and Toby hitch a harness to Ben, not to plow, but to pull dead trees from the watering hole, Loreen still didn't see how he thought to enclose an entire field with his skimpy supply of water-soaked wood.

It was a question she decided was well worth asking, as the trampled field had been neglected since he'd taken up the fool notion—or more fittingly, suicidal notion—of building a fence in cattle country.

"Billy's not going to like it," she told him when he came to the house for a dipper of cool water.

"Probably not," he agreed. "The outfits around Fort Worth don't like it either. But homesteaders are doing it just the same. Hell, I didn't think it was right when I herded cattle, but now I'm on the other side of the fence. Had we already planted, we would have lost everything."

"If you put up a fence, you may lose your life. Billy thinks he can run his cattle anywhere and everywhere in the territory. I guess that's why he's buying up most of it, or using unscrupulous methods in order to convince people to sell." She glanced behind her. "He uses the watering hole on our property—always has, and I imagine that's the reason he wants the farm. Besides, I don't see how you're going to build a fence with that sorry woodpile you've collected."

"Ever heard of barbed wire?"

The mere mention of the term struck fear into her heart. "I've heard of it. The cattlemen are convinced the spiked wire will injure their herds. Billy won't even let Mr. Johnson order it for his store. Manny Crawford—he has one of the few farms still occupied in the area—went off to another town and brought some home with him. Billy's boys just cut it as fast as he could put it up."

"Does he have any left?"

Loreen placed her hands on her hips. "I suppose he must. He didn't get far before Billy convinced him that fencing in his fields wasn't a wise decision. I believe a threat was made against his young wife and their new baby."

Jake didn't respond. He appeared to be lost in thought. Loreen didn't care for the determined set of his jaw, or the thoughts she suspected were rolling around in his head.

"For a man who doesn't believe in fighting, you sure are trying to stir up trouble."

"Where's Wren?" he asked, glancing around.

"She's in the house finishing off the last of the candy. I'm surprised it lasted this long."

"I need a word with her."

Curious, Loreen followed him into the cabin. Wren sat on the floor, what few treasures she had left clutched in her sticky hand. When Jake squatted beside her, she opened her palm.

"Want one?"

Loreen's lips twitched when he quickly declined the child's offer.

"Wren, remember the money I gave you?"

She nodded. "I hid it just like you told me to. And I didn't tell anybody."

"What money?" Loreen asked.

Jake ignored her. "Where did you hide the money?"

The child cocked her head to one side. She pinched her lips together. Her little brows furrowed. "I don't remember."

Jake ran a hand across his eyes. "Did you hide it in the house, or outside?"

Wren's face brightened. "Outside. I remember thinking Lori might find it in the house."

"Where outside?"

She screwed up her face again. "Don't remember."

He glanced at Loreen, his expression one of helpless appeal. Loreen mouthed the words, *You gave her money?*

Obviously realizing she would be of no help to him, he turned his attention back to Wren. "I need you to think real hard about where you hid the money, Wren. I need it for something."

"But you gave it to me," she reminded him.

There went his hand across his eyes again. "I gave it

115

to you to give to Loreen if she needed it, remember? But that was when I thought I was leaving, and I didn't leave, so now I'd like to have the money back. Understand?"

The child nodded again. "You're a taker-backer."

When Jake looked offended, Loreen realized he didn't know beans about handling children. Loreen couldn't believe he'd entrusted money to a five-year-old child and believed he would ever set eyes on it again. Still, her insides turned a little mushy at learning he'd given them his last cent. She walked over and bent down beside them.

"Let's play a game," she said to Wren. "We'll have a treasure hunt."

Excitement danced in Wren's eyes. "What treasure?"

"The lost money. Let's see if we can find it."

After popping the rest of the candy into her mouth, Wren jumped up. "I'm ready," she mumbled.

"No, you're not." Loreen held out her hand. "That's too much candy. You'll choke. Spit it out."

Reluctantly Wren leaned forward and emptied her little mouth. Loreen glanced at Jake, wondering if he had taken note of the correct strategy to use when dealing with young children. He looked horrified, his gaze glued to the slobbery, sticky mess in her palm.

Rolling her eyes upward, she walked into the kitchen. She dipped her hand into a bucket of water resting in the dry sink, then placed the sticky sweets on a plate to dry. There was no use in throwing the candy out, as Wren would only complain about her missing stash later. Loreen wiped her hands on her apron and joined Wren and Jake.

"Now we can go."

Once outside, Wren ran ahead of them, searching.

Because Wren looked inside barrels and under rocks, Loreen was convinced the child truthfully had no idea where she'd hidden Jake's money.

"I wouldn't count on seeing that money again," she said.

Although Jake's expression appeared grim, he shrugged. "It wasn't much anyway. But maybe we won't need much to buy fencing that's just going to waste."

Loreen secretly hoped the money stayed hidden. Although she saw the sense of fencing the field, and Jake had been right—they would have lost everything had they already planted—she didn't want to give Billy more reasons to harass her family.

"Hey, I thought you were only going for a drink, Jake!"

She turned and saw Toby headed toward them. "We decided to have a treasure hunt," she called.

He stopped, staring at her and Jake as if they'd both lost their minds. "A what?"

She looked at Jake, deciding he should explain. He said nothing until Toby joined them.

"I gave Wren a bandanna tied up with money the day I rode out. I told her to hide it and give it to your sister when supplies started to dwindle. Now I need the money—"

"And she can't remember where she hid it," Toby finished for him. He shook his head. "I've heard of men doing some dumb things before, but—"

"I have faith in Wren," Jake interrupted. "She'll remember." His gaze strayed to the little girl. Wren had picked up a rock no bigger than her toe and looked beneath it. He sighed. "Eventually."

They'd searched the farm for the better part of an

hour when Wren had a revelation. She came racing from the back of the cabin shouting, "I remember, I remember!"

Loreen sat on the porch, having already given up. She jumped to her feet. Rather than run to her, Wren ran into Jake's arms. He hefted her high in the air. She squealed with delight.

"I knew you could do it," he said to her. "Now, where is the money?"

She pointed. "In there."

The man holding her frowned. "Toby and I already searched the barn."

"I buried it beneath the dirt," she explained. "I'll show you." He tried to put her down, but Wren held on. "Carry me, Jake. I'm tired from all that hunting."

Loreen suspected Jake was tired, too. He'd spent the entire morning searching for more trees to pull from the pool behind the cabin. She supposed swimming lessons had fallen by the wayside, but every evening since Jake and Toby had made their agreement, he'd taken her brother out to shoot his rifle.

The two had developed a bond of sorts, and as she watched Jake walk toward the barn holding Wren, her little arms wrapped around his neck, she had to wonder if she'd made the right decision by allowing him to stay.

"Aren't you coming with us, Loreen?" Wren called.

Loreen walked after them. Upon entering the barn, she found her younger brother laughing. "What's so funny?" she asked.

When Toby only laughed harder, she glanced at Jake. He wasn't laughing. He wasn't even smiling.

"It seems after I left, Wren decided to bury the money in the stall where I kept my horse."

She moved toward Jake and a very sober little girl.

Loreen couldn't see why Toby found Wren's hiding place so humorous. Once she reached them, she glanced into the stall. There stood Jake's beautiful mare . . . it was what she was standing in that brought about Loreen's enlightenment as to why Toby was laughing and Jake was not.

"I've been meaning to muck out that stall," Jake said. "I just haven't found the time."

"You ain't mad at me, are you, Jake?" Wren whispered.

He bent down and lifted her into his arms. "No, Wren. You picked a good place to hide the money."

Wren leaned forward and patted his mare on the head. "For such a pretty horsie, she sure can make a mess."

"She sure can," he agreed.

"Wren, let's go the house and get lunch on the table," Loreen said.

The little girl made a face. "What good is all that bread you've been baking when there ain't no butter to spread on it?"

"There isn't any butter," Loreen corrected. "And there isn't any butter because to have butter, we need a cow."

"Pa should have never sold ours to Mr. Crawford. He already had two milk cows."

"He needed the money," she said. "And Mr. Crawford does well enough selling milk to folks in the area too poor to have a cow of their own."

Wren sighed dramatically. "Well, I miss that old cow. And our chickens, too."

"You hated those chickens, Wren Matland," Toby said. "You used to come in crying because they pecked your toes. You were scared to death of them."

"Was not," Wren countered.

"Were too," Toby shot back.

Loreen supposed a contest of "was not, were too" would follow. She also suspected Jake wouldn't put up with their nonsense for long. But when she glanced at him, he hadn't seemed to notice the bickering. He stared at the mare in an appraising manner, the same way he'd looked at Loreen the day he married her.

"Toby," he said, "find old Ben. We'll hitch him to the wagon. Even if we dig up the money, it isn't much. Not enough to get everything we need. I have an idea."

A skitter of alarm raced up Loreen's spine. An idea had occurred to him the night of the stampede, too. She hoped this one, unlike the last, didn't hold the potential to get them all killed.

Jake guided the old plow horse down a rutted trail that supposedly led to the Crawford farm. Loreen had insisted they have lunch before hitching up Ben, and Jake was chomping at the bit to see if his new idea would pan out. He glanced over his shoulder, his gaze sliding over Toby and Wren before settling with regret upon the pretty sorrel mare tied to the back of the wagon.

She was fast as a prairie fire, high-spirited and fine-boned. What she wasn't was a horse suited for life behind a plow. She had neither the strength nor the stamina to endure the grueling pace he'd imposed upon Ben during the past few days. At present, he had little use for the mare, and the farm needed a milk cow, a few chickens, and barbed wire to fence in the field. He hoped Manny Crawford had a mind to do some trading.

"You're not going to trade that fine animal for a few rolls of barbed wire, are you?" Loreen asked.

"What I trade for will depend on whether Mr. Crawford's in a trading mood."

"My father thought highly of Manny Crawford," she said. "The rest of us haven't spent much time around him, or his wife."

He lifted a brow. "I figured neighbors got together, helped each other out."

"Not around here. Everyone sticks to their own."

"Because Billy prefers it that way," Jake predicted. "He's used the oldest war strategy in the book: divide and conquer."

"I suppose you're right," she agreed. "The Crawfords settled here three years ago. Mrs. Crawford seems a little odd. She doesn't look much older than me, but she never speaks to anyone. The few times I've seen her in town, she walks with her head bowed. She had a baby, who I guess should be going on two years old now."

"She sounds like someone who could use a friend. Maybe a young woman around her own age."

Loreen cut her gaze sideways at him. "I haven't had a friend since we moved out here."

"Then it sounds like you could use one, too."

"I don't have time for friends," she informed him. "And what's the use of making them when—" She cut herself off, glancing meaningfully toward Wren.

Jake made no comment. He didn't have any friends either. Not a drifter who strayed from one place to another. Not a man running from the law. He had to keep reminding himself of what he was, of his past, every time he looked at Loreen and wanted to kiss her.

She deserved better, and he had no doubt that once she left Miller's Passing, some man would snatch her up and make her his. Hopefully a decent man, one who would accept Wren and Toby into the bargain and love them as his own.

That was exactly what she needed, Jake told himself, dismissing the jealousy he felt over imagining Loreen with another man. And that was what Toby and Wren needed, as well. They were both good kids, and they deserved someone far better than him: a man they could look up to and be proud of—again, not a man such as himself.

"There it is," Loreen said. "I don't know what the Crawfords will think about a wagonload of strangers suddenly showing up on their doorstep."

"I imagine they'll be happy to have company," Jake said, hoping he sounded enthusiastic.

A second later a shot sounded. Dirt kicked up in front of the wagon and Ben shied. Jake quickly brought him under control. "You kids get down!" he shouted, helping Loreen to scramble to the back of the wagon. Jake tied off Ben's reins and jumped from the bench seat. He raced to the back of the wagon, where the mare was tied. The horse reared.

"Easy now," he soothed, then shouted, "Hold your fire! We're not armed."

"Who the hell goes there?"

"Jake Winslow! I have the Matland children with me!"

A figure stepped from the brush. He was taller than an oak tree and about as broad. He squinted toward them. "I couldn't see who was coming. Figured you were a wagonload of Billy's boys come to give me grief."

"Maybe you should get yourself a pair of spectacles before you kill someone!"

The man winced, then waved them forward. "Come on in," he called.

"Toby, Wren, are you both all right?" Jake asked.

Two heads popped up. "We're fine," Toby said.

"Loreen?"

She appeared, her bonnet somewhat askew. "That was some welcome," she said sarcastically, righting her bonnet.

"I guess I need to remember that folks around here are about as skittish as this mare." He untied the horse from the wagon and led her prancing toward the front of the wagon. Rather than drive the wagon, Jake took hold of Ben's harness and walked them in. He questioned his sanity regarding barbed wire, the trading of his horse, and the sense of approaching a man holding a gun.

Chapter Ten

The man stood in front of a sod house. A woman appeared on the porch, holding a small child. When the barking started, the mare reared again. Jake tightened his hold, glancing around. A dog—actually, it looked more like a wolf—came creeping from behind the house.

"Wolf, go on about your business," the man said to the dog.

Only after the animal turned and disappeared did Jake breathe a sigh of relief. The mare, obviously disturbed by the dog's scent, reared again.

"Whoa," Jake said, trying to calm her.

"That's one fine-looking piece of horseflesh," the man said, propping his rifle against the porch before he approached him. He stuck out his hand. "Manny Crawford."

Jake had trouble holding the horse and shaking

hands at the same time, but he managed. "Jake Winslow."

After an awkward pause, Manny lifted a bushy eyebrow. "So you're the new husband?"

"Yes," Jake answered.

The man glanced toward the wagon and Loreen, his rough features softening. "Sorry about your folks," he said. "Your pa was a good man. I'd have stopped by to pay my respects, but I didn't know he'd passed on until I made a trip to town yesterday and heard the news."

Loreen nodded, her blue eyes turning watery for just a moment; then she placed her hands on Wren's and Toby's shoulder. "Thank you, Mr. Crawford. Our pa always spoke well of you."

If in fact he'd been the mighty oak he resembled, Jake suspected the man's leaves would have quivered. He sniffed, then seemed to pull himself together. "So to what do we owe the pleasure?"

Now came the sticky part. "I understand you have one milk cow too many. I have one horse more than I need."

Crawford's eyes ran appraisingly over the mare. He glanced toward the plow horse and frowned. "I suppose it's the old one you've come to trade."

Jake smiled. "No, I need him. It's this pretty, well-bred mare I'd like to trade."

"Her for a milk cow?" he asked, suspicious.

"She's worth more than a milk cow," Jake agreed. "I thought you might throw a few other things into the bargain."

A gleam entered Manny's eyes. He was obviously a man who appreciated a good trade. "Get the little one out of the wagon. Your wife and the child can go into the house with my Gretchen. Us men will see to business."

It was a rare occurrence, but Jake took to Manny Crawford immediately. And he liked the way Manny included Toby in their dealings. The boy puffed up and jumped from the wagon, quickly coming to take the mare's lead rope. Jake went to the wagon and helped Wren and Loreen down.

"She's a little shy, my Gretchen," Manny said quietly. "She comes from sturdy German stock, but it's taken her some time to learn our language. She still gets a bit tongue-tied at times. Embarrasses her something fierce."

Those few words explained why the townspeople found the young wife odd. Jake wondered if Loreen had just arrived at the same conclusion he had. When he glanced at her, her cheeks were bright pink. She'd obviously put the puzzle together.

The young woman was a foreigner, which in some people's eyes counted as a mark against her. If that wasn't bad enough, she couldn't speak the language well, another reason she might be ridiculed and teased.

"I'm very anxious to meet Gretchen," Loreen said. Her gaze cut to Jake. "I could use a friend."

Manny's grin couldn't get any wider. "Come on. I'll introduce the both of you."

Jake didn't think any two people looked less suited for one another than Manny and Gretchen Crawford. First off, Manny was about fifteen years older than his young wife. Second, regardless that her husband claimed she came from sturdy German stock, Gretchen was no bigger than a minute. Manny was red-haired and ruddy, Gretchen dark-haired and pale-skinned.

She was a beauty, though and Jake suspected that if anyone gawked at the couple, it was because they wondered how a big, rough-looking man like Manny had managed to snare himself such a prize.

The big man introduced everyone, and Gretchen, shy to a fault, could hardly bring herself to say hello. Manny slapped Jake on the shoulder and steered him away from the house. Jake glanced back, hoping things between Loreen and Gretchen would warm up. Right now, they looked like two beautiful statues.

"Aren't you going to ask us inside?"

A blush exploded in Loreen's cheeks. Leave it to Wren to add to an already uncomfortable situation. "Wren," she scolded, "where are your manners?"

The child looked rightfully outraged. "Where are hers?"

Loreen wanted to crawl beneath a rock. "I'm sorry," she apologized. "Wren has never been one to watch her . . . what she says," Loreen finished, afraid Wren would stick her tongue out and try to look at it again.

"She is right," Gretchen said. "My manners are as bad as my English. Please come inside."

They followed her into the house, and Loreen gasped with surprise. Although on the exterior it was as typically unattractive as most sod houses were, Gretchen had decorated her home beautifully.

"It's lovely," Loreen whispered, glancing about at the fine china figurines, the lace doilies and beautiful homemade quilts spread over the crude furniture.

"Old family . . . what are they called?"

"Heirlooms," Loreen provided.

"Yes. They belonged to my parents, and theirs before them. We came to America three and a half years ago. My parents died of sickness on the trip over the ocean. I arrived with all of our treasures, but nothing else. I did not know what would happen to me. Manny, he is what happened. He rescued me."

Although Loreen had also lost her parents, and she supposed Jake had rescued her as well, she thought Gretchen's story sounded much more romantic. Or maybe it was the light that entered Gretchen's dark eyes when she spoke her husband's name. Theirs was clearly a marriage born of love, not convenience.

"This is little Samuel," she said, placing her child on the floor. "He has been keeping me from my baking."

In the kitchen, Loreen saw that the woman was in the process of making a pie. "Wren and I can keep an eye on him while you finish," she offered.

Gretchen appeared indecisive. "He is a footful."

Wren burst into giggles. Loreen wanted to reach out and stifle her.

"I said something wrong," Gretchen ventured.

"It's not a footful," Wren informed her. "It's a handful. I know because that's what Loreen says I am."

Beneath her pale complexion, Gretchen blushed. "I should not even try to talk to people. I always embarrass myself." She hurried into the kitchen.

Loreen frowned at Wren. "You've hurt her feelings."

Wren's big eyes widened. "I didn't mean to. It was funny."

"It wasn't funny to her."

The child now looked as if she would cry. Loreen hugged her and sighed. "Wren, you are a footful, too. Play with Samuel."

As most often happened, Wren's tears disappeared as quickly as they had appeared. She walked over to the toddler. Loreen watched them, smiling when Wren tickled the boy under his chin and he began to giggle.

In the kitchen, she heard the rattle of pots; then Gretchen appeared at the table, her back to them as she went about her pie making.

A few minutes later she let loose a string of words Loreen couldn't understand. Her stance expressed what her words hadn't. Gretchen was clearly vexed.

Loreen walked into the kitchen. "Is something wrong?"

Gretchen pointed to the dough she'd been trying to roll out for the pie crust. "I can never do this. My Manny, he loves pie, but my crust is always bad."

"A little shy on flour and lard," Loreen said. "Do you mind if I try my hand at it?" She nodded toward the sticky dough.

"Please," Gretchen pleaded. "I will make us tea, *ja?*"

Tea? Loreen couldn't remember the last time she'd had such a luxury. "Tea would be lovely, Gretchen."

As the two women went about their tasks, Loreen couldn't help but think of her mother. She missed the shared comradeship of two women bustling around a small kitchen together. Jake had been right—again: she hadn't realized how badly she needed female companionship, a possible friend. Heaven knew it had been a while since she'd had one.

Of course, Loreen couldn't lay all the blame on the folks of Miller's Passing. Her family had moved so that she could start over, but the past wasn't easy to put behind her. The simple truth was, Loreen hadn't felt like a carefree girl of sixteen when the Matlands settled in the small community of Miller's Passing. She'd felt wise beyond her years—as if she didn't deserve friendships built around a lie. And she certainly had no desire to attract the attention of any decent boy her age. She hadn't considered herself worthy.

"Would the little girl like a fresh glass of milk?" Gretchen asked after walking back to where the children were playing.

Wren led Samuel to the kitchen table. "I sure would," she said, then seemed to recall her manners. "Thank you."

Loreen smiled at her while Gretchen poured their drinks. A second later, her smile faded. Wren dipped her finger in Gretchen's apple pie filling, then stuck it into her mouth. She made a horrible face.

"Wren," Loreen whispered, "that's not polite."

When Wren's lips continued to pucker and she started to wipe her tongue on the sleeve of her dress, Loreen chanced a glance at Gretchen. Noting her back was turned, she sampled the pie filling herself—and nearly choked. The apples were sour.

She first thought a household shortage of sugar and cinnamon to be the reason. But then, all the necessary staples were displayed on the table. Perhaps Gretchen hadn't finished preparing the filling.

"Here is tea," Gretchen chirped, carrying two dainty china cups to the table. She walked back to the counter and returned with two tin cups of milk. Wren snatched up her cup and drank greedily.

"The dough is ready, too," Loreen said. "I hope you don't mind, but I've already placed it in the pie plate."

Gretchen eyed her crust enviously. "You have done this before," she said flatly. Heaving a sigh, she walked around the table and started to pour the filling into the crust.

"Wait," Loreen blurted. "Ah, I always stir and taste my filling again before I pour it in the crust."

The young woman snatched up a wooden spoon, gave the filling a stir, and tasted it. She winced, then shrugged. "It tastes the same as always. Bad."

When she tipped up the bowl to pour again, Loreen placed a hand on her arm. She nodded toward the filling. "I hate to keep interfering, but can I—"

"You can make this better, too?" Gretchen asked hopefully.

"I believe I can."

The bowl was thrust toward her. "Strudel I can make. Pie I am not so good with. But for my Manny, I keep trying."

"You speak very good English," Loreen told her while she set about adding more sugar to the filling. "I doubt most people could learn another language as quickly as you have."

"The right words do not always come." Gretchen settled in a chair across from her. She hefted Samuel into her lap and kissed him. "And the accent, I fear, will never go. Because the words sound different when I say them, I will always be a stranger in this country."

"I like the way you talk," Wren piped up. "It's because you don't sound the same as everyone else that makes you special."

Gretchen smiled at the little girl. "Thank you, Wren. Would you play with Samuel again while we have our tea?"

Wren scrambled down from her chair. "Can we go outside?"

After a nervous glance toward the door, the young woman said, "If you stay by the porch. We have a dog I do not trust."

Recalling the wolflike creature, Loreen shuddered.

131

"Maybe you'd better play inside, Wren. That dog is running around loose."

"Wolf?" Gretchen asked, then shook her head. "He is harmless once Manny tells him to go. It is the other one I worry about. The she-wolf. She trusts no one, and I'm afraid she will bite. I make Manny keep her in a cage until dark."

Loreen shivered again. "Where is the cage?"

"A good distance behind the house. But if the children stay by the porch, they should be safe."

"Wren, can I trust you to keep Samuel in the front of the house?"

The girl nodded. "I'm older. I can watch him."

This was a new experience for Wren, Loreen realized. She had always been the baby, the one looked after. She supposed it made her feel more grown-up to be around a two-year-old.

"All right, then. Go on outside." After Wren clasped Samuel's hand and led him away, Loreen said to Gretchen, "We'll take turns keeping an eye on them."

Gretchen nodded in quick agreement. Loreen finished her filling preparation, poured it into the crust, and placed another crust on top. While Gretchen popped the pie in the oven, Loreen checked on the children. They were playing in the dirt next to the porch. She returned to the table, took a seat, and began sipping her tea.

"It seems ages since I've had a nice cup of tea."

Gretchen joined her, her dark eyes filled with sympathy. "Manny told me about the trouble with your family. The sickness that has taken your parents. I am sorry."

And Loreen knew she truly was, because she had

experienced the same grief herself. "We aren't so different, are we?"

A smile lit the young woman's face. "No. And now, also the same, you have a husband to help ease your suffering. I know like others, you are wondering why I married a man older than myself. And Manny, he is not as nice to look at as your man, but he has a good heart. I knew from the moment I met him that I loved him. Was it the same for you?"

Loreen lowered her lashes. When it came to their husbands, she and Gretchen's similarities ended. She couldn't tell the young woman the truth, or even that she hardly knew Jake. Her life seemed destined to be cluttered with one lie after another. And a lie was nothing to base a friendship on—and certainly not a marriage. Still, she had to say something.

"The first time I saw Jake, I-I thought him very handsome," she said, which was the truth.

Gretchen sighed appreciatively. "It is hard not to notice." She promptly added, "But it was not his face that captured your heart, *ja?*"

"No, it was not," she said, wishing they could end the conversation.

She was thankful when Gretchen rose and checked on the children. Loreen sipped her tea. She nearly choked when the young woman asked if she and Jake wanted other children.

"Other children?"

Gretchen returned to the table. "Your younger brother and sister are now yours to raise. Do you want babies of your own?"

The possibility hadn't been given much thought. However, she knew that she and Jake wouldn't have children together. Since she never intended to marry in truth, she supposed future children were out of the question.

"You'd better check on the pie," she said, thinking any answer but a bold-faced lie would sound suspicious. "I'll check on the children."

As Gretchen hurried to the stove, Loreen rose and walked outside. Wren and Samuel were chasing each other in circle, giggling. She smiled at their carefree antics. Although little Samuel had his father's coloring, in her mind's eye she imagined a little dark-haired boy playing with Wren—one that looked like a miniature Jake. Loreen quickly chased the vision away.

"Manny will know I did not bake that pie," Gretchen said, joining her on the porch. "It already looks too pretty."

They watched the children play and spoke of the weather, about sewing and gardening. In exchange for helping her with the pie, Gretchen gave Loreen a small sack containing various seeds for planting her own garden. A while later Gretchen went back inside and brought the pie out to cool.

The men ambled toward the house. Jake led the milk cow that Loreen's father had once traded Manny Crawford for money. Gretchen's husband carried a cage containing two hens and a rooster.

"Your man is a stubborn trader," Manny called to Loreen. "I thought that damn horse would cost me my whole farm before it was all said and done."

"Manny, I know that word is bad," Gretchen fussed. "Do not say it in front of the children."

When he grinned broadly at them, it was difficult not to grin back. Even his young wife lost most of her bluster. "You already have a good horse, husband," she reminded him.

"I bought the mare for you. It's high time you learned to ride."

"Horses are for pulling, not riding," she said, but her pretty blush said the gift pleased her.

"Do I smell pie?" Manny put the chickens in the buckboard and hurried to the porch. He eyed the pie, licked his lips, and glanced up at the women.

"I reckon Loreen must have made this."

Gretchen stiffened for a moment; then she burst out laughing. "I told you he would know I did not make such a pretty pie," she said to Loreen.

A smile crossed Loreen's lips, but she sobered when she caught sight of Jake staring at her. He was in the process of tying the milk cow to the back of the wagon. And the way he looked at her made her face hot.

He smiled slightly, and just like as his handsome face, his mouth was hard not to notice. And the feel of it against her lips was a stimulating memory impossible to forget.

"I can tell by the way he looks at you, and you him, you will have other children," Gretchen whispered beside her. "Many children."

Chapter Eleven

Jake kept the old workhorse at a slow pace on the trip home. He'd traded for everything he'd intended to come back with and gotten more than he planned in the bargain: a new friend. Loreen seemed content sitting beside him as well. She seemed satisfied by her new friendship, too, if somewhat melancholy.

He wondered if they were having the same thoughts, if an afternoon spent with two people so obviously soft in the head over one another had made her life seem lacking in comparison. Jake tried to shake off his fanciful musings. He hadn't answered Loreen's advertisement with any hope of finding a life such as Manny Crawford lived: one tied to a woman and children. His future was tied to a past that dictated what he could and could not have.

Loreen was a could-not. Wren, Toby, and children

born from his own seed were could-nots. He'd be damn lucky if he even managed to have the solitary, peaceful life that he'd hoped for in Miller's Passing. Yet it was a small town few people had heard of—a place to blend in and disappear.

Wren's squirming in the back of the wagon returned his thoughts to the present. "Don't get close to the barbed wire, Wren. It can cut you."

His warning also brought Loreen from whatever reflections had kept her quiet for much of their journey.

"I wish you would have left that behind," she said. "I think Gretchen was relieved to see you carting it off."

"Probably because Manny has a mind to try his hand at fencing again. It's one of the reasons he bought those dogs. He figures with them roaming the farm at night, someone might think twice about cutting the wire."

"But first he's probably going to wait and see what happens to us," she muttered softly enough for only his ears. "And those dogs, as you choose to call them, are more dangerous than the scum he thinks to run off with them. Did you know they have to keep the female caged during the day?"

Toby stuck his head between them. "I saw her."

Loreen twisted around on her seat. "You what?"

"Toby." Jake sighed. "I told you to keep that to yourself."

"Keep what to himself?" she demanded.

"Manny warned us about the female. He said she hadn't warmed up to them and he didn't know if she could be trusted or not. Of course that made the boy curious. I told him he could have a look as long as he kept his distance."

137

The boy's sister visibly shuddered. "You shouldn't have let him go anywhere near that dog. Think what could have happened if she'd somehow managed to get out?"

"I might be dead," Toby provided. "She looks more like a wolf than the other one. Her eyes glowed in the darkness of the cage, and then she showed me her fangs." He lifted his fingers and measured out two inches. "They were this long and dripping with spit, or maybe blood from something she'd killed the night before. I couldn't tell for sure."

"Toby," Loreen whispered harshly, "you'll give Wren nightmares."

"I ain't scared," Wren said, but she scrambled over Toby and climbed into Jake's lap. "That dog probably just needs a friend."

Jake laughed at her logic, then sobered. "Keep your distance from that dog, Wren. She's been mistreated by someone. A dog that can't trust, can't be trusted herself."

Rather than appearing frightened by his warning, Wren's big eyes filled with tears. "That's sad," she said.

Transferring the reins to one hand, Jake brushed his fingers through her curls. "You have a soft heart, Wren. But that she-wolf, she's had a hard life. As long as she believes everyone wants to hurt her, she won't overcome her past. Because she can't learn to trust, she can't learn to love. She'll remain what she is—trapped in a cage."

Wren burst into sobs. Jake hadn't been trying to upset her, but to enforce all the reasons why Wren should stay away from the dog. He glanced helplessly toward Loreen. Her face was red, her eyes suspiciously moist as well.

"What's the matter with you?" he asked her.

She blinked back her tears. "N-Nothing," she stammered. "I feel sorry for her, is all."

He laughed, trying to ease the tension. "I suppose you're crying, too," he said, turning to look at Toby.

Toby wasn't crying. He was staring straight ahead, his body tense. "I wish we had that she-wolf with us. I'd let her out and hope she is mean. We have company."

The house had come into view. A horse was tied to the front porch, the door to the cabin was standing wide-open.

"I guess whoever he is, he doesn't know it isn't polite to enter someone's home when they aren't there," Jake said.

"This ain't no social visit," Toby responded. "That horse belongs to Billy Waylan."

The man who belonged to the horse stepped out of the cabin. He held a white piece of clothing in his hand. As they pulled up in front of the cabin, Billy shoved his hat back on his head and grinned at them.

"Well, there you are," he called. "I was beginning to think you folks grew some sense and lit out of this place, but then, Loreen wouldn't leave all her unmentionables behind, now, would she?" He brought a soft nightgown to his face and inhaled deeply. "She sure smells sweet."

One of Jake's hands tightened on the reins; the other gently nudged Wren from his lap. He didn't like the thought of Billy going through Loreen's things, touching them as if, by doing so, he could touch her. It took a good deal of willpower, but his expression reflected none of his inner turmoil.

Jake knew the thing to do when dealing with Billy was to keep his temper in check—especially in front of the children. He climbed down from the wagon, reaching to assist Wren and Loreen. Once the Matlands were all unloaded, he turned to Loreen.

"Take Toby and Wren into the house," he said softly. "Bolt the door." Jake walked them up the porch steps, then placed himself between the family and their unwanted guest. He snatched the nightgown from Billy's hands, shoving it into Loreen's as she passed. Once the door closed and he heard the bolt slide into place, he turned from Billy and walked back to the wagon.

"You folks could use some lessons in hospitality," Billy drawled.

"You're not welcome here," was all Jake said in reply. He led Ben toward the barn without a backward glance. Of course, he knew Billy wouldn't take the hint. His kind never did. He had just put the milk cow in the stall his horse had occupied when Billy sauntered through the open doors.

"It appears as if you're settling in." He nodded toward the cow, then eyed the contents of the wagon. A frown shaped his mouth when he spied the barbed wire. "I can't figure you, Winslow. You're either very brave or very stupid."

Jake hefted the crate of chickens from the back of the wagon. "I'm what you might call a dangerous combination," he said dryly. "I'm a little of both."

Billy laughed, then shook his head. "I think you're just plain stupid, and that's all. I want you gone, Winslow. Get on your horse and ride out."

After placing the chickens on the ground, Jake said, "That's a problem. I traded my mare for this fine milk cow and these chickens. Guess I'm stuck here."

All traces of humor faded from Billy's face. "What

am I going to have to do to get my message across? Kill you?"

Jake pretended to consider the matter. "That would seem the logical solution. Of course, you'll want to wait until your gang of hoodlums is around to spur you on. I don't think you have the guts to kill me without them."

Billy's face turned redder than that of a man two days in the desert without a hat. "For a coward who won't fight, you have a smart mouth. I didn't bring my boys along because I wanted to spend time with Loreen . . . alone. Figured you might watch the children for us while we—"

"You figured wrong," Jake interrupted. He was trying like hell to keep his temper under control, but Billy was sorely aggravating the attempt. "I have work to do, and Loreen doesn't want to spend time with you. It'd be best if you rode out and didn't show your face around here again."

His suggestion clearly held no appeal for Billy. The man's skin turned a darker shade of red. Like himself, Jake suspected Billy was trying to keep a tight rein on his anger. But why? Why hadn't the man just gunned him down in cold blood? Was he afraid of the—

"You don't understand at all, do you?" Billy said. "I run Miller's Passing. When I tell someone to jump, they ask how high. When I want something, I take it. That's just the way it is."

Jake made a pretense of studying the chicken crate, afraid that if he even so much as looked at Billy, he'd resort to violence. "We're not in Miller's Passing," he reminded Billy. "You're on my land, and I want you off. That was the last time I'll ask you politely."

Billy snickered. "Since you ain't a fightin' man, I can only assume that the next time you ask me to leave, you'll just use harsher words. Besides," he continued, moving toward him, "I wanted to have a little fun with Loreen before I go. You know I was in her room? I laid on the bed and smelled her on the sheets. It made me harder than that dirt out yonder you're trying to plow."

A drop of sweat traced a path down Jake's temple. His hands were clenched into fists, but he said nothing.

"I figured as long as I was there, I might as well relieve my—"

Jake snapped. He pulled back his fist and landed a punch before Billy completed whatever obscene sentence he was about to say. The blow knocked the man off of his feet. He didn't stay down for long. Jake blocked his jab and delivered another solid blow to the man's gut. Too far gone with temper, he grabbed Billy by the collar and shoved him up against the side wall of the barn. Jake pinned him there, one hand against his throat.

"Don't ever touch Loreen's things—or her—again! Don't speak her name; don't even look at her! Do you understand?"

Choking noises followed. Jake realized the bully's face had turned blue. Disgusted with Billy, and with himself for stooping to his level, Jake released him. In the whip of a snake's tail, Billy went for his gun. Jake lunged forward, wrapped his fingers around Billy's wrist, and banged his hand against the wall until he dropped the weapon. He kicked it aside, reached down, and scooped it up. The tables were turned.

"Go ahead," Billy goaded him. "Shoot me."

For a second Jake was tempted. Sorely tempted. But then he spotted the water trough outside the barn door, walked over, and pitched the gun in the water. "If you try to fish that gun out, I'll have to drown you. Now get off of my land."

Sporting a welt nearly as big as the state of Texas, Billy bent and retrieved his hat. He beat the dust from it against his leg. "You *are* stupid, Winslow. You should have killed me when you had the chance."

Although Jake didn't much feel like it, he smiled. "I reckon another one will come along."

"You can count on that," Billy said; then he stormed from the barn.

Jake walked outside and watched him roughly grab his horse's reins, mount up, and ride away. Only after Billy disappeared did he breathe a sigh of relief. He hadn't refrained from violence, but then he also hadn't killed Billy or been killed by him. Not yet, at least.

Damn the man for pushing him too far. Jake walked to the water trough and dunked his head, thinking he should have done his cooling off before he let his fists fly. When he came up for air, he saw Loreen's reflection in the water.

"What happened?"

"We exchanged a few words," he answered, slicking back his hair. Deciding that further details were unnecessary, he reentered the barn with the intention of unloading the wagon.

"Words?" she repeated, following him inside. "What kind of words?"

Loreen wasn't slow. Jake didn't suppose she'd believe that he and Billy had been discussing the weather. "Heated ones," he answered. "After we exchanged these heated words, I asked him to leave, and he did. That's what happened."

She didn't appear to believe him. Her pretty blue eyes narrowed. "You asked him to leave, and just like that he went. Docile as a lamb?"

"I never compared him to a lamb. He left growling like a lion." Jake hefted a roll of barbed wire from the wagon. "You'd better put those chickens in the coop. Midnight might get off of his lazy hide and come to investigate. I'm sure he's caught their scent by now."

"Billy didn't try to kill you?"

"I never said that."

She blocked his path to the wagon. "You're not saying much of anything."

Jake ran a hand over his face. "Well, I will say this: I don't think we've seen the last of Billy. Keep your guard up . . . and wash your sheets."

Loreen wasn't listening, Jake realized. She took his hand in hers. "Your knuckles are bleeding."

He glanced down and winced. "Damned barbed wire."

When Jake looked back up, he met Loreen's intense regard. She stared deeply into his eyes, as if she were trying to probe his mind. He suspected she didn't believe that barbed wire was responsible for his swollen, bleeding knuckles. He didn't see any reason to tell her that he'd dug his grave a little deeper with Billy Waylan. She had enough worries.

Although he tried to remain passive to her touch, Jake found it difficult. Loreen's beauty always startled him. He couldn't help but respond to her nearness and to the warm touch of her hand still holding his. As he'd done earlier with Billy, he fought to keep control over his emotions. He told himself he didn't want to kiss her. Kissing her would only complicate an already complicated situation.

Loreen released Jake's hand. She had the oddest feeling he wanted to kiss her again; then she wondered if it wasn't *her* who wanted the kiss. An afternoon spent with two people in love had obviously affected her. She supposed it was only natural to wonder what it would be like to be married to a man she loved, instead of one who came as part of a bargain. Then Jake's explanation to Wren about the she-wolf, and why she would always be trapped in a cage, had hit too close to home. As if that weren't enough, Billy's visit had shaken her.

And she wouldn't question why, when she'd been barricaded in the house with the children, it was Jake's life she feared for and not her own. Damn his bargains. She wouldn't let herself want him to kiss her. Not ever.

He stared at her for a few more minutes, then moved away. From beneath her lashes, she watched him unload another roll of barbed wire. She had half a suspicion that Jake hadn't cut his knuckles on the barbed wire, but on Billy's face. It was only a suspicion, and not a very sensible one. If he'd hit Billy, he'd surely be a dead man. Wouldn't he? Billy had become enraged by far less before, and Jake's odd brand of nonviolence—she couldn't decide whether it were cowardly or heroic—would never protect him from that.

Jake was strange. She imagined there was more to him than met the eye, certainly more than he'd be willing to expose about himself. . . . She caught herself.

145

That wasn't really her business. Jake wasn't part of her plans for the future. Lifting the crate with the chickens, she started toward the door. She'd almost made it outside when she recalled something Jake had said to her earlier. She turned back to him. "Did you tell me to wash my sheets?"

Chapter Twelve

When Jake told Loreen that Billy had been in her bed, she had assumed that meant he'd climbed in and wallowed around on her sheets, and she'd ended up burning them along with her nightgown. That was a good two weeks past, and as yet, Billy hadn't paid them another unwanted visit. Loreen couldn't quite believe their good fortune. The hens were producing eggs, they had fresh milk daily, and Jake had plowed a small vegetable garden next to the cabin.

That was where she sat at that very moment, little Wren helping her bury the seeds Gretchen had provided. She glanced across the field. Jake had almost finished stringing the barbed wire, and Toby, growing it seemed by leaps and bounds due to their generous supplies, could now handle some of the plowing. They had a way to go before they could plant, but at the rate Jake pushed himself, it wouldn't be long.

She couldn't fault his determination. He didn't have a lazy bone in his body. And it was his body that kept stealing Loreen's attention away from her gardening. The grueling pace he'd set for himself during the past two weeks had hardened his already fit physique. Jake thought nothing of removing his shirt during the heat of the day, seemingly unaware of the distraction he represented to her.

The muscles in his arms and back flexed while he wrapped a strand of barbed wire around a post, then pulled the wire taut. A light sheen of sweat made his sun-darkened skin glisten in the sunlight. Watching him labor was a chore in itself. Or Loreen assumed so, because her heart beat faster and the sun suddenly seemed hotter.

"You like Jake, don't you?"

Realizing that Wren had taken note of her distraction, Loreen quickly returned to her gardening. "How are you doing with those seeds?" she asked, ignoring the question. She smiled when the little girl proudly displayed her empty apron. "I think you might be a farmer, Wren."

Wren looked as if she were trying to decide whether she wanted the title. A moment later she proved that Loreen's ploy hadn't managed to derail her train of thought. "You must like him or you wouldn't have married him, right?"

Loreen had hoped Wren was too young to question the marriage, and, because of the girl's age, she and Toby had decided to keep Wren in the dark about the bargain she'd struck with Jake. Poor Wren—she'd been in the dark all of her life, living a lie the same as Loreen.

"You should like someone if you marry them," she agreed. "But sometimes people get married for other reasons. And sometimes they don't always stay married."

"They don't?" Wren asked, her little face registering surprise. "Why not?"

After removing her sunbonnet, Loreen fanned her face and wondered how she would explain the three of them leaving to Wren when the time came. "Sometimes the husband and wife want to live in different places."

"Oh," Wren said. Her mouth twisted into a frown. "The same as they sometimes want to sleep in different places?"

It had never occurred to Loreen that Wren would question the sleeping arrangements between her and Jake. She assumed Wren was too young to ponder such an adult matter; then she thought she understood why the child had asked.

"Are you asking because Mama and Papa slept in the same place?"

Wren nodded. "If Jake would sleep with you, then when I go to bed at night, I could pretend you and him are my new mama and papa. Then maybe everything wouldn't seem so different."

Tears suddenly threatened Loreen's eyes. She blinked them back. It wasn't that she herself didn't miss her parents and her older brother. She simply had too much to do each day to dwell on their loss. Loreen set her sack of seeds aside and opened her arms. "Come here, Wren."

The little girl quickly scrambled into her lap. Loreen ran her fingers through Wren's red curls. She'd waited an eternity to reclaim something precious that had been snatched away from her—waited too long to hear Wren call her what she truly was, instead of who the child had been led to believe she was. It was bitter-sweet for Loreen to say her next words.

"If it would make you feel better, you can call me Mama."

Wren twisted around to look at her. "I can?"

"If you want," Loreen told her, tears almost over-whelming her again.

Wren worried her bottom lip with her teeth. "But most folks know you're not my real mama."

"That's true," Loreen said, her voice catching for a moment. "But it's up to me to raise you now. To take care of you until you're grown. Don't you think that makes me your real mama?"

A shadow fell across them, interrupting the conver-sation. Loreen glanced up to see Jake standing before them, his shirt thrown over one shoulder.

"Are you ready for swimming, Wren?" he asked.

The child shot off of Loreen's lap and ran to him, jumping into his arms. "I like swimming," she said. "You should get in the water, Lor— Mama." At the lift of Jake's eyebrow, Wren explained: "Loreen's going to be my new mama."

"She is?" Jake glanced at Loreen oddly.

Loreen felt her face flush. "Wren is missing . . . I didn't see what harm it would do for her to call me her mother. I *am* responsible for raising her now."

"I guess I see the sense in that," he responded.

"And that means you're my new papa," Wren told him. "It does?"

His horrified expression nearly made Loreen laugh, but it was no laughing matter. Wren couldn't come to think of Jake as her father. She had the feeling she'd

150

already have enough trouble convincing Wren they had to leave when the time came. An serious attachment to Jake would only complicate matters.

Wren grinned at Jake. "Now you can sleep with her."

Jake lifted a brow. He cut his gaze at Loreen. "Is that so?"

"Wren," Loreen quickly interjected. She rose and grabbed up the sack of seeds. "Let's go inside so you can strip down to your underwear. If you don't hurry, Toby will beat you to the water."

The thought of Toby arriving at the swimming hole first was all the encouragement Wren needed. She struggled until Jake lowered her to the ground, then took off in a flash of red hair.

"Don't ask," Loreen said before hurrying after Wren.

"Maybe you should join us today," he called. "You do need to learn to swim."

Loreen wouldn't have the likes of Jake Winslow telling her what she did or did not need. After her near-drowning experience, she had trouble sticking her toe in the water, much less her whole self. But she had enjoyed watching Jake teach Toby and Wren during the past two weeks. He was patient with them, and the children immensely enjoyed their afternoon swimming sessions.

Wren had stripped down to her chemise and pantalets by the time Loreen walked into the cabin. After Loreen placed her seeds on the table, she scooped the child's worn dress from the floor and walked to the rocker. "We need to talk about . . ." Her voice trailed off when she realized that Wren had already left the cabin. She sighed, laid the dress over the back of the rocker, and hurried outside. Toby raced past from the direction of the barn. One of his chores before swimming was to unhitch the plow horse and put Ben in his stall to rest.

Loreen debated over whether to watch the lesson. Since she refused to participate, it seemed a sinful indulgence to sit on the shore, especially with so many chores to be done daily. Still, she enjoyed the escape from her tedious tasks, and, as always, they would be waiting for her when she returned.

The sounds of splashing and laughter reached her long before she came upon the swimming hole. The children's enjoyment brought a smile to her lips. Jake had found a way to break up the monotony of their days as well. When she reached them, a frightening scene greeted her. A rope had been tied to the branch of a tree that hung over the incline, and Toby was dangling in midair. A moment later he let go.

Her heart raced as Loreen ran to the edge of the incline. She glanced down, relieved to see Toby's head above the water. Jake was well within rescuing distance should the need arise, and Wren waited in the shallows.

"That didn't look like much fun," the little girl said.

"Toby forgot to swing first," Jake responded. "I'll show you both how."

Jake swam beside Toby until they reached the shallows. The incline jutted out over the water, shielding the bank below. Loreen moved closer to the edge and looked down. A few minutes later someone grabbed her waist and pushed her forward. She squealed in fright until she realized the hands still held her, and she hadn't fallen over the incline. Turning her head, she encountered Jake.

"That was not funny," she scolded.

He grinned. "If you knew how to swim, it might have been."

He looked so handsome dripping wet that Loreen had trouble being annoyed by his antics. She also had trouble ignoring the feel of him pressed against her backside. He wore nothing but a pair of drawers that tied at the top, ended just below the knee, and, when wet and clinging, left little to the imagination. She knew because he'd worn them swimming every day for the past two weeks.

"Your attire is a concern to me. I think you should take more care with modesty when swimming in the company of a little girl," she said.

His breath tickled the back of her neck. "I have. I usually swim naked."

She turned to face him, careful to keep her gaze above waist level. "You may have not have noticed, but you might as well be naked. Your unmentionables cling indecently when wet."

He smiled. "That's the difference between big girls and little girls: big girls notice such things and little girls don't."

Her face suffused with heat. "It's very noticeable," she defended.

He smile widened. "That water's still damn cold, but thanks for the compliment."

"It was not a compliment." Her face grew hotter. She had no idea what the water being cold had to do with anything. "I simply thought you might be unaware of the problem."

His smile faded. He lifted a brow. "I've been swimming in my drawers for two weeks. You took your sweet time to call the 'problem' to my attention."

Loreen tried to concentrate on his face. She could drown in his deep-set, thickly lashed, ·stormy blue eyes. A droplet of water traced a path down his cheek, dropped to his neck, and continued the journey down his chest. She quickly snapped her gaze back up, realizing she had been following the drop's decent.

"It didn't occur to me until last night, when I was lying in bed, that Wren might take notice of your . . ." Her voice trailed off. That hadn't come out right. "What I meant to say is—"

"You were lying in bed thinking about me last night?" His brow rose higher.

"I was thinking about your drawers," she specified, then bit her lip. "I mean . . . oh, hell, we were discussing Wren, remember?"

"Hey, Jake, are you still up there?" Toby called from below.

Children were a blessing, Loreen decided then and there. Jake was still watching her, a quizzical expression on his face, so she said, "I believe you were about to show Toby and Wren something else I probably won't approve of."

He ran a hand over his face. "I need a dip in cold water. If Wren hasn't taken note of my . . . differences before, having you tell me you've been lying in bed at night thinking about me has only made them more noticeable."

The temptation to drop her gaze to the vicinity of his drawers was almost overwhelming. Her will prevailed. Loreen stared him straight in the eye. He laughed.

"But seriously, Loreen," he said. "You should learn to swim. You never know when you might take a tumble in the water. You wouldn't want it to be up to Toby and Wren to save you."

It hadn't occurred to her that refusing to participate

in the swimming lessons might someday place Wren or Toby in jeopardy. "I suppose you're right," she admitted. "But what will I wear?"

His gaze lowered thoughtfully to her clothing. "A dress is too bulky. Best strip down to your underwear like the rest of us." When she purposely narrowed her gaze on him, he smiled. "I won't look."

Loreen didn't know if she should trust him. She hadn't been able to trust herself as far as not stealing glances at him while he traipsed around indecently clad. Still, as he said, learning to swim was important. Right? "Promise?" she asked.

He sighed. "I guess you're just going to have to trust me, Loreen."

She didn't trust him, not completely, but Loreen definitely wouldn't have him thinking her a coward.

Her hands automatically reached for the buttons of her dress. Jake's gaze lowered for the slightest second; then he quickly glanced back up at her. She thought she heard him swallow loudly; then he took off, jumped into the air, grabbed the rope, and swung out over the watering hole. He let go, drew his knees up to his chest, and made a huge splash upon entering the water. Whoops from below greeted his efforts.

Loreen thought him a madman, but had to secretly admit that one might experience a certain amount of exhilaration in swinging in midair before plummeting to the water below. Still, she couldn't see herself soaring like a bird. Not without being, as always, worried over the consequences. Despite her lack of an adventuresome spirit, she continued to undress, making sure Jake kept his gaze averted, as he had promised. She tried not to think about the water, and the fact that she was terrified of drowning.

Chapter Thirteen

Jake was in the process of telling Wren she wasn't big enough to swing on the rope by herself when a flash of white on the bank captured his attention. Loreen stood there, a vision in chemise and drawers complete with worn stockings. Her hair hung loose around her shoulders, curling around the shape of her full breasts. He quickly averted his gaze, as promised, but he'd already seen far more than he considered comfortable.

"Lori!" The five-year-old he'd been arguing with suddenly squealed in delight.

Wren had obviously already forgotten her decision to address Loreen differently. Recalling Loreen's flush of pleasure when the child had called her mama earlier caused Jake to ponder the elder sister's reaction. Something about it struck him as odd. But then, maybe picturing Loreen as a mother had seemed strange to him.

It shouldn't have, though. She was old enough for children of her own. Some girls married as early as thirteen, and had a passel of children by the time they reached Loreen's age. That struck him as odd, too. Why hadn't she found herself a husband before now?

"You ain't wearing your stockings into the creek, are you?" Wren called.

To add to his discomfort, Jake imagined Loreen rolling her stockings down her long legs. The sudden appearance of Toby beside him helped bring his ardor under control. They had a staredown, Toby obviously daring him to look at his older sister while she stood half-naked on the bank.

"Get in, Lor—Mama," Wren called. She turned to her brother. "Loreen is gonna be my new mama," she proudly announced. "And Jake's gonna be my new papa. They're going to sleep together."

The boy's eyes widened, then narrowed on Jake. "Is that so?" he repeated in the very words Jake had said earlier, only Toby's tone held no amusement.

"Wren and I need to have a talk," Jake said. "I'll explain the way of things to her."

"See that you do, and that the way of things is as it should be," Toby grumbled, but he took Wren and moved toward the bank.

The sounds of splashing followed. Loreen yelped, so he assumed the children were splashing her. The thin chemise she wore would soak up the water quickly, exposing the pink hue of her skin beneath. He supposed the clinging material would mold itself to her breasts, calling attention to the darker rose hue of her nipples beneath the sheer fabric. He swallowed loudly again. The water was cold.

Her nipples would be standing at attention, straining, perfect little buds that would fit nicely into his mouth. He shook his head, trying to dislodge the visions, trying like hell to keep his promise to her. Jake tried staring across the pool into the barren distance. He stared until his eyes began to sting.

Gradually he noticed the children's voices fading. They were probably climbing the incline to try the rope again. He swam out deeper, knowing approximately where Toby and Wren should land. Then he wondered about Loreen. Where was she? Still wading out into the water? Or shivering, erect and deliciously wet on the bank?

"Jake?"

He turned, realizing she wasn't far away from him, and thankful that her body was completely submerged beneath the water. Then he realized she was headed for a drop-off.

"There's a drop," Jake started to warn her, but too late—she disappeared beneath the surface. She popped back up a minute later, gasping for breath. He waited for her to regain her footing. She didn't.

Jake dove beneath the water and swam to her. He grabbed her around the waist and propelled her backwards. They surfaced with her arms around his neck. He thought she might choke him to death.

"It's all right," he tried to calm her. "I have you."

"W-Why didn't you tell me there was a drop-off?"

She looked truly terrified. Jake brushed her long hair from her eyes. "I tried to but you went under before you heard my warning. See that big stick?" He nodded toward his marker. "I put it there today. That's were the drop-off is, so Toby will know, and the other one is a way up where the water gets too deep for Wren to touch bottom."

"You might have called that to my attention before I waded out too far."

"I wasn't looking, remember?"

"Oh, right," she said, still clinging to him.

In that instant Jake became uncomfortably aware of the difference between imagination and reality. Loreen not only had her arms around him; she'd wrapped her legs around him as well. Cold or not, the water couldn't douse the fire that sprang to life below the surface. Insisting she learn to swim might not have been such a good idea.

Jake waded back to the place where she could touch bottom and was about to let her go when Toby and Wren sailed through the air, releasing the rope in unison. Wren squealed before they hit the water.

He kept his gaze glued to the spot where they went under, relaxing only when they surfaced. To his credit, both swam toward him, proving that his patience over the past two weeks had paid off.

Once the children reached them—Wren holding on to Toby because she couldn't touch, Toby barely able to himself—the boy frowned at them.

"Loreen, why are you hanging on Jake like that?"

"Because I can't swim!" she answered shortly.

Wren began to giggle, and Toby's frown deepened. "You should be able to touch bottom."

Her gaze locked with Jake's. He grinned weakly before releasing her. "Toby, Wren, I can't watch you and teach Loreen to swim at the same time. Go on back to the house. Dry off and hang your wet clothes on the line."

Wren grumbled, and Toby narrowed his eyes on him again. Jake needed to have a serious talk with the boy, too. He was as bad as his elder sister, thinking every man wanted to get Loreen on her back.

"He's right," Loreen said. "I can't concentrate if both of you are swimming around out here. Jake can't give all of us his undivided attention."

"If I go, can I have some candy?" Wren wanted to know.

Jake answered automatically. "No," he said. "You can do what you're told without having to be bribed. And Toby, you're old enough to mind without being told twice."

Wren pouted and Toby offered him a final warning glance, but both children moved toward the bank. When Jake looked at Loreen, she wore a strange expression. He wasn't sure she approved of his stepping in with the children. Hell, he wasn't sure he did. He'd sounded like what he supposed was suspiciously close to being a father.

"Are you ready to learn to swim?" Jake asked.

She glanced out over the watering hole. "If I don't want to drown should I happen take a tumble in the creek or need to help one of the children, I don't see that I have a choice."

He liked Loreen's attitude. "First, you need to learn to stay afloat, and how to tread water. It doesn't matter how strong a swimmer you are; if you don't learn tactics to save your strength, in some situations, knowing how to swim won't save you."

His words obviously were not a comfort to her. She paled. "I'm terrified of the water," she admitted. "I keep remembering how it felt to be trapped beneath the surface."

"That's why you need to do this, Loreen. Otherwise your fear will only grow."

"All right. What do I do first?"

"I'll teach you to float first. We can do that in the shallows."

She looked relieved. "I'll be more relaxed if I know I can touch bottom."

A while later, Jake wasn't at all relaxed about being able to "touch bottom." Rather, he was tied in knots from not being able to touch hers. Loreen was floating on her stomach, his arms beneath her to help keep her afloat. Her wet drawers displayed her tempting bottom to full advantage.

"Why don't you try floating on your back?" he suggested, flipping her over. It wasn't a good idea: he had more to look at. A lot more. Jake released her. "Better yet, why don't we call it a day?"

Once she gained her footing, she frowned. "But I was just getting the knack of it. Can't you teach me a little about actually swimming?"

Torture. She might as well have asked him to tie a rope around his waist and let her drag him naked through a brier patch. "I should get back to work."

She lowered her lashes demurely. "Please?"

"Wren's the spitting image of you. Especially when she's trying to get her way about something." Jake said, looking at her thoughtfully.

Loreen's lashes lifted. "She looks more like my older brother, Joseph. His hair was red."

Loreen tried to slow the fast beating of her heart. She wasn't certain why, but Jake's comparisons between herself and Wren unnerved her. Or maybe it was the thoughtful way in which he regarded her—like a man trying to fit a puzzle with a missing piece together. She didn't want him to know about Wren. It wasn't any of his business.

"Just a while longer," she said, hoping to distract him from dwelling too long on her and Wren's similarities.

He rolled his eyes skyward, but waded toward her. She tried her best to keep her thoughts focused on the lesson. Loreen listened to Jake's patient instructions, and tried to ignore the fact that they brushed up against one another often. The entire situation was indecent, both of them wearing nothing but their water-soaked underthings, displaying far more of their bodies than was proper.

"I believe I can do it on my own now," she said, and wasn't certain, but thought she heard him breathe a sigh of relief. "What do I do next?"

"Give yourself a push off the bottom and kick your legs," Jake instructed.

Loreen couldn't get her feet high enough in the water to make progress. Jake appeared beside her, and just as he'd done while teaching her to float, he slid his arms beneath her stomach to help support her weight. Loreen splashed, thrashed, and, eventually, realized Jake's arms no longer held her up. She was actually swimming, and on her own!

"I did it!" she shouted. "I swam."

He grinned at her. "I knew you could."

Loreen was so excited about her accomplishment that she jumped forward and threw her arms around his neck. Without thought, she pressed her lips to his in a brief kiss. Only after the contact ended, and they were staring at each other, did she realize her emotions had gotten the best of her. Neither of them moved or spoke.

Jake looked deep into her eyes. His head bent and his lips brushed hers again. She pulled back, then leaned forward, their mouths barely touching, teasing. The sun beat down on her from overhead, but she didn't think it was responsible for the warmth flooding her veins. His mouth closed firmly over hers, igniting the flame of her passion.

She melted into him, their wet bodies and the heat between them making the air around them feel like steam. Her hands roamed his magnificent body, touching him as she'd wanted to do for so long. He cupped her breasts and brushed his thumbs across her nipples.

The sensation made her gasp; then his lips were on her neck, her shoulders, and moving steadily toward her straining peaks. She felt herself swell into his palms, aching deep inside for him to kiss her there, to take her into his mouth. As she leaned back, her lashes fluttered open, the incline coming into view. She blinked. Toby stood there, watching them, his face bright red.

"Oh, God," she said with a moan, shoving Jake away. He pulled her close again, his mouth seeking hers. "Toby," she whispered. "He's watching us!"

His head swung around, his gaze searching the incline. The passion drained from his face. "Get out and get your clothes. I'll handle this."

"He's my brother," she said. "I'll talk to him."

Loreen's legs felt shaky as she made her way to the bank. She grabbed up her clothes and hurried up the incline, although she had no idea what she would say to Toby, how she would explain her behavior when she didn't understand it herself. He met her the moment she made it to the top, and she didn't have to say anything. Toby seemed intent on doing all the talking.

"What are you doing, Loreen?" he demanded. "Trying to get yourself in trouble? You're acting like a whore!"

A hand flew defensively to her throat. Heat flooded her again, but it was a result of embarrassment and shame, not desire. She supposed she was acting the wanton, thinking with her body and not her head. Still, Toby saying such to her made her angry.

"Don't you dare speak to me that way," she said. "You have no right to insult me!"

"Don't I?" he shot back. He looked as though he would say more, but his gaze strayed to a spot behind her.

"Go to the cabin, Loreen," she heard Jake say. "Toby and I need to have a talk."

"I told you—"

"Go on, Loreen," Toby interrupted. "I'm the man of this family, and I'll handle this."

It sounded like a dangerous combination to her: one man, and one boy who thought himself a man, trying to settle a dispute over something that should have never happened—something that had happened, nevertheless, and with her just as responsible for the trouble as Jake. She saw Wren coming from the cabin and didn't want the girl to witness this particular confrontation. She would let Jake handle Toby first; then she would talk to him.

The moment Loreen made it to the cabin, took Wren's hand, and disappeared, Toby charged him. Jake stumbled back a step, but didn't fall. Toby swung at him, and Jake thought that in all fairness, he should probably allow the boy to get in a couple of good punches. But this wasn't the way he wanted Toby to learn to deal with his temper.

The second time Toby swung, Jake easily ducked

the punch. "You want to be the man of this family, you'll have to start acting like one," he said.

Toby's face colored. "If I'm to follow your example, I guess that means I should go around trying to get all of my friends' sisters in trouble."

Jake lowered his guard for a moment. Did that mean Toby considered him a friend? Toby landed a solid blow, and damned if the boy couldn't pack a wallop. Jake stumbled back. He rubbed his throbbing jaw.

"I guess I deserved that," he said. "But if you want to be treated like a man, you'll have to learn to say more with your mouth, instead of with your fists."

"I got some things to say," Toby said in a growl, but delivering a punch had obviously relieved some of his frustration. He lowered his fists. "I saw you and Loreen kissing."

"There's nothing wrong with two people kissing," Jake said. "As long as it's a mutual agreement," he added quickly. "It was a mutual agreement. And harmless."

"It didn't look that way to me."

Jake had to remember, that Toby wasn't five like Wren. The kiss he and Loreen had shared had started out harmless enough, but it had moved past that fast. "I am attracted to your sister," Jake admitted. "But I respect her, too. I wouldn't shame her by taking advantage of her innocence."

And that wasn't a lie. Jake would never set out to purposely seduce Loreen, although he couldn't swear that if she were willing, he wouldn't go as far as she wanted to go with him.

"You respect her?" Toby asked.

Jake's brow lifted in surprise. "Shouldn't I?"

Toby's face darkened, but he didn't answer.

165

"I hope *you* respect her, as well," he said, annoyed at Toby's lack of response. "She's taken care of you and Wren just fine, as far as I can see. There's nothing she wouldn't do for either one of you."

"She causes trouble," Toby said quietly. "I don't guess she means to, but when I saw you kissing her, I got scared."

Feeling awkward, Jake touched the boy's shoulder for a moment, then quickly withdrew his hand. "Scared of what?"

"Scared you're gonna hurt her. If you're staying, and we're not, why'd you go kissing her?"

A good question. "I don't know," he answered honestly. "I guess because I am attracted to her. But I'd never hurt your sister. I can promise you that, Toby."

"I want your word," Toby demanded.

At least Toby now seemed to value his word. Jake hoped he wasn't lying when he said, "You have it."

Toby gave him another hard look before he nodded. "We should get back to work," he said.

"We will," Jake agreed. "As soon as you apologize to Loreen for what you said to her earlier." He fixed Toby with a harder look than the boy had given him. "I figure you're old enough for me to say what I'm going to say. Never call any woman a whore. I don't care if she is one; you show respect to all females. And you especially show respect to those you love."

Another blush crept into Toby's cheeks, and Jake knew it wasn't anger, but shame over what he'd said to his sister that caused it. "I shouldn't have said that to her," Toby admitted.

"Tell *her* that," Jake warned him, then grabbed the boy and steered him toward the cabin.

Chapter Fourteen

Once Toby came from the cabin, looking properly sorry for his words to Loreen, and nodding to Jake that he'd done as instructed, Jake tackled like a man possessed the barbed wire fence he had yet to string on the north end of the field. He worked the rest of the day, stopping only long enough to get a drink. Even when dusk started to settle in and Toby had long since gone in for supper, Jake continued to push himself.

The muscles in his arms and back were screaming by the time he finished stringing the fence. On legs leaden with exhaustion, he made his way toward the barn to put away his tools. He was surprised to find who awaited: Loreen with his supper and Wren in her nightclothes.

The moment their eyes met, Loreen blushed. "I've tried to keep it warm for you," she said, indicating where she'd set his meal. "Unless you plan on working yourself to death, you need to eat."

Jake swore he could fall asleep where he stood, but his belly felt as if it were chewing on his backbone. He put away his tools and eased himself onto the open end of the buckboard, placing his plate in his lap.

"What are you doing out here this late, Wren?" he asked before shoveling a spoonful of food into his mouth.

"Lo— Mama says you're not sleeping with her. I told her you were so, and I wouldn't go to bed until you went into the back room with her."

He glanced at Loreen and lifted a brow.

"I've tried to explain that you would rather sleep out here in the barn, but she insists that you wouldn't."

"There's a problem with my sleeping in the house," he said to Wren, placing his plate aside. The child stepped forward and held up her arms for him to lift her. Jake hefted her up into his lap despite his aching muscles.

"What is the problem?" she asked seriously.

That was when he drew a blank. How to explain that he and Loreen weren't married the way other people were married? He knew Loreen had kept their bargain from Wren, and he saw the logic in not trying to explain what a child her age couldn't understand. Jake's gaze scanned the barn while he tried to come up with an answer. His gaze snagged on two glowing eyes in a dark corner of the barn.

"Midnight," he said.

"Midnight?" the child repeated.

Jake nodded. "That cat has taken to curling up beside me at night. I don't know if he could sleep without me."

A frown puckered Wren's brows. He had obviously

presented an argument worth consideration, in her young mind. "I don't want Midnight to be lonely," she said. A moment later she came up with a solution. "Midnight can sleep in the house with you and Loreen."

"No," her older sister spoke up. "You know the rules, Wren. Animals aren't allowed in the house. Midnight doesn't have manners. And you don't want him to sleep out here all alone, do you?"

Grudgingly, the little girl shook her head. "I guess not."

Loreen's soft sigh of relief almost made Jake smile. "Now, young lady, will you please go to bed?" she asked.

Wren wrapped her arms around Jake's neck. "I want my new papa to tuck me in."

He kind of felt as if he'd been kicked in the gut again. Jake brushed Wren's wild curls from her eyes. "Wren, I think 'papa' is a grand title. One someone has to earn. I haven't been around long enough to have earned such a compliment. I don't even look like a papa, do I?"

She eyed him. "No. You're too skinny and don't have long whiskers. My old papa felt like a soft pillow, and he used to tickle me with the hair on his face."

Jake smiled fondly down at the little girl. "For the time being, I think it would be best if you just called me Jake."

"All right," Wren grumbled. "But will you still tuck me in?"

"We need to let Jake finish his supper, Wren," Loreen fussed. "He must be starving."

Truth be known, Jake was almost too tired to eat,

but he gathered the girl in his arms and eased his weight from the wagon. "Just tonight," he told Wren. "And you have to go right to sleep."

With a shake of her red curls, she said, "I promise."

After Loreen took his plate, the three of them headed toward the cabin. Jake thought the house had a cozy, lived-in look about it, one that would suite him fine once the Matlands were gone. Then he'd have the whole place to himself. He'd sleep in that feather bed in the back room—but he'd sleep there all alone.

Toby raised a brow upon seeing him in the house so late, but said nothing. Jake paused at the ladder to the loft. As worn out as he was, it looked a mile high.

"Toby, fetch me some firewood before it gets too late," Loreen instructed. "And Wren, Jake is tired. You'll have to climb up by yourself."

Toby laid his whittling aside, and Wren reached out and grabbed the ladder. Jake flashed Loreen a grateful glance, then climbed up after Wren. There wasn't much room in the loft, and he had to walk bent over. The children had makeshift beds and straw mattresses. Wren quickly scrambled beneath her covers.

"Well, good night, Wren," he said, then turned to leave.

"Wait. That's not all there is to it. Don't you know nothing about tucking in little girls?"

He grinned at her cross expression. "I'm afraid I don't."

She patted the place beside her. "Come here and sit down."

"Yes, ma'am," he teased, his back aching in his bent position. Jake sat on the edge of her bed. "Now what do I do?"

"Pull the covers up around me snug," she instructed.

"Like this?" Jake pulled the worn quilt up over her face. She began to giggle. The covers were suddenly thrown back.

"Not like that, silly. Up around my shoulders."

"Oh." Jake made a pretense of fussing over the covers, pulling them up, then down, to one side and then another until Wren began to giggle again.

"You're funny, Jake. I like you."

She had the most angelic features, especially for the fiery nature she possessed. Jake touched her nose. "I like you, too." And he did. Immensely.

"Now kiss me good night and leave me alone." Wren sounded much more mature than her five years. "I'm sleepy."

"Yes, Your Majesty." Jake bent over her and kissed her cheek.

"What's a majesty?"

He tucked a corner of her blanket around her chin. "A queen. You know all about queens, kings, and princesses, don't you?"

She shook her head.

"Then I'll tell you a story." At the excitement that entered her eyes, he added, "But only a short one. I'm sleepy, too."

Jake launched into a fairy tale. As he spoke, Wren's eyes grew heavier. By the time he finished, she was fast asleep. Jake started to rise, then noticed Loreen sitting on the floor a short distance away.

"Who told you that story?" she asked softly.

"My mother. Years ago. I can't believe I even remembered it." Upon reaching her, he wondered if the soft glow in her eyes was genuine or a trick of the light.

"It was very nice. And kind of you to humor Wren and tuck her into bed."

171

"I don't imagine there will be much Wren can't have if she just asks. She's a heartbreaker."

Loreen smiled. Jake started down the ladder with the intention of helping her down. He did so at a speed reflective of the day spent too long at work. Loreen was almost upon him by the time his feet hit the floor. She turned around before he could step away.

Their bodies brushed and, exhaustion be damned, his senses stirred. Her blue gaze locked with his, and he knew they should discuss what had happened between them at the watering hole earlier.

"Did Toby apologize?" he asked, just to make certain.

She glanced down. "Yes, he did. Is he responsible for the bruise along your jawline?"

"Yes, he is."

Slowly her gaze lifted. "I guess we both needed some sense knocked into us."

He could use a little at the moment. "I'm sorry. It was my fault. I got carried away."

"Not everything is always your fault," she said softly. "Maybe both of us are trouble-prone."

She didn't douse his desire by admitting as much to him. Her ability to shoulder responsibility for her actions made him all the more attracted to her. And it was his attraction that made him step away from her. It turned out to be a good decision, since Toby came rushing inside, banging the door against the cabin wall.

"I need my rifle," he huffed. He glanced around frantically. "Those bastards are cutting the fence!"

In two long strides, Jake made it to the door. He saw dark shapes moving around in the field. It didn't really surprise him. Deep down he'd known Billy wouldn't let his beating go unpunished. He stopped Toby when the boy thought to push past him, rifle in hand.

"What are you planning to do?"

"I'm gonna shoot them," Toby answered. "You've been stringing that fence for a week!"

"Then I guess this is *my* problem."

The boy's chest heaved with emotion. He shoved the rifle into Jake's hands. "All right. You handle it."

Jake stepped out onto the porch, Toby hot on his heels. He aimed the rifle toward the sky and shot.

"You ain't gonna hit none of them that way," Toby said.

"Didn't plan to hit anyone," Jake countered. "I worked myself half to death over that fence, but barbed wire isn't worth killing a man over. There's very little that is."

He shot a couple more times in the air, and as the men raced for their mounts and the thundering of horses' hooves could be heard, he lowered the rifle and returned to the house. Loreen stood by the loft, then hurried over when he sat back down at the table to finish his meal.

"What happened?" she whispered.

"Nothing," Toby grumbled. "Jake just shot in the air to scare them off. They didn't get what they deserved for cutting that fence."

"I have more barbed wire," Jake informed him dryly.

"Yeah, and if you string it again, they'll only cut it again," the boy fumed.

As Jake finished supper, he mentally admitted Toby was right. They needed to plant, and soon. He couldn't keep restringing fence week after week. They'd never

173

get a crop in the ground. Still, he didn't need the law poking its nose around if he shot someone—even in self-defense. Plus, he had new principles, and they weren't worth throwing away over wire.

And he was damn tired of getting little sleep during the night in order to stand guard, as he'd been doing. He had to think of something, and even as the thought entered his mind, a solution came to him. And this idea, like all the others he'd had, wouldn't please Loreen. Not at all.

Chapter Fifteen

Loreen was furious. All of them were squeezed together on the front bench seat of the buckboard, headed for home after a pleasant afternoon spent with Manny and Gretchen Crawford. She'd been surprised when Jake, with the fences down and plowing to do, had declared that they all needed an afternoon off. Of course, now she understood—he'd had an ulterior motive.

"Wren, turn around and stop staring," she said tightly. "That animal would probably just as soon gobble you up as look at you."

"She's not mean," Wren declared. "She's just scared. She needs a friend."

In response, Loreen glared at Jake.

"Stay away from her," he warned Wren. "Manny said she's only growled at him, but she might bite if she feels threatened. I got her to protect the farm at night, not to be a pet."

"And who's gonna guard us from her?" Toby asked before Loreen could pose the question.

"We'll all have to be careful," he answered. "I'll keep her in the cage during the day, and there will be no going outside once I let her out. With things the way they are, no one needs to be roaming around in the dark anyway."

"You've added to our troubles by taking that wolf off of Manny's hands." Loreen sighed, then quipped, "We don't need more danger dogging our heels."

"That'd be a good name for her," Toby said. "Danger."

"Her name is Princess," Wren informed them all. She turned around again. "Hello, Princess," she called sweetly.

Loreen cast a fearful glance over her shoulder. The wolf actually pricked its ears and regarded Wren intently—probably trying to decide how long it would take her to digest the child. Loreen turned back toward the road.

"I imagine the minute you let her out of the cage, it will be the last we see of her," she said to Jake. "I hope you didn't pay Manny anything for her."

"No," he responded. "But I did agree to help him raise a new barn once I get the crop in. I hope he'll do the same for me someday."

A new barn would be nice, but then, that wasn't really any of Loreen's concern. What Jake did with the farm once she and the children were gone was none of her business. Placing them all in danger in the meantime was.

"I really wish you would have discussed bringing

the wolf home with me," she said. "You've only made an uncomfortable situation more so."

When he lifted a brow, she supposed he knew what she meant. Loreen felt confused about their relationship. They shared a common goal, but lately that didn't seem to be all they shared. She had enjoyed kissing him at the watering hole that day—liked the sensation of his mouth moving over her skin. No other man had made her feel the emotions Jake did. Desire? She certainly never thought she'd experience that with a man—any man.

"I suspect that this wolf is more snarl than snap," he said. "She's frightened and mistrustful, but in time I think she'll come around."

"She's not afraid of me," Wren informed them. "Maybe because I'm little."

Loreen cast Jake another dark glance, then turned to Wren, thinking the subject should be changed. "You acted very grown-up today watching after Samuel. He likes playing with you."

Honestly, Loreen had spent a wonderful afternoon with Gretchen. Her friend had promised to help Loreen sew new dresses for herself and Wren. Gretchen couldn't bake, but she was quite an accomplished seamstress.

"I like Samuel, too," Wren said. "Can we get a baby?"

So much for pleasant conversation. "No," Loreen answered, maybe a bit too firmly. She tried to control the blush she felt rising in her cheeks when Jake smiled and Toby lifted a curious brow. "We cannot have a baby," she stated, hoping to end the discussion.

"Why not?" Wren insisted. "Where do babies come from, anyway? And how do folks get one?"

Loreen removed her bonnet and began fanning her face. Jake's grin stretched. Toby's eyebrow lifted higher.

"I'm not sure," she answered, cutting her gaze toward the driver. "Maybe Jake knows."

Toby laughed, but Jake did not. He sobered considerably. "I asked my ma the same thing when I was about your age. I wanted a brother. She told me babies grow in flower gardens."

Despite her discomfort over the subject, Loreen almost smiled. Wren frowned.

"We don't have a flower garden," she said sadly.

"No, we do not," Loreen agreed.

Wren stayed quiet for a few minutes, then said, "I bet Jake can get us seeds." Her little face turned up to him. "You can plant flowers, can't you?"

Jake shifted uncomfortably on the bench seat. "I don't know, sweetheart. To my knowledge, I've never planted any flowers. I'll have my hands full just trying to plant maize."

"Then Loreen and I will plant them," she decided. "We'll grow us a baby."

Toby laughed again. Loreen wanted to box his ears.

"What's so funny?" Wren asked the boy.

Before her brother could blurt out an answer Loreen felt certain would only add to Wren's confusion, she said, "I think the flowers have to be planted by a man and woman who want a baby. Then a wish has to be made upon a star for a baby to grow in their garden."

"Oh." Wren's brows puckered. "That sounds like a lot of trouble."

"It is," Loreen assured her.

Loreen was thankful when Wren said nothing further, but the child's thoughtful expression worried her.

She assumed Wren was searching for flaws in her explanation, which would soon lead to more questions. The cabin came into view, and Loreen breathed a sigh of relief. From what she could see, they had no unwanted visitors and nothing looked out of place.

"Wren, as soon as we pull up beside the cabin, run inside and set the table for me. Toby, stoke the stove."

"But I wanted to watch Jake unload Princess," Wren complained. "I need to show her Midnight and tell her she's not to eat him."

"I wanted to see if she tries to bite Jake's hand," Toby said.

Again Loreen shot Jake a dirty look. He took control.

"Toby, Wren, do as your sister tells you. Neither of you needs to get too close to the dog. Not until we see if she can be trusted."

Loreen's laugh purposely held no humor. "We already know she can't be trusted. That's why Manny let you have the animal."

His gaze met hers. "Don't you believe in second chances?"

Jake always asked questions that made Loreen uneasy—as if he had insight to her past, as if he knew things about her he shouldn't know. She'd been given a second chance five years ago, and now her life was a shambles.

"We're not referring to a person," she answered. "We're talking about an animal, a wild dog who is obviously part wolf. If anything happens to one of the children because of her, I'm holding you personally responsible."

"What's 'sponsible mean?"

She glanced down at Wren, realizing this matter should be discussed in private. "Nothing, Wren," she answered as they pulled up in front of the cabin. "Go inside now and do what I asked."

Toby jumped down from the bench seat and held out his hands for Wren. He took the child and placed her on the ground, his gaze passing over Jake and Loreen.

"Are you gonna milk while you're in the barn bending Jake's ear?" he asked his sister.

"I'll see to it," she answered stiffly. "Once you get the stove going, feed the chickens and gather the eggs."

Jake flicked the reins and they moved toward the barn. He jumped down and opened the doors. Loreen took the reins and drove the wagon inside. She didn't wait for Jake's assistance to move from her perch atop the bench seat. Nor did she hesitate to express her concerns regarding his actions.

"I should have put my foot down and demanded you leave that she-wolf behind," she huffed. "What were you thinking, Jake?"

He went around the front of the wagon and began unhitching Ben. "I was thinking we needed some protection around here during the night. I can't stay awake and guard you, the children, and the farm, then work all day. Something had to give."

She had no idea he'd been standing guard over them during the night. He must be exhausted. "You should have told me. We could have taken turns."

His laugh was as flat as hers was earlier. "I couldn't sleep knowing you or Toby were roaming around in the dark. You both need to be bolted safely inside the cabin come dark."

"But that dog . . ." Loreen pleaded, her gaze moving to the cage in back of the wagon. The animal had cowered down, and it growled low in its throat. "The children . . ."

Jake led Ben into his stall and approached her. "I won't let Wren or Toby come to any harm. You're going to have to trust me, Loreen. And that's all I have to say about the matter."

Loreen wanted to stamp her foot in frustration. Jake could be as stubborn as a gravy stain. "The first time that dog even so much as looks at Toby or Wren the wrong way, she's gone. I'll get the rifle myself and see to it."

That brought a lift to his brow, but he said nothing. He moved around her and approached the cage. The growling grew louder with each step he took. The milk cow let out a frightened bellow that almost made Loreen jump out of her skin.

"She's scaring the other animals," Loreen said in a hiss.

"They'll get used to her." Jake pulled a pair of worn work gloves from his back pocket and slipped them on. "And she'll get used to them. I'm not putting her outside to suffer the elements." Despite the wolf's growling, Jake opened the cage door. "Throw me some rope," he instructed.

Loreen looked around frantically, found a long piece of rope, and pitched it to him. When he stuck his hands inside the cage, she squeezed her eyes shut. There was a lot of growling, and she wished she'd gotten the rifle before he attempted to unload the wolf. Loreen didn't like the idea of shooting anything, but she would if it became necessary.

"What's happening?" she asked, her eyes still closed.

"I've tied her up. I'm going to unload the cage and get her back inside."

Upon opening her eyes, she half expected to find Jake bloody from bites. She didn't see any blood. "Didn't she try to bite you?"

He hefted the heavy cage and lumbered toward a spot in the corner. "No. She's scared, not vicious, just as I thought."

"It's a little early to be making assumptions," Loreen warned him, but her gaze strayed to the wolf. She'd hunkered down, shaking. Loreen's heart softened. *Poor animal,* she thought. *Afraid of her own shadow. Mistrustful of all humans.* When Jake approached the wolf again, she didn't feel quite as sorry for the animal.

"Be careful," she whispered.

He leaned forward and snatched the rope from around the wolf's neck. Loreen realized the animal could attack either of them. She froze, as did the wolf.

"That wasn't smart," she said quietly. "Now she's free."

Jake stood very still, his eyes trained on the beast. "She doesn't want to be free," he said. "Watch her."

The wolf turned around in circles, her tail tucked between her legs. She whimpered, spotted the cage, and made a mad dash for safety. Jake walked over and closed the door.

Only then did Loreen remember to breathe. She let out a long sigh, and was suddenly furious with Jake again. "She could have torn us both to shreds!"

He walked over, lifted the back of the buckboard, and removed his gloves. "I didn't think she would. I played a hunch."

"You could have been wrong," she persisted.

He glanced at her and did the oddest thing: he smiled. "You're beautiful when you're riled, Loreen Matland. Your cheeks turn a pretty shade of pink, and your eyes sparkle like the stars."

A flush of pleasure merged with her ire, but she wouldn't let Jake sidetrack her. "I'm still mad about the dog," she declared. "Flattery will get you nowhere."

He joined her, tenderly brushing a strand of hair behind her ear. "I don't suppose so. I imagine you've heard every pretty word a man can think of."

Although she hadn't heard a polite compliment in a while, she'd heard her share of false flattery in the past. Pretty words were only tools a man used to chisel away at a woman's heart—to whittle her down until she crumbled. At his closeness, she took a step back.

"I need to milk," she blurted.

"I'll see to the milking," Jake offered. "Send Toby to fetch the bucket later. The cow's a bit edgy. She might kick."

Which brought them back to the subject of the dog. "I hope you know what you're doing."

"I've milked before."

"You know I'm not talking about the cow."

"Loreen." He said her name with a sigh. "If I had a silver dollar for every minute of the day you spent worrying over something, I'd be a rich man." He placed his hands upon her shoulders. "You need to loosen up."

When his strong fingers began to knead the tension from her shoulders, *relaxed* wasn't exactly what she felt.

183

"Stop," she said quietly.

His fingers ceased, but he didn't remove his hands from her shoulders. "You're about as nervous as that she-wolf. When are you going to realize I won't hurt you, or try to take advantage of you at every turn?"

She hadn't been worried about what Jake might do, but what *she* might do while they were alone. Her feelings for him didn't make sense, especially given the fact that she didn't plan on staying around.

Loreen pulled free from him and turned toward the door. "I'd better see to supper."

Once inside the cabin, she found the table set and the stove stoked and going. She'd cooked beans the day before with salt pork. All she needed to do was warm the beans and bake corn pone.

"You did a nice job on the table," she praised Wren. The little girl didn't complain nearly as much anymore when asked to help. Loreen suspected, with regret, that it was because Wren felt like part of a family again. "Want me to teach you to make corn pone?"

The child nodded enthusiastically.

"Where's the milk?" Toby asked.

"Jake offered to handle the chore, since the dog has the cow spooked. He said to send you to fetch the bucket."

Toby went willingly, no grumbling about fetching or carrying. She realized Toby no longer seemed to mind spending time with Jake, or working beside him. Toby's temper had much improved, as well. She supposed Jake had been a good influence on her brother.

"Can I stir?" Wren asked.

"Of course you can. I think you have a real talent for stirring."

Wren giggled. "You think I can do everything good."

Loreen touched her button nose. "I guess I do."

"What's talent?"

With a sigh, Loreen began mixing the ingredients for corn pone, knowing she would have to explain until Toby arrived with the milk. Luckily her brother didn't take long. Once the meal had been prepared, she sent Toby to fetch Jake for supper. The boy returned, informing her he'd said he was busy and to go ahead without him.

Annoyed that the man could never seem to appear on time for supper, Loreen fixed him a plate. She spooned up beans for Toby and Wren, crumbling pieces of corn pone into the mix; then she set off for the barn again. She had no desire to tarry, just to give Jake his supper and make a hasty retreat. Given her conflicting emotions of late, being alone with Jake probably wasn't a good idea.

Chapter Sixteen

After she entered the barn, Loreen drew up short at the low sound of Jake's voice. She glanced around nervously, wondering who would be paying them a visit at this late hour. Loreen didn't see anyone. In fact, she couldn't even locate Jake. Edging around the wagon, she saw him stooped down in front of the wolf's cage. The soft words he spoke to the animal made her lips twitch. She came close to smiling when the animal only growled at him in response.

"I don't think she's going to be taken in by pretty words either," she said.

Jake jumped at the sound of her voice. He straightened, turning to look at her. "I thought it was worth a try," he admitted, his face flushing slightly at being caught. "What are you doing in here?"

Loreen lifted his plate. "Nothing irritates a woman more than having her cooking go unappreciated. And nothing tastes quite as bad as cold beans and corn pone."

"Cold stew taste worse," he joked, but approached her.

"Would you rather come to the house?"

He shook his head. "I planned on sharing my rations with the dog. If pretty words don't appeal to her, food might soften her."

A shiver raced up Loreen's spine. "She might rather have you as a meal."

After taking his plate, Jake settled on the back of the wagon. "You sound almost concerned over my well-being, Loreen."

"I'm concerned about all of us," she countered. "Mostly Wren."

"Me?"

They both jumped. Loreen turned to see the little girl standing at the barn door.

"What about me?"

"What about you is right," Loreen said. "What are you doing out here?"

"I finished my supper and put my plate in the dry sink," the little girl answered. "I wanted to tell Princess good night." She held out a bowl. "And to bring her some supper, too."

Loreen gave Jake another dirty look. "I told you, you're not to go near that dog."

"But she likes me," Wren insisted. "She told me so. When I looked at her in the back of the wagon, I sent her a secret message. I told her she didn't have to be afraid of me, and she said she wasn't."

Jake put his plate aside and slid off of the wagon.

"It'd be nearly impossible for someone not to like you, Wren. But that wolf—"

"Princess," she demanded.

187

He sighed. "But Princess isn't a person, and we can't trust her. Not yet, anyway. Now go on back to the house and get ready for bed."

Wren's rosebud mouth formed into a pout. "I hate being the littlest. Everyone tells me what to do. Why can't the two of you plant a flower garden so there will be someone littler?"

Loreen groaned. "We're not going to discuss that again. And you're stalling for time. Go back to the house, and take the bowl with you. I don't think that wol—Princess would care for beans."

The child looked as if she wanted to argue further, but her shoulders slumped in defeat as she turned and went back outside. It took Loreen all of one second to pounce on Jake.

"Now do you understand what we're up against?" she asked angrily. "Wren trusts everyone and everything. It doesn't matter what kind of animal it is." She paused. "Well, besides chickens, Wren thinks all creatures are her friends."

"I do see," Jake admitted. "And I guess you were right this time. I should have never hauled the wolf home with us. Tomorrow I'll take her back."

Relief washed over her. "Promise, Jake?"

He stepped forward and drew her close. "I never aimed to place any of you in danger, especially not Wren. You know that, don't you?"

Blast those deep-set blue eyes of his. Loreen always felt a little dim-witted when he turned them on her. She nodded dumbly. Sensations all too familiar when he held her rushed to the surface. The shortness of breath, the pounding of her heart, the weakness in her limbs. Most damning of all was the lack of willpower to do anything except stare helplessly back at him.

"She does so like beans."

Jake and Loreen both froze. The pounding of her heart increased, then felt as if it rose to her throat when she realized who had spoken, and from what vicinity of the barn.

"Oh, my God," she whispered. "Wren!"

A hand was suddenly clamped over her mouth. Jake dragged her to the side of the wagon, where a terrifying sight shifted into view. Wren had come back in and opened the cage, and the wolf was out, gobbling down the bowl of beans the child held in her hand.

"Screaming will only startle the animal," Jake said in Loreen's ear. "Be very quiet and very still."

At her nod, he took his hand away from her mouth. Loreen tried to remain calm despite her terror. A moment later, Toby strolled into the barn.

"I was beginning to wonder—"

"Shhh!" both Jake and Loreen hissed.

"What is it?" he whispered.

Jake motioned him forward, and Loreen watched her brother's face drain of color.

"Wren, sweetheart," Jake called softly, but it wasn't the child who responded. The wolf glanced up and growled.

"Hush up, Princess," Wren scolded. "That's my family. Your family now, too. Don't go growling at them."

To Loreen's surprise, the wolf returned to her eating. "Wren," she tried. "Honey, please set the bowl on the ground and come here. But don't run. Walk very slowly."

"I can't come yet," Wren informed her. "I have to introduce Princess to Midnight."

Horror quickly returned as Wren set the dish down

and scrambled beneath the wagon, only to return a moment later holding a squirming cat. Loreen struggled in Jake's arms, but he held her fast.

"Those two won't get along," he warned Wren. "That wolf will try to eat him, and the cat will scratch you."

"Will not," Wren responded smugly. "Midnight, stop trying to get away. This here is Princess, and she's my dog. Princess, this here is my cat, and you're not to eat him, understand?"

The cat was suddenly shoved in the wolf's face. Loreen wanted to close her eyes, wanted to scream or rush forward to snatch Wren from the inevitable confrontation between the animals. Instead she stood frozen, waiting for the violent scene to unfold. The wolf leaned forward and sniffed Midnight. The cat sniffed her as well. The wolf's mouth opened, fangs gleaming; then a pink tongue emerged and gave Midnight a sound lick on the face. Unimpressed, Midnight turned his attention to the food.

Shocked, Loreen watched the wolf return to her meal, from all indications willing to share with Midnight. Wren petted both animals while they ate. Words were finally muttered. And if Loreen had been thinking them, and she suspected Jake had, as well, it was Toby who said, "Well, I'll be damned."

Damned was truly what Jake believed the Matlands were when he'd first learned about the circumstances surrounding them. Now, as he settled back on his makeshift bed made of straw, he wasn't so sure their future didn't look favorable. He'd spent the week nearly breaking his back to make up for lost time. The barbed wire was now restrung, the plowing finished, and he'd dragged a log across the ground to settle the dirt and break up larger clods.

Tomorrow they would plant. He couldn't quite believe they'd actually made it this far, and without his having to shoot Billy or one of his boys, or be shot by them. His good fortune made him nervous, and he figured Loreen and her constant worrying had rubbed off on him. He smiled thinking of her cool attitude toward him all week. That woman hated to be wrong.

Princess, it seemed, adored Wren, and even showed signs of a soft spot for the blasted cat that kept curling up next to Jake each night. Jake had to admit, it was a strange phenomenon. The wolf still growled when the rest of the family came too close to her, but one word—or sometimes even just a look—from Wren, and she quieted. The child had a gift when it came to animals.

Jake chuckled to himself. Imagine animals reading a person's thoughts, or vice versa. He hoped the little spitfire couldn't tell what *he* was thinking, or she'd be asking questions again—questions about why he kept thinking about Loreen. About kissing her and touching her. About lying naked with her, their legs entwined and their bodies slick with the sweat of passion. He'd been around Loreen for a while now. He'd assumed that with time, some of his attraction would have died away. That had hardly been the case.

It was the little things about Loreen that drew him to her: the way she smiled and her eyes grew warm when she watched Wren, the softness of her voice when she spoke to the child. It was clear to him that Loreen thought the sun rose and set on her younger sister, and although he knew she loved her brother as well, her love for Toby seemed somehow different. Maybe more natural as how one sibling should feel about the other.

He thought at times that Loreen took her new role as Wren's mother too seriously. But then, she was raising the child—and what did he know about women? Maybe all of them took to the role with practiced ease. God-given instincts, he guessed. Loreen had hers and he had his. His went on the alert. The subtle sound of feet crunching on dirt reached his ears, and in the distance he heard the soft nicker of a horse. Jake lay very still, listening. When the wolf began to growl, he knew he hadn't been imagining the noises.

Silently he crept from his bed and went to the door. He cracked it an inch. There were dark shapes descending upon his field. Billy's boys were back, and all of them, he suspected, were armed with tools to cut the fence. Jake swore softly. He moved to the corner of the barn where the cage rested, the wolf inside still growling low in her throat.

"All right, Princess. This is where you earn your keep." The dog hadn't been out of her cage at night before. Jake had allowed her to roam loose around the barn a couple of times, but only when the door was closed.

"There're men outside who don't belong here," he said quietly. "Run them off." He opened the cage and the wolf crept out. She went immediately to the door, and although Jake feared he would never set eyes on Princess again, he opened it and let her out. Then he waited.

The wait wasn't long. He smiled when the cussing and shrieking began. His smile stretched when growling and tearing noises followed. He couldn't help but laugh out loud when one of the men screamed, "Run!" The commotion was enough to wake the dead, so it didn't surprise him to see the glow of a candle appear at the cabin window. He only prayed Loreen and the children would stay inside until the men were gone.

Shots were fired, and his gut clenched. He hoped none of the bullets had found its mark. He scrambled outside, running out into the field.

Sounds of Princess's barking brought him a measure of relief. The animal was still alive, at least at the moment. As the animal's barks faded into the distance along with the sounds of the fleeing men, he worried she might chase them all the way back to Billy's place. Hoping the wolf wouldn't lose her way and become lost, he walked from the field, headed back to the barn.

The soft creak of the cabin door drew his attention. Loreen stepped out onto the porch. The candle she held cast a golden halo around her unbound hair, as well as silhouetting the shapely form of her body beneath her white nightgown.

"Jake?" she whispered, her gaze finding him standing in the dark.

"Go back to bed," he said. "It's over."

She stepped down from the porch and approached him, and Jake mentally groaned. It was the loneliest time of night, and he'd been fighting his feelings for Loreen for too long to deal with this attack on his senses. She wasn't safe out here when the moon was full and emotions ran strong—not safe with him. But she obviously didn't have the same instincts he had, because she kept walking toward him.

Chapter Seventeen

"What was that ruckus?" she asked.

"Billy's boys, come to fix my fence again."

In the candle's glow, her expression turned to one of concern. "I'm sorry, Jake. All that work for nothing."

He smiled. "I imagine my fence is still intact. I introduced them to Princess."

Nervously Loreen glanced around. "She's out? Running wild?"

"She took off after Billy's gang. It may be the last we see of her."

By the candle's glow, Loreen appeared as if she were choosing her words. "I can't say it would upset me not to see her again. But it would break Wren's heart. She's become attached to that wolf in a very short time. Still, I don't trust the animal. I never have and probably never will."

Vulnerability, or just plain foolishness—Jake didn't

know which of the two—made him ask, "I know you don't believe in second chances, but do you believe that people can change?"

She moistened her lips with the tip of her tongue. "We're not referring to people. We're discussing an animal."

The issue was important to Jake. What had happened to him a year ago in a small bank in Kansas had forever changed him. He needed to know if Loreen believed that even the worst of men could become decent. Why he needed to know, he wasn't ready or willing to question.

"Then let's talk about people," he said quietly. "Do you believe they can change?"

An irritated sigh escaped her. "Are we discussing me? Because if you're going to give me another lecture—"

"Hell, Loreen," he swore, "why does everything have to be about you?" Annoyed with himself for even starting the conversation, and just as irritated that what she thought of him mattered, Jake turned back toward the barn. "Go to bed."

He stormed into the barn and kicked one of the wagon wheels. Jake had headed down a dangerous path with Loreen. Why would he want to confess all of his sins to her? Why would he want her forgiveness?

"I'm sorry."

The flame's glow chased the shadows from the barn. Jake turned to see her place the candle on a board.

"You're right. I do seem to assume everything is about me. But it isn't because I'm prideful or vain; it's only because I find so many faults in myself."

His temper immediately cooled. "From where I'm standing, they're hard to see."

Her shoulders stiffened. "Do you think being pretty is all a woman has to be?"

"No," Jake quickly assured her, closing the distance between them. "You are pretty, Loreen. More than pretty, but that's not all I see when I look at you. You have a strength you're not aware of, a stubborn streak a mile wide, and a sweetness about you despite your sharp tongue."

"And here I thought you were going to try to fill my head with flattery again," she said sarcastically. "But we aren't talking about me, remember? You wanted to know if I thought a person could change. Change in what way?"

He silently cursed himself again for asking her in the first place. She had her own plans and he had his; they weren't the same. There was no need to confess his past to Loreen—he had no call to share his secrets with her.

Still, he found himself asking, "Do you think a bad person can become a good one? Or do you believe that once a person has strayed, they can never walk the straight and narrow again?"

She cocked her head to the side in a manner he found endearing—sweet but distracting. The position left a long strip of her neck exposed. It was a stretch of territory he'd like to explore.

"I believe a bad person can become a good one given the right circumstances, or the other way around. Are you asking if a person should be condemned for the rest of her life because of her mistakes? I suppose it depends on the mistakes."

If the first part of her answer filled him with hope, the last part dashed them upon the rocks. His was not a simple mistake. It was a very bad one. If Loreen knew who and what he really was, she wouldn't be standing alone with him in a candlelit barn in nothing but her nightgown. She wouldn't lower herself even to speak to him, much less to allow him to kiss her.

And he wanted to kiss her badly—to kiss her while she still believed cowardice was the worst of his traits, to kiss her while she naively assumed the hands touching her belonged to a farmer. While the candle flickered and sent light dancing upon the walls, while the night slept and the innocent slumbered in it, he wanted to kiss Loreen as if there were no tomorrow, because in his circumstances, he never knew. Tomorrow could just as easily find him swinging from a rope as planting a field of grain.

"You'd better go inside," he said.

She glanced around, fumbling with her nightdress nervously, but she made no move to follow his suggestion. "I'm wide-awake. Maybe we could talk some more."

"Talk about what?"

Her gaze wouldn't meet his. "Mistakes," she answered, chewing her bottom lip in a manner he'd come to recognize. She wrestled with something, but whatever it was, his own struggle was worse. The longer she stood before him, the harder it was to refrain from touching her.

"We can talk about mistakes," he answered. "And the one you're making right now."

She lifted her gaze abruptly. "What mistake?" she whispered, and her lips looked so petal soft, so tempting, he had to turn away from her.

"I want to kiss you," he answered bluntly. "And if you don't go, I'm going to, whether you ask me to or not."

He expected to hear her scramble from the barn in a hurry. What he heard instead was complete silence. Jake turned back to her. Loreen's lips parted slightly, and he figured that was as much an invitation as the fact that she was still standing there. He thought she might not have heard his warning, but she wasn't deaf, and he'd be damned if he gave her another one.

Closing the distance between them, he pulled her into his arms. He didn't bother with tender explorations or gentle persuasion. Jake kissed Loreen hard and deep, channeling his fears, his doubts, and his passion for her into the fusion of their mouths.

His ardor frightened her. He knew because she tried to pull away. He softened his claim on her lips, soothing the sting with light kisses, teasing until she responded. He kissed her tenderly, holding himself back because he wanted Loreen to know he wouldn't hurt her. Not ever.

Gradually the kiss shifted, became more intense. Loreen returned his ardor with a passion that surprised him, her tongue dipping into his mouth to tease his, her hands beginning to roam.

Caught up, he didn't realize he'd maneuvered her to his straw mattress until he'd gently lowered her to the blankets. Jake still had the presence of mind to question what the hell he thought he was doing—but he lacked the willpower to stop himself. Their lips remained joined as his fingers reached for the buttons on her nightgown. She didn't stop him, not after the first button or the second. Not even when he'd unfastened all of them.

She opened his shirt, running her hands over his chest. He sucked in his breath at the feel of her ripe breasts against his skin, groaned when he filled his hands with her, and what little control he still had left slipped away.

Loreen felt herself slipping away, swept up in a whirlwind of emotion, lost in the heat of seeking mouths and roaming hands, of bodies pressing against one another in a dance as old as time. Somewhere in the far recesses of her mind, she knew important boundaries were being crossed.

But reason could not battle passion, and Jake made her feel things she had never felt before. She came alive beneath his mouth and hands. With him, the memories of pain and humiliation she'd suffered five years ago faded. Only he could slip past her defenses of shame and guilt to touch the woman inside of her—the woman who still wanted to believe that the joining of two souls could be beautiful, despite the ugly past that haunted her.

Her breasts swelled into his palms, the friction of his callused fingers teasing her nipples into hard buds of sensation. The feel of his mouth where his hands had once been intensified the torture. She felt as if she might explode. His gentle sucking created a tension in her, started a pulse deep in her very core, a throbbing that pounded between her legs. She knew what she wanted, and that she could want him in that way—want him inside of her, ripping, tearing, hurting—shocked her back to reality.

She clasped his head between her hands and made him look at her. "I'm afraid," she whispered.

His eyes were bright with either the glow of passion or the flickering flame of the burning candle—she wasn't certain which.

"What are you afraid of, Loreen?"

"I'm afraid you'll hurt me."

He pressed his forehead against hers. "I would never want to hurt you."

"But you would," she said, sadly resigned to the fact. "You would hurt me to get what you want."

Pulling back to look at her, he sighed. "I don't know any more about a woman's pain the first time than you do. Nothing except what I've heard, but I do know how to give you pleasure without hurting you."

Besides what he'd already done to her, Loreen couldn't see things going any further without the degradation surely to follow. "How?"

His lips brushed hers softly. "To show you, you'd have to trust me again."

Trusting Jake had been a slow process, and under the present circumstances, might be impossible. He believed her fear stemmed from ignorance, when in fact it resulted from the opposite. She *had* been a fool once, trusted with all her heart, and she'd paid dearly for the mistake. But Jake was different. What he made her feel was different.

"I'll try," she compromised.

He claimed her lips again in a slow, melting kiss that turned her blood to fire. The burning trailed a path from her mouth to her breasts, where he lowered his lips to trace the circles of her nipples. He suckled her straining peaks, teasing them with his tongue, causing a pulsing to begin again somewhere deep inside of her—that insistent ache that spread through her and settled between her legs. His fingers were there a moment later. Loreen tensed.

"I promised I won't hurt you, remember?"

She wanted to believe him. And he'd asked for her trust, so Loreen willed herself to relax, trying for the first time in a very long time to place her faith in a man. At least she wore her cotton pantalets, and, as yet, he hadn't attempted to remove them.

His touch was gentle. He stroked her breasts and the throbbing place between her legs, and he kissed her. The pleasure grew, became more intense, and rather than relaxing, she felt as if she were being tied in knots. Breathing became difficult, as did focusing on anything other than the building sensation inside of her.

When he broke from her lips and paid homage to her aching breasts, she arched against him, against his mouth, against the fingers lightly stroking her through the thin fabric of her underclothes.

Heat flooded her lower regions. The throbbing beneath his fingers drove her to desperation. She pressed harder, moved in rhythm with his fingers, and still it wasn't enough to end the torture. "Please, Jake," she whispered, although she didn't know exactly what she begged him to do.

She groaned in agony when his fingers ceased to stroke her, only to moan in ecstasy when he slid his hand inside her underclothes, touching her with no boundaries between them.

Embarrassment should have claimed her, shock that he touched her in so intimate a place, but some primitive need pushed modesty aside—left room for only him, only the beating of her heart and the pulsing of her flesh beneath the steady stroke of his fingers.

His lips were on her ear. She heard the labored sound of his breath, the low groan in his throat, and felt the hard length of him pressing against her leg. His body moved against her with the motion of his hand, and only the fact that he remained fully clothed from the waist down kept panic from overwhelming her passion.

"Let go," he whispered in her ear. "Take what you want."

She didn't know what she wanted, but she knew she wanted something, and she wanted it badly. Her thighs began to tremble. She pressed against him harder, faster, the gathering sensation reaching a painful crest; then her world burst apart.

A tide of pleasure, hot and sharp, rocked her. A low, animal sound escaped her lips. Her nails dug into Jake's shoulders. She shuddered, shook, and said things to him no decent woman would say, things she hadn't even known she knew the meaning of—but words he obviously did.

He pressed his arousal harder against her; then he groaned and rolled away. Jake sat up, burying his head in his hands, his breathing fast and ragged. Loreen stared at him in awe. She'd never experienced any-thing like the pleasure he'd just given her, had never known it was possible.

She felt reborn, as if the world, at least in this moment, was a place of mystery and intrigue, a place of wonder. However, Jake, she noted, didn't seem to share her rapture. He looked as if he was in pain. She felt as limp as a rag doll, but managed to lift herself to a sitting position.

"Jake, are you all right?"

Slowly he lowered his hands to look at her. His gaze dropped to the front of her gown, which she realized gaped open, revealing a good portion of her breasts. He groaned and glanced away from her.

"Go to the house, Loreen. Go now."

His voice held an edge. Loreen wondered if he was angry with her. Or was he repulsed? Was he sickened by her brazen behavior? Did he think she was a woman of the lowest standards to allow him to do what he'd done?

With trembling fingers, she quickly buttoned her nightgown. Her legs were shaking, but she managed to rise. The intense pleasure she'd felt only moments before turned to unbearable pain. Her eyes started to sting.

"I'm so ashamed," she whispered brokenly, then rushed toward the door.

Strong hands grasped her shoulders and wheeled her around before she escaped. Jake pulled her close. "You have nothing to be ashamed of, Loreen. I promised I wouldn't hurt you, and somehow I have. I've given you shame when all I wanted was to give you pleasure. I've made you think you're weak, when it is my own weakness I'm fighting." He kissed her softly. "At this moment, I want you more than I've ever wanted anything. Can you feel how much I want you?"

He pressed against her, and the hard length of him made her breath catch in her throat.

"I asked you to trust me, but now I can't trust myself. That's why I told you to go. That's why I have to make you leave."

Warmth flooded past the chill of rejection she'd experienced a moment past. She wanted him, too—wanted to give him the same pleasure he'd given her, to sacrifice herself, for surely allowing him to join his body with hers would kill her. She shuddered slightly at the thought.

"You would be the death of me," she said, unknowingly expressing her fears aloud.

Jake lifted her chin, forcing her to look into his eyes. "What?"

Since she couldn't lower her chin, she lowered her gaze. "Us. We could never . . . I mean, it wouldn't fit. . . ." her voice trailed away.

He laughed, surprising her. "We would fit, Loreen," he assured her. His expression sobered. "It might be a tight fit, like a fine glove stretched snug—" He took a deep breath. "Damn." He stepped away from her. "Go, Loreen. Leave before I ask you to trust me again— trust me to give you the same pleasure I gave you earlier, but this time, with the part of me you fear."

She knew her gaze widened. "I don't see how that would possible. Not after . . ."

His blue eyes pinned her. "Not after what?"

Oh, God, she'd almost told him, almost allowed the secret she'd been carrying around with her for years to slip past her lips. He thought her innocent. It was that innocence he desired. He didn't know her, wouldn't want her if he knew the truth. No decent man would.

"I have to go," she said, frantic to escape. "I don't know why I allowed this to happen. We both know it shouldn't have."

"Sometimes things that shouldn't happen do," he said. "But you're right: we both know better."

She supposed she'd secretly hoped he'd argue with her, explain to her why they couldn't seem to keep their hands off of one another, and give her reasons to doubt her decision to leave. Loreen knew that for her, her attraction to Jake was not merely physical. What he felt for her obviously was, and she realized she was making a fool of herself again.

When he stepped toward her again, looking as if he meant to say more, she rushed outside and ran to the cabin. She couldn't bear to hear him tell her, as he had the day she'd met him, that sometimes two people liked what they saw and there was no use denying it. She wasn't that shallow, and she hoped Jake wasn't, either. If he was, she'd just made another bad mistake. If a woman trusted a man with her body, she should be able to trust him with her heart. And she didn't know if she did trust Jake with her heart, or if she could. Not yet.

Chapter Eighteen

Breakfast was strained to say the least. Jake wasn't in the best of moods. He'd spent the night tossing and turning again. Even a late-night swim in chilly water hadn't doused his desire for Loreen. And he had no right to desire her, to do what he'd done with her last night.

She had no idea who he really was, what he'd done, or why he'd answered her advertisement for a husband. Sure, he'd been tempted to tell her, but he hadn't; instead he'd taken liberties with her he had no right to take, felt emotions for her he had no right to feel.

He'd tried to win her trust without earning it, not in the way he should: by confessing his sins to her, by telling her he'd begun to question the decision he'd made a year ago to run. He'd even thought of asking her what she thought he should do to right his wrong. But he hadn't done any of that, because he'd taken the coward's way out again.

He wasn't sure Loreen knew him well enough, trusted him enough, to hear the truth and believe him, and that made what they'd done together wrong. He knew it and she knew it, and knowing had made the tension between them this morning feel as thick as Loreen's homemade butter.

"Loreen said Billy's boys tried to cut the fences again last night," Toby commented. "She said that wolf ran them off."

"*Princess* is her name," Wren reminded her brother. She turned to Jake. "Is Princess all right? She didn't get hurt, did she?"

In the process of setting a plate of flapjacks on the table, Loreen glanced at Jake, her worry over how Wren would react to the dog's being missing unmistakable.

"Princess is fine," he said. "I thought she might get lost, but she crept into the barn sometime before dawn and went right back into her cage."

The little girl frowned. "I don't see why she has to stay in that nasty cage anymore."

"Because she wants to," Jake remarked, filling his plate. "I left the door open last night, but she doesn't want to come out. She's not ready to let go of her past."

A fork clattered noisily against Loreen's plate. Jake lifted his gaze. At the strange expression on her face, he raised an eyebrow.

"But why can't she?" Wren asked. "She knows I won't hurt her." Her big blue eyes widened. "Maybe she doesn't know *you* won't hurt her, Jake."

He poured molasses over his flapjacks. "I've tried to show her, but I guess she's not ready to trust me yet." When the elder sister's fork clattered to her plate again, he asked, "Are you trying to play music, Loreen? Or are you going to eat?"

Toby laughed "She's edgier than a long-tailed cat in a roomful of rockers this morning."

Loreen jumped up from her chair. "I'm not very hungry. Princess can have my breakfast."

"The rest of mine, too." Wren pushed her plate aside and rose. "I'll feed her."

"Sit down, Wren." Jake pulled her plate back. "You haven't eaten enough, and the dog doesn't need all that food. Manny must have fed her too well and given her too little running room. She's as fat as a pig."

"Is not," Wren argued.

"She is, too," Toby countered.

Stepping forward to spear two flapjacks with her fork, Loreen said, "She is fat, Wren. A-And I'll feed her."

Both children's mouths fell open when she walked out of the cabin, plate in hand.

"But Lor— Mama is scared of that wolf," Wren whispered. "Why'd she do that?"

A ready answer came to Jake: Loreen would rather face the snarling, growling wolf this morning than him. "You two finish your breakfast and do the dishes for Loreen," he said to the children. "We need to get the planting started, and it will take all of us."

"Me, too?" Wren asked.

Her excited expression made him smile. He rose from the table, then touched her little nose. "I have a very important job for you."

"You do?" she said softly. "What is it?"

"I'll tell you when I get back. I'd better check on your sister."

"She's my mama now," Wren reminded him. "And Toby's."

"Loreen ain't my mama," the boy grumbled. His gaze lifted from his plate. He stared right at Jake when he said, "But I reckon she can rightfully claim Wren as her own."

Something in the boy's eyes, in his tone of voice, struck Jake as odd—as if Toby were trying to divulge information without actually spelling it out.

"And why would that be?" he asked.

The boy's gaze stayed to Wren. He shrugged. "Wren's still little. She needs a mama. I'm nearly grown."

Although the explanation was reasonable, Jake had a feeling it wasn't the entire truth. Just as he suspected, Loreen had secrets she had yet to uncover. What had she been about to say last night after she'd expressed disbelief that a man could give a woman pleasure with the part of him that made him male? She'd said she couldn't believe it, not after . . .

She hadn't finished the sentence, but he remembered how her face had suddenly gone pale, the haunted look that had entered her eyes. Something she didn't want to tell him had almost tumbled from her lips. And Jake suddenly suspected he knew what that something was. If he had hit upon the truth, it made his blood turn cold in his veins. It made his fists clench into balls of anger. He wanted answers from her, and he wanted them now!

* * *

Princess accepted the food, but Loreen still felt nervous about getting too close to the animal. She glanced around the barn, waiting for the dog to finish so she could take the plate back to the house for a good scrubbing. Her gaze landed on the blankets folded neatly on top of the bench seat of the buckboard. Jake's blankets.

The blankets she'd lain on with him last night. Loreen felt the walls closing in on her. There were too many reminders here of what had happened between them—what she had foolishly allowed to happen. Another reminder, the strongest one of all, appeared inside the doorway of the barn. His stormy expression took her off guard. His strong jaw looked clenched, and his blue eyes were ablaze, but not with passion.

"He raped you, didn't he?"

Her hand went automatically to her chest. "What?"

Jake stormed toward her. "Billy. He did more than try to kiss you and tear your dress that day in the alley. He raped you."

She was so shocked by the accusation, she couldn't speak. Jake shook her gently.

"Tell me," he demanded.

"W-Where did you get such an idea?" she whispered, freeing herself from his hold. "Billy's intentions toward me are hardly honorable, but as yet, he hasn't been brave enough to carry out his threats."

His bluster faded. "I assumed . . . that is, after what you said last night, or almost said, I thought you'd been—"

"What did I say to make you assume any such thing?"

Jake looked her square in the eyes. "You said, 'Not

after . . . ' And you were voicing your doubts that a man could give a woman pleasure with his . . . well, you remember."

She did remember. And she recalled the horror she'd felt at almost blurting out the truth—the same terror she knew now at being confronted. She'd hoped that with so many other mistakes she'd given Jake to dwell upon the previous night, this small one would have fallen through the cracks.

How could she explain her reluctance to believe that intimacy between a man and woman would be anything but painful and degrading without telling him the reason? The answer was simple: she didn't have to tell him anything.

"You have made a wrong assumption," Loreen said stiffly. "Now, if you'll excuse me." She tried to step around him. He wouldn't let her.

"It wasn't what you almost said; it was the way you looked afterward. The pain and suffering I saw in your eyes. Something has happened to you, Loreen. Something you're trying to hide from me. Tell me what it is."

Her heart pounded wildly inside her chest, but her fear had ebbed, replaced by righteous indignation. "I don't have to tell you anything. What may or may not have happened to me in the past is none of your business." Anger brought tears to her eyes. "You have no right to question me, to judge me. We have a bargain, an arrangement, and it doesn't include—"

"Our bargain wasn't supposed to include what happened last night either. After all we've shared that wasn't in the original bargain, if someone or something has hurt you, I thought you might want to tell me."

The temptation to confess almost overcame her. If

she wanted to end the dangerous attraction between her and Jake, the truth would do it. But she couldn't bring herself to tell him. And the reason why, the true reason, scared Loreen to death: she cared what he thought of her. Cared deeply.

Not for a moment when she'd placed the advertisement for a husband, did she believe the arrangement would turn into more, that her heart might become compromised in the bargain. An emotional involvement with Jake was not an option. Therefore, she had to say something to chase the concern from his eyes.

"As I said, my life is none of your business. And what would you have done had Billy raped me? Given him a good tongue-lashing?"

Her strategy worked. The concern drained from his expression. A cool mask settled in its place. "If that little jab was meant to castrate me, it won't work. Whether you like it nor not, I am a man. And you didn't seem to dispute that fact at all last night."

Loreen tensed. "You are no gentleman to keep bringing up last night."

"I've never claimed to be a gentleman," he countered. "And it seems as if things just keep popping up between us."

She was not amused by his phrasing. Noticing that the dog had cleaned the plate and gone back to her cage, Loreen scooped up the dish.

"We have planting to do," she reminded him. "I think it would be best if we kept our minds on work and kept our distance from one another. I'll fetch the children and meet you in the field."

As if she were an officer in the calvary, he gave her a mock solute. Loreen flounced past him, refusing to let him know how touched—or how frightened—she'd

212

been by his delving into her past. The less he knew about her, and her growing feelings for him, the better off she'd be. She and Jake were slowly, but steadily, reaching their goal. One crop, that was all she needed to bring in. Nothing must compromise her plans to escape.

His original goal had been compromised, but Jake would be damned if he would let last night fill his head with nonsense. He could have no more fanciful notions that there could be more between him and Loreen than a cold agreement. She'd made herself clear earlier: she wanted to share nothing further with him. She wanted distance between them, so he'd give it to her.

He flicked Ben's reins to move the plow forward. Jake would harrow the ground, and Loreen would plant the maize. Toby would follow behind with a rake to move the dirt over the seeds, and, true to his word, Wren had a very important job. She walked with Toby, scaring off the birds as they tried to eat the seeds.

Determined to keep Loreen out of his mind, he threw himself into his work. He managed for a good long while; then the touch of Loreen's hand on his arm made him pull Ben to a stop. The worry in her eyes alerted him to danger. He quickly followed the direction of her gaze. A spiral of dust could be seen coming from the road.

"Get Toby and Wren inside," he said.

The thought of Billy's gun he'd fished from the water trough surfaced. He'd hidden it away inside his saddle packs. Jake squelched the temptation to retrieve the weapon. Hiding behind a gun was a coward's way. Toby had his rifle in the house. The boy knew how to use it, too.

Ronda Thompson

As the dust grew closer, Jake took up a position in front of the cabin. A whine sounded. He glanced down to see Princess sitting beside him. The dog acted peculiar. He knew her eyesight and hearing were far better than his. She didn't growl or act as if danger approached. Just the opposite: she scurried away to the barn and her haven, the cage.

A few minutes later, when a buggy came into sight, pulled by his once-prized mare, he knew why the dog felt no need to protect her new territory. Jake bounded up the porch steps and pounded on the door.

"You can come out!" he called. "It's the Crawfords!"

The door was immediately flung wide. Loreen's cheeks were flushed with pleasure. "Gretchen's coming?" She hurried onto the porch. "But I have no tea," she fretted. "No pie. Nothing to offer—"

"Calm down. They might be just stopping by on their way into or from town. Maybe they don't intend to stay."

"Not staying," she repeated breathlessly. "Of course they're staying."

"We are in the middle of planting," he reminded her.

Loreen glanced down at her dusty dress, noticed the seed sack still slung over her shoulder, and groaned. "I am not at all presentable." She removed the sack and shoved it at him. "Stall them while I tidy up."

The door was almost closed when she jerked it back open. She reached out, grabbed a dirty-faced Wren, and pulled her inside. Loreen stuck her head out.

"You and Toby at least beat the dust from your clothes."

A loud whack followed the closing door. Since Toby had set about brushing off his clothes, Jake figured he

214

should do the same. He was about to step down from the porch when the cabin door opened again. Loreen and Wren stepped outside, their faces clean, their hair smoothed, and if he wasn't mistaken, Loreen was wearing a different dress. The quick transformation was surely a small miracle.

Before he could comment on the matter, the Crawfords pulled up in front of the cabin. Jake had to admit the sorrel mare he'd traded to Manny looked as sharp as an arrowhead pulling his fancy buggy.

"Gretchen," Loreen called, hurrying down to greet the woman.

The excitement in her voice made Jake smile. That was what all the fuss was about: she was happy to see her friend and wanted everything to be just right. The dark-haired German girl looked equally pleased to see Loreen.

"I told my Manny it was not proper to visit people who are not expecting company. Forgive our bad manners."

"Nonsense," Loreen said. "You must call on us whenever you wish. Please come inside."

"Can't," Manny piped up. "We're on our way to town, but Gretchen wanted to drop off some of her strudel and her fine sausage for you."

Loreen's cheeks flushed. "I have nothing to trade."

"Why must everyone trade in this country?" Gretchen blustered. "It is a gift from one friend to another. I want nothing in return."

"Loreen would be happy to bake the pies for your barn raising," Jake offered.

Manny's face turned red. "Uh, I guess I didn't mention it would be just the two of us, Jake. They don't have barn raisings in Miller's Passing like regular folk. No dancing or such. The folks are afraid of—"

"Let me guess," Jake interrupted. "They're afraid of making Billy mad, or worse, having him join the party?"

"That's the short and long of it," Manny answered.

"What about you, Crawford? Are you afraid of stepping on Billy's toes?"

The giant appeared rightfully outraged. "I fear no man. But I feared for my wife and child when Billy cut my fences and threatened my family. I've taught Gretchen to shoot since then, and she's a fair sight better than I am. I'm not as worried now."

"Then prove it," Jake suggested. "Have yourself a real barn raising."

Manny scratched his whiskered chin. "With dancing and food? Would you like that, Gretchen?"

His wife paled. "And people?" she whispered.

Her husband frowned. "It'd be damn good for you, woman. It's time you tried to mix with these folks."

"I will think on it, husband."

Jake suspected the thinking was already over. Gretchen was clearly terrified of the prospect of entertaining people she believed didn't accept her in the community.

"Here are your strudel and sausages," Gretchen said, handing the items to Loreen. "Have you cut out the dresses you want me to sew for you and Wren?"

Shyly, Loreen nodded. "I have, but you've already done so much for me. I would like to do something for you."

A hint of a smile crossed Gretchen's lips, as if she were waiting for just such an opportunity. "You can come to town with me and Manny. And little Wren, too."

The rosy hue of excitement on Loreen's face quickly faded. "Oh, I . . . well, it's Saturday and"—she indicated the field with a sweep of her hand— "we're planting today."

Manny finally took the time to survey the field. He grunted in satisfaction. "I see your fences are still up. Don't tell me that wild she-wolf is responsible?"

"Her name is Princess," Wren informed him sweetly. "And she likes me and my cat."

With some amusement, Jake watched Manny's mouth drop open. "The hell you say!"

Wren's eyes widened. "I didn't say that."

Gretchen poked her husband in the ribs. He blushed for cursing in front of the children. "Well, are you gals coming with us or not?"

As Jake watched Loreen's gestures and her expressions, he realized she was still frightened about going into town. The farm had become her prison, and he wasn't going to let it continue. He saw no reason for her not to go, not with the Crawfords for companions.

"You and Wren should go," he said. "I'll have to give Ben a rest before long. You won't be gone long, will you, Manny?"

The giant shook his head. "Just going because Gretchen wants some new buttons and a bonnet. If it wasn't Saturday, I'd send the gals on their way and help you plant."

"Get back before dark and I may put you to work."

Loreen grew more nervous with each minute that passed. Jake wouldn't soften. For her own good, he walked over and hefted Wren into the buggy. He turned to Loreen. "Run into the house and get some money from your jar. We need tea, remember?"

She went, but he sensed that it took all of her willpower to do so. He thought the trip would be for her own good. Jake hoped he wasn't making a mistake.

Chapter Nineteen

The only consolation Loreen found from being in Miller's Passing on a Saturday—when most of the neighboring farm folk came into town, Billy Waylan included—was that the woman with her was even more frightened than she was. Loreen feared one man. Gretchen was afraid of the whole town. And shortly after departing the buggy, Loreen had begun to understand why.

While women smiled and nodded at Loreen, they did not so much as acknowledge Gretchen's presence. It was if Manny's wife did not exist, as if she were a ghost with no form, instead of a warm, spirited German girl with dark hair and kind eyes. Their treatment of her friend made Loreen furious—mad enough to forget her own fears in light of Gretchen's unhappiness.

They were inside Mr. Johnson's mercantile looking at buttons while Wren and Samuel stared longingly at the candy counter. There were a few women milling about the store. One of them was Hetty Johnson; the woman only helped her husband on Saturdays, when there was the chance for gossip. Loreen took Gretchen's arm and steered her toward the store owner's wife.

"Mrs. Johnson, you know Gretchen Crawford, don't you?"

The woman glanced around the store as if searching for something. "I believe we have met. Her husband introduced her when they first settled here."

When Hetty refused to look at Gretchen, Loreen felt her anger increase. "Gretchen and Manny will be having a barn raising in about two weeks. They'd love for you and Mr. Johnson to attend."

Hetty's gaze snapped to Loreen. "A barn raising? No one has had one of those in years. . . . You know that, Loreen . . . Winslow, is it now?" The woman looked around the store. "Is your new husband in town?"

"He's planting," Loreen answered. "And don't you think it's time there were more social occasions? It's getting to where no one even knows their neighbors. If the townswomen had more functions to attend, you'd sell more material and sewing supplies."

Appealing to Hetty's business sense earned Loreen the woman's complete attention. "I suppose that's true. We hardly sell anything but sturdy cotton for work clothes. My husband won't let me order any fancy hats or bonnets because he knows the women have no place to wear them."

"That's a shame," Loreen said, trying to fight her annoyance. "You might want to mention to Mr. Johnson that if he doesn't have a mind to attend the barn raising, Manny might take his lumber business elsewhere."

One of Hetty's brows lifted. "Why, Loreen. That almost sounded like blackmail."

Loreen smiled. "We both know it isn't an uncommon practice here in Miller's Passing. But I suppose you're just not used to being threatened by anyone but Billy Waylan."

The woman's face turned red. "Mr. Waylan owns the mortgage on our store. If it wasn't for him, we wouldn't be in business, nor could the Clay's who own the livery or—"

"None of you own your businesses, Mrs. Johnson," Loreen interrupted. "Billy owns them, and he owns the lot of you along with them."

For the first time, Hetty glanced at Gretchen. "If you wanted an ally in this town, Mrs. Crawford, Loreen was not the one to choose. Everyone knows Billy Waylan wanted her for a wife. She's only made matters worse for our town by defying him, and her stubbornness will end up getting that handsome new husband of hers killed, the same as it did her brother."

Hetty Johnson might as well have taken a broom to Loreen and beaten the spirit from her. Now she had more guilt to add to her seemingly endless supply. Had Billy been taking out his anger with her on the townsfolk? Had he been terrorizing them even worse since she'd married Jake?

"I am proud to call Loreen my friend." Gretchen stood straight, staring down her nose at Hetty Johnson. "She has shown me more kindness during the past two weeks than this town has shown me in two years. She is not afraid to embrace what is unfamiliar to her. You shame her when you should honor her spirit. She will not be walked upon by this bully who holds you all in his hands as if you were puppets. If this one woman can stand up to him, why can we not follow her example?"

The store owner's wife paled. Her gaze strayed past Loreen and Gretchen, then widened. It was a natural response for a person to wonder what had struck obvious horror into Hetty Johnson. Loreen glanced over her shoulder. It was the same thing that made the taste of terror rise in her own throat: Billy Waylan.

As soon as he stepped away from the doorway, the mercantile cleared out. Since his gaze was leveled directly on Loreen, she knew that any attempt to flee with the others would be pointless. Hetty quickly abandoned the two women, mumbling that she had to see to something in the back.

"Well, aren't you two a prize pair," Billy drawled, strutting toward them. "My sweet Loreen and the pretty dark-haired foreigner." He stopped to fondle a lock of Gretchen's hair. "Your English is getting good. Now what was it you were saying, darlin'?"

Instead of shrinking away from Billy, Gretchen leveled a cold stare on him. "I said what I choose to say. To you, I choose to say nothing."

Billy released Gretchen's hair. He sighed. "I do believe you're getting as uppity as my Loreen. It might be wise of you to choose another friend."

"She isn't my friend," Loreen said. "There's no call for you to bother her."

He glanced between her and Gretchen and laughed. His teeth were crooked and tobacco stained. "I won't bother her . . . this time. Run along, Mrs. Crawford. I'd like some private time with Loreen."

For an awful instant, Loreen thought Gretchen would refuse to leave. Loreen's gaze strayed meaningfully toward the candy counter, where the children stood, still engrossed with eyeing the treats. The German girl understood her message: she needed Gretchen to get the children away from the situation, and hopefully her friend would go in search of her husband.

Gretchen walked to the counter. "Come, children, we will get candy later."

Loreen held her breath, expecting Wren to pitch a fit about not getting a treat right then and there. But the little girl turned, spotted Billy, and, to her credit, took Gretchen's hand without a fuss. The three of them almost made it to the door before the bully walked over and snatched Wren up.

"I don't think this one is yours," he said to Gretchen. He grinned at Wren. "You can stay in here with me and your sister."

When Wren began to struggle and Gretchen glanced helplessly at Loreen, anger overrode fear. Loreen marched over to Billy.

"Let her go this instant!" She reached for the child, but Billy turned away.

"I ain't gonna hurt her, Loreen. I'm gonna get her some candy." He walked to the candy counter holding a squirming Wren.

Billy's ploy was obvious. He would hold Wren to keep Loreen from bolting for the door. She glanced at Gretchen and mouthed for her to leave and find Manny. The woman's eyes conveyed reluctance, but she finally nodded and hurried outside with Samuel.

"Now, what kind of candy would you like, little girl?" Billy drawled. "Or would you like some of each?"

"I like candy, but I don't want none from you!" Wren said. "And my name is Wren, not little girl."

With a chuckle, Billy sat her on top of the counter. "You're as feisty as your sister, ain't you?"

Wren glared at him. "Loreen ain't my sister no more. She's my mama."

He turned his head, regarding Loreen with a lifted brow. "Then I guess that'll make me your papa when I marry Loreen."

"Jake's gonna be my papa," the child informed him. "And you can't marry Loreen 'cause she's already married."

"Accidents happen," he said. "Loreen might not be married for much longer."

When Wren's big eyes filled with tears, Loreen could stand no more. She stormed to the counter and pushed Billy out of the way. She'd obviously taken him by surprise, because he didn't react soon enough to keep her from lifting Wren from the counter and quickly placing her on the floor. When Billy made a lunge for the child, Loreen blocked his body with hers.

"Run!" she shouted at Wren. "Go find Gretchen!"

The little redhead raced for the door and ran outside before Billy could stop her. He shook Loreen violently.

"I just wanted to buy her some candy!" His fingers dug into her arms before he seemed to gain control over himself. Billy shoved Loreen away, but kept himself between her and the door. She rubbed her arms, praying Manny would arrive soon.

"That little gal makes me near as mad as you do. She's got your spunk, too."

Loreen hadn't felt nearly so courageous when she'd first spotted Billy standing at the door. Her fear of the man now made her sick with self-loathing. "You leave Wren alone," she said. "If you ever touch her, I'll kill you." And Loreen knew her words were true.

His cocky grin settled back into place, but the smile didn't reach his eyes. They were as cold and unfeeling as a snake's. "I don't like it when you threaten me, Loreen. And you shouldn't keep telling me what I can and can't do. I give the orders around here, and I expect people to follow them. You need to get that through your stubborn head if we're ever gonna get along."

"We are *never* going to get along," she ground out. "If you'll excuse me, I've finished my shopping and want to leave."

His jaw dropped for a moment, but the coldness in his eyes remained. "I don't want to hurt you, Loreen. I don't want to hurt that little girl, but unless you start showing me more respect, I'm afraid that's the only way you're gonna learn not to make me mad."

It was on the tip of her tongue to tell him he already was mad—crazy as a loon. Loreen knew she shouldn't push him to violence. He'd just threatened Wren, and the thought of his hurting the child kept her quiet. The silence ticked past until the soft sound of a throat clearing shifted her attention to Mr. Johnson, who stood behind the counter.

"You've run off all of my customers, Billy," he said. "How will I pay you what I owe you if I don't have any business?"

Billy grinned at the man. "That sounds like your problem, Johnson. And I've decided you're not to have any more dealings with Loreen or her kin, or with anyone who calls her a friend. If she wants to eat or feed her family, she'll have to come begging to me."

"But that's not fair," the storekeeper argued. "Loreen always pays her debts. She's never accepted credit."

The bully shrugged. "Life ain't always fair. You do as you're told or I'll take this store away from you, understand?"

Mr. Johnson stared him down for a good split second; then he lowered his gaze. "This store is all I have, but I can't stand here and do nothing while you make Loreen stay against her will."

Slick as a rock smoothed by rushing water, Billy drew a gun. "Then you'd best not stand there. Go on to the back with your wife."

The storekeeper glanced down the barrel of the weapon and swallowed loudly. He flashed Loreen an apologetic look and hurried away.

"Damn coward," Billy muttered, replacing his gun in its holster. "That's what I like about this town: it's full of them. Speaking of which, where's your new husband?"

Although he'd just classified Jake as a coward, Loreen wondered why Billy's gaze scanned the front windows nervously.

"He's busy," she said quietly.

Billy ambled toward her. "I've seen how busy he's been. I'm gonna kill that dog. The damn animal took a bite out of one of my men. I'm going to teach those idiots to shoot; then I'm gonna cut those fences of yours. Know what else I'm gonna do?"

With each step forward Billy took, Loreen took one back. She wanted to stand her ground, but the thought of Billy putting his hands on her, possibly trying to kiss her or worse, ate away at her courage.

"I'm gonna run my cattle through your field. Kill your man. Burn your house. Do whatever I have to do to give you no choice but to come begging to me. No one tells me no. No one takes what should be mine. No one!"

His eyes were blazing. He reminded Loreen of a child throwing a temper tantrum. She'd backed herself into the corner where Mr. Johnson kept his dry goods. As the smell of strong spices assaulted her, she realized there was nowhere to run. But Billy didn't press his advantage. Instead he moved toward the counter and grabbed a jar of licorice sticks.

"You give this to your little girl. Tell her it's from me. When her sister comes to her senses, there will be lots more sweets for her." He shoved the jar into Loreen's hands and grinned lewdly. "She's a pretty thing. In a few years when you're all used up, I can see letting that little piece of fluff step into your shoes."

The thought of Billy considering Wren with such vile intentions enraged Loreen. She reached behind her, grabbed a handful of spice, and threw it in Billy's face. He hollered and began rubbing his eyes. Loreen bolted around him and ran for the door.

Frantically, she searched for signs of the Crawfords. She spotted the buggy coming from the livery at full speed. Loreen ran out into the street, thought about waving her arms, then realized she still held the jar of licorice and threw it to the ground. The glass broke. Manny hadn't even brought the buggy to a stop when Loreen jumped up on the side and scrambled inside.

"Go!" she shouted.

He flicked the reins, shouted, and they were off in a cloud of dust. Loreen stuck her head out the side. She

227

squinted through the dust. Billy stumbled from the store and out into the street, still rubbing his eyes. She saw him trip over the broken jar of licorice. He fell, jerked, rolled to the side, and clutched his knee. She hoped he'd cut his leg. Oh, no. He'd soon realize how and on what he'd injured himself. He would know she had thrown his gift to Wren in the dirt.

Loreen made a realization of her own: she was a bigger fool than Jake. His actions of stringing a fence and siccing a dog on Billy's boys might have bought the shovel, but what Loreen had just done had surely dug their graves. If she told Jake what had happened in town, what Billy had said about Wren, he might be angry enough to confront the bully. And as crazy as she suspected Billy was, words wouldn't do Jake a bit of good. Billy would kill him this time.

"What happened?" Manny asked. "What did that varmint do to you?"

Trying to slow the racing of her heart, she measured her words carefully. "He didn't hurt me. He's just what Jake says he is: a lot of wind."

Gretchen cast her a skeptical look. Wren slid her tiny hand into Loreen's, and so help her God, she'd do worse than throw spice into Billy's face if he ever touched a hair on her little girl's head.

"I think it best that we don't tell Jake about . . . well, that Billy and I exchanged words. It will only upset him, and he might do something foolish."

"Jake wouldn't want you keeping that from him," Manny argued. " 'Sides, he might be just the man to put that bully in his place. Which is six feet under," he added.

Loreen leaned forward. "Jake doesn't believe in

228

fighting. He won't carry a gun. And Billy wouldn't think twice about . . ." Her gaze strayed to Wren. "Do you understand what I'm saying?"

Manny nodded. "He don't carry a gun? Then you're right. If he won't defend himself, no need getting Billy any more stirred up."

"How do you stir someone up?" Wren wanted to know. "With a spoon?"

She smiled weakly at her daughter. "Honey, I want you to do something for me. It's a grown-up thing."

Wren puffed up. "I'm growing up," she declared.

And she seemed to be doing just that before Loreen's eyes. She helped out around the farm, and her control over the candy, her greatest weakness, showed Loreen her little girl was maturing. It broke her heart. She wanted the time to be Wren's mother back, the five years she'd already lost. She took a deep breath.

"If we tell Jake about what happened in town, about Billy bossing me around and trying to make you take candy, it will upset him. Make him sad. You don't want to hurt Jake, do you?"

Wren shook her head. "No. I love Jake."

Tears blurred Loreen's vision. She blinked them back. "Then this has to be our little secret, okay?"

Wren twisted her lips, her brow furrowing. "Isn't that lying? Is it all right to have a secret, Mama?"

That was a touchy subject. "As long as it doesn't hurt anyone," she answered. "Or as long as it keeps someone else from getting hurt."

"That's what we're doing, right?"

"Right," she answered, but somehow, even though she was only trying to protect Jake, Loreen wasn't sure she was doing the right thing. It seemed underhanded. Still, better to be untruthful than to see him dead, she reasoned.

"I won't tell," Wren agreed. She turned to Samuel and began tickling him, proving that she was, in fact, still a very young child, despite her bouts of maturity.

Loreen leaned back against the seat, relieved. She'd done what she thought was best for Jake. Now she must do the right thing where the Crawfords were concerned. For their own protection, she must tell them they couldn't associate with her any longer. Billy had taken her brother from her, threatened her home and family, and he would try to take anything else that became precious. That would include the only true friends she had.

Chapter Twenty

The secret was killing her. Loreen felt as if she were deceiving Jake, never mind that she'd kept silent for what she first believed was his safety. A week had passed since she'd gone into town with the Crawfords. Day after day, her conscience preyed upon her, and Loreen realized she'd made a mistake by not telling Jake about the confrontation.

She'd placed him in further danger by allowing him to remain ignorant of the threats Billy had made. She'd spent the week watching him and Toby dig a ditch—a watering ditch, as Jake called it—and as her conscience continued to work on her, she knew she had to right her wrong.

During the past week, she'd kept a vigil over her family, thankful that Princess seemed content to follow Wren wherever she went. But the dog's behavior of late had only added to Loreen's feelings of impending disaster. Animals, she'd heard, could sense danger long before people could. The dog had spent the last few days creeping around the farm, looking in every nook and cranny, as if she were searching for something . . . or maybe someone.

The dog's uneasiness strengthened her resolve. Loreen vowed to tell Jake what had happened in town that very morning. She'd use taking his breakfast out to him as an excuse to get him alone. She prepared the last of Gretchen's delicious sausage, and called for Toby and Wren to come and eat. Her brother was first down the ladder.

"Sure smells good," he said, settling at the table. "Is that more of Gretchen's sausage?"

"That's the last of it, so eat slowly. Wren!" She glanced expectantly up at the loft.

"She's not up there," Toby said, his mouth full. "I thought she'd already come down."

"I didn't see her." Loreen glanced at the cabin door. "She must have slipped outside while I cooked." She sighed. "Well, I'll round her up while I take Jake his breakfast."

She dished Jake a healthy portion of eggs and sausage, then moved toward the door. Once outside, she expected to find Wren sitting on the steps petting Princess. There was no sign of either the little redhead or the dog.

"Wren!" she called on her way to the barn. There was no answer. She squeezed through the crack left open during the night for Princess to come and go, not bothering to knock. It was a mistake. She caught Jake getting dressed.

"Ah, I'm sorry. I should have said something before I barged in."

"You seem to have a habit of catching me at a disadvantage."

Loreen stood there for a moment before she wheeled back around, her gaze scanning the barn. "I thought Wren would be in here."

Jake glanced up from buttoning his shirt. "I haven't seen her. Wren! Are you in here?"

No answer. The plate in Loreen's hand began to shake. "She's not in the house, either."

He shrugged. "I'm sure she's around somewhere."

Rushing forward, Loreen shoved Jake's plate into his hands and hurried for the door. Once outside, she called for Wren again but received no answer. She ran back into the house. "Has she come in?"

Toby glanced up, his mouth full. He shook his head.

Loreen raced through the house to the back porch. "Wren!" she shouted. Her gaze roamed the area and darted toward the watering hole. A horrible thought occurred to her. Loreen scrambled down from the porch and nearly collided with Jake.

"Did you find her?"

Her voice was frozen. She shook her head and hurried down the path leading to the water.

"I don't think she'd go near the water." Jake fell into step beside her. "I told her I'd tan her hide if I ever caught her messing around alone down there."

Words still wouldn't come. Loreen continued on, her fear growing, her heart pounding wildly inside her chest. There was no sign of Wren at the watering hole—no small body floating facedown in the water. Then she remembered the dead trees Jake had pulled from the pool. Maybe he hadn't gotten all of them.

He must have read her thoughts, because suddenly

he raced toward the incline. He grabbed the rope swing and swung out over the deep end, dropping into the water. Loreen made her shaky legs work, running to the top of the incline, where she collapsed.

Eternity. That was what it seemed like to her, watching Jake surface, take deep breaths, then disappear again. She was about to strip and join him in the search when his head popped up again.

"There's nothing down here!" he yelled.

Tears of relief streamed down her cheeks. She tried to control her gasps for breath while watching Jake swim to the bank. Then, one frightening possibility behind her, the next reared its ugly head: Billy. The thought surfaced as Jake joined her.

"He's taken her," she whispered, the words barely making it past her paralyzed throat.

"What? Who?" he demanded.

"Billy," Loreen rasped; then the words frozen inside of her spewed forth in a gush. "He threatened us last week. He said he'd kill you and the dog. He said he'd burn the house, destroy the crop. He tried to give Wren candy, and he said he didn't want to hurt her, but if I didn't show him more respect . . ." She paused to catch her breath. "I threw the candy on the ground and the glass broke. He cut his leg—"

"Loreen." Jake shook her. "You're babbling. Did you say Billy threatened to hurt Wren?"

"He said ugly things. Things I won't repeat. He took her to get back at me! To teach me a lesson!"

The fear in his eyes changed to something else. "Why didn't you tell me?"

She cursed herself for not filling Jake in on Billy's

threats the very day it had happened. "I-I was afraid you'd do something foolish."

"You were right." He rose, storming toward the house.

Although Loreen's knees still felt weak, she roused herself and caught up to him. Toby met them before they reached the house.

"Did you find her?"

Loreen shook her head and Jake said nothing; he just kept walking. The boy fell into step beside him.

"That dog ain't around, either," he said. "I took my scraps out to the barn, but she wasn't there. What's going on?"

When Jake wouldn't answer, the boy turned frightened eyes on Loreen. "Where's Wren? What's going on?"

"I think Billy might have taken her."

Toby drew up short. "Billy? Why would he do that?" He hurried to reach them. "He couldn't snatch her from under our noses. And besides, that dog wouldn't let him. . . ."

Her brother had made the connection. The wolf was probably dead. Billy would have taken care of the animal before he'd attempt to kidnap Wren. Loreen could only assume he'd waited until early this morning, when Wren had gone outside to the outhouse, to snatch her. Which at least would mean he hadn't had her for long.

She and Toby followed Jake into the barn. He grabbed his bridle and went into Ben's stall. A few minutes later, he slung his saddle over the horse's back. Loreen gasped softly when he removed a six-shooter from his saddle packs.

235

"Where'd you get that?" Toby asked in a hushed whisper.

"I took it off of Billy the last time he was stupid enough to show his face around here."

Loreen couldn't imagine Jake getting enough of a jump on Billy to unarm him. And why hadn't Billy simply taken the gun back? She started to ask Jake, but after he spun the barrel of the gun and shoved the weapon back into his pack, he led Ben from the barn.

"What do you intend to do with that gun?" Loreen asked, following him outside with Toby behind her.

His eyes were hard, a stormier shade of blue than normal, when he turned them on her. "If Billy has taken Wren, and if he's harmed one hair on her head, I intend to kill him."

Loreen was too shocked to respond. Toby was obviously shocked as well, because neither of them said a word as Jake mounted up and rode away.

"I knew he wasn't a coward," Toby said proudly.

Jake might not be a coward, but he wasn't a fighting man, either. He'd get himself killed by confronting Billy in a gunfight. Now, tangled in her worry for Wren, Loreen feared for Jake's life.

"We have to stop him," she said frantically, racing for the road. "He's going to get himself killed!"

Toby easily caught her. "What are we going to do? Run all the way to town?"

"If we have to," Loreen yelled.

They had made it to the road leading to Miller's Passing when Toby reached out and pulled Loreen up.

"Look!" He pointed behind them. "Someone's coming. Maybe we can hitch a ride."

She shaded her eyes, recognizing the Crawfords'

buggy moving toward them. Loreen ran to meet them. Manny had barely reined the pretty mare to a stop when Loreen jumped up on the side of the buggy.

"You have to take us to town! Wren's missing and—"

"Hi, Mama," a familiar voice chirped. A little head popped up from the backseat of the buggy. "What's the matter?"

"Wren," she said in a gasp. Loreen reached inside the buggy and pulled her out, holding her tight. "Where have you been?" she choked out. "We thought—"

"We found her walking down the road," Manny interrupted. "She said she was looking for her dog."

Tears of joy and relief coursed down Loreen's cheeks. She hugged Wren tighter, then wanted to spank the girl for scaring the life out of her. "You are never to go off like that without telling me," she scolded. "We didn't know what had happened to you!"

"I didn't mean to walk so far," Wren said, her bottom lip trembling. "But I couldn't find Princess, and I thought she might be lost. I got a sticker in my toe," she added with a sniff. "I want Jake to get it out."

Loreen's elation came crashing down around her. "Jake," she whispered. "Oh, my God, we have to stop him."

Jake cursed the day he'd traded his fast mare to Manny Crawford. Old Ben gave him all he had, but the big-boned horse possessed about as much speed as a lame turtle. Jake's legs were chapped from his wet pants rubbing against his legs. As he rode, his rage grew. Thoughts of Billy taking Wren from them, visions of the girl's tiny face etched in fear, of her crying and begging to go home, made him forsake all vows he'd made after the tragic turn his life had taken in Kansas a year ago.

He'd told himself there was no right side of a gun to be on. That drawing a weapon on a man was a coward's way of settling a dispute. But Jake had never had someone threaten something precious to him. And during his stay with the Matlands, Wren had become more than a feisty little girl with red hair who spoke her mind and knew how to wind him around her finger: she'd become part of his heart.

His senses stirred when the hazy image of a town took shape before him. Jake cursed the fact that he'd have to stop at the mercantile and get directions to Billy's ranch. If he had to ride much farther, the horse might give out altogether.

He couldn't have hoped for more. Jake spotted Billy and a few of his boys coming from the saloon. Wren wasn't with them, which meant the monster had left her alone somewhere. The closer he came to Billy, the more his rage grew. By the time he reached the laughing men, Jake had lost control. He jumped from the saddle and landed on Billy, knocking him to the ground.

"Where is she, you son of a bitch?"

To say he'd caught the bully off guard was an understatement. Billy's eyes were as round as two plug nickels as he stared up at him. Jake rose, hauling the man to his feet. He shoved him backward.

"I said, where is she?"

A crowd had already began to gather, Jake noted, seeing shapes appear from the corners of his eyes.

He'd forgotten it was Saturday again—exactly one week since Billy had threatened Loreen. Billy noticed the crowd as well, and acted accordingly. He grinned evilly.

"You've got some nerve, putting your hands on me, plow boy. But before I beat the living daylights out of you, I want to know what you're accusing me of."

"You know damn good and well why I'm here," Jake ground out. "What have you done with Wren?"

Billy scratched his whiskers. "Wren? Don't know nobody named that."

Jake stepped forward and shoved him again. "Loreen's little sister. I know you've taken her."

"Ohhh." Billy drew out the syllable. "The little red-headed spitfire. The one who thinks she's too high and mighty to take candy from me? That the gal you're talking about?"

"Stop stalling and tell me where she is," Jake warned. "I've had a gullet full of you riding roughshod over everyone in this town, lording it over these people because they owe you money. I don't owe you anything, and I won't allow you to keep threatening my family."

"Well, ain't you the brave one," Billy said. "You're making me look bad in front of these folks, maybe giving them ideas." He paused to run an evil eye over the townsfolk. "Tell you what I'll do: you draw against me, and I'll give you the location of the little girl. How does that sound?"

Fixing a cold stare on the bully, Jake said, "Dead men can't talk."

Billy snickered. "Those are mighty big words for a

man who refuses to wear a gun." He moved his dirty
jacket behind the holster strapped to his hip. "Now
what have you got to say?"

His steely gaze never wavering, Jake opened his
jacket. Billy's eyes lowered and widened.

"Hey, that's my gun," he said.

"Yes," Jake agreed. "The same one I took from you
the day I gave you a well-deserved beating and ran you
off my place."

Jake's publicizing Billy's humiliation at his hands
obviously didn't sit well with the town bully. He narrowed his beady eyes to mere slits. "Let's see if you
know how to use that gun."

Jake didn't trust Billy enough to turn his back on
him, so he took ten paces backward. The murmurs of
the crowd died. Silence settled over Miller's Passing,
broken only by the soft sound of a gasp somewhere
behind him. Jake could have sworn it belonged to
Loreen, but there was no way she could have made it
to town on foot in the short amount of time he'd been
in Miller's Passing.

It was clear Billy had no intention of divulging
Wren's whereabouts, but Jake wasn't worried. He
didn't plan on actually shooting the lowlife. A show
of skill would probably be enough to scare this wind-
bag into telling him the girl's location. He lowered
his hand to his side and waited. The sun was blazing
hot, not yet fully in the sky. It was directly behind
Billy.

That didn't matter, though. Seeing Billy's face
wasn't necessary. Jake had a sixth sense about these
matters. He would know the second Billy decided to
go for his gun. The second came. Billy reached but

Jake was faster; he had his gun trained on the bully before he ever cleared leather. The snake froze, his gaze darting from Jake's waistband to the gun in his hand as if he couldn't believe his eyes.

Jake marched forward, the gun pointed straight at Billy's face. The man began to back away but came up flush against a horse tied to the hitching post outside the saloon. Jake advanced until his gun's barrel rested directly against Billy's forehead. His opponent made a whimpering noise and fell to his knees.

"Please don't kill me," he said in a croaking voice.

"Give me your gun," Jake demanded.

Billy fumbled with his holster and handed Jake his weapon. He tossed it into the nearest watering trough.

"I'm going to ask you one more time: where's Wren?"

"I don't know," Billy whined. "I swear I don't."

A liar's word didn't count for much in Jake's opinion. He felt a rage coming on, that this man had harassed Loreen—the whole town, for that matter—for so long and gotten away with it. He cocked the six-shooter.

"One more time. Where is—"

"Jake!"

He froze. The voice belonged to Loreen. He turned his head, his gaze searching the crowd. In the back, standing beside Manny Crawford's buggy, he found her. Loreen's face was an ashen hue, but it was her eyes that made his gut twist. They were wide with shock, as if she couldn't believe what she had witnessed.

And he suspected she'd been standing there through the entire confrontation. That was when he noticed she wasn't alone. Manny stood beside her, and in his arms he held the little girl whose disappearance had driven Jake to violence.

Manny and Gretchen wore curious expressions, but it was Toby who made Jake feel the worst. He stood in the buggy, admiration shining in his eyes. In a moment ruled by anger, Jake had undone everything he'd tried to teach the boy. He'd stooped to the level of the snake whimpering before him.

He looked around. While he held Billy temporarily at bay, there was still the threat of his gang. "Tell your ruffians to throw their weapons in the water trough," he instructed Billy.

For a moment Billy looked as if he might refuse, so Jake pressed the barrel of the gun harder against Billy's forehead.

"Do what he says," Billy instructed his boys.

After the last weapon had been soaked, Jake lowered his own gun. "Don't make me mad again," he said softly to the bully. "And don't come near my family."

He walked to the water trough and added his weapon to the collection. When he turned back toward where Loreen had been, all he saw was the dust from Manny's departing wagon. Jake walked to old Ben and swung up in the saddle. As he reined him toward the farm, a solitary clapping began. It belonged to Mr. Johnson, who owned the mercantile.

The man's approval didn't make him feel better. Once, he'd believed the speed of a gun could win him respect and honor among men, but he'd learned there was no glory in killing.

A gun had made him a wanted man, and now it had done worse. By resorting to its power, he'd shattered the trust he'd worked so hard to build with Loreen, and he'd made a lie out of everything he'd tried to teach Toby.

Breaking his vow never to draw a gun again had taught him another hard lesson in life: the only thing worse than not having a family to call his own was finding one and then losing it.

Chapter Twenty-one

Loreen felt betrayed. Jake hadn't told her the truth about himself. By acting as if he didn't believe in settling disputes with a gun, he'd as good as lied to her. She hadn't witnessed any gunfights firsthand, but even an idiot could figure out that Jake was fast on the draw—real fast. When he'd first ridden onto her farm, she'd wondered if he was an outlaw. She'd since dismissed the possibility.

His actions this afternoon forced her to reevaluate her opinion of him. After the Crawfords departed, Gretchen leaving the dresses she'd stitched, which was the reason the couple had been on the road to their farm, she'd shut herself and the children up in the cabin, grappling with her hurt and anger. As close as she and Jake had become, as intimate as they'd almost been, she felt both used and foolish. What else hadn't he told her?

"Why can't I talk to Jake?" Toby demanded for the second time.

"And I want to see if Princess has come back," Wren insisted.

"Hush, both of you," Loreen said. She'd been pacing the small living area for nearly an hour, trying to bring her temper under control before confronting the man living in her barn.

"Toby, I'd like to speak with Jake first. He owes me an explanation for what happened in town."

"What did happen?" Wren asked, her forehead puckered.

"Jake put Billy in his place," Toby told her. "Didn't you see how fast he drew that gun? Didn't you see Billy begging and groveling in the dirt?"

"Toby," Loreen warned. "Don't glorify what Jake did. He said he wouldn't stoop to Billy's level, and at one time that made me believe he was a coward. Then I began to realize he was right. I thought it more courageous of him to have beliefs and to stick by them. Now I don't know what to think. Did you see how close he came to killing Billy? Unarmed? Wouldn't that make him just as wrong?"

"Are you mad at Jake?" Wren asked softly.

Loreen didn't answer. Wren was clearly confused by what had taken place in town, and Loreen wasn't sure how to explain matters. Toby took the liberty of answering for her.

"She's mad," he said. "And she should be happy." The boy glanced at his older sister. "You wanted someone to protect us in the beginning. Well, Jake's proven he can. What is there to be angry about?"

Her brother, Loreen realized, was still too young to

understand what she felt. Jake had been a faceless name when he'd come to her, a person she didn't know. He'd wormed his way into the children's hearts, and she supposed into her own. During the weeks they had spent together, she thought she'd come to know him. She'd begun to trust him. Now he seemed like a stranger again—a truly dangerous one.

"I want both of you to stay inside while I speak with Jake. You can scrounge us up something to eat."

"But that's your job," Toby said.

"And I'm too little," Wren added.

"Don't argue," Loreen warned. "Not right now."

Both children wisely headed toward the kitchen. Loreen smoothed the wrinkles from her dress before going outside. While she made her way to the barn, she tried to bring her anger under control. She wanted to discuss what had happened in town with calm dignity. The moment she set foot in the barn and saw Jake gathering the shovels, her dignity fled.

"You lied to me," she said.

Her accusation received no response. Jake grabbed his shovels and walked past her into the bright sunshine. Loreen hurried after him.

"Did you hear me?" she demanded.

"I never lied to you," he countered smoothly.

His calm only added to her anger. "But you didn't tell me the truth, either. Who and what were you before Miller's Passing?"

He stopped, digging a shovel blade into the ground with force. "I told you, I was punching cattle at a ranch when I saw your advertisement. And as I recall, you said my reasons for marrying you weren't important."

Loreen placed her hands on her hips. "Things have changed since then, wouldn't you agree?"

Jake looked at her. "Have they?"

She wanted to stamp her foot in frustration, but she wouldn't give him the satisfaction. "I would think so."

"I had thought so, too," he said quietly. "I foolishly believed you had come to trust me, but you haven't. If you trusted me, you would have told me what happened in town last week."

She wouldn't allow him to turn the conversation around. "I explained why. I thought you might confront Billy and get yourself killed."

"Well, as it turned out, I did end up confronting Billy. Am I dead?"

"That is the *point* of this discussion! You led me to believe you don't settle disputes with a gun; then you pull one on Billy and humiliate him in front of the whole town. And it wasn't that you resorted to violence; it was the skill you displayed while doing it! I want to know how you came by your rather remarkable abilities!"

His eyes turned a darker shade of blue. "And I want to know what else you're hiding from me! I want to know why you're warm and willing in my arms one minute and scared to death of me the next. I want to know if whatever made you afraid of living, of loving, happened before or after you moved to Miller's Passing. I'd like to know—"

"We aren't discussing me," she reminded him hotly. "I thought I made it understood—"

"Then let me make something understood. If your past is none of my business, mine is none of yours."

To further annoy her, he pulled the shovel from the dirt and walked toward the ditch he and Toby had been digging. Loreen had a good reason to follow him. More precisely, two good reasons.

"But you are my business," she said. "I must consider Toby and Wren's safety."

Jake threw the shovel on the ground, cursed loudly, and turned toward her. "If you don't know anything else about me, you know I'd lay down my life for those two kids. It's not Toby and Wren you're worried about; it's us—what happened, what still is happening. But I have to tell you, Loreen, nothing can continue to happen if you can't trust me."

He was right. It was just as well if he kept his secrets and she kept hers. She suddenly felt afraid again, but this time she only feared the love growing inside of her. And it wasn't Jake she didn't trust; it was herself. Loreen had learned five years ago that her heart couldn't be trusted.

"You're right," she said. "We are none of each other's business. Who or what you are isn't my concern. Getting myself and the children off of this farm and out of Miller's Passing is. Go back to work."

She turned from him and went to the cabin. Toby brushed past her the moment she entered, obviously anxious to speak with Jake. Loreen only hoped Jake handled her brother's questions better than he'd handled hers.

Wren sat at the table, her big eyes sad.

"You know you're in trouble, don't you?" Loreen asked the child.

She nodded miserably.

It was tough being stern with a child who'd only recently, and by a bad turn of events, become rightfully hers. Loreen knew that to be a proper parent, a loving parent, she must discipline Wren.

"You know better than to go off without telling anyone," Loreen began, and when Wren burst into sobs, it took all her willpower to continue. "I know you didn't mean to frighten everyone, but you did. You caused a lot of trouble, and you're to promise me you will never go off without telling someone again."

Wren nodded, sniffing loudly. "I was just worried about Princess."

"I'm worried about her, too," she admitted. The dog really had disappeared, and Loreen felt awful about that. "But that still doesn't excuse your just running off to look for her and not telling me. I have to punish you."

Wren's eyes widened. "What are you going to do?"

Loreen supposed a swat wouldn't hurt the child, but she couldn't bring herself to punish Wren physically. She knew what would sting worse. "I'll have to give you extra chores for a week, and there will be no sweets. No pie, no cookies, none of your favorites."

For a moment Wren's eyes filled with tears again, and Loreen thought she'd throw a tantrum. Then she showed some of the recent maturity of which Loreen had only caught glimpses. "Yes, ma'am."

Because she'd accepted her punishment well, Loreen said, "Before we weed the garden together, why don't we go see if we can find Princess?"

The redhead snapped to attention. "Really?"

Loreen opened her arms, and Wren jumped up and rushed into them. "I promise I won't ever scare you again."

Smoothing the child's curls from her wet cheeks, Loreen said, "The punishment still stands, mind you."

Wren nodded against her, and together they strolled from the cabin. Although Loreen had a dozen chores to do, she walked with Wren toward the barn. For her daughter's sake, Loreen felt obliged to help search for the dog. Truth be known, she, too, was concerned for the animal's welfare. The wolf had tried to protect them, and had grown to love Wren—she supposed the least she could do was return the favor.

While Wren called for the dog and searched the barn, Loreen pondered what had happened in town earlier. Would Billy leave them alone now? Or had Jake only thrown a match on kerosene? She had trouble believing the bully would allow a set-down in front of the town to go unpunished.

Still, Jake had made the man grovel, made him beg for his life. Maybe Billy had learned a lesson about harassing people he thought were too scared to retaliate.

Lost in her thoughts, Loreen realized she no longer heard Wren calling Princess or scrambling around the old barn. Curious, she began to look for her. She found her sitting on the floor next to the haystack. Her eyes were wide as she stared into what appeared to be a tunnel dug at the bottom of the stack.

"Wren?" Loreen called.

Her head turned in Loreen's direction. Wren's wide eyes filled with tears. "I found her," she whispered. "She's just lying there, and she has rats eating on her."

Jake wondered when Toby's curiosity would get the best of him. They'd been digging for a while, and Toby still hadn't said a word about what had happened earlier. He felt the boy's regard often, glancing up to see pride shining in his eyes—and it annoyed the hell out of Jake.

"There's nothing to be smug about," he finally said. "What I did today was wrong."

Toby ceased his digging. "I can't see how it could

be. You stood up to Billy for us. You stood up for the whole town."

The object of Toby's adoration threw down his shovel. Jake wiped the sweat from his brow. "And I also went back on my principles when I drew a gun on Billy. I became no better than him. There's no honor in being stronger or tougher or faster than another man— not when you hold it against him."

"But he deserved it," the boy argued. "He's had it coming for a long time."

"That may be so," Jake had to agree. "But his punishment wasn't for me to decide. When a man takes the law into his own hands, he can get himself into trouble. Right and wrong become clouded issues. Innocent people get hurt, sometimes killed."

"But Billy's not innocent," Toby pointed out.

"He was innocent of taking Wren. That was the crime I called him to account for."

"But some men should die," Toby persisted. "Killing a killer doesn't make you one. Not if you're only defending your family."

Jake motioned him toward the water bucket. "All right, Toby. I'm not saying sometimes a man isn't forced into killing in order to defend his family, or even himself. I'm saying, make damn sure that there's no other way. Life is priceless, Toby. And if a man becomes too unfeeling about death or killing, then what's to say the next time he kills, it won't be because a mercantile owner sold him some bad goods, or someone looked at him wrong on the street?"

Toby lifted the dipper from the water bucket. "No, that wouldn't be right."

"Killing is never right," Jake stressed. "Sometimes it becomes necessary, but it's never right. That goes whether you're talking about men or beasts. Don't shoot anything you can't eat, wear, or isn't threatening your family or property. If I ever catch you shooting at sparrows for the fun of it, I'll take that rifle away from you."

The boy got huffy. "Hell, I wouldn't shoot at something living just for fun. You know I wouldn't."

Jake tried to relax. "I know. But know this about me. I'm just a man. I'm no hero. I make mistakes, and today was one of them. I don't imagine Billy will take being humiliated in front of the town sitting down."

Toby made a snorting noise. "He won't bother us again. Not after today."

Taking the dipper from the boy, Jake said, "Don't count on it. Meanness is like a dust devil dancing in the desert. It just keeps growing."

Loreen's brother waited until Jake finished his drink before asking, "How did you learn to draw a gun so fast?"

He supposed the question was inevitable. He didn't see any point in not telling him the truth. "When I was boy, not much older than you, I ran away from my pa's farm. I thought the measure of a man was determined by the speed of his gun. I took to practicing with a six-shooter I stole from my father's house."

Jake paused to remove his sweat-soaked shirt. "I talked big, and I showed off with that gun, thinking I impressed people wherever I went. It wasn't until later, much later, that I realized the only men I impressed were the ones just like me. The ones with no family of their own and nowhere to call home."

"I was impressed," Toby said.

Jake looked out over the plowed field and the surrounding countryside. "The measure of a man should be determined by the sweat on his brow. By the number of friends he has and the love he feels for those closest to him. If you envy me anything, Toby"—he nodded toward the farm—"envy me this."

"I do," the boy said quietly. "I still don't want to go, but I reckon the place will be in good hands with you."

The compliment pleased Jake. He and Toby were making headway. Maybe he could still smooth over the damage he'd done today—with Toby, though probably not with Loreen. He'd belittled her for a lack of trust in him, when in truth, he was no better. He didn't trust her enough to tell her the reason he'd answered her advertisement. Jake wanted to, but telling her wouldn't change what he'd done. It wouldn't change anything.

He was about to turn and resume his digging when he caught sight of Wren racing toward them.

"Jake, Toby, come quick. I found Princess!"

When she reached them, Jake scooped her up in his arms. "Is the dog all right?"

Wren nodded, trying to catch her breath. "I thought she was dead and had rats chewing on her, but she ain't dead. And Loreen says them rats are puppies."

Toby and Jake looked at each other; then they all headed toward the barn. The sight he came upon made him laugh. There were eight of them, squirming little balls of fur all fighting for their mother's milk.

Jake wasn't sure what was the hardest to believe: that none of them had associated the dog's weight with her condition, or that Loreen held Princess's head cradled in her lap, praising her softly for her accomplishment.

"What in tarnation are we going to do with all of them?" Toby asked.

"Keep them," Wren answered matter-of-factly.

"We can't keep them all," Loreen told her. "We couldn't possibly feed this many dogs. Besides, puppies are for sharing. If you love them and treat them nicely while they're young, they'll make good pets for other families."

"I guess we can share a few of them," Wren said.

"Manny's dog must be the father," Jake speculated.

"Puppies have mommies and daddies?"

Loreen's glance told him he'd already said too much, but Toby continued, "All living things have mommies and daddies."

Wren's little forehead puckered. "If babies come from flower gardens, where do puppies come from?"

Jake and Loreen both groaned.

Chapter Twenty-two

Puppies, Loreen ended up telling Wren, came from brier patches. As soon as the child became old enough, Loreen would have a lot of explaining to do. The pups were now three days old, and Loreen had to find plenty for Wren to do or she'd pester the mama dog and her pups to death.

"Wren, we never did get the garden weeded," she called as the child crept toward the barn. "Come see to it while I hang the laundry."

Wren did an about-face, her shoulders slumped in disappointment. "I was gonna check on the puppies."

"You checked on them a minute ago and said they were all doing fine. If you keep bothering them, Princess will take them and move away."

Wren's eyes immediately registered alarm. "Move where?"

Walking to the child, Loreen bent to her eye level. "I was just teasing you. Princess wouldn't leave you."

She breathed a sigh of relief. "Why *do* folks move off, anyway?"

This was Loreen's chance to plant a seed. "The world is a big place. People like to see all the different parts of it. Wouldn't you like to see something besides the farm and Miller's Passing?"

"See it, or live in it?" Wren asked.

"Well, both," Loreen answered enthusiastically.

Her red curls bounced when Wren nodded; then she shook her head.

"Does that mean yes or no?"

"Yes, I'd like to see it, but no, I wouldn't want to live anywhere except here with you and Jake. And Toby," she quickly added. "And old Ben, Midnight, Princess, the puppies. Oh, and Brown Eyes."

Loreen's spirits sank. "Brown Eyes?"

"That's our milk cow," Wren explained. "I just figured out she didn't have a name, so I thunked her up one."

Despite her disappointment, Loreen couldn't help but smile. "You thought her up one." She touched Wren's nose. "You need some schooling."

The child frowned. "But we ain't got a school."

Another idea occurred to Loreen. "Other places have schools. Big houses where lots of children go and learn together."

She'd gotten Wren's full attention. "Lots of kids?"

"Children you could play with," Loreen tempted her further. "Wouldn't you like that?"

"I guess so," Wren admitted. "Could Jake, Toby, and all of the animals come with us?"

Loreen worried her bottom lip with her teeth for a moment. "Well, maybe just you, me, and Toby."

"Then I won't go," the child declared. "Jake wouldn't like to be left here alone. Families are supposed to stay together."

Loreen sighed. She withdrew the spade from her apron and handed it to Wren. "Be careful in the garden. Don't cut yourself and don't dig up any of the plants. They're just starting to sprout up."

Wren took the shovel and skipped toward the garden.

"And don't run with that spade," Loreen warned.

Grabbing her basket of wet clothes, Loreen began to hang them on the line. Sooner or later she would have to tell Wren they were leaving Miller's Passing. Doing so would obviously be met with opposition—not only from Wren, but from Toby as well. Her brother had worked hard to prove his dedication to the farm, and she had to admit she'd developed qualms about taking away his birthright.

Her gaze strayed to where Toby and Jake labored. As usual for early afternoon, Jake had removed his shirt. It proved difficult for Loreen to keep her eyes off of him.

His skill with a gun still bothered her, although Toby had told her how he'd come by it. Loreen was more than a little hurt that he couldn't have told her the same story he'd told her brother.

But then, she hadn't answered his questions, either. They were supposedly none of each other's business, and Loreen would do well to follow Jake's example and keep her thoughts focused on work.

Although sprouts were shooting up in the field, they were still far from being grown. The past three days of digging from sunup until sundown had produced results for Toby and Jake, however, and she watched them throw their shovels on the ground and grin at one another.

Toby turned toward her. "We're gonna see if it works!" he shouted. "Come watch!"

Wren darted from the corner of the house at a full run. Fortunately she wasn't carrying the garden spade or Loreen would have boxed her ears. She hung her last article of clothing and made her way toward the group. Toby raced to the watering hole. He disappeared shortly, hidden by tall, dry grass.

"Ready?" she heard him shout.

Jake cupped his hands to the sides of his mouth. "Open the chute!"

They waited, all watching the ditch. A few moments later, water began to rush down the trench and into the dry field. Fascinated, Loreen watched the water journey to each neatly trenched row.

. "It works!" Toby joined them, puffing from his run.

"I think it does," Jake commented.

Wren ran to the edge of the field and tried to race the water's procession. Jake offered Toby his hand.

"I couldn't have done this without you."

Toby pumped his hand enthusiastically. "And it wouldn't have gotten done at all if you hadn't thought of it. Isn't it great, Loreen?"

She saw no reason to act unimpressed. "It certainly is. Imagine not having to look to the sky for rain! Of which there is very little in this part of the country."

"We'll still have to pray for rain so the watering hole doesn't go dry," Jake said. "But there should be plenty to get this crop up."

"Yahoo," Toby hollered. He started to dance, which

made Loreen and Jake laugh. Wren spotted his antics and joined him. The two held hands and went around in circles. The next thing Loreen knew, Jake had taken her hands. It seemed silly, childish, but his smile was contagious, and it brought Loreen a sense of light-heartedness. It lifted some of the weight she carried on her shoulders.

She laughed out loud when he spun her around, the blue sky dotted with white fluffy clouds passing behind him in a blur; then the innocence of the moment died. His gaze locked with hers. A current passed from his hands to hers, a delicious sizzle that ran the length of her arms. More than static laced the air. The undeniable attraction they felt for one another rested between them.

Jake was the first to break contact. He released her hands, and the moment drifted away with the harmless clouds passing overhead. He drew his arm across his forehead.

"Sure is hot today." He turned to Toby and Wren, who'd ceased their shenanigans. "What do you say to a well-deserved swim?"

Both children whooped in delight.

"Toby, go down and shut off the chute. The plants are delicate; too much water can wash them away."

"And you, young lady, go change into your old underclothes," Loreen instructed Wren.

The children left, and with their departure an awkwardness settled between Jake and Loreen. She was still painfully aware of him—of the strength in his arms, the sheen of his sun-darkened skin, the coarse hair around his copper-colored nipples, and the dark trail that disappeared inside the waistband of his pants.

"The ditch was a good idea," she finally said, pretending a preoccupation with her fingers.

"I was thinking. It wouldn't be much trouble to lay some pipe, veer off from the ditch, and build you a pump. It'd save you several trips a day to fetch water. Would you like that?"

To say she wouldn't would sound silly. "A pump would be nice, but suit yourself. The place will be yours. With any luck, I'll be leaving soon."

The words sounded ominous. Jake said nothing, which only increased the tension.

"I'm sure you'll marry again someday," Loreen commented, not particularly liking the sound of that either. "Your wife would most likely appreciate the pump."

"And what about you? Will you marry again?"

Although he'd asked in a casual manner, a muscle in his jaw jumped. He wouldn't glance at her, so she had trouble detecting any emotion in his stormy eyes.

She sighed. "I certainly don't foresee myself as being another man's wife." Loreen suddenly realized she'd indicated that she saw herself as Jake's. "I mean, becoming any man's wife."

He did look at her then, his brow cocked. "I thought all women wanted marriage and children."

"I already have children," she said dryly. "And I can't see that I'd like someone bossing them around."

Some distant point captured his attention. "Is that what you think I do?"

"Of course not," Loreen answered. "You're wonderful with Toby and Wren. They seem to adore you."

A tinge of red crept into his face, and Loreen suspected his blush stemmed from pleasure.

"I mean, they seem to like you," she corrected.

"I like them, too."

He turned his gaze on her, and Loreen had the odd-est feeling he was going to add that he liked her as well. Wren came running from the cabin, slamming the door loudly, and ending the intimate conversation.

The child started for the pool, saw Jake, and came toward them. Suddenly the redhead stopped. She looked up at Loreen, and if ever a guilty expression had been seen, Wren wore it now.

"Forget your bloomers again?" Loreen asked.

Wren shook her curls.

"Have an accident?"

Again Wren indicated the negative.

"What's the matter, Wren?" Jake asked.

She coyly lowered her gaze and pointed behind her. Loreen searched the cabin, finding nothing amiss. The clothes were all still on the line; then she spotted the garden. A few of the plants had been dug up.

"Wren?" she asked. "What have you done?"

Rather than answer, the little girl resorted to tears. She let out a caterwaul that could have probably woken Samuel Crawford from his nap two land sec-tions over. Jake, to Loreen's irritation, quickly scooped the child up in his arms.

"Don't coddle her," Loreen warned him. "I told her not to dig up the plants, and she did it anyway. I want to know why, Wren."

Wren sniffed loudly. "I got to thinking, and seeing as I like puppies so much, I thought we'd plant a brier patch instead. That way we can have puppies all the time."

Loreen's mouth dropped open. "We needed that food, Wren. What are we supposed to eat now? Puppies?"

The child began to cry in earnest, and Loreen wanted

to snatch back her question. Jake gave her a dirty look, which didn't help matters. He set Wren on the ground.

"Go back inside the house and wait for us."

Wren had the good sense to glance at Loreen for permission. "Go ahead," she said stiffly. Once Wren moved from hearing distance, Loreen faced Jake with tight lips.

"You baby her too much," she accused.

"And you didn't handle that well. Puppies? We're going to eat puppies?"

Her cheeks stung with anger and embarrassment. "What she did was very wrong. Our supplies are dwindling and we need fresh vegetables. Billy told Mr. Johnson he wasn't to trade with us anymore. Us or anyone who calls us a friend!"

Jake removed his hat and beat it against his leg. "I see there's yet another thing you failed to mention to me."

"I meant to tell you," she said more calmly.

After cramming his hat back onto his head, Jake asked, "Have you gone hungry a day since I set foot on this farm?"

"No," she admitted.

"She dug up only a few of the plants, not the whole garden. Wren should be punished," he admitted. "But bear in mind that it was you who told her puppies came from brier patches. When I was five, if someone had told me that, I'd be looking to plant stickers, too."

"Wren has to learn that she can't just go doing anything she gets a notion to do. She has to learn serious consequences might follow."

Jake's gaze rolled upward. "You have a real fixation on consequences, don't you?"

"I have a problem with Wren misbehaving!" she

shot back. "And I have the right to punish her. She's *my* daughter!" When his eyes widened slightly, Loreen quickly added, "My, ah, responsibility." She drew herself up, daring him to say something about her reference to being Wren's mother, and praying he wouldn't.

She was thankful he didn't, but the intensity of his stare made her more nervous. Loreen had no choice but to lower her gaze.

"I think Wren has spirit," he said. "I like that she's not afraid to act on her impulses. I like her sass and her bluntness. I imagine she's a lot like you were at her age."

Loreen didn't think she'd ever heard a compliment and an insult rolled up together. He started to walk away. "Hold on," she said. "You told Wren to wait for us in the cabin. Us. You and me. You didn't think I handled the situation well; I want to see how you would handle this."

Chapter Twenty-three

Wren's punishment had ended. Her chores were lessened, she'd eaten cookies that afternoon, and as for the punishment Jake had dished out for digging up some of the garden, Wren had managed to suffer through one full day of not seeing the puppies. It was late afternoon and Jake paced outside the cabin, waiting for Loreen and Wren to come out so they could attend Manny's barn raising.

Toby had taken up a stick for whittling, which suggested that the females might not make an appearance anytime soon. Jake felt edgy, like a schoolboy attending his first dance. Manny Crawford had come by two days prior and brought Loreen a bag of apples, claiming he had a hankering for her pie again.

Loreen had been baking ever since, and six pies sat in the wagon, ready to be gobbled up, although Jake couldn't see how only two families could devour them all in one evening. Jake felt obligated to tell Manny about Billy's instructions that Mr. Johnson not trade with anyone who called the Matlands friends. But the giant had claimed he wouldn't be told who he could or could not have dealings with, and the matter had been settled.

The cabin door opened, and all other thoughts were forgotten. Two angels stood before him, their pretty dresses exactly alike, their hair piled atop their heads with soft curls dangling down to their shoulders.

As he stood there staring at them, Jake figured that if Loreen had realized that by dressing herself and Wren alike, right down to the same hairstyle, she had only strengthened his suspicions about the pair, she might have done differently.

Sisters could strongly resemble one another, but apart from their hair and age, Wren and Loreen were mirror images. He supposed he could still be wrong, but he didn't think so. His gut instincts told him Wren was part of a secret Loreen hid from him.

"Ain't you gonna tell us how pretty we look?" the little girl asked, placing her hands on her hips.

Her sassy stance made him smile. "You are just about the prettiest girl I've ever laid eyes on."

His answer made her frown. " 'Just about' don't mean the prettiest," she informed him.

He laughed out loud. "I stand corrected, as I fear most men will in your company, Wren Matland. You are, in fact, the prettiest girl I've ever seen."

She grinned broadly at him and bounced down the steps. Jake lifted her into the wagon. He turned to find Loreen still standing on the porch.

"I suppose you're waiting for your compliments, too?" he asked, joining her on the porch.

"Yes, please," she answered, lifting her nose, but spoiling the effect with a girlish giggle.

Jake walked in a slow circle around her. He didn't imagine there was more beautiful woman in all the world. Although the material he'd purchased was little better than homespun, the bodice hugged Loreen's breasts becomingly and accented her small waist. The lace around the collar and cuffs was a nice touch, contrasting nicely with Loreen's sun-kissed skin.

"How does a man compliment perfection?" he asked once he faced her again.

Loreen's eyes narrowed. "It's taken me three hours to prepare for this social. Try."

As with Wren, her sauciness made him laugh. He sobered, staring into her soft blue eyes. "I've told you more than once you're beautiful. Sometimes outer beauty fades once the inside person emerges. To me, you grow more beautiful every day."

Two bright spots of color surfaced in her cheeks. She fanned her face. "Oh, my," she said breathlessly, then walked past him and down the steps.

The journey to the Crawfords' didn't take long. Jake heard the clacking of hammers against wood long before he reached the sod house. The sight of several wagons and buggies lining the road made him pull up on the reins. He turned to Loreen. Her eyes were as round as he imagined his own were.

"They came," she whispered. "The whole community must be here."

Not the whole community, Jake suspected. He was willing to bet Billy Waylan and his gang hadn't taken up hammers to help to the Crawfords.

They all climbed from the wagon and approached the gathering. The closer they drew to the house, the more excited Wren became, and the less excited Loreen appeared to be.

"You wanted to show off that new dress," he reminded her. "Aren't you pleased so many people have shown up to help?"

"I'm wondering why," she remarked. "Most of the women of Miller's Passing haven't said two words to Gretchen Crawford. Why are they here?"

"Maybe they've decided it was time they were more neighborly," Jake answered, but he was wondering the same thing—not just about the women, but about the men as well.

She cast him a skeptical glance, but said nothing more. Once they came upon the house, the answer became clearer. As soon as they were noticed, the women rushed forward, not to greet Loreen, but to fawn over Jake.

"Let me take those pies, Mr. Winslow," Mrs. Johnson from the mercantile said. "We can't have our town hero doing women's work."

A titter of female laughter followed. Jake didn't smile back at the women. The hairs on his neck started to bristle. He had a bad feeling about the barn raising, or rather, about the reason so many folks had shown up to help.

"Hey, there's Jake Winslow!" a man called from the area where the men were working on the new barn. Several laid down their hammers and approached them. Within minutes they were surrounded. Jake felt like a prize hog at a county fair.

"Could we get you a drink, Mr. Winslow?" Mrs. Johnson chirped. "A cool glass of lemonade, or would you prefer something stronger?"

"I *prefer* just plain Jake," he answered. "And what I'd like is a hammer. I came here to raise a barn."

Mr. Johnson stepped forward. "I brought plenty of hammers, but we don't want you busting up your hands." He laughed. "We'll help Crawford raise his barn. Any friend of yours is a friend of ours."

If Jake didn't have a cast-iron stomach, he might have become sick. Once, he had believed his skill with a gun could earn him respect from other men. What the good people of Miller's Passing offered him wasn't respect; It was dependence. They'd be nice to him because they wanted something in return. They wanted him to protect them.

"Loreen told me Billy said anyone who was a friend of ours wasn't welcome to trade in your store, Mr. Johnson."

Andrew turned red. "Well," he blustered, "that was before. And Billy and his boys have gone off to Dodge to trade cattle. It's market time, and time for all of us to breathe a sigh of relief they're gone. Maybe he won't come back."

Just the mention of Dodge made Jake uncomfortable. "I wouldn't bet money on it, Mr. Johnson." Jake edged his way through those gathered, heading toward the barn.

Loreen couldn't have been prouder of Jake. He'd made the townsfolk look like groveling idiots, and he had steered clear of any references to gunfighting. The fact that he didn't readily accept their friendship also pleased her. Friendship was something that should be earned with respect and kindness, not with a weapon, and not because they wanted something in return.

"Well, Loreen," Mrs. Johnson gushed, "I do believe that is the prettiest dress I've seen for some time. The stitching is very impressive. I didn't know you were such a talented seamstress."

While the women admired her dress, Loreen searched for Gretchen. She spotted her standing near the house, and from the miserable look on her face, Loreen assumed none of the women had bothered to make her feel accepted.

"Actually, my good friend Gretchen Crawford stitched this dress for me," Loreen said. She walked through the crowd and took Gretchen's hand, pulling her forward. "Her father was a great tailor in Germany, did you know? Her mother created gowns for royalty. Gretchen comes by her talents naturally, and I told her she should open her own shop."

"Royalty!" one woman whispered, obviously impressed.

Mrs. Johnson shoved her way to the front of the group. "Gretchen Crawford trades in my store," she said, as if everyone present didn't, seeing as the Johnsons' Mercantile was the only one in Miller's Passing. "We have even spoken on several occasions," she bragged.

When Gretchen stiffened beside her, Loreen squeezed her hand. Mrs. Johnson should have been put in her place, but Gretchen's acceptance had to begin somewhere, and the store owner's wife was as good a place as any to start.

"And just last week Gretchen told me there wasn't a finer mercantile in the country," Loreen said. "So modern and well stocked."

Hetty Johnson blushed becomingly. "I certainly take that as a compliment. And Gretchen dear, you *should* open your own shop. I can't sew worth a hoot. I'll be your first customer."

"Mrs. Crawford, are you up on the latest styles?" Gus Sims's wife asked. "I would love to have a dress with a bustle."

In the silence that followed, Loreen realized Gretchen felt reluctant to speak. Loreen squeezed her hand again.

"W-When I first came to America, I docked in Boston. I made sketches of the fashions there."

Hearing Gretchen's accent seemed to remind the women present that she was a foreigner. Loreen said in a carefree manner, "Don't you adore her accent? It makes her sound so mysterious and uncommon."

"She is uncommon," one woman reluctantly agreed. "And a beauty."

"So refined," Mrs. Johnson offered. "A breath of fresh air."

"Look at the darts on this dress." A woman stepped forward. "Do you think you can do anything with them?"

Gretchen released Loreen's hand in order to study the darts. "*Ja,* I can fix this."

The woman smiled, then frowned. "Are you terribly expensive?"

After cutting her gaze slyly at Loreen, Gretchen said, "For my friends, I am very reasonable."

In an instant, all of the women wanted to become Gretchen's friend. Loreen slipped away from the group. Maybe buying friendship wasn't the best thing, but once the townsfolk got past their silly prejudices, Loreen was certain Gretchen could find a true friend or two in the bunch. She noticed Wren and Samuel playing with a group of children.

Toby had joined Jake and the men. Loreen found the

scene very pleasant. She felt a part of the community for the first time. How wonderful it would be if this sort of comradeship between the townspeople could continue.

"You are sneaky, Loreen."

She turned to find Gretchen standing behind her. "I don't know for a fact that your mother *didn't* sew gowns for royalty," Loreen said.

"She was a well-respected seamstress," Gretchen admitted. "But I would not brag about such a thing."

"You didn't," Loreen reminded her. "I did."

Gretchen laughed, hugging her. "One true friend is worth more than a hundred who are false. The others"—she nodded toward the women who had resumed various jobs—"I do not care about them."

"But you must," Loreen insisted. "You'll need friends and I . . . I'm not staying in Miller's Passing."

The woman's brow puckered. "Where are you going?"

Loreen knew that to be a true friend, she had to tell Gretchen the truth about her marriage and her plans to escape Miller's Passing.

Chapter Twenty-four

Evening had started to settle across the land when the men marched toward the tables of food. Jake was surprised to see Gretchen Crawford surrounded by women, and more surprised to see Loreen sitting alone. He approached her.

"Hard to have a party of just one, isn't it?"

She smiled at him, but there was little humor in her expression. "I had to give my ears a rest."

"What's going on there?" He nodded in Gretchen's direction.

"Gretchen has gone from having a mother who sewed for royalty to being descended from royalty herself. It's amazing how far a group of woman can stretch a tiny tidbit of gossip."

"Who started the rumors?"

Her smile widened. "I did."

Jake pulled up a chair and sat beside her. "That was a nice thing to do. Why aren't you with her?"

Loreen's gaze lowered. "I told her the truth—about us and about my plans to leave Miller's Passing. I thought it would be best if she made new friends."

"I imagine she will," he commented quietly. "That doesn't mean you can't still be her friend until . . . well, until then," he finished.

He realized he had a problem accepting that Loreen and the children were leaving. Jake also realized that if he didn't have his past hanging over his head, he might just try to talk Loreen Matland into staying. His thoughts made him uneasy. That certainly hadn't been part of the bargain. Past or no past, Loreen didn't want to live in Miller's Passing—not with him or any other man.

Jake glanced around and spotted Wren speaking to Mrs. Johnson from the mercantile. The woman listened intently to whatever the child said, glanced in their direction, and began to laugh.

"What's that precocious child up to?" he mumbled.

"I don't know," Loreen answered. "Wren's probably telling Hettie about the puppies, and where they came from."

He grinned at her. "Well, that's your own fault for filling her head with lies."

Loreen didn't take his teasing well. She looked thoughtful for a moment, then sighed. "Everyone is lining up at the tables to eat. We should join them."

Jake rose and took Loreen's hand. As usual, the ever-present current passed between them. They were both getting good at pretending not to notice it, though. The food was plentiful. Gretchen's sausage

273

went fast, but not as quickly as Loreen's apple pies. She was declared the best pie baker in the area and, some ventured, the best in the state.

The praise, along with her acceptance among the women, made Loreen's eyes sparkle and her smiles frequent. Jake couldn't stop watching her, couldn't keep pride from swelling inside his chest. He knew she had secrets. Who didn't? She had fears, and with good cause. She had strength she hadn't yet tapped, and a spirit that, although battered, had not been broken.

She was a prize any man would fight for, die for, but she could never be his. Not unless he became the man she deserved, or at least made the effort, even if he died trying. He had to confront his past; to earn Loreen he'd have to become honest.

The sound of a bow being drawn across a fiddle distracted him from his thoughts. Manny Crawford began playing a jaunty tune. The evening took on a festive air. As men hurried to pull tables out of the way, Wren took Samuel's hands and started to dance with him. Couples joined in, and soon sounds of fiddling, foot stomping, and clapping filled the night.

Loreen settled beside him. She pointed at Toby, who'd managed to coax a pretty young girl into dancing, and they both smiled. After a while Loreen began tapping her toes. Jake tugged at his collar.

"I don't know how to dance," he said, anticipating her. "But if you have your heart set on it, I'll give it a try."

"We don't have to dance," she quickly told him. She tapped her toes a few minutes longer, then jumped up and grabbed his hands. Loreen led him into the fray.

"Take my hand like this, and place your other one on my waist."

Deciding that dancing couldn't be all that bad if he got to touch her, Jake did as she asked.

"This is a simple waltz; you should be able to pick it up quickly. Follow my lead."

He'd thought, the first day he met her, that Loreen was the type of woman a man would follow to hell and back. She was also the type a man made a fool of himself over. Which he felt certain he was about to prove.

Loreen's feet were killing her. Or rather, Jake's feet were killing hers. She'd never met anyone more uncoordinated when it came to dancing. They had danced several dances, and he hadn't improved. Since he seemed to do everything else well, his inability to catch on surprised her. She tried not to wince when he stepped on her foot again.

"Sorry," he muttered stiffly, and she heard frustration in his voice. That he continued to try, even though people were ogling them, kept Loreen from becoming overly impatient with him. She had, in fact, tried to steer him away from the makeshift dance floor more than once. He refused to surrender to his lack of skill.

"I thought you wanted to sample Gus Sims's rum," she tried.

"Am I embarrassing you?" He lost count of his steps and did further damage to her feet.

"I could use a rest is all. And, to be honest, you look like you could use a drink."

Reluctantly he took her hand and led her away. Loreen thought she heard a collective sigh of relief from those still dancing. She tried not to limp while following him to a table, where he poured her a glass of lemonade.

Jake handed her the drink, and they walked toward the rum keg.

A group of men were gathered around the keg, laughing. They became suspiciously quiet when they noticed Jake's presence among them. Gus Sims hurried to pour him a glass.

"You must be powerful thirsty," he remarked.

One man snickered, then quickly disguised it as a cough.

"You fellows weren't discussing my dancing abilities, were you?" Jake asked dryly.

Loreen found it amazing that a group of half-drunk men could become sober so quickly.

"We were just remarking on what a handsome couple you and Loreen make," Gus supplied.

"You look nice together," another added.

Jake took a sip of rum and ran his steely gaze over the men. "As long as we're not dancing, right?"

The group looked at a loss for words until Jake smiled at them. Then they all burst into laughter.

"I do believe you're the worst dancer I've ever seen," Gus admitted, slapping Jake on the back.

"No, you're the worst, Gus," one man argued. He flapped his arms and strutted like a rooster. Loreen smiled as the men continued their antics, including Jake in their silliness. She slipped away, moving farther from the gathering in order to breathe the night air and stare at the full moon above.

The men had relaxed around Jake, and the reason, she supposed, was because he refused to allow them to treat him as in any way superior to them. As she heard their muted laughter from the short distance, a calmness settled over her. Jake would have a good life in Miller's Passing. These people would become his friends.

Maybe together the town could put an end to Billy's tyranny. She could leave Jake with a clear conscience.

"Are you trying to hide from me?"

Startled, she turned to find him leaning against a tree. "I wanted a moment to catch my breath," she answered. "And you should mix more with the townsfolk."

He shrugged away from his position. "Why would I want to stand around with a bunch of ugly men when I can be out here beneath a full moon with you?"

Her heart sped up a measure when he stood before her. The night shadowed his chiseled features, but she had already memorized his face, his every expression.

"Well, we should get back," she said, noting the nervousness in her voice.

"There's no hurry," he countered. "Wren and Toby are still dancing. I spotted them before I saw you standing alone in the moonlight."

"It is past Wren's bedtime," she insisted. "I imagine everyone will be leaving shortly."

He stepped closer. "All the more reason we should have one last dance."

She stifled the groan that immediately rose in her throat. Perhaps being honest had its merits. "Jake," she began hesitantly, "dancing doesn't seem to be your strong suit."

To her surprise, he laughed. "That's a nice way of putting it. You're right; I'm awful."

"Yes, you are," she agreed. "Which greatly surprises me. You seem so adept at everything else you do."

His smile widened. "Anything in particular?"

"You swim well," she quickly offered. "And the way you string a fence is pure poetry. The grace with which you work is like a dance in itself. Your movements have a rhythm, which is all dancing is—following the

277

beat of the music and the movements of the person you're dancing with."

He took her glass and set it on the ground. "Show me again."

She could see there would be no dissuading him. Loreen waited until the music began. It was a slow waltz. She took Jake's hand in hers, and he placed his other on her waist.

"Remember the steps?"

"The steps don't help me." He pulled her close. "And I can't follow the movement of your body when you stand so far away."

Dancing this close would be considered indecent in public, but since they were more or less alone, Loreen saw no harm in obliging him. After a bad start, they began to move together, flow together, dance together. She held her breath, waiting for him to step on her feet, but he didn't.

Since words would only break his concentration, she kept quiet, marveling at how effortlessly he followed her movements. A few seconds more, and she became aware of other things: of his body moving against hers, the feel of his breath against her hair. She glanced up and caught him staring at her.

Their gazes met and held, their bodies still moving in perfect time. It seemed only natural that their lips should meet as well. A not-so-subtle cough had her jerking away from him. Gretchen stood not far from them.

"Wren is asking for you," she said. "I think she is ready to find her bed."

"Oh, yes, we should be going." Loreen hated the husky sound of her voice. She and Jake walked to where Gretchen stood.

"It was a wonderful social," he said to Gretchen. "Thank you for inviting us."

"Thank you for coming," she responded politely.

Jake turned to Loreen. "I'll get Ben hitched up and meet you and the children at the wagon."

She nodded, then watched him return to the gathering. The silence between herself and Gretchen seemed awkward. "We were just dancing," she mumbled.

Gretchen raised a brow. "I saw you . . . dancing." Her smile was much too smug as she took Loreen's arm and steered her back toward the guests. "I do not think you are going anywhere, my friend."

Wren looked exhausted. Loreen gathered her empty pie plates and said her good-byes. She spotted Toby still flirting with the young girl he'd danced with, waved for him to come along, and led Wren to the wagon. Toby raced past them and jumped into the back. Jake lifted Wren into the wagon, and she scrambled to snuggle beside Toby. Loreen imagined the children would be asleep before long.

Jake lifted her up to the bench seat and hopped up beside her. They rode in silence. Words seemed unnecessary. They hadn't kissed, even though they'd come close—of course, neither of them had to admit that. She had greatly enjoyed the barn raising, the food, the dancing, and the comradeship of others.

The social had given her a glimpse of what life could be like in Miller's Passing if people stood up for themselves: neighbors helping one another, a husband in truth by her side. A man to dream with, hope with, share with . . . Not just any man. Jake.

Only he stirred her passions, made her feel more than beautiful. But did she dare believe he could forgive her for past mistakes? Her parents, God rest their souls, had convinced her that her past would mark her as unworthy, convinced her that she must take her secret to the grave or risk condemnation from decent folks. Perhaps they were right, but Loreen couldn't honestly give her heart—or anything else—to Jake unless she first gave him the truth.

"You're quiet," he commented. "Did you have a fun at the social?"

"Yes," she answered. "I found the entire evening very enjoyable."

"Even my stepping on your feet?"

She laughed. "All right. Maybe not everything."

He pulled the wagon to the side of the road. "Seems to me we didn't finish that last dance. Not the way we intended to."

A glance to the back of the wagon found Toby and Wren asleep. Loreen turned to Jake. "What do you mean?"

"You know what I mean. I was going to kiss you, and I think you were going to let me. Am I wrong?"

Although she saw the sense in telling him he was mistaken, she was tired of lying, and tired of fighting her feelings for Jake.

"No," she said. "You weren't wrong."

He leaned toward her, and she met him halfway. Their lips had barely brushed when a shot suddenly rang out. Old Ben lunged forward. Another shot sounded, whizzing past Loreen's nose.

"Get in the back!" Jake yelled, trying to control the horse.

"What's happening?" Toby called, awake now.

"Stay down, all of you!" Jake snapped the reins and let Ben have his head.

Loreen fell into the back of the wagon, trying to

shield Toby and Wren with her body. The buckboard bounced each time they hit a rut or a rock, knocking them all painfully about. She heard more shots fired, but they seemed to be fading into the distance.

Nevertheless, she continued to lie on top of the children. As they raced at breakneck speed toward home, Loreen prayed they would all make it there in one piece.

The ride seemed to last forever, but soon she felt the wagon slow to a stop. She poked her head up and Jake was already down from the bench seat.

"Is anyone hurt?"

"I think we're all okay," she answered. "Toby, Wren, are you all right?"

Toby said he wasn't hurt, but Wren could only sob. Her brother bounded over the side of the wagon.

"Grab your rifle in case they've followed us," Jake instructed the boy. "Come here, Wren."

She rushed to him and he lifted her out. "You don't hurt anywhere, do you, sweetheart?"

"I'm just scared," Wren answered.

Jake set her down. "Run inside the cabin. Get up into the loft, under your bed."

As Wren ran to do his bidding, he turned to Loreen. "Are you all right?"

"Just shaken up." She accepted the hand he offered her. "Who do you think it was? Robbers?"

With a slight groan, Jake lifted her from the wagon. His jaw was clenched tight. "You know who it was. Billy. He must not have left for Dodge yet. I guess he has decided that since can't outdraw me, he'll have to shoot me in the back."

Loreen knew he was right; still, she hoped they were merely random victims chosen for robbery.

"Maybe it wasn't Billy. And the most important thing, if it was, is that he didn't succeed. Let's hurry into the house."

She started for the cabin, noticed Jake wasn't following, and turned around. He leaned heavily against the wagon.

"Jake? Are you coming?"

He nodded, took a step, and stumbled. Loreen rushed forward to catch him. He fell into her arms, then slid to the ground. That was when she felt the wetness on her hands. It was the stickiness of blood.

Chapter Twenty-five

Loreen had dug the bullet out of him three days ago, but Jake had lost a lot of blood. He'd drifted in out of consciousness, sometimes lucid enough to eat, most times too weak to care. She supposed he was lucky the bullet hadn't damaged him beyond repair: an inch higher and it would have pierced his lung. Regardless, she wasn't sure he would pull through, and the thought of losing him was almost more than she could handle.

"Is he better?"

Toby and Wren stood at the doorway to her bedroom, where Jake had been sleeping, both as solemn as judges since the shooting.

"I think he's a little better," Loreen lied to the children. "But I'm having trouble getting him to stay awake long enough to eat." She motioned Wren forward. "Come talk to him, honey. Maybe you can get him to wake up."

Wren approached the bed. "What do I say?"

"Just talk about anything you want. If he opens his eyes, you come fetch me."

"All right," Wren said, but her voice caught. Her eyes filled with tears. "He looks funny. Not like himself."

Jake's usually dark complexion had paled, and he was so horribly still. He felt cold to the touch as well. Loreen didn't think that was a good sign.

"He just looks that way because he doesn't feel good right now," Loreen explained. "As soon as he starts to mend, his color will return."

"Jake won't die, will he?" Wren asked, fear clouding her usually clear blue eyes.

"Of course he won't." Loreen wondered if it was the right thing to say. Should she give Wren a false sense of security about something she had very little control over? "Well, we're going to pray he doesn't," she amended. "We're going to do our best for Jake."

"I'll tell him the story he told me," Wren decided. "The one about kings and queens. And then I'll tell him about Princess and how those pups are growing."

"I'm sure he'd like that." Loreen rose from the bedside, stretched her back, and walked out of the room. Toby followed close on her heels.

"What do we do today?" she asked him.

"I think the crops need more water, and of course everything needs to be fed. I can do the feeding, but someone has to stand by the chute and stop the water."

"I'll handle the chute. You just holler when you want it closed."

Toby was silent for a moment; then he blurted, "He ain't going to die, is he, Loreen?"

She stopped and turned around. Toby looked as if he might cry, too. "I don't know, Toby."

"But it ain't fair," he said in a choked voice. "Everyone we care about gets taken away!"

Supposing she couldn't argue that issue with him, she did the only thing she knew to do and hugged him. He cried, and it was the first time she'd seen him break down since the loss of their brother and parents. She let him cry, holding him until he quieted.

"Would it be so bad, Loreen?" Toby asked. "So bad if you and Jake stayed married, and we all lived here together?"

The question surprised her. "I don't guess it would be bad," she admitted. "It just wouldn't be right. Jake and I don't, well—and Billy, he's always going to be a problem. I thought you didn't want Jake in our lives . . . in mine."

Toby shrugged; then his eyes watered again. "He already is a part of our lives, isn't he?"

Yes, she thought. Loreen felt her own eyes start to sting as well. She didn't know what to tell Toby. Loreen wasn't sure how Jake really felt about her, or the possibility of their staying on the farm with him. Yes, it was clear he wanted her, but wanting her to be a permanent fixture in his life was far different. She knew that, if nothing else. Also, she wasn't certain how she felt about it all.

"I don't know, Toby," she whispered. "Now isn't a good time to think about that. We're both tired and we're all worried about Jake. We have to take care of him and the farm right now. We'll worry about everything else later."

He nodded, and together Loreen and Toby went outside to do chores. She returned often to check on both Wren and Jake. By evening, Wren had fallen asleep curled up next to the wounded man.

The picture they made tugged at Loreen's heart-strings. She wished in that moment that Jake truly was Wren's father. He would love her, protect her with his life, do all the things the child's real father had refused to do.

He stirred, and she quickly moved to the bedside. A sheen stood out clearly on his forehead. He felt hot to the touch. Loreen hurried to the doorway.

"Toby," she whispered frantically.

The boy appeared, a half-eaten bowl of soup in his hands.

"Come take Wren up to bed. Jake has a fever."

Toby set his bowl aside and hurried to do her bidding. "How can I help?"

"I'll need cold water. As soon as you've settled Wren, fetch me a bucket."

Loreen went to her wardrobe and pulled out a worn nightdress. She started tearing it into strips. Jake tossed against the bed sheets, mumbling incoherently. Loreen feared he'd reopen his wound. She hurried to the bed, placing her hands on his shoulders in an effort to quiet him. Sick as he was, he still maintained the strength to shove her hands aside. He sat bolt upright in bed, his eyes wide and staring into hers.

"I didn't mean to do it," he rasped. "I didn't mean to shoot him!"

She froze. *Shoot who?* He was obviously having some sort of nightmare. His eyes were glazed over, and sweat trickled down his temple. Jake settled back against the pillows, but it was his next whispered words that made her blood turn cold.

"I gotta run. I gotta disappear."

That long-ago conversation they'd had flooded her memory. Jake had said that Texas was a place that could swallow a man whole, make him disappear. Was he hiding from someone? She also recalled the slight relief he displayed upon learning there was no law in Miller's Passing. Had Jake been looking for a hideout when he answered her advertisement? A place the law might not find him?

"Here's the water." Toby came into the room with a bucket. "I hope it's cold enough."

"Go on to bed," she instructed, hoping Jake didn't say anything else, not in front of Toby. "I'll tend to Jake."

"But I want to help."

"I know you do." She subtly steered him from the room. "But I may be up all night, and one of us has to get rest. If I need you, I'll call you."

"All right," he reluctantly agreed. "But I'll sleep in the rocker so you won't have to wake up Wren."

She mussed his hair. "You're a good help to me, Toby. I don't know what I'd do without you."

He blushed, but she saw he was pleased by her compliment. Loreen had decided she should praise him often, treat him as more of a grown-up than she sometimes did. But for now, she had other matters to tend. Drawing a shaky breath, she reentered the bedroom.

She closed the door, turning to stare at the man lying in her bed. Her first reaction had been to automatically jump to the worst conclusion. But now that she'd calmed somewhat, she tried to find other explanations.

For all she knew, Jake had just been having a nightmare. True, she had wondered if he was an outlaw at one time, and true, she'd allowed her suspicions to resurface after seeing him draw against Billy, but the obvious seemed impossible. Jake didn't have a killer's nature. He was a good man, a fair man—but was he an honest one?

The fact that she hadn't been honest with him either, not from the beginning, and not since she'd come to know him, brought her shame. Little wonder she couldn't trust anyone, not when her life had become one lie after another.

How could she judge Jake when she didn't know if he had deceived her or not, and for what reasons, if he had? She couldn't. Loreen piled her rags next to the bucket Toby had fetched. She poured water into the basin and began to sponge Jake's fevered skin.

There was only one truth that mattered to her: the truth in her heart. Jake wasn't a cold-blooded killer. She'd misjudged men in the past, but not this time. Or at least she prayed she wasn't wrong. She would believe in her intuition, believe in Jake. At least until he proved her wrong.

Jake felt as if he'd been kicked in the side by a horse. His mouth had no saliva and his stomach growled loudly. He pried his eyes open, wanting to shut them against the daylight. He glanced around, surprised to find himself in Loreen's bed, more surprised to see her sitting across the room in a chair, asleep. For a moment he couldn't remember how he'd come to be there, but then events came rushing back to him.

He'd felt the bullet's sting when it had entered his flesh, but there had been no time to worry over being shot. All he'd been able to think of was getting Loreen and the children home to safety. Other memories came to him, the sound of Wren's voice telling him a story, and the feel of Loreen's gentle touch, cool against his burning skin. He tried to sit, but his limbs felt weak. He coughed due to the dryness of his throat.

Loreen came straight up off her chair. She hurried over to him. "Jake?" she whispered.

"Can't a man get a drink around here?" he rasped.

Her smile looked brighter than the morning sun. She ran to the door and flung it wide. "Toby! Wren! Jake is talking! He wants a drink!"

Rushing to the basin, she dipped him a cup of water. She sat beside him, holding his head while he sipped. "Not too much," she warned him. "Too much will only make you throw it back up."

He knew that, but rather enjoyed her fussing over him. Wren and Toby appeared in the doorway, both puffing wind. Neither looked sure whether it was all right to enter.

Jake weakly motioned them inside. "You two been staying out of trouble?"

Both broke into smiles and ran to the bed. Wren crawled up beside him, her movement causing him to bite back a groan.

"Careful, honey," Loreen cautioned her. "Jake is sore. Don't jostle the bed too much."

Wren flashed him an apologetic smile, but launched into questions. "Did you hear me tell you the story, Jake?"

"I do remember hearing the story," he told her. "And you told it very well. And I remember you talking about Princess and those pups, too."

"They're starting to run all over the place," she informed him.

Jake tried to smile, but even that hurt. He looked past Wren at Toby. The boy's eyes were suspiciously moist. "How about you, Toby? Have you been seeing to things while I've been laid up?"

"Loreen and I have," he answered. "Got some weeds trying to choke our plants. We're gonna yank them today."

"All right, that's enough for now," Loreen said. "Jake needs to take it easy. Wren, dish up a bowl of soup for him, and Toby, you'd better start on the chores. I'll join you shortly."

Wren kissed him on the cheek, and Toby, obviously uncertain what to do, stepped forward and offered his hand.

"Glad you ain't dead," he said.

Although Jake figured that, due to his weakened state, his return shake was less than manly, he couldn't help but smile at Toby's bluntness. "I'm glad, too."

"Out," Loreen ordered, steering the children toward the door. "Wren, holler at me when you've dished up the soup."

Once the children were gone, she returned to the bed. Loreen placed her hand against his forehead.

"No fever," she announced.

"How long have I been lying here? Two or three days?"

Her perfectly arched brows lifted. "A week."

"A week?" he echoed, struggling to sit.

Loreen put her hands on his shoulders. "And it will be a lot longer if you pull out the stitches I sewed into your side. Too bad Gretchen wasn't here. She'd have done a better job."

"I guess no one knows about this," he said.

"No one but those responsible," she countered.

"And they probably don't know if they succeeded in shooting anyone. I imagine Billy was in Dodge and he got one of his boys to do his dirty work. Gives him an alibi. But he'll be back, and he'll want to see if they managed to kill you."

"Yeah, he'll be back," Jake said coldly.

Loreen sighed. "The question is, what are we going to do about him?"

He liked that she'd said "we." "I can't let this one go, Loreen. It might be different if he'd only come after me, but he could have just as easily shot you or one of the children. I can't let him get away with that."

"I know," she agreed softly. "But you're in no condition to confront him now. You need to get your strength back. And hopefully we have a little time before he returns from Dodge."

The dark smudges beneath her eyes bespoke the hours she'd already spent tending to him. He reached over and took her hand. "Thank you."

Her eyes misted, but she blinked back the tears. "I was afraid you might not make it. Afraid you might not come back to us. I would have"—She stopped to draw a shaky breath. "I would have been sorely disappointed if you hadn't."

His heart gave a funny lurch. He had the impression that Loreen's disappointment stemmed from more than not having him to help with the crop. He lifted her hand to his lips and kissed it gently. "I had a lot to come back to."

Their eyes met. Loreen leaned toward him, and Jake had the oddest notion that she was going kiss him. The partially opened door slammed against the frame. Loreen jerked up straight. Wren stood there with his soup, most of the contents, he suspected, leaving a trail from the kitchen to the bedroom. She smiled. Jake loved Wren deeply, but damned if she didn't have the instincts of a spinster chaperon.

Chapter Twenty-six

A few days later, Loreen allowed Jake to sit on the porch for short periods of time throughout the day. She knew he was mending, because he'd become almost impossible to keep stationary. His color had returned, and along with it, a fair amount of his strength. He still tired easily if he tried to do too much, but he ate like a horse, and she figured that was a good sign.

She bent over in the field, going after a stubborn weed with the hoe. During the past two weeks, she had discovered something she'd never known about herself: Loreen liked the feel of soil between her fingers and toes. She even liked the smell of dirt.

"Hey, yonder comes Mr. and Mrs. Johnson from the mercantile!" Toby shouted, running in from the field.

Loreen rose, dusting the dirt from her dress before she followed her brother. She couldn't have been more surprised to see the Johnsons' buggy pull up in front of the cabin. Jake had risen and walked down the porch steps to join Toby.

"Loreen," Mrs. Johnson chirped. "We haven't seen your bunch in town and thought we'd stop by to check on you on our way to the Crawfords'. Manny and Gretchen were in town last Saturday, and Manny remarked that he thought it odd that Jake hadn't been over to help him finish up his barn."

"I've been laid up," Jake explained.

"Nothing too serious, I hope," Mrs. Johnson said.

Loreen and Jake exchanged a glance.

"I was shot in the back the night of the barn raising. We were attacked on our way home."

Mrs. Johnson gasped, bringing a gloved hand to her mouth. "Oh, my word."

"Any idea who shot you?" Andrew Johnson asked.

Again Jake's and Loreen's eyes met.

"I think we all know who'd like to see me out of the way," Jake answered.

A frown settled over the man's mouth. "Billy was supposed to be in Dodge. Did any of you see that it was him?"

"Billy doesn't kill anyone in front of witnesses," Loreen answered bitterly. "But we know it was him behind it. Maybe he put off his trip—lying to you folks to get an alibi—then he'd have the opportunity to shoot Jake on our way home from the barn raising. Or maybe he hired someone."

The mercantile owner looked nervous. "I think I heard Billy and his boys ride through town late last night. I received a telegraph a couple of days ago that a gang who'd robbed a bank in Dodge last year and killed a clerk had been brought in. I had kind of hoped

294

Billy might be tied up with that bunch. Wouldn't put it past him."

"Maybe you could telegraph Fort Worth and tell them about our trouble here," Loreen suggested. "We can let the law handle—"

"No law," Jake said quietly. "Without actually seeing Billy and his boys shoot at us, it would be our word against his."

"Wretched man," Mrs. Johnson muttered. "I'd like to see that Billy Waylan put away somewhere."

Loreen wondered why Jake had looked uncomfortable when Mr. Johnson mentioned Dodge—and why he didn't want the law involved in their problems.

"Well, we're glad he didn't get away with murder again," Andrew said. "Is there anything we can bring you from town?"

"Not as yet, but we might have to purchase some potatoes and such. Wren weeded our garden a little too well."

"Oh, that reminds me," Hetty blustered. "I brought a small stash of seeds for Wren. She told us she'd dug up a few of your plants, and wanted to replace them." The woman began searching the back of the buggy, saw the little girl emerging from the barn, and called, "Wren, I have those seeds you wanted!"

Wren came running, her red curls bouncing. "You brought them?" she said with a gasp, her face flushed with excitement.

Mrs. Johnson cast a smug glance toward Jake and Loreen. "I sure did."

"Oh, thank you, Mrs. Johnson." Wren hugged the woman. She took her small sack and ran into the house.

"That was very kind of you, Hetty," Loreen said.

"Oh, it's nothing," the woman said, smiling. She wore a strange expression, almost amused. "Actually, these are a few rare seeds Gretchen gave to me. Some sort of plant she grew in Germany. She says you should plant them quickly, though. The season is already late."

"We'd better be off," Mr. Johnson told his wife. "I don't like to leave the store closed for long."

"Gretchen is going to sew me a new dress," Hetty said to Loreen. "I told my husband he'd better get me over to the Crawfords' before she's covered up with orders."

"That's wonderful." Loreen was thrilled that Gretchen would be given an opportunity to make both extra income and new friends in the community. "Give her my best."

"I'm sure once they hear what's happened to Jake, they'll both be over to check on him," Andrew said, helping his wife back up into the buggy. He glanced at Loreen. "You know, those pies of yours were the best I've ever eaten. If you'd like to start selling them in my store, I'd let you keep most of the profit."

A flush of pleasure crept up her neck. "Thank you, Mr. Johnson. I'll consider your offer."

He hopped up into the buggy, nodded smartly to everyone, and flicked the reins. Loreen, Toby, and Jake stood, watching them leave. Jake's arm went around her waist.

"I told you your pies were good."

This time she knew her flush of pleasure stemmed from more than Jake's compliment. She liked the subtle touches exchanged between them of late. They had a sweetness about them, not as strong an emotion as when passion flared between them, but one almost more satisfying. What she didn't like was the cloud that had gathered over their heads since Mr. Johnson said Billy had returned.

"Loreen, why don't we look at the garden?" Jake suggested. "Discuss a few things."

When he glanced at Toby, she understood he wanted to discuss the fact that Billy had returned. Toby didn't seem to be paying them any mind. He was watching the Johnsons' buggy move down the road, a brooding expression on his face. After a moment, he turned and went inside.

"What are we going to do?" Loreen asked again.

"I need to confront him."

Loreen placed her hands on her hips. "Not in your condition. You'll be no match for him."

"He's going to come see if I'm still alive—I'd rather go surprise him. I want you and the children out of the way."

"Jake—" She started to argue, but the cabin door slamming drew her attention. Wren stood on the porch, her precious sack of seeds clutched between her hands.

"Toby's doing something wrong," she said.

Sighing, Loreen said, "Go back into the house, Wren. You can tell on Toby later."

Wren chewed her bottom lip, a habit, Loreen realized, the girl had picked up from her. "He took his rifle, and he snuck out the back door. He said I wasn't to tell you, so I figured he must be doing something wrong."

"Damn it," Jake swore. "He's going after Billy."

"Oh, my God," Loreen said in a croak. She started to run toward the road, but Jake stopped her.

"He's not dumb enough to walk all the way to town. I figure he's in the barn trying to saddle up Ben. You and Wren go back inside. I'll handle this."

She wanted to argue with him—Toby was *her* brother. Then she realized Jake could probably handle the boy better than she could. Maybe he'd listen to Jake. She prayed he would. Loreen took Wren inside, deciding she'd better have a contingency plan, just in case Toby wasn't in a listening mood.

Jake breathed a sigh of relief. He'd been right. He watched Toby try to saddle Ben from outside the barn door, took a deep breath, then walked inside.

"Getting yourself killed isn't going to help anyone."

Toby jumped at the sound of his voice, but continued to saddle the horse. "I should have known Wren wouldn't keep her mouth shut."

"And she did the grown-up thing by telling," Jake countered. "What you're doing is childish."

The boy set his jaw. "I'm doing what has to be done."

"You gave me your word you'd let *me* handle Billy, remember?"

Tears came close to filling Toby's eyes. "And you said if you couldn't protect us, I was to do it. You're not in any shape to take care of Billy, but I am."

Jake chose his words carefully. "You're growing into a man, Toby. But you're not there yet. You know I can't let you go."

Toby pulled himself up to his full height. "You can't stop me."

Impatiently, Jake ran a hand through his hair. Even that action caused him to hurt. "I reckon I can try."

Glancing at Jake's side, Toby said, "I don't want to hurt you." His eyes filled with tears again. "It's you I'm doing this for, too. Billy killed my brother. Soon as he figures out you're still alive, he's gonna come here and try to finish you off. I can't let him." Toby's voice cracked when he added, "I-I love you, Jake."

A bullet was nothing compared to the feelings that ripped through Jake. He and Toby had come a long way since the day he had married Loreen. Jake alone had come a long way. He came to Texas to hide, to disappear, never realizing there was one thing no one could hide from, and that was love.

"I love you, too, Toby. That's why I can't let you go."

Despite his earlier confession, Toby's watery eyes hardened. "I know you're not a coward. And I know you have your principles and all; I respect that about you. But Billy, he ain't got no principles, and this time you're wrong. Words aren't gonna stop him, and scaring him with a gun won't stop him, so that leaves it up to me."

"You're right about Billy," Jake agreed, moving toward the boy. "He's as bad as they come. But Mr. Johnson gave me an idea about how to handle this situation, one I rejected at first due to my own fears—but it's time to face those and do what's right for all of us. Give me the rifle, Toby."

He held out his hand, waiting. Toby glanced at Jake's hand, then back at Ben then outside. In a split second, Jake saw something in Toby's eyes shift, and he knew he'd make his move. He tensed, expecting Toby to lunge at him. He wasn't prepared when the

boy smacked Ben sharply on the hindquarters, startling the animal.

Jake banged up hard against the barn wall, Ben
nearly running him over as the horse raced outside.
The breath had been knocked out of him, his side
screamed in pain, but he tried to grab Toby as the boy
darted past him. He missed.

His boot got caught on something and he tripped.
Scrambling up, Jake ran outside. Ben was standing not
far away, but Toby hadn't quite managed to mount the
horse. He was lying facedown in the dirt. Loreen stood
over the boy, her heavy cast-iron skillet gripped
between her hands. She threw the frying pan aside and
quickly knelt beside her brother. Jake rushed over and
bent down next to them.

"I tried not to hit him too hard," she whispered. "I
didn't know what else to do. How to stop him."

Jake touched the knot already rising on the back of
Toby's head. There wasn't any blood. He helped
Loreen flip the boy over. Toby opened his eyes.

"What happened?" he mumbled.

Jake smiled down at him. "You had a run-in with
Loreen's heavy skillet. You know, the one you introduced me to a while back?"

Toby groaned as Jake and Loreen helped him to his
feet.

"Let's get him inside and to bed," Loreen said. "I
want a closer look at that bump."

"Oh, my head," Toby complained as they helped him
up the steps and into the cabin. Wren jumped to her feet.

Before she could ask questions, Jake said, "Wren,
go outside and lead Ben back into the barn. Don't try
to unsaddle him; you're too little. Just tie him up and
I'll tend to him in a minute."

The child opened her mouth—Jake suspected to argue—but he gave her a warning glance and she hurried outside. They made their way to the back bedroom and eased Toby down on the bed.

"You shouldn't have hit me with that frying pan," Toby accused his sister. "And I thought you said violence was wrong." He sulked, glancing over at Jake.

"I hope she knocked some sense into you," Jake responded.

"Hush up, both of you," Loreen scolded, probing Toby's head with her fingers.

"Ouch, Loreen," Toby grumbled.

"It's not bad," she pronounced. "You've had bigger knots on your head than that one. I barely hit you."

Knowing the boy just needed some time to cool off, Jake turned toward the door. "I'd better see to Ben."

Loreen glanced up at him; then her gaze lowered and she frowned. "You're not going anywhere. You're bleeding."

Chapter Twenty-seven

The next morning, freshly bandaged and tired from a fitful night spent sharing a bed with Toby—he had to make sure the boy didn't run off—Jake joined Loreen and Wren on the porch. He'd spent the entire night thinking. He had a lot on his mind, a lot to do, and wasn't sure how long he had before Billy called his hand. His side still ached, and he knew he had to mend better to carry out his plans. When Mr. Johnson had mentioned that a gang of outlaws who'd robbed the bank in Dodge and shot a man last year had been brought in, Jake knew his days were numbered.

"You shouldn't be up yet," Loreen said without glancing at him.

He sat beside her on the steps. She and Wren were looking at the seeds Mrs. Johnson had brought the previous day. There were only about five of them, and they were rather strange-looking seeds to be vegetables.

"I've been idle too long," he complained. "You've had to take up my slack in the field and take care of everyone besides."

She surprised him by saying, "I haven't minded. You know, dirt smells good. It feels good when you run it through your fingers and crunch it between your toes."

From the corner of his eye, he watched her stare out proudly over the field. The crop was coming along nicely. If he wasn't careful, she'd realize she didn't really need him at all. But then, maybe that would be for the best.

"Well," he said uncomfortably, "I'm itching to get my hands in the dirt again."

"You can plant my seeds," Wren offered.

Any job would have pleased him, but he cast the girl a stern look. "You dug the plants up; you should be the one to replace them."

"That's exactly what I told her," Loreen agreed. "Get the spade and plant your seeds. Not too deep," she called when Wren grabbed the tool and walked down the porch steps. "But not too shallow, either." She sighed. "Maybe I'd better help her."

"I'll do it," Jake offered. "I can at least tell her how."

"Make her do all the work," Loreen warned him.

He laughed. "There's not much work involved in planting five little seeds." Jake rose and walked down the steps. He joined Wren in the garden. He spotted a couple of yellow squashes that were ready. All in all, Wren hadn't done much damage the day she'd decided she wanted to plant brier bushes. Now she had her spade poised, making a whole in the ground. Jake squatted beside her.

"Not too deep," he warned. "There, that's about right. Now drop the seed in and cover it back up."

She shook her head. "I want to make all the holes first."

He shrugged. "Go ahead."

After Wren had dug five holes in the ground, he handed her the seeds. She dropped them. Suddenly clutching her finger, she let out a loud wail. Loreen materialized in a second.

"What happened, Wren?" She bent beside the child. When Wren kept wailing and clutching her finger, Loreen's gaze darted to Jake. "What happened?"

"I don't know," he answered above the noise. "Wren, let me see your finger."

She held out her hands. They were covered in dirt. "I don't see anything," he said.

"Let me look." Loreen snatched Wren's finger from him and studied it. "I don't see anything either. Wren, honey," she soothed the child. "Go inside and wash your hands so I can see what's wrong."

Wren jumped up. She sniffed loudly and stared at the ground. "But my seeds. I dropped them."

"Jake and I will pick them up and put them in the holes. Run along and get your hands clean so I can look at your finger again."

Loreen started digging around for the seeds. Jake watched Wren skip toward the cabin. Odd, she wasn't crying anymore.

"I'm missing one," Loreen said. "I only have four seeds."

Jake helped her search, finding the last seed. Together they hurriedly dropped the seeds in their holes and covered them up. Wren appeared in an amazingly short time. Her hands were still dirty.

"My finger stopped hurting," she said.

A suspicion arose in Jake's head that Wren's finger

304

had never hurt to begin with. Loreen, he noted, was more gullible. Her brow puckered.

"Let me see it again," she demanded.

Wren thrust a dirty finger in her face. Loreen wiped Wren's finger with her apron and squinted at it. "You have a splinter."

"I do?"

The surprise in Wren's voice almost made Jake smile. Also, it wasn't even the same finger Wren had complained hurt earlier. Sneaky. She'd found a way to get out of doing her work. Jake started to say something, then decided to let Wren think she'd gotten away with her ploy. He'd have a talk with her later. Jake had to admire the child's ingenuity, but he felt sorry for anyone who had to raise her on their own. It would be a big job.

"Go into the house and wash those hands," Loreen ordered. "Check on Toby and put my sewing box on the table. I'll be in shortly to dig that splinter out."

Wren didn't appear nearly so pleased now. Pouting, she walked back toward the cabin. She wasn't skipping.

"There's some squash ready," Jake said. "Looks like a few beans need to be picked, too."

Loreen's beautiful features lit with pleasure. "I've been so busy, I haven't had time to check on the garden."

"I'll pick," Jake said. "You've been doing too much around here."

"We both will," she insisted. "I don't want you opening that wound again."

With the mention of his injury, and with all that had happened yesterday still fresh, the pleasure faded from her face. Jake's confrontation with Toby had opened his eyes. When Toby had said he loved him—and Jake realized he loved the boy as well, loved Wren, and yes, more than anything he loved Loreen—he'd known it was time to do what he should have done a year ago: face the consequences of his actions. He had to be the man they thought he was.

"Why are you looking at me like that?"

He'd been staring at Loreen instead of working. Memorizing her face. And, he realized, along with his decision to do the right thing came the pain of letting go. Letting go of her. Letting go of all of them.

"I don't think I should sleep in the house anymore," he said. "I'll start sleeping in the barn again."

"Too drafty." She immediately dismissed the idea, plucking the squashes from their vines. "You're not healed enough to risk getting sick."

"I'm well enough to want you when you sneak into the room to check on me late at night."

Although her cheeks turned a pretty shade of pink, she didn't glance away from him. "I suppose there are things left unfinished between us," she said. "Unfortunately, now is not a good time to . . ."

"Discuss them?" he supplied.

"Yes, discuss them," she agreed. "I'll make you a proper bed in the barn tonight after supper." She rose, the vegetables gathered in her apron. "I'd better get the splinter out of Wren's finger before it gets infected."

She briefly touched his shoulder. His skin tingled where her hand had rested. Jake would offer to get the children settled after supper; then he could slip out to the barn before Loreen finished making his bed. There was no point in putting off what he had to tell her. He'd put it off for too long.

* * *

306

Loreen stroked the she-wolf's coat, smiling at the wobbly antics of her pups as they tried to maneuver in their small den. Princess licked her on the cheek. It was the first time the animal had shown her such affection.

"Thank you, Princess." She wiped her wet cheek with the sleeve of her dress. "I think."

Midnight rubbed against her, demanding equal attention. She scratched his back. "Miss your sleeping companion?" she asked. "Against my better judgment, I'm giving him back to you tonight. Lucky cat," she muttered.

She truly envied the cat, Loreen suddenly realized. She desired Jake, wanted to be with him, even knowing what she did about intimacy. And that baffled her. Certainly there would be pleasure in his arms—up to a point. It was the act of joining her body with his that frightened her. And afterward . . .

More than her fear of consummation raised doubts in her mind. Jake's confession while under his fever's influence gave her a good reason to deny her desires, a good reason not to trust him—that along with his strange behavior yesterday when Mr. Johnson had mentioned Dodge and she'd suggested getting the law involved with their troubles.

Still, he had been right. They had no proof it was Billy who shot at them. And Loreen had no evidence that Jake was running or hiding from anyone. He'd asked her to trust in him many times, and she had. This was another instance where she had to believe the best of him.

Loreen gathered hay to put in the dog's cage. Princess hadn't slept there since her pups were born, but she felt that if Jake were to get any rest, the female and her brood should be confined during the night. The cage was big enough for mother and children, and Loreen set a dish of food and water inside.

"Come here, Princess," she called. The dog trotted over, followed by her playful pups. "Inside," she said, and felt a little guilty when Princess glanced inside the cage and whined. "I know. It's not your den anymore, but it's where you're going to sleep at night until those pups are older. Come on. Get inside."

Although the animal was clearly not happy with the arrangements, she slipped inside the cage, the pups following her. Loreen closed and locked the door. She rose, intending to fix Jake's bed. It took her a few trips to the haystack, but she made him a soft mattress before spreading a thick blanket over the straw. When she rose to fetch the sheets, Princess began to growl low in her throat.

Loreen glanced around, noticed that the door stood slightly ajar, and wondered if she'd closed it or not. The rifle she'd brought along lay on the back of the buckboard. Maybe Princess had just been voicing her displeasure over the sleeping arrangements, but Loreen thought it best not to take chances. She edged her way around the buckboard. Her fingers nearly closed around the rifle before someone grabbed her. Loreen was jerked away from the weapon and shoved up hard against a wall of the barn, the barrel of a pistol thrust in her face. At the end of it stood Billy Waylan.

"Where is he?" he rasped, and she smelled the liquor on his breath.

She froze, not only at the threat of the gun, but because she knew why Billy had come. He'd sneaked onto their farm to make sure Jake was dead. But did he already know he wasn't? According to Mr. Johnson, Billy hadn't been back long. Jake was in the house, tending to Wren and Toby. She couldn't let Billy burst in there and threaten them all, so she played a hunch.

"He's dead," she whispered.

The news didn't affect Billy as she'd hoped. He frowned, which at first led her to believe he already knew otherwise. "Hell," he cursed. "I had plans for him."

For a moment Loreen had felt as if her heart had stopped beating. Now she felt it lurch. He obviously didn't know Jake was still alive. But her relief was short-lived. He grinned, displaying his ugly teeth.

"But, then again, I have plans for you, too. And now I don't have to worry about being interrupted."

Almost as if to prove him wrong, Princess growled loudly again. "Tell that dog to shut up, or I'll put a bullet between its eyes!"

"Princess, hush!" she automatically called, then realized that if Billy fired a shot, Jake would know they were all in danger. She didn't want to sacrifice the dog's life for her family's, but she would.

The dog momentarily quieted, Billy glanced around. He spotted the mattress she'd made on the floor. His gaze swung back to her, full of suspicion. "Who's that for?"

"Me," she said, trying to keep her voice calm. "I figured you'd come sneaking around here. These walls are thinner, easier to hear through, and I wanted the children safely bolted inside the cabin. I knew the dog would alert me if—"

"The dog's caged," Billy interrupted. "How can she protect you if she's locked up? You're not lying to me, are you, girl?"

His suspicions could be the death of Jake. Loreen had to think fast and ignore the fear rising inside of her. "She has pups. I just wanted them out of the way while I made the mattress; then I planned on letting her back out."

"You're acting very levelheaded, Loreen." He lowered the gun. "Ain't you afraid of what I'm going to do to you?"

She was terrified. Not only did Billy smell of whiskey, but his body reeked of uncleanliness.

"Take what you want and leave," she said. "I'll give myself willingly if you won't bother the children." Maybe she could find some way to overcome him if he were distracted.

His beady eyes glazed over, and she nearly gagged when he licked his lips and leered at her. He lifted his gun.

"We'll just take this along for the ride in case you change your mind."

He grabbed her arm roughly and shoved her toward the pile of hay on the ground. Loreen's feet felt leaden. He shoved her again and she tripped, the mattress breaking her fall. Billy loomed above her, and the anticipation on his face more than terrified her; it made her angry. Her gaze strayed to the gun in his hand. If she could wrest the weapon away from him, she had no doubt she would kill him and end his threats to her family for good.

"Unbutton your dress," he rasped hoarsely.

She didn't respond as quickly as he wanted, so he leveled the gun on her.

310

"Do it!"

His raised voice cause Princess to growl again. The gun swung toward the cage. "Tell her to be quiet."

Loreen battled what she knew to be the easiest way to alert the others and the growing affection she felt for the dog. "She doesn't like it when you threaten me."

Billy seemed to consider the matter, then shook his head. "A shot would only bring them young'uns from the house. Then I'd have to deal with them before I can have my fun with you. I've waited too long already." In a deadly quiet voice he said, "Unbutton that dress like I told you."

Her fingers trembled when she reached for the top button of her dress, partly from fear, but mostly due to her growing rage that Billy had managed to place her at his mercy. She'd been smart enough to bring the rifle with her, but too ignorant to keep the weapon within easy reach. If she could get her hands on a gun, she'd blow the lewd grin right off of Billy's face.

His breath started to come faster as he watched her, his gaze trained on the flesh exposed with each button undone. Her attention volleyed back and forth from his eyes to the gun he'd already unconsciously lowered. There was no way she could make a lunge for the gun, though, not sitting on the ground with him standing over her.

"It will be easier to get this dress off if I stand up," she said.

He quickly motioned with the gun for her to do so. Loreen rose slowly, afraid any sudden movements would shift his attention from his lust to the fact that he'd unwisely allowed her equal ground. She contin-

ued to open her dress, displaying her body, while carefully moving closer to him. His pistol hung limply by
his side, forgotten while his eyes roamed over her. For
Loreen, undressing had become only a means to an
end—Billy's end. The end of his tyranny, of his killing
and raping without consequences.

She shrugged the dress from her shoulders, using the
ploy of stepping from the material bunched at her feet
to get within grabbing distance of his gun. Billy's
breath, now coming in fast gusts of air from his mouth,
hit her full in the face. She tamped down her nausea,
and when he reached to touch her, Loreen made her
move.

The cold feel of steel teased her fingers; she
grabbed—but the gun was suddenly yanked from her
and shoved into her face.

"You bitch," Billy said in a growl. He twisted a
handful of her hair in one hand, and with the gun
pointed against her head, he forced her back and down
onto the straw mattress.

"Thought you were gonna get my gun away from
me, didn't you?" He straddled her and, still holding
the gun, he tried to fondle her. "You wanna play rough,
that's all right. I like it rough."

Billy jerked the gun away, and to her surprise tossed
it out of reach. "I don't need no gun to get what I want
from you. Let's get started."

She immediately bucked, trying to unseat him. Billy
was too heavy for her to do more than jostle him. He
drew back a hand to slap her, but suddenly the barrel
of a rifle was aimed at his temple. On the other end of
the rifle stood Jake.

"Get off of her," he said in a low growl, and his
voice shook as much as his hands did.

Loreen knew he wasn't shaking out of fear, but because he was trying to control his desire to blow Billy's head clean off then and there. Billy glanced down at Loreen, a moment of almost ludicrous hurt registering on his face.

"You lied to me, Loreen."

Chapter Twenty-eight

"Get up!" Jake ordered, pushing the barrel into Billy's temple.

The bully lifted his hands. "I'm moving," he said. "Don't shoot."

Relief washed over Loreen, both with Billy's weight lifting from her body and with the knowledge that Jake had spared her from the worst degradation she could imagine.

"Are you all right, Loreen?" Jake asked, never taking his eyes off of their enemy.

She scrambled up. "I'm all right. He didn't . . ." Her voice trailed off.

"Where's his gun?"

In her mind, she had marked the spot exactly where Billy's gun had landed—marked it with the hope that she'd somehow manage to get her hands on it again, either before Billy raped her or afterward. Loreen walked over and picked it up.

"You've given me a moral dilemma," Jake said to Billy. "I was planning on letting the law handle you, but now you've made me angry. You've got me thinking I should just kill you where you stand, and we won't have to bother with you anymore."

Sweat ran down Billy's face. "I think you should let the law handle me," he said nervously. "You don't believe in killing, remember?"

In the short silence that followed, the sound of a gun cocking sounded like bones breaking. Loreen realized it was from the one in her hand. "Jake may have his principles, but I don't. Not after what you've done to me and my family."

Billy's Adam's apple bobbed. "Now, *you* wouldn't shoot me, Loreen. A sweet thing like you."

She took a step toward him. "It's hard to be nice to a man who killed my brother, shot my husband in the back, and just tried to rape me."

"Me?" he asked, his gaze lowering to the gun in her hand before he swallowed loudly again. "No one saw who shot your brother. No one saw who shot your man. And rape?" He chuckled nervously. "I was just funning with you."

"I'm not laughing." Loreen took another step toward him. She felt cold and hard inside—and justified. "But I do want proof of your crimes. Admit you killed my brother."

Billy smiled at her. "I'm innocent," he said. "And if you shoot me, you're gonna hang. It'll be murder, plain and simple."

There was nothing uncomplicated about the emotions that were rushing through Loreen. Billy had fed on her fear over the years, cowed her, humiliated her, and she couldn't give up the hate inside of her. It gave her the need to demand justice. And only one kind seemed fitting for a cold-blooded murderer. But first she wanted his confession.

"You're not innocent. Admit you killed my brother!"

When Billy continued to smile at her, Loreen lost the thin thread holding her rage at bay. She marched toward him, aiming the gun at his head.

"Loreen!"

Jake's voice shifted her attention. He hurriedly lifted the rifle, but Billy was quicker. She still held the gun, but Billy's hand was wrapped around hers, and the pistol was now pointed at her head.

"Drop that rifle!" he shouted at Jake. "Drop it or I'll kill her."

He did so immediately.

"Kick it over here," Billy ordered.

Jake hesitated for a moment, but when the pain of the gun biting into her soft skin made Loreen gasp, he did as Billy instructed. The murderer shoved Loreen forward. She stumbled, then felt Jake's arms around her. When she turned to look at Billy, he had both weapons trained on them.

"Whew," he said with a laugh. "That was intense, wasn't it?"

Bile rose in Loreen's throat. She had no doubt Billy would kill them both.

Billy stood there for a moment, obviously savoring the upper hand. Then he said, "Now *I'm* faced with a dilemma. I'm glad you're alive, boy. There are so many possibilities to this situation. I can tie you up, Winslow, and rape your woman while you watch. Then I can kill you while she watches. Then I can rape her again."

Loreen felt Jake tense, and, knowing he was close to losing control, she held on tighter to him.

As he wiped the sweat from his forehead with his sleeve, Billy's breathing became labored with excitement. "But I did have another plan for you, Winslow, and as difficult as it is to give up the one I just told you about, the other one will work more to my advantage."

He began to pace, although he still held both weapons trained on them, and his eyes as well. "You see, if I kill you, then Loreen would be a witness and I'd have to end up killing her, too. And you've both got them damn townsfolk starting to think for themselves now. They'd probably put it together and do something foolish, like try to see me hanged." He sighed. "Then I'd have to kill everyone, and hell, who'd be left to terrorize?"

"You're insane." Jake expressed exactly what Loreen was thinking.

Billy's hand tightened on one of the guns aimed at them, and Loreen thought he'd forget any plan save killing them. He licked his lips, then eased his finger back off the trigger.

"You ain't the first to think so," he said. "I'm not crazy. I just like doing bad things and getting away with them. If you ain't a coward, Winslow, meet me in town tomorrow. Noon. Whooee, am I glad you're not dead." He laughed, and his gaze lingered on Loreen. "You come along, too. Maybe we can find us an alley and finish what we started here tonight."

Billy backed toward the door, his weapons trained on them. The moment he disappeared, Jake started after him. Loreen held on to his arm.

"What are you going to do? You don't have a gun," she said. "He'll just shoot you down!"

Jake was shaking again, grappling with himself, and Loreen knew she had to penetrate the fog of his rage. It was the same rage that had her intending to kill Billy just a short time ago.

"Be smarter than I was," she said, and her foolish actions rushed up to assault her, along with a delayed reaction to the attack. She began to tremble. "I let anger and my thirst for revenge nearly get us both killed!"

He glanced down at her. "You had every right to be angry, and every right to seek revenge."

"I know that," she whispered. "But I let passion cloud good judgment when I got close enough for Billy to grab me and the gun. Now we have to be sensible. There's more at stake than our lives."

"Toby and Wren," he said suddenly, moving again toward the door.

Loreen followed him outside to the cabin. She'd all but forgotten that all she wore was her underwear—until the night breeze danced against her bare skin. Going back to don her clothes, she followed. Jake checked on Toby while Loreen climbed the loft to make sure Wren was in her bed asleep. She'd just reached the bottom of the ladder when Jake appeared beside her.

"She's asleep," she whispered.

"Toby, too. Stay here and keep the door bolted. I have something to do." He left her standing alone.

If Billy had wanted to kill them tonight, Loreen knew he could have done so. The children were safe, for the time being. She crept quietly into her room. Toby slept in it, so she fetched her robe. She shrugged into it and out of the dress that now felt soiled from her run-in with Billy, then went back outside. She saw Jake come out of the barn, a lantern in one hand and what appeared to be a shovel in the other.

It took Jake more than one try to unearth what he'd been searching for. He lifted the object, still wrapped in canvas, then carefully peeled back its covering. The gun, well oiled, gleamed in the lantern's glow. He lifted it, tested its balance, and marveled at how well it fit in his hand. He'd hoped it would seem awkward to him, as if it didn't belong in the hands of a farmer. But he was who he was.

"What's that?"

Rising, he faced Loreen. Despite the ordeal she'd been through, she looked beautiful. He moved his hand into the light, showing her the gun.

"I buried this the day I decided to stay. I thought that if I buried the gun, I could bury my past along with it." He ran his fingers over the polished steel. "But my past is probably about to catch up with me, and even if it doesn't, I am man enough now to meet it head-on. Thank you for making me that man."

Tears glistened in her eyes. "You did something really wrong. You killed someone, didn't you, Jake?"

Her question surprised him, but then he realized it shouldn't have. Loreen was too smart not to ask herself why he'd agreed to this marriage, why he'd displayed the skill of a gunman when dealing with Billy.

"How long have you known?"

She shrugged, and her calmness greatly surprised him. "You said some things while the fever had you. I guess I've been waiting for you to tell me."

"You've suspected I might be a killer all this time and you didn't question me? Didn't throw me out? You nursed me and let me spend time with Toby and Wren. Why?"

"It was an accident, wasn't it?" She looked up at him expectantly, but her faith couldn't erase his pain.

He ran a hand through his hair and laughed bitterly. "Yes. But that doesn't fix it. And how could you know that?"

Loreen stepped toward him. "I knew it because I've come to know you, Jake. This trouble you're in, it has to do with Dodge, doesn't it?"

Kicking dirt into the hole he'd dug, Jake nodded. "My real name is Jake Walters. I walked into a bank in Dodge one afternoon during a holdup. There was only one gang member inside, getting the rest of the money. I was cocky about my talent with a gun. Without thinking, I drew, but the outlaw pulled the clerk in front of him. My bullet found the wrong target. He shoved the dying man at me, and while I grappled with what I had just done, he ran out of the bank. A woman stepped inside and started screaming. She thought I was one of them."

"Why didn't you explain what had happened? Explain—"

"Because I wasn't the kind of man anyone would believe," he interrupted. "I was a drifter, a gambler, a braggart, and I never stayed in one place long enough to make friends. I had no one to come to the defense of my character, and no character worth defending. It took me all of a split second to reach that sorry conclusion about myself, so I took the coward's way out. I ran."

She touched his cheek gently, startling him. "I'm sure that at the time it seemed like your only option, but you should have gone back, Jake. You should have told them the shooting was an accident."

His fingers wrapped around hers, and he felt the night chill upon her skin. "I know that now, but I didn't and still don't think the law would have believed my story. So as payment for my sins, and for being a coward, I have a wanted poster with my face on it—one claiming I'm a murderer."

"So it's the gang Mr. Johnson said had been brought in that you're associated with," Loreen realized. "And you were trying to hide out in Fort Worth, trying to lie low with a ranching outfit when you saw my advertisement."

Jake felt awful all over again. He picked up the lantern and started for the barn, deciding that Loreen shouldn't be out in the night air in just her underclothes and a robe.

"This sounded like the perfect opportunity to start over," he said as he walked. "A small town in the middle of nowhere, a woman who wanted nothing from me except to help her raise a crop so she could return to the east. I figured there would be no law here—or I strongly counted on it." He laughed. "And then I rode right smack into trouble's arms."

They walked into the barn, and the stronger light displayed her guilty flush. "I didn't tell you the truth either. I knew no man in his right mind would have answered my advertisement had I told him about our troubles."

"And I knew that if I told you I was a wanted man right off, you wouldn't have believed in my innocence."

Slowly, her gaze lifted. "But I believe you now."

Jake's heart constricted. He hadn't killed her trust in him. "It's been a long time since anyone has believed in me. I appreciate that, but what means more to me is your believing in yourself." He placed the lantern and his gun on the back of the buckboard before turning to her. "While I lay injured and weak, you ran this farm just as well as I could have done. And you stood up to Billy tonight, Loreen. It was a brave thing you did. You don't need me anymore."

She pressed her fingers against his lips. "No, Jake. You're wrong. I do need you. I needed you to help me find my own courage. And I need you still."

She stood on her tiptoes and her lips brushed where her fingers had been. Jake slanted his mouth across hers. Passion immediately flared. She clung to him. He held her tight, damning the past—and damning the future, because without Loreen and the children, he didn't have anything. He kissed her chin, her neck, further impassioned when she pressed urgently against him. His hands slid inside her robe, cupping her full breasts.

She moaned softly, then steered him toward the straw mattress on the ground. Jake went willingly, eagerly, desperately wanting to hold her, to touch her before the chance was taken from him, possibly forever. He kicked the blanket aside, easing Loreen down into the soft hay.

He kissed her neck, then went lower when she

opened her robe. Her soft moan of pleasure urged him on. He kissed her breasts through the thin fabric of her chemise; then her hands were in his hair, pushing him away.

"We must stop."

Jake did so immediately. He sat up. "I'm sorry, Loreen. I want you so much. I know it isn't right, not with the past still—"

Again she placed her fingers over his lips. "I didn't ask you to stop because of your past; I asked because of mine. You shared your secret with me, and I must share mine with you."

Chapter Twenty-nine

The heat of passion had darkened his eyes, but they were filled with another warmth, as well: the warmth of caring. Loreen knew she was doing the right thing, the only thing she could do if she truly loved him.

"There's nothing you can say that will change the way I feel about you," he said.

Her chest tightened, but she meant to see her confession through. "You can't know that until you've heard the truth. I'm not what you think I am, Jake. I'm not pure and chaste. I-I've been . . ." The words stuck in her throat.

Jake's strong hand settled over hers. "You've been raped, haven't you? Before you came to Miller's Passing. That's why you're afraid of being with me. You're afraid I'll hurt you."

He hadn't made the telling easier, but more difficult.

"I was about to say I've been with another man, and no, Jake, he didn't rape me. I gave myself willingly, because he said that if I loved him, I would prove my love for him."

The coldness she feared might enter his gaze did not, but confusion clouded his eyes. "I don't understand. If you loved him, and he loved you, then why—"

"He didn't love me," she interrupted quietly. "I thought he did, because he said the words and he promised we'd be married. His father owned the mercantile my father worked in, along with several business. I thought being pretty was enough to elevate me to his social standing in the community. It wasn't until after I had given myself to him that I realized he had played me for a fool."

"He wouldn't marry you?" Jake whispered.

She closed her eyes for a moment, reliving the humiliation all over again. "He wouldn't even look at me. He acted as if I'd suddenly become dirty, undeserving of his love. And he told other boys about us and what we'd done. They said things to me, horrible things. I wanted to die of shame."

Jake reached out and took her hand. "And then to add insult to injury, you found out you were carrying his child."

Her heart lurched, her gaze snapping to his.

Jake stared at her. "I figured out Wren was yours a while back. You took to the role of mothering her too naturally. And when you look at her, it's with the love a mother feels for her own child."

"My parents took her away from me when she was born," Loreen said softly. "They said it was for her own good as well as mine. They said people would call her a bastard, and call me a whore. Wren was born on our journey west, in the back of a prairie schooner where I hid most of the trip in my shame. My mother had padded her clothing and claimed the child was hers when she came, so the other people traveling with us wouldn't know she was in fact her granddaughter."

"Why didn't they just pass you off as a young widow who'd lost her husband?" he asked.

"I begged them to, but my ma said it always caused a raised brow when a young girl showed up in a new town with a baby, claiming to have been widowed. She wanted me to have a fresh start, and she wanted Wren to have a father." Tears filled her eyes at the memory. "So I let them take her from me, and I watched another woman—one who'd lost her own baby along the journey—nurse her because my mother said her milk hadn't come down. I sat there with my breasts aching, and my heart breaking, while the child I had loved since the first time I saw her became my sister."

"Did her father know about her?" Jake asked.

Loreen nodded, dislodging the tears gathered in her eyes. "When my pa found out, he was livid. He went to his employer and demanded that the man's son marry me. Mr. Allison said I had a bad reputation among the boys, and Wren could be another's child. He gave my father the money to move to Texas, saying he never wanted to see us again. Thinking back, I don't imagine we were the first family he'd had to pay off because of his son."

When Jake's grip tightened painfully around her hand, Loreen said, "You're angry with me, aren't you?"

He turned to look at her, and his eyes were indeed filled with rage, but they softened upon seeing her.

"I'm mad as hell at that son of a bitch who misled you. I'd like to get my hands on him."

"But it was *my* fault," she whispered. "I was too foolish to see him for what he really was. I couldn't see past his handsome face or hear beyond the sweet lies he told me. He used and humiliated me, and it was my own fault for trusting him."

Jake rose, his fists clenching and unclenching at his sides. "Good God, Loreen. Wren is five; you couldn't have been more than sixteen. You hadn't done enough living to know who you could or could not trust. The bastard seduced you. He's the guilty one, not you!"

Her family had never said as much to her. They had refused to talk about her mistake. Instead they had chosen to pretend it had never happened. They had encouraged Loreen to pretend, as well. Her parents had helped create the lie, but they hadn't helped her deal with the shame, the guilt, or the horrible loss she felt when her child had been taken from her arms and given a lie to live, as well.

"If he's guilty, why is it me who has had to pay?"

Jake settled beside her again. "Because he wasn't man enough to take care of his responsibilities. The only mistake you made was to fall in love with the wrong man. Now you're older, stronger for what you've suffered, and you won't make the same mistake again."

"I once believed my parents' deaths were my fault. Even though my father often spoke of moving to Texas when he acquired the funds, I wanted to blame myself for the fact that we did come. I realize now that what happened to them could have happened anywhere." She took a steadying breath. "And Joseph. He didn't

327

die because of me. His death was terrible, but noble. He died being the kind of man he'd grown into. Defending what he believed—that no man had the right to take what didn't rightfully belong to him or to terrorize others."

Jake squeezed her fingers, and Loreen stared into his eyes. Jake was the reason she had seen past her self-pity and her hate. If he hadn't come into her life, taught her to trust and love again, she might still be living a lie. There were no words to thank him for all he'd done for her, so Loreen leaned forward and kissed him.

The touch of their lips was as gentle as a butterfly's kiss. Loreen placed her arms around his neck and tried to draw him closer. When he pulled away, her heart felt as if it had dropped to her stomach.

"Don't you want me now?" she whispered.

Hurt entered his gaze. "You know me better than that. I want you more than I ever have, because there are no more secrets between us. But I don't want you to be afraid of me. Of any part of me."

"I'm not afraid of you, Jake," she assured him. "And I don't want to be afraid of being with you, but I know what being intimate with a man is like. I know about the pain and the embarrassment. It wasn't the way *he* told me it would be." She paused, the humiliation she thought she'd put behind her quickly resurfacing.

"He hurt me and he didn't care. He wouldn't stop—even though I was crying, begging him. After he'd finished, he told me I was a baby. He said I wasn't a woman or I'd know that when men and women joined, it was for the man's pleasure, and that the woman was to lie there quietly and do her duty."

Jake's hands were trembling again, the rage back in his voice when he said, "He didn't deserve you,

Loreen. He lied to you. I understand that a woman experiences pain when she loses her virginity, but he could have obviously been gentler—and after the pain, he could have given you pleasure. He could have if he wasn't a selfish bastard who cared nothing about your feelings!"

His outrage deepened the love Loreen already felt for Jake. She lifted his trembling hand to her face, her own somewhat shaky, and kissed it. "All right, then. Show me how it should be."

He didn't pull away from her this time. Their lips met in a tender kiss. And then, as before, gentleness soon gave way to fiery passion. Jake let her pull him down onto the straw, sliding her chemise off of her shoulders. He kissed her neck, the pulse beating at the base of her throat, then her breasts as he worked the chemise down to her waist.

She brought him back to her lips, wanting to feel his skin against hers. Slowly she unbuttoned his shirt, pushing it from his shoulders. Her fingers met with the bandage tied around his wound.

"Your injury," she said, worried he might not be up to finishing what she had willingly started.

"It's nothing," he assured her with a smile. "I promise I won't even notice it."

She kissed the bandage, then kissed his chest, running her tongue around the copper circles of his nipples. He sucked in his breath sharply, then recaptured her lips.

Heated kisses were exchanged while Jake undressed her. He teased her nipples as she'd done to him, then sucked and nibbled until she arched against him. When his hand slid between her legs, she felt none of the inhibitions she'd felt the first time he had touched her. She knew he could give her pleasure beyond imagination.

Loreen suddenly wanted to give him pleasure as well, and she reasoned that if his touch could excite her, hers might do the same to him. It took a great deal of courage, but she reached for the waistband of his pants. His hand settled over hers.

"I don't want to do anything you don't want to do," he said against her neck.

"I want to touch you," she whispered. "The way that you're touching me."

"God." He groaned, but removed his hand.

She unbuckled his belt, then began unfastening his pants. The task proved difficult, and she could only assume that his arousal added to the problem. Jake took over, quickly shucking the rest of his clothing. She envied his lack of modesty, and tried not to jerk away when he settled against her again.

Instead she touched him, running her fingers along the long, smooth length of his shaft. She liked the sound of his breath catching in his throat, and the low moan that followed. Once again he stopped her.

"Am I hurting you?" she asked.

He sank his teeth softly into her neck for a moment, then raised his head to look at her. "No, you're not hurting me. You're driving me insane. If you don't stop, making love to you won't be the way it's supposed to be. It'll be over."

She didn't want anything to be over between them—not ever—so she released him. He'd made her hot, achy, and she longed for the intense pleasure he'd given her before—the building sensation that led to an explosion.

He must have read her thoughts. He bent over her, kissing her before dipping down between the valley of her breasts. He traveled lower, igniting her skin with hot kisses until his mouth caressed her where his fingers had earlier. She felt a moment of alarm, but only a moment, because sensation soon blocked everything else from her mind.

Heat wound a path up her legs. Her thighs trembled and still he continued, pushing her onward toward sweet release. It found her surprisingly quickly, that sudden seizure that clenched her insides and made her arch upward. The explosion ripped through her, tearing his name from her lips; then she floated back down, the tranquil tide of warmth wrapping her in sheer contentment.

Jake wouldn't allow her to slip away, though. His lips teased hers until she responded again. She wrapped her arms around his neck, aware now of the hot, moist feel of his flesh against hers. He kissed her until she became breathless, until she began to tingle and pulse, until she wanted him again. When he gently nudged her knees apart and she felt him between her legs, she instinctively tensed.

"Don't be afraid," he whispered. "Trust me."

She willed her body to relax because she *did* trust him. She trusted him with her life, and she trusted him with her heart. She turned her head and found his mouth. He kissed her deeply. His tongue and body both slowly penetrated her.

His tongue inched deeper into her mouth, while below, she felt him filling her. She squeezed her eyes together, anticipating pain, but there wasn't any. There was none of the knife-sharp jarring she'd felt once before.

331

The size of him, and the pressure as he continued to inch his way inside, made her gasp softly, but she couldn't identify what she felt as pain. His breathing had become rapid, and he rested his forehead against hers as if he battled some unseen force. As she recalled, it hadn't taken Wren's father long to complete the act. Perhaps this was all there was to it.

"Am I hurting you?" he asked.

"No." She thought from the way he trembled that he might be the one in pain. "Am I hurting you?"

He pulled back to look at her, a half smile settling over his mouth. "You're killing me."

Alarmed, she tried to move. That only seemed to cause him more pain. He groaned, pressing down to keep her still.

"You're killing me because you feel so good."

He kissed her again. It was a deep, wet kiss that made her pulse leap; then he began to move inside of her. He moved with grace and strength, and before long she felt the first sparks of a bonfire of pleasure that threatened to consume her entirely.

Jake knew the moment he had her completely, the first moment her body wholly understood the needs of his own. She moved with him, digging her nails into his shoulders. Making love to Loreen was nothing like he'd imagined, because his imagination could not have competed with this reality. Not with the hot, velvet feel of her wrapped around him, or the sweet moans he elicited from her.

Nothing he'd ever experienced in his past could compete with this. He could have easily already spent himself. He'd given her pleasure, but even that wasn't enough for him. His own pleasure had to wait. He'd deny himself to see her breath catch in her throat, to see her eyes widen and feel her arch against him in rapture once more.

And so he held back, loving her with steady strokes, withdrawing, only to penetrate again, and always with gentleness until she wanted more. When her hips ground against his and her nails dug deeper into his back, he gave in. Jake loved her less gently, harder, faster, ever closer to utter surrender.

Loving her became agony, torment of the sweetest kind, and he thought he'd lose his battle, but she surrendered first. She moaned, a sound from deep inside her, one that spurred his own release. As she clung to him, pulsating around him, he exploded. He shuddered, helpless to stop the flow of his seed.

Jake held her tightly, the ravages of his climax still pounding in his ears. He cursed himself for putting her at risk. She was still innocent, and he should have been strong enough to take precautions, man enough to see that there were no consequences to their lovemaking. Even as he thought it, he realized there would be consequences either way. She snuggled her head beneath his chin.

"Now I understand," she whispered softly.

Worried, he ran his fingers through her hair. "You understand what? That I'm still a wanted man? A person can change, but they can't change their circumstances. I'm trouble for you, Loreen."

Instead of pulling away, she snuggled closer to him. She sighed, a sinfully contented sound. "Then I've never felt safer than in trouble's arms."

As she drifted away in mind, if not in body, Jake

stared at the rafters above. What had he thought? That Loreen's forgiveness of his crimes could banish them altogether? Loving her had not released the past's hold on him. It had only strengthened it. He'd known what he had to do for a long time. Now, if he ever wanted any chance of happiness—for himself or Loreen—he had to go through with his decision.

Chapter Thirty

Loreen woke in the oddest of places: the old rocker inside the cabin. She tried to remember how she'd come to be there; then the night came rushing back to her. She smiled. Stretching lazily, she vaguely recalled Jake carrying her inside the house at some ridiculous hour. She'd been half-asleep, and he'd obviously not known what to do with her. Toby had still been sleeping in her bed.

Her smile stretched, and she fingered the blanket he'd wrapped around her. She was glad that at least he'd had the sense to realize they shouldn't be caught by the children, wrapped around one another, lying in the hay. She wondered if she still had time before Toby and Wren woke to sneak back out and make love with him again. It was a thought. A sinfully delicious one.

With a sigh, she rose. A good scrubbing was what she needed after a night spent loving Jake. Loreen slipped into her room. Toby snored loudly, and she smiled down at him. After gathering clean clothes, Loreen slipped outside and started toward the watering hole. The sun wasn't up, and the moon still hung low in the sky.

She hummed while she took the path to the bank below the incline. Once she stood naked, she glanced out over the pool. Her gaze snagged upon a shape. It was the shape of a man. He rose from the water, wet flesh shimmering with the beginnings of the dawn light. Loreen waded out to him. He opened his arms and she went willingly into them.

He kissed her deeply, his tongue moving inside her mouth, his hands roaming her wet skin. She touched him, too, marveled over him, worshiped him. He cupped her bottom, lifting her up and onto his ready sex. She wrapped her legs around him, and together they moved, the water gently lapping around them to the rhythm of their bodies. The water grew more frenzied as their demands upon one another became urgent.

Straining against one another, the waves of ecstasy broke over them quickly. Gasping with the fury of her climax, Loreen clung to Jake. He held her tight, his own heavy gasps merging with hers. After the waters had calmed, they climbed out. Loreen found her blanket, watching Jake snatch his up and wrap it around him. Together they walked up the incline. They held hands until their journey took them in different directions: his to the barn, hers to the cabin.

It wasn't until Loreen was back inside and had quickly dried and dressed for the day that she realized they had not even a spoken a word to each other. Cer-

336

tainly they hadn't exchanged the most important ones. She tried to recall if Jake had, even once during the night told her that he loved her. A little ashamed, she realized she hadn't said the words either.

Before she could dwell overlong on the matter, the sun broke through the windows. She heard Toby stirring, and she knew she had to begin the day's chores. Loreen felt starved. She admitted, with a deep sense of contentment, that, although man could not live by bread alone, neither could he live solely on love. She went into the kitchen and began preparing breakfast.

Jake brought her a bucket of fresh milk halfway into her preparations. Their fingers touched when he handed her the pail, lingering for a moment more than necessary. Toby sat at the table, and it was his regard that made her pull away.

"Feeling better?" he asked her brother.

"My headache's gone," he answered, flashing Loreen a dirty look.

"Good. I need you to come help me for a minute before Loreen has breakfast ready."

Loreen watched her brother follow Jake from the cabin. She liked how well they got along together. They worked well together, too, and she had no doubt they could make the farm prosper. And Wren, well, the child thought Jake could do no wrong. But he had done wrong; the dark thought intruded upon her happy musings. And along with the memory of a night filled with passion in Jake's arms was also the thought of the horrible man who had begun what had led up to their lovemaking: Billy Waylan.

He was a black mark that smudged the picture of her happy future. It was, she knew, a future that had taken a different turn since Jake had gotten shot. But then, maybe she'd known before that. Maybe she'd known from the first day she and Jake had stood before the preacher, and he'd kissed her boldly, that she would never want to leave him.

Wren appeared, rubbing the sleep from her eyes. "Smells good in here," she mumbled.

"About time you woke up," Loreen said with a smile. "I need an extra pair of hands."

The child lifted hers. "These hands?"

"Those are the very ones I was hoping for," Loreen answered.

When Wren giggled, Loreen walked over and swept her up into her arms. She tickled her, making the child laugh harder. Wren threw her arms around her neck and kissed her on the cheek.

"I love you, Mama," she said.

Loreen suddenly felt as if she'd died and gone to heaven. She had her child back, and she had the man she loved outside in the barn. That thought caused her to frown. She'd have to work on getting him inside the cabin—and into her bed each night.

"I love you, too, Wren." She hugged the little girl tight.

Wren pulled back and studied her. "You look different this morning."

A burst of heat settled in Loreen's cheeks. "How do I look different?"

The little girl smiled. "You look happy."

Laughing, Loreen hugged her again. "I am happy. I think today might just be the best day of my life."

This was the worst day of Jake's life. He stared into Toby's trusting eyes, and the words he had to say seemed to lodge in his throat.

"Well, what do you want me to do?" Toby asked for the second time.

Jake took control of his emotions. "I want you to make me a promise."

One of Toby's dark brows lifted. "A promise?"

"Actually two promises," Jake corrected. "The first one is, I want you to promise you'll take care of Loreen and Wren for me."

The boy paled. "I don't see why you'd be asking me to make that promise. Not unless . . ."

Turning from him, Jake slipped an item wrapped in cloth from his saddle pack. He unwrapped the gun, watching the boy's eyes widen at the sight of the weapon.

"The second promise I want you to make to me is that you'll never let something as cold and unfeeling as this take away everything you care about."

Toby's gaze snapped up to his face, confusion clouding his eyes. Jake placed a hand on his shoulder.

"This gun once meant everything to me. I loved it, I worshiped it, and then I let it destroy me. Not only did I take an innocent life with a cold lump of steel, but it ended up taking my life. And now it will take all that's become important to men. Loreen, you, and Wren."

"What are you saying?" Toby whispered.

"I'm saying I have to right the wrong I've done. I have to answer for my sins. I'm a wanted man, Toby. I came here to hide like a coward."

"You're not a coward!" Toby shouted. "You were never a coward!"

The prickly sensation of tears stung the back of Jake's eyes. He grabbed the boy and held him. "Bravery stems from love. I didn't have that until I came here, and all of you taught me what bravery truly is.

You've given me the courage now to do what I know I must."

Toby pulled back from him angrily. "You're going to turn yourself in, aren't you?"

"I have to."

Tears—of both anger and love—filled Toby's eyes. "No, you don't. I know you. You wouldn't do anything wrong—not unless there was a good reason, or unless it was an accident. You can stay here, hide like you planned."

Sadly Jake shook his head. "You know me better than that, too. I'm only doing what I should have done a long time ago. What I'd have done in the beginning, if I'd had people who believed in me the way you do to speak on my behalf."

"How do you know they wouldn't have believed what you did was an accident?" Toby demanded.

The truth hurt, but Jake thought Toby deserved to hear it. "Because I wasn't any good. When I was younger, I'd spent time in jail for petty theft. I got in a lot of small trouble. Then I took to practicing with a gun. I told you about that. I was a gambler, a drifter, a man with too much time on his hands and too little to occupy himself with. I figured the law would take all of that into account, and just assume I'd moved on to bigger crimes."

"What happened?" Toby asked.

Jake told him the story, the same one he'd told to Loreen last night. He added, "You heard Mr. Johnson talk about getting a telegram from Dodge that those gang members have been brought in? Scum like them aren't going to say I wasn't part of the gang. They'll probably say I was, just out of meanness. Posters are going to start going up again, and the law's going to start looking for me. As far they know, I'm the worst one of the bunch. I'm the one who killed the clerk."

"So your only option would be to run again," Toby reasoned.

"That isn't an option," Jake reminded him. "It might count favorably toward my innocence if I turn myself in. Then, well, I'll just have to take my chances."

"They don't sound like very good chances," Toby said.

"That's why I need you to make me those promises."

The boy wiped a sleeve across his eyes. "But what about Billy?"

"I'll handle Billy. I'm going into town to have Mr. Johnson wire the sheriff in Dodge that I'm coming to turn myself in. And I'm taking Billy with me."

"He won't have to mind to go," Toby warned him.

Jake glanced down at the gun still clutched in his hand. "That's why I'm taking this along. If I have to use it, I will, and you understand that, too, don't you?"

Toby nodded. "I understand."

"You haven't given me your word yet."

Instead of answering, Toby flung himself into Jake's arms.

Loreen's sunny mood had started to darken. Breakfast sat on the table, in dire threat of becoming cold. Men. They never showed up on time. When Toby came in and quietly approached the table, she couldn't swear to it, but she thought he looked as if he'd been crying.

"Is everything all right?" she asked.

He shrugged, but wouldn't meet her gaze. "Jake wants to talk to you. In private," he added.

A flush of pleasure rose in her cheeks. Maybe he'd realized, as she had, that they hadn't said those important words to one another—either last night or early this morning.

"I'll fix him a plate," she chirped, happily doing so.

"Can I come?" Wren asked.

"Private means alone," Toby informed her. "A-And I brought a couple of them pups to the porch. When we're done eating, we can play with them."

Loreen flashed Toby a grateful smile for his ingenuity in making certain she and Jake would not be disturbed. Odd, but he didn't smile back at her. He just dug into breakfast with what appeared to be gusto, but upon closer inspection, amounted to his just scooting food around on his plate.

A little rattled by Toby's behavior, Loreen grabbed a fork, set it on Jake's full plate, and hurried outside. As she drew closer to the barn, her anticipation grew. It seemed like an eternity since Jake had kissed her, held her. The fact that it had been only a few hours had her giggling. As soon as she entered the barn, her smile faded. Jake's things were all packed up, his saddle and bridle resting on the ground.

"What are you doing?"

"I'm leaving, Loreen."

The plate in her hand dropped to the floor. Midnight and Princess were on the spot immediately to see to the mess.

"Leaving?" she whispered.

He moved toward her, and in an unconscious act of denial, she began backing away. He didn't let her get far. His hands settled on her shoulders—hands that had stroked her, touched her, made love to her.

"I've just been through a tough good-bye with Toby. I explained to him about my trouble with the law, and why I have to leave now and face the consequences of my actions."

"What about your actions with me?" she asked angrily, going from hot to cold so fast she shivered.

His fingers brushed her lips. "What happened between us last night was beautiful, but it was ill-timed. I should have waited—we should have waited," he corrected. "Until I had my trouble behind me."

"There's a chance you can't put it behind you," she ground out. "A chance you'll hang!" He tried to pull her closer, but she knocked his arms away, all her happy hopes shattering around her. "Don't touch me. Is this just another excuse to run, except this time away from me? Are you just like *him?* Now that you've gotten what you wanted, you—"

"Damn you for saying that to me," he interrupted, his eyes suddenly as angry as she knew hers were. "Don't you know how much this is killing me? How it's tearing me apart to leave you?"

"Then don't," she begged. "Don't go."

He reached for her again, and she let him pull her into his arms. "The law will be looking for me again. I can't have them riding in here with the assumption that I'm a cold-blooded killer and shooting at anything that moves. You know I'm doing the right thing, Loreen. And if you'll just think about it for a minute, you'll agree that it's the only thing I can do. I won't have you living in fear. I have to face my past."

She didn't want to think about him leaving her—not even for a second. Loreen pulled away from him, trying to protect her heart, because he'd just shattered it.

"Then go," she said bitterly, turning away from him. "Go get yourself killed."

The warmth of his hand hovered over her shoulder; then it was gone. "The crop will be ready in a couple of weeks. Manny can help you harvest, and Mr. Johnson will give you a fair price. Then you'll have what you wanted: the money and the freedom to leave."

After all they had shared, how could he still believe leaving was what she wanted? "I want the farm," she snapped.

"What?"

She wheeled around to face him. "The farm. It's Toby's birthright and the only home Wren has ever known. Neither of them wants to leave, and I don't either. Not anymore."

He ran a hand through his hair impatiently. "But you said you hated this place."

"I did, or I thought I did." She glanced outside. "But I must have more of my father in me than I knew, because I've grown to love this land."

"You're a confusing woman, Loreen. And a confused one at the moment. Do what I asked and give this some thought. You'll see it's the only thing I can do. The right thing."

Loreen wouldn't give him permission to go off and get himself hanged. She could only hope he wouldn't get far down the road before he realized he was making a mistake. If he didn't, then she'd have to deal with her circumstances.

"Good-bye," she said, stiffly turning from him. She nearly tripped over Wren. The child struggled, her arms loaded down with puppies. Loreen's gaze immediately shifted to Jake. He was staring at Wren with such raw agony in his gaze that her heart softened. She quickly hardened it again.

It was anger that made her decide he could just deal with her rejection, and with telling Wren good-bye as well. She marched toward the cabin, joining a somber Toby. They didn't speak; both just stared out over the field. A few minutes later she felt Wren slip her hand inside hers. She glanced down at her, and the sight of those big blue eyes filled with tears broke her heart for the second time that day.

"He's coming back," the child whispered. "I know he will. Then he said he'll be my papa if you'll let him. You *will* let him, won't you, Mama?"

Her own eyes close to tearing up, Loreen glanced behind her. Jake stood on the road. He opened his mouth as if he would shout something, but she quickly turned back around. Whatever he had to say wouldn't make a difference. Not now. Instead of answering Wren, she said, "Let's get to work."

Chapter Thirty-one

It lasted about an hour, Loreen's pretense that she was perfectly fine with Jake's leaving, that hoeing the weeds trying to choke her precious maize was the most important thing in her small world. Then she admitted it was just no good. There was no good in lying to herself. She needed to think about Jake, and about his decision.

The first thought that popped into her head was that he didn't love her—Couldn't love her the way she loved him, or he wouldn't have left. Instead he had selfishly decided to turn himself in. To risk his life for the sake of what? A name?

"Walters," she fumed. That wasn't his name. To her, he would always be Jake Winslow, the man who'd ridden cockily onto her farm and married her. The man who had taught Toby the wisdom of avoiding violence, and who adored Wren, no matter her true parentage.

Jake Winslow was the man they'd all grown to love, and to Loreen, Jake Walters was just someone she had never met, a stranger who'd made a mistake—and yes, it was a horrible mistake, but one he should bury in his past for the sake of Loreen and the children. For his own sake. She stewed for a few minutes more; then the truth slapped her full in the face.

She knew what it was like to live a lie, to wonder who might discover her secret, and when. And it was never for herself that she'd allowed Wren to be taken from her, but for the child's welfare. She hadn't wanted Wren to suffer the sins of her mother.

She hadn't wanted the child to be called a bastard, to know that her father didn't want her, or even care what became of her. Jake had left, had made the decision to turn himself in, not because he didn't love them, but because he did. Like her, he didn't want those he loved most to suffer for his mistakes.

"You shouldn't have let him go like that," Toby said beside her, a hoe in his hands as well.

"Like what?"

"Acting all mad at him for just doing what he knows he has to do."

"Are you taking his side?" she asked.

"Only because he's right and you're wrong," her brother answered. "No one wants him to stay more than I do, Loreen. And it ain't just about the farm. He's like a brother to me now. I had one snatched away, and God gave me another. I need him—to tell me things and show me things only a man can tell and show another man."

She raised her brow at his reference to himself as

a man, but didn't say anything. "What do you suggest I do?"

Toby removed his hat and wiped the sweat from his brow. "If I was you, I'd go after him. I'd make things right with him, because, hell, Loreen, he not only is going off to face justice, he's going off to see that justice is done. He's going to confront Billy first."

Her knees nearly buckled. Of course he would. Why hadn't she thought of that? Jake wouldn't leave her and the children without making sure Billy had been dealt with first. The blood in her veins turned cold.

"Billy told him to meet him in town today. At noon. He said he had plans for him."

"An ambush, I bet," Toby worried. "We should go and help him. Maybe he hasn't made it to town yet."

"*I* should go," Loreen stressed. "And try to talk some sense into him about this decision he's made, no matter how noble it is." Her mind was suddenly teeming with ideas. They could run, all of them together— escape the law, escape Billy. Just load up what they could and take off. But then her idea was snagged on the first setback: Toby.

"If you had to give up the farm, Toby, if you had to for Jake, would you?"

Tears filled his eyes. "I would, Loreen. And he knows that I would."

Could she say Jake knew she felt the same? To her shame, she could not. She hadn't told him she loved him, that she would risk everything for him, give up the farm, and even the dream she had once had of finding a secure, safe life somewhere else. If he still refused to return with her, she would go with him.

If he couldn't convince a judge of his innocence, she would try. And if both of them failed, if they sentenced

Jake to a rope, she wouldn't let him die without her by his side. He had stood by her; now she would stand by him, no matter the outcome.

"I want you to hitch up the wagon for me and stay here with Wren. If I can't convince Jake to return with me, I'll come home and take Wren to the Crawfords'. If I have to, I'll be going to Dodge to see if there's any way I can help him. You'll have to stay here and run the farm, but Manny will help you."

"I'm proud of you, Loreen," Toby said quietly. "I'm ashamed I ain't said it enough, and I've been mean to you before. I've known from the day Wren was born she wasn't my sister. Even though I was young when she came, I remember you swelling up, and I heard you laboring with her inside the wagon."

He paused to gather himself. "I figured if Ma and Pa didn't want anyone to know, you must have done something bad. That's when I took to blaming you for everything bad that's happened to us. I'm sorry for the way I've acted. And Jake, well, I thought you'd made a mistake with him and would get hurt again, but I was wrong about that, too. Both of you have taught me that even people we love make mistakes, and the best thing to do is just keep loving them anyway."

She grabbed Toby and hugged him. "I love you, too, Toby. A minute ago, I thought you weren't yet a man, but I'm wrong. You are a man, and I'm so proud of you. I know our parents would be, too."

Toby hugged her back, then returned to business. "Jake's got a good head start on you. You'd better get moving."

It wasn't an ambush . . . exactly. When Jake finally made it into town, he found Billy waiting for him, and he had company: a man with a tin star pinned to his chest. A man, Jake suspected, who had come all the way from Dodge to meet with him. He found the situation ironic. Here he was with the intention of making his way to Kansas to turn himself in, and Billy had saved him the trouble.

"That's your man," Billy shouted, pointing at Jake. "Not Jake Winslow, the town hero, but Jake Walters, a murdering son of a bitch."

If Billy expected him to bolt or make a run for it, Jake imagined he'd be sorely disappointed by his next move. He kept walking toward the men, noting the now familiar faces lining the streets. Manny and Gretchen Crawford were among the townspeople. Jake felt a moment of shame that he'd deceived not only Loreen and her family, but these good people as well.

"Don't try to deny it!" Billy shouted, although Jake hadn't said a word. "I found out about you while I was in Dodge. Spent a night in jail for getting in a fight, and lo and behold, if there wasn't a poster with your face on it tacked up on the wall. I knew you weren't no farmer!"

Billy had presented Jake with one problem: how could he deal with the bully if he let himself be taken into custody right then and there? He couldn't leave Loreen and the children behind knowing Billy was still on the loose. That left him one option.

"Sheriff," he said upon reaching the men, "arrest this man." He nodded toward Billy. "He's a murderer, and he's robbed the good people of this town. Charged outrageous prices for their businesses. Worse, he keeps them under his thumb and terrorizes them with a gang of gunmen."

The smug look on Billy's face gave way to shock. "H-He's lying," he stammered. "I'm a respected businessman in this community. Tell the sheriff it's so," he ordered the townspeople, narrowing his gaze on the group.

No one said anything for a moment. Manny Crawford finally spoke up. "Billy Waylan has cut my fences, destroyed my crops, and threatened the lives of my family."

"I've paid for my store twice over," Mr. Johnson from the mercantile joined in. "Billy keeps putting more against the loan, and what can I do but pay him or lose everything I've worked for?"

"He's done the same to me," Gus Sims said. "By right, my saloon should be paid for, but Billy keeps upping the loan, says he'll burn it down and hurt my wife if I give him any lip."

The sheriff, who'd been eyeing Jake suspiciously, turned his gaze on Billy. "Sounds like *you're* the varmint around these parts."

"They're all lying," Billy fumed. "They are doing it for him! He's the man you should arrest!"

Reluctantly the sheriff regarded Jake again. "The woman who gave a description of Jake Walters was pretty shook up. She couldn't remember much, but you do resemble the poster."

If Jake could be certain the sheriff intended to do something about Billy, he would have confessed. As it stood, he couldn't do anything.

"Jake Winslow has lived here all of his life," Hetty Johnson shouted. "He's a farmer, and I don't think he's ever even been to Dodge."

"When did he commit this crime he's supposedly guilty of?" Manny demanded.

"About this time last year," the sheriff answered. "This Jake Walters had in been in town a couple of days. He's the one a woman said she saw in the bank during a holdup. He shot the bank teller and then he ran out and rode away. Funny thing is, she said he rode in the opposite direction of the gang members. Even odder, we rounded those boys up a few days ago. Their leader had been killed, but none of 'em seemed to know who I was talking about when I mentioned Jake Walters."

"Well, our Jake isn't the one you're looking for," Manny said. "Last year about this time, he was helping me harvest my crop."

"That's a bold-faced lie," Billy said with a snarl. "Jake Winslow rode in about three months ago. Claimed he was Loreen Matland's sweetheart from back east come to marry her. Now I figured out she didn't even know him. She just wanted some man to protect her."

The sheriff lifted a brow. "Who'd she need protecting from?"

Billy's silence proved damning. Jake had a big lump in his throat again. These people had rallied around him, lied outright for him. He didn't know why they would. They must know he was the Jake Walters the sheriff had come to arrest.

"You said he killed someone," the sheriff reminded Jake. "That's a mighty serious charge."

"He killed my wife's brother. And he shot me in the back. He sneaked onto our place last night and threatened me and my wife."

"He ain't got no proof." A trickle of sweat ran down the side of Billy's face. "He's lying, I tell you."

The sheriff, an older man, one who looked past his prime to be rounding up outlaws, sighed. He was clearly confused about which man to arrest. "Can your wife verify that this man killed her brother?" he asked Jake.

Now came the tricky part. "No. We don't have any proof, and all I have as proof about last night is my word."

The smug look that stole over Billy's face made Jake sick to his stomach. Exactly what he feared might happen looked as if it would.

"Jake's word is good enough for me!" Manny Crawford shouted.

The sheriff raised a hand, as if he knew more references to Jake's good character would follow. "I'm the law, and unless I know someone personally, I can't just accept a man's word. Are you Jake Walters or Jake Winslow?"

To lie now would be to discredit everything he now stood for. "I am Jake Walters," he admitted. "I'm the man you're looking for."

A hush fell over those gathered—all save one. Billy laughed. "I told you he was the murderer you're looking for. Hey, is there a reward on him?"

The sheriff frowned at Billy. Jake had the impression the lawman was a man quick to make judgments, and his opinion of Billy Waylan wasn't a good one.

"I think there's a small one," he admitted. "But if this man is leaving a wife behind, maybe you'd do the gentlemanly thing and give the money to her."

Billy's grin stretched. He looked Jake straight in the eye. "Oh, I'll give it to her, all right."

That was the wind that snapped the branch for Jake.

He stepped forward and grabbed Billy by the throat. "Don't go near Loreen!"

"Or you'll do what?" Billy taunted. "Come back from the grave after you've been hanged and kill me?"

"Break it up," the sheriff warned, pulling the two men apart. He said to Billy, "All men are entitled to a fair trial and are innocent until proven guilty. You may be counting your chicks before they hatch."

Billy had the sense to realize he'd almost made a mistake by taunting Jake. He settled down, but Jake still saw an evil gleam of satisfaction in his eyes.

"This wife of yours," the sheriff said to Jake. "Is she here? I'd like to ask her a couple of questions."

Jake glanced at the ground. "No, she's not here."

"Too bad," Billy said. "Too bad she's not here to see who and what you really are."

"I know who and what Jake is."

Jake jerked his head around, surprised to see Loreen standing behind him. From the condition of her bonnet, she looked as though she must have pushed old Ben to his limits. She stepped up to the sheriff, her head held high.

"He's a good man. A fair man. And an honest one. If he ever shot anyone it would only be in self-defense, or because it was an accident."

"You can't believe her," Billy spit.

The sheriff lifted a brow again. "Seems to me you don't think I can believe anyone in this town except you. That strikes me as odd."

"Hell, they'd all lie," Billy said to the man. "I own their businesses, the mortgages on their farms. They'd like to see me gone, arrested unfairly so they don't have to pay their debts."

Without commenting, the lawman turned to Loreen. "Does this man own your property?"

"No, sir," she said, lifting her chin higher. "But he'd like to, and me along with it. We have water," she explained. "Billy Waylan has been terrorizing my family and this town for years. He shot my brother in cold blood because he stood up to him for molesting me in an alley."

The sheriff's gaze shifted to Billy.

"She's a lying bitch," he said in a growl.

Jake stepped in again, but this time he landed a solid jab to Billy's jaw. The bully stumbled back. "Watch what you call my wife," Jake threatened him.

For a second Jake thought Billy would go for his gun. The bully's hand strayed toward his hip, then moved back up. Billy knew he still held all the cards.

"I'll have to ask you to keep your temper," the sheriff said to Jake. "Although I can't much blame you for losing it," he added dryly.

"Now, Mrs. . . ." He seemed at a loss.

"Loreen," she quickly provided.

"Loreen, did you have any proof this man called Billy Waylan shot your brother?"

Jake watched her gaze drift downward. "No, sir," she answered softly.

The lawman sighed again. "Hold out your hands, Walters. I'll have to cuff you."

The small whimper of distress he heard from Loreen slashed into him. He had no choice but to do as the sheriff instructed. The cuffs were nearly around his wrist when someone cried out.

"Hold it, Sheriff!" Gus Sims, the saloon owner,

stepped forward. Having everyone's undivided attention made him fidget. He glanced at Jake and said, "I saw Billy Waylan shoot Joseph Matland, Loreen's brother. He shot him in cold blood."

A murmur ran through the crowd. Billy's face turned bright red. "He's lying, too!" he shouted. "He's lying because he owes me money!"

"I did hear you say he owned the mortgage on your saloon," the sheriff said. He scratched his head, then smiled at Billy. "Sounds to me like you'd better come along to Dodge until we can sort this out. See who's lying and who isn't. We can have a hearing on the matter." He frowned. "Besides, after I let you out of my jail for being drunk and disorderly, I found out a girl over at one of the saloons had been badly beaten by one of her customers."

A muscle jumped in Billy's jaw. "I imagine that happens a lot in a whore's profession."

The sheriff nodded. "But, unfortunately, most of them don't survive the kind of beating this girl took. This one did, and she said she'd never forget the man's face who roughed her up. I'm wondering if she shouldn't have a look at yours."

Sweat popped out on Billy's upper lip. "You can't make me go with you," he said, his tone cocky. "You've got nothing on me but a bunch of liars sticking up for one another."

Although an older man, the sheriff turned a deadly look on Billy. "I'm the law. I can make you do whatever I damn well please."

Billy's gaze strayed to Jake. "This is his fault. He's turned these people against me. He married my woman. Him and his so-called principles, making these folks believe they can live a different kind of life in Miller's Passing. Thinking they can get together behind my back and socialize, stand up to me. I ain't had nothing but trouble since he stepped foot in this town. He's got to pay for what he's done to me."

The town bully's eyes shifted, and Jake read the decision in them a second before Billy went for his gun. Jake went for his, too. One shot was fired. A bright red stain spread over the front of Billy's shirt. The bully glanced down, then back up at Jake in disbelief, then crumpled to the ground.

That Billy was dead, Jake had no doubt. He hated that he'd been the one to kill him, but Billy had left him no choice. The sheriff had drawn his own weapon, but now he bent and placed his fingers against Billy's throat. He stood a moment later and looked at Jake.

"He's dead, but he drew first, and that didn't leave you any choice." The man frowned. "It seems there's been a lot of trouble going on in this town." He glanced at Billy's hoodlums, all standing quietly, staring down at their dead boss.

"Were you boys involved in this shooting that took place? The death of Joseph Matland?"

Horace, the dumb one, shook his head. "Billy done the killing. That kid walked up and punched him and Billy just drew his gun and shot him right between the eyes. We didn't have no part of that. Billy sent us ahead to Dodge so he could stay and shoot Winslow after the barn raising. He caught up to us late, and we didn't have nothing to do with that woman he beat up in Dodge."

"Them boys are Billy's henchmen," Manny Crawford said. "They might have just been following orders, but they've cut fences and caused trouble around here, too."

"Billy threatened to kill us if we didn't do what he

said," Horace defended himself. "One of the boys left two years ago and Billy shot him in the back. Said he knew too much, that we all knew too much."

"Has Billy cheated these people on their mortgages?" the sheriff asked.

Horace nodded again. "He done about every bad thing a person could think of."

The sheriff sighed. "I'm not in the mood to haul the lot of you off to jail." He glanced at the dead man on the ground. "Take your boss and bury him; then you boys head out of here and don't come back. If I catch even a whiff that you've shown your faces in Miller's Passing again, I'll get me a posse and we'll come after you. Understand?"

All of Billy's gang nodded. A couple of men picked Billy up and slung him over his horse. "What about his property? His cattle and such?" Horace asked. "Can we—"

"No," the sheriff was quick to answer. "Feel lucky I'm letting you take the clothes on your back. If Billy's robbed these people, I say they should split his property among themselves. Of course, your mortgages are all free and clear now," he said to the people gathered.

A cheer went up. The sheriff smiled, but it faded when he looked at Jake. "You know I still have to take you in."

Jake held his hands out for the cuffs.

"No!" Loreen stepped between him and the sheriff. "Tell him it was an accident, Jake!" she demanded. "Tell him what happened!"

"He can tell it to the judge," the sheriff said, but his expression was sorrowful when he glanced at Loreen. "I'm just the man they sent to get him. I don't have any leeway to decide if he's innocent or guilty."

"If Jake and Loreen say whatever Jake did was an

accident, then that's so," Manny Crawford insisted. "We know these folks. They're good people, both of them."

Jake noted the sheriff's nervousness as the crowd began pushing forward, surrounding them.

"I appreciate your standing up for me," he said, his gaze settling upon Manny before encompassing the whole group. "All of you. If I'd have made the kind of friends in Dodge that I have made here, I would have never run from the law. But the sheriff has to do his job, and I have to answer for what I've done, whether it was an accident or not. Clear a path and let us pass."

"I'll need that weapon," the sheriff reminded him. "Though I don't figure the cuffs are necessary."

Jake handed him his gun.

"You got a mount?" the man asked.

He shook his head.

"Someone get this man a horse," the sheriff called.

No one made a move. "We don't have any to spare," Mr. Johnson from the mercantile said. "Do we?"

Everyone shook their heads. The sheriff cursed softly. He drew a sleeve over his brow. "I need a drink. You all come inside the saloon, and let's discuss all the reasons you expect me to let this man go free."

Chapter Thirty-two

Loreen's legs were trembling so badly she could hardly make it up onto the plank sidewalk in front of the saloon. Jake took her arm and helped her.

"You shouldn't have come," he said softly. "Where are the children?"

"Toby's watching Wren," she whispered. "When do we make a run for it?"

His brow shot up. "What?"

She made a pretense of tripping to stall for time. "A run for it," she repeated, her voice low and frantic. "You don't think the children and I are going to let you go, do you?"

He smiled at her, but the crowd pushed them both inside the saloon. Gus Sims went behind the bar, and, women present or not, he began setting up glasses and liquor.

"Bring me a whiskey," the sheriff said, settling at a table. He motioned Jake to take a seat across from him.

Loreen didn't sit down with them. She thought better on her feet. She had to come up with a plan to rescue Jake.

"Where's that drink?" the sheriff bellowed, and a plan came to her.

Loreen walked to the bar and picked up a heavy bottle of whiskey. "I'll give it to him, Gus," she said, starting to move off; then she turned back. "Why didn't you speak up about Joseph a long time ago? I could have wired the law with proof!"

A guilty flush spread over the saloon owner's face. His gaze darted toward the sheriff. "I was lying," he whispered. "I didn't see nothing."

She figured her eyes widened to the size of tea saucers. "You lied?" she whispered back.

He nodded. "But it doesn't matter now. You see, I figured Billy would panic if he thought he was going to get taken off to jail. And he did. His gang admitted he killed your brother, so there was no harm done."

She smiled at him, reaching across the bar to touch his hand briefly. He smiled back; then her attention became focused on her plan. She walked up behind the sheriff slowly. Her heart started to pound, her palms to sweat. She hated to do what she was about to do, but she couldn't see that she had any choice.

Lifting the bottle over the sheriff's head, she closed her eyes and dropped her hand. The bottle's descent suddenly halted. She opened her eyes to see Jake's hand grasping the bottle.

"What the hell are you doing, Loreen?" he asked, his expression disbelieving.

361

The sheriff frowned at her. "I'd say she was getting ready to club me over the head with that bottle."

"I think Loreen intends to rescue me," Jake explained. "She isn't by nature a violent person."

"Get over here and sit down," the sheriff ordered her. "Across from me, where I can keep my eye on you both."

Deflated because her plan had failed, Loreen did as the man instructed. He narrowed his gaze.

"Why in tarnation did you do that?"

Loreen didn't see in any point in lying. "Because Jake is kind and good, and he's not guilty of murder. Not in truth. I can't let you take him from me. I love him."

Jake turned toward her, and the sheriff was forgotten. The whole town was forgotten. His eyes met hers; then he took her hand.

"I could die tomorrow and never be as happy as I am right now. I love you, too, Loreen, and that's why even if you'd knocked this man out cold, I couldn't run again. I never cared much for Jake Walters, but I like Jake Winslow, and I like him because he's the man you helped make me. I love you and the children too much to let you live in the shadow of my shame."

"And I love you too much to let you go," she whispered.

He leaned toward her and their lips brushed before the sheriff's loud cough brought them back to their predicament.

"You two are about to turn my stomach," he grumbled, then glanced around. "Any food around this place?"

Gus Sims disappeared in the back, Loreen assumed

in search. Jake squeezed her fingers; then the sheriff demanded their attention once more.

"Guess you'd better spit it all out, young fellow. Tell me what happened in Dodge."

"Yes, tell us what happened, Jake," Hetty Johnson urged. The sheriff gave the woman a dirty look, then nodded for Jake to proceed.

Having heard the story, Loreen barely listened, instead taking the opportunity to memorize the deep sound of Jake's voice. She'd known he loved her before he said the words, but there was nothing in the world as sweet as hearing them. Billy was gone, and she felt that her family was truly safe for the first time in years. That along with Jake's admission were heady realizations.

When Jake stopped talking, the sheriff poured himself a drink and gulped it down. "Heard you were cocky, a braggart, and a no 'count drifter. That's the man I expected to find today. Instead I find a man who's been hiding out in a no-name town and not only has the townspeople lying and defending him, but has this pretty young woman telling him she loves him, and willing to get herself into trouble by clubbing a man of the law over the head so you can escape."

"She probably wouldn't have followed through," Jake quickly assured the man.

Loreen gave him a dirty look. "I would, too."

The sheriff cleared his throat, recapturing their attention. "The point I'm getting to is, even though you have this pretty woman willing to go to those extremes for you, you stop her, and then tell her you won't run away with her nohow. What are you, stupid, Walters?"

Bristling, Loreen said, "He certainly is not stupid. He's honorable!"

A smile stole over the sheriff's lips beneath his thick, gray mustache. "Exactly."

Her heart started to beat at an alarming rate. The sheriff poured himself another drink, then fixed both of them with a steely glance. "If Jake Walters was a cold-blooded killer, he'd have gunned me down outside right after he took care of that other feller. Or he'd have let you club me over the head and not given a damn what trouble that might get the both of you into. I'm a fair judge of character. In my line of work, a man has to be. I believe you that the shooting was an accident."

She must have been holding her breath, because Loreen felt it leave her lips in a long sigh of relief. Then Jake had to go and spoil her fast-rising hope.

"But will anybody else believe me?" he asked.

"I believe you, Jake," Manny Crawford said, stepping forward. "A cold-blooded killer doesn't pull a town together the way you have. That kind of man doesn't stand up to men like Billy while doing his best to avoid violence."

"We believe you, too." Mr. Johnson stepped forward, pulling his wife up beside him, who in turn grabbed Gretchen and little Samuel. More faces formed a circle around the table, all willing to place their trust in Jake. When she saw his eyes water, she felt so proud of him—so proud to love him and be the woman he loved.

The sheriff held his hands up to quiet everyone. "My guess is that all these folks would be willing to come to Dodge to speak on your behalf, and I also believe their doing so would see you cleared of this crime."

Loreen's heart leaped with joy. She began to throw

her arms around Jake, but the sheriff gave her a warning glance and she contained herself.

"But that sounds like an awful lot of trouble. All of you have businesses and families to see to. It could take a good month or more to get the circuit judge to listen to the case."

Loreen didn't know what the man was leading up to, but he'd better spit it out, because she was becoming worried again.

"What are you suggesting?" Jake asked point-blank.

"Earlier, outside, I said I didn't have any say in whether you were innocent or guilty. Truth is, I've been a lawman for a long time, and there are many people who set store by what I say. Figure as long as you promise to stay put, I can go on back alone and get your name cleared."

It was difficult for Loreen to keep her mouth from dropping open. Jake had to open his again and cause trouble.

"Why would you do that?"

The sheriff smiled. "Not for you, Walters, although you seem to be a good man." His gaze landed on Loreen. "I'm doing it for her. It sounds like she's had enough trouble. Besides, she said something about her and the children needing you." He frowned. "You've already got children?"

Jake glanced at Loreen, and the love and joy in his eyes made it, indeed, the best day of her life. "We have a daughter," she said.

He lifted her hand and kissed it. "Guess I'd better make you an honest woman," he leaned close to whisper. "What if they still want me to go before the judge?" Jake turned to ask the sheriff.

He shrugged. "Don't figure they will, but if they do,

I'll wire the mercantile and send for you. I trust you to show up."

Jake nodded. He glanced at Loreen and she nodded, too.

"Guess you're free to go then."

"Free?" Jake said, as if awed by the possibility.

Loreen could no longer contain herself. She threw her arms around his neck and kissed him. A loud cheer went up from the townspeople. Then they were surrounded and pulled up from their chairs, hearty slaps falling on Jake's shoulders and the women hugging Loreen. Jake took her hand and tried to pull her through the well-wishers.

"Hold up," the sheriff called.

For an awful moment, Loreen thought their good fortune was about to end, that the sheriff had suddenly changed his mind.

"Seems to me this town needs a sheriff," he said, his gaze leveled on Jake. "Sometimes being on the wrong end of a gun when it goes off does a lot to make a man learn to respect life, the power of a weapon, and the law. I imagine you've learned your lesson. After we get your name cleared, if these good people want to vote you into office, I'll come down and swear you in."

"I'll vote for him," Mr. Johnson said. "And we can afford to pay you a salary, since we don't have to pay Billy extra anymore."

Jake didn't know what to say. His head reeled from being assaulted with so many emotions. He'd found a place where he fit in, where he was loved and could love in return—a place to settle down and grow old. He didn't really mind the possibility of being sheriff. It would be extra income, and Miller's Passing had the makings of a peaceful town without Billy Waylan and his gang terrorizing everyone. He glanced at Loreen.

"I think my wife has her heart set on my being a farmer," he said.

She smiled at him. "I'll love you no matter who you are. You know that. Besides, we already have a farmer in the family."

He returned her smile. "I guess Toby will end up getting his birthright after all." To the townspeople he said, "I'm touched by your support, and your belief in me. I'll give the matter some thought."

"Ain't you two got young'uns to tend?" the sheriff called.

Jake wondered if the lump in his throat would ever go away. He released Loreen and walked back over to the man. He extended his hand.

"Thank you for giving me a second chance," he said.

The sheriff shook his hand. "No thanks necessary. It was these friends you've made and that woman you love who gave you the second chance. See that you don't make them—or me—sorry."

With a nod, he turned back to Loreen. He still couldn't quite believe his good fortune. He was free— free to love Loreen and Wren, to be Toby's brother in truth.

They would all stay in Miller's Passing together. They would raise crops, and he guessed he might be the sheriff. Loreen could sell pies in Mr. Johnson's mercantile, and between all of them, they would survive. He couldn't wait to start his new life.

"Well, what are you waiting around for?" the sheriff grumbled. "Go home."

Keeping his gaze glued on Loreen, Jake walked

away from the man who'd ended up being his savior, rather than his prosecutor. He took Loreen's hand again and led her outside. They both broke into a run, headed for old Ben, waiting patiently hitched to the wagon.

Jake jumped onto the bench seat, then helped Loreen up. He kissed her, right there in the middle of Main Street. Her arms went around his neck, and she melted against him, their passion a mixture of joy and desire.

"Let's go home," she whispered, and besides her telling him she loved him, those were the sweetest words he'd ever heard.

They didn't tarry, although Jake wanted to pull to the side of the road, take Loreen in the back, and make love to her again. Toby would be worried, and no telling what Wren might have gotten into under his supervision. When he pulled onto the road leading to the cabin, he stopped for a moment. Both he and Loreen stared out proudly over their ripening crop. Toby spotted them and came running. Jake flicked the reins and they lumbered forward.

"What happened?" Toby shouted, running alongside the wagon. "Do we need to hurry and throw our things together?"

Jake stopped the wagon and jumped down. He faced Toby with a lump still in his throat and his eyes misty.

"We don't ever have to run again," he said. "None of us. The sheriff believed me, and he's going to see that my name is cleared."

Toby, on the verge of manhood, did a very un-grown-up thing: he rushed forward and threw his arms around Jake like a little boy might. Jake hugged him back. "You've made me a rich man, Toby." He pulled Loreen into the hug. "All of you have."

"What about Billy?" Toby worried.

Billy, Jake thought, was probably in hell, where he belonged. "He won't bother us anymore," Jake answered. "He won't bother anyone."

The boy looked him in the eye and nodded, and Jake suspected that was the last time he'd ask about the bully. He realized one family member was missing.

"Where's Wren?"

"She's in the garden," Toby answered. "She's been staring at the ground for nearly the whole time you've been gone, and she ain't said two words."

Worried that his leaving had traumatized Wren, Jake and the rest of the family hurried toward the house. They found Wren just as Toby had said, staring at the ground.

"Wren?" Jake said. "I've come home."

She glanced up. "I knew you would," she responded. "You had to, because I wished upon a star. Part of what I wished was that you would be my papa. You couldn't be my papa if you didn't come back. Papas are supposed to stay around forever."

He reached down and snatched her up. "That's just what I plan to do—stay around forever and be your papa."

When he glanced at Loreen, he expected tears of happiness to be shimmering in her eyes. Instead she stared thoughtfully at the ground.

"She wished upon a star," she said quietly. Her gaze lifted abruptly. "Wren, what did you plant in the garden?"

The little girl smiled. "Oh, I didn't plant anything. You and Jake did, remember?"

Loreen placed her hands on her hips. "And what did Jake and I plant?"

The child's smile stretched. "Flowers."

Jake's gaze met Loreen's. "Looks like Wren is determined for us to have babies."

Her gaze widened. "We planted five seeds."

He winced. "Maybe all of them won't come up."

"I guess it'd be all right if we just had one baby," Wren decided. "Two would be better."

With his past behind him, his name cleared, Jake realized he very much wanted other children—brothers and sisters for little Wren. But did Loreen? As if she read the question in his eyes, she smiled.

"I think we can manage two."

Hugging Wren tighter, he said, "I imagine we're going to have our hands full with this one."

Toby stepped forward, then glanced between Jake and Loreen nervously. "Uh, Wren. Since Loreen is your mama now and Jake is your papa, that means I have to be your uncle."

Her mouth turned down. "You can't be my brother no more?"

He shook his head sadly.

Wren gave the matter a moment of thought. "I ain't never had an uncle before, have I?"

"No," Loreen answered, brushing the curls from her daughter's eyes.

Wren shrugged. "I guess I got one now."

They all laughed and hugged, the reunion interrupted by Princess and eight pups almost old enough now to be weaned. Wren struggled down from Jake's arms and started playing with the pups. With a grin at Jake and Loreen, Toby turned and started back toward the field.

"Think we could find a few minutes alone?" Jake whispered to Loreen, nuzzling her ear.

"Depends on what you plan to do with those few minutes," she answered.

"You know what I plan to do."

She pulled back from him, looking far too prudish to be the same woman who had waded into the pool naked earlier that morning.

"In town, I believe you said something about making an honest woman of me. If you're going to give Wren and me your name, shouldn't it be your real one?"

"Will you marry me, Loreen?" he asked.

Tears filled her eyes. "The day I met you, I thought I should have my friends around me, family, a choice, and most of all love. You've given me a chance to have all of those. We'll have another wedding. A real one."

"And you've given me a new beginning, and a family of my own."

Leaning toward her, Jake kissed Loreen, the touch of their lips interrupted by the little girl playing with puppies at their feet.

"Don't forget what you're supposed to give *me*," Wren reminded them.

He smiled at the woman he loved, then shrugged. "She always could wrap me right around her little finger. I imagine she'll get her way about this, too."

Jake glanced at the garden, and damned if he didn't see a tiny sprout, where they had planted the seeds, struggling up from the ground to drink the sunlight.

Loreen lifted a brow. "She probably already has."

Lair of the Wolf

Chapter Six

Deana James

On January 1, 1997, *Romance Communications*, the Romance Magazine for the 21st century made its Internet debut. One year later, it was named a Lycos Top 5% site on the Web in terms of both content and graphics!

One of *Romance Communications'* most popular features is The Romantic Relay, an original romance novel divided into twelve monthly installments, with each chapter written by a different author. Our first offering was *Lair of the Wolf*, a tale of medieval Wales, created by, in alphabetical order, celebrated authors Emily Carmichael, Debra Dier, Madeline George, Martha Hix, Deana James, Elizabeth Mayne, Constance O'Banyon, Evelyn Rogers, Sharon Schulze, June Lund Shiplett, and Bobbi Smith.

We put no restrictions on the authors, letting each pick up the tale where the previous author had left off and going forward as she wished. The authors tell us they had a lot of fun, each trying to write her successor into a corner!

Now, preserving the fun and suspense of our month-by-month installments, Leisure Books presents, in print, one chapter a month of *Lair of the Wolf*. In addition to the entire online story the authors have added some brand-new material to their existing chapters. So if you think you've read *Lair of the Wolf* already, you may find a few surprises. Please enjoy this unique offering, watch for each new monthly installment in the back of your Leisure Books, and make sure you visit our Web site, where another romantic relay is already in progress.

Romance Communications

http://www.romcom.com

Pamela Monck, Editor-in-Chief

Mary D. Pinto, Senior Editor

S. Lee Meyer, Web Mistress

Meredyth stared into the dying fire. A tiny, defiant flame leapt in the heart of what had once been a mighty log. Now that pitiful light was all that remained. Soon it would be extinguished. A melancholy symbol for the House of Llewellyn.

She had pulled the soft, gray pelts up over her shoulders and rolled onto her side, facing away from the bed. Behind her she could hear the heavy, even breathing of her husband. Yet not her husband. Not fully. Not yet. She didn't want to surrender her body to the Wolf.

She'd been appalled at the heat that had stirred inside her at the sight of his scarred chest. When he'd pulled off his jerkin and knelt beside her, she had felt a pang deep in her belly. Black hair had curled silkily over his swarthy skin; a warrior's muscles had flexed

377

beneath it. The sight had made her throat go dry, and she'd felt her heart thrum faster in her chest.

Such evidence of the shear physical power of the Wolf had been overwhelming. She doubted that even her father or any of her brothers could have overcome such a man.

He could have taken her if he had desired. As he'd leaned above her, meeting her gaze, his dark eyes reflecting the light of the flames, she'd begun to tremble deep inside. Aware of his strong, long-fingered hands mere inches from her breasts, she had stiffened in alarm, feeling a prickling sensation deep inside her. She had wanted to cross her arms for protection.

But both she and her people needed more than her frail arms for protection from the Wolf. Especially those in the dungeons. She was their only hope. Her fealty was their freedom. Yet when she swore the oath, they would become the villeins and serfs of Longshanks' Wolf. No! Better to perish than place her hand beneath his boot! Her hot Welsh blood blazed in defiance.

Alas, she realized, her father and brothers had taken that road, and it had led nowhere but to death. She sighed, trying to reason her way through the impossible.

If she swore the oath without completing the marriage contract, then all would be void. And if she lied in a matter of honor, no one would ever believe her again.

As she stared at the fire, the last tiny curl of flame died. The log fell apart with a snapping sound and a flash of sparks.

So could she die, as could all those in the dungeon.

Their lives could be snuffed out in an instant, and this would be the Wolf's lair. In a few years she would be forgotten, the name Llewellyn gone. Her father's name, her brothers' name, and her own.

She turned. The room was dark. Dark as a dungeon. Quiet as a cat, she sat up and gathered the throw made of wolf pelts around her. The undercoat was soft as velvet, the fur tantalizing where it brushed her skin.

A trembling began in her belly as she rose to her feet. The darkness seemed impenetrable, the room already growing chill. Yet she could hear his breathing, strong, deep, even. The sound was somehow hypnotic, calling to her.

Her bare feet tentatively crossed the floor. She closed her eyes, frightened at what she was about to do.

For her people, she thought. For the Llewellyn name, so that some part of that noble family would remain here in their ancestral castle. For her own soul, so she could live in truth. And, in truth, for her own body, which even amid her fears was letting its desires be known.

Before she could lose her nerve, she fairly lunged the remaining few feet and flung herself onto the bed, the wolf pelt billowing like a cape.

The Wolf met her with a growl, grappling for her wrists. In fierce silence he forced her back into the pillows, pinning her to the bed. One muscular leg captured her thighs.

She struggled mightily, fearful he would kill her. What a fool she was! Then she realized that she had been so bedeviled by her own fears, she'd not thought how pouncing on him in the dark would seem. He feared she'd come to kill *him.* "I have no weapons, Wolf," she whispered. "No dagger, this I swear."

379

His iron grip on her wrists eased. He leaned closer in the darkness, his weight pressing on her breasts. "You took a dangerous chance, Lady Meredyth, leaping into a man's bed like that."

She had to swallow the knot of terror in her throat. "I leapt before my fear could drive me back."

"Fear, my lady?"

She couldn't answer, so tight was her throat. He was overpowering her with his masculinity—the size and heat and scent of him.

Then, out of the darkness, his roughened cheek brushed hers, and he kissed the corner of her mouth.

She gasped and tried to turn aside, but his lips captured hers, kissed her fully. She opened her mouth to protest. His tongue slid into it, meeting hers. And the sensation was as overwhelming as the rest of him.

Finally he released her wrists, and she had thought he would lift himself off her. But he did nothing of the sort. Instead, he ran his hands possessively over her shoulders and down her arms. Then one hand glided down her side and up over her belly.

She drew in her breath.

His hand didn't stop at her waist, but moved onto her breast. She gasped and involuntarily arched her back.

He gently squeezed her flesh at the same time he deepened his kiss, and Meredyth was overcome with a torrent of sensations she had never known. His fingers satisfied the odd ache they created, while another began deep in her belly. And suddenly she didn't want to be free of him or his bold, questing hands. She wanted more of everything, and something she couldn't name.

This desire was unseemly, her mind protested. She had come to Sir Garon to sacrifice herself for her people, for her family name. She hadn't come to find pleasure. She couldn't enjoy him. She couldn't let her body betray her. If she were to keep her self-respect, he should need to wrest from her what she would give him only grudgingly.

In a burst of panic, she tried to tear away the hand that brought such traitorous sensations to her breast.

"What the—?" Sir Garon's voice was thick, muffled against her mouth.

She slapped at him. He gasped and then cursed as she sank her fingers into his thick hair and pulled. Her whole body convulsed with her panic and anger.

"Take me!" she cried. "Take me and get it over with! I hate you!" She slapped at him again. "I hate you!"

He captured her wrists again, pushing them above her head, laughing in her ear.

"Don't you dare laugh at me!" She was almost weeping now, in a painful mix of frustration and shame.

He clasped both her wrists in his left hand. His right closed over her breast. She stared up at him fearfully. His thumb and forefinger closed over her nipple. It was hard and eager beneath her linen gown. As his fingertips toyed sensuously with the swollen bud, Meredyth heaved and bucked with chagrin and desire.

"No," she pleaded. "Don't."

"Don't what, my lady?" He was chuckling, his mouth close to her ear. Then his lips closed over her earlobe and gently tugged.

Again Meredyth was awash in unprecedented sensations, every inch of her responding to his gentle, sensual ministrations. Her mind commanded her body to fight him. Her spirit demanded that he take her by force, not seduction. But as his fingers and lips continued their hypnotic magic, she trembled from her scalp to the soles of her feet. The muscles of her belly tightened and shivered with the violence of her passion. In one last effort to throw him off, she frantically bucked upward.

He gently but thoroughly pressed his body down to meet hers. "My bride, my dearest wife, you stir me so," he whispered.

Her body flamed at the sweet words and the sweet weight now upon her. Whatever she would think of herself on the morrow, she could no longer summon the will to fight him.

She turned her head, but this time to seek his kiss. Their mouths locked on each other as if they could never get enough. His hands caressed her breasts, molded the curve of her waist, of her hipbones. His thigh slid up and down, caressing the tops of hers and the base of her belly.

She moaned, dissolving in sensations.

His weight left her, and she gasped in disappointment. Her eyes flew open, but the darkness was profound. She couldn't even make out his shape. But then his hands boldly glided down hers, tracing her shape, finally reaching the hem of her gown.

He lifted it and pulled it upward, over her. Chill air struck her legs, her belly, her ribs, her breasts, and she moaned softly at being thus exposed.

"Sit up," he commanded huskily.

She did so.

"Raise your arms."

She might have been his slave, so smoothly did she obey his commands. Could a slave love a master? she wondered in confusion even as he completely divested her of her clothing and lay her back, naked, against the warm bed linens.

She had thought he would take her swiftly. She had expected pain. But instead, his fingers caressed the insides of her thighs. He pushed them gently apart, bestowing caresses where she had never imagined they could be given.

Meredyth's flesh began to burn and throb, her body feeling suffused with her blushes. Moaning in helplessness and desire, she reached for the anchor of his powerful shoulders, pulling him toward her, urging him.

"Do you want me, Lady Meredyth?" he whispered in the darkness.

Of course, she wanted him, though she could scarcely admit even to herself just how much. But she surely could not to admit it to him. He could not make her do so, could he?

"Lady Meredyth?" he prompted, his breath feathering against her ear, his heated touch making her tremble and flush.

She moaned softly. If he would only spare her this admission, she could still keep some part of herself inviolate.

"Shall I leave you, then, my lady?" His lips brushed her ear. "Perhaps you wished merely to join me in my bed to keep warm?"

She groaned. He wouldn't spare her. Longshanks' Wolf was too fierce. He would exact his tribute with no mercy. She set her teeth against her lower lip.

He took his hand away. "Shall I leave you to sleep, my lady?" he repeated.

She desperately wanted his hand back at the aching core of her. Despite her best efforts, one word escaped her lips. "No."

"Then so be it." He positioned himself between her thighs.

She could feel the powerful male part of him against her, and her heart leapt into her throat. Her body shuddered. He began to enter her, and she made a tiny whimpering sound as the pressure built.

Then he put his mouth over hers and drove himself forward. Like a dagger through silk, he split the virginal tissue and buried himself deep within her body.

She had steeled herself against pain that didn't come. Instead, she felt him fill her, stretch her, and her desire quickened.

"Is it bad, my lady?" he whispered, his voice solicitous.

She wanted to hate him for being kind, for caring about her. She should tell him that it was agony. She should spoil his pleasure for him. Instead, she gave her head the barest shake. "No."

"Ah." He began to move then, slowly.

From the first, she matched his rhythm. Instinctively, as though they had danced this dance a half a million times, she clung to him, raised her hips to his. Involuntarily, her muscles clasped him. She could feel them tightening within her belly.

He groaned. "My sweet bride. Dear, sweet Meredyth."

"Wolf," she whispered. She set her teeth to keep back a keening cry. Something was happening within her body. Was this the pain she had been expecting, this sensation, mounting in her thighs, her belly, her breasts?

Every muscle, every fiber of her body was strung tight as lute strings vibrating together. And then she exploded in a momentous crash of feeling that was beyond any pleasure she had ever known.

The sunlit courtyard was so bright. Her husband had had her brought to its very center, where his men-at-arms had spread the Persian carpet that ordinarily formed the floor of his campaign tent.

On it had been placed two curule chairs, one his from the same tent, and one she recognized as her father's. It had long stood beside the fireplace in the solar.

The courtyard was full of her people, summoned by the Wolf's men, waiting in sullen silence for they knew not what. In a small knot to one side, still fettered, were her father's loyal men—the steward of Glendire, the captain of the old castle guard, and several yeomen who had offered resistance to the English invaders.

Like her, they blinked in the sunlight as Dame Allison led her forward. At her lord's command, Meredyth had been dressed in her bridal finery.

Immediately, the knowledgeable in the courtyard began to mutter among themselves at the sight of her hair, which had so long hung down her back beneath her veil. Now, though cropped much shorter, it was threaded with blue ribbons that matched the background on the Wolf's banner.

She cringed inwardly. She knew what her people were seeing. She was virgin no more. She'd given herself to the Wolf. Yet the worst was still before her.

Sir Olyver Martain surveyed her with what looked to be a leer. His stare seemed to undress her, making her feel soiled, as if he was imagining the physical coupling that had taken place between the Wolf and herself the night before. She lifted her chin contemptuously. He could imagine, but he would never know what joy she and the Wolf had found.

Sir Olyver's expression altered. His eyes narrowed as if he read her mind, and his lips seemed to contort with anger. Instantly, however, all emotion was extinguished by a bland smile.

The onlookers began to mutter, and Meredyth looked around.

Sir Garon Saunders, Longshanks' Wolf, came out of the castle and strode across the courtyard, accompanied by the priest who had married them.

With proper ceremony, he took his place in front of his chair. The priest stood on his right, and Sir Olyver reluctantly took his place on the left.

Meredyth felt Dame Allison's hand on her elbow, guiding her until she was standing in front of Garon, her back to her people. She could almost feel their strength and sympathy reaching out to her. She could say the word, and a terrible battle would begin. But she would not say the word.

The Wolf looked into her eyes, and the expression he read there seemed to please him. He then looked up and beyond her. "Now, people of Glendire," he announced, "I have taken your lady in marriage. The daughter of Llewellyn is now the wife of Saunders."

The silence behind her was heavy, almost menacing. She could imagine they were thinking she had been raped. The Wolf was a fool if he thought he could win her people in this way.

386

"As a bridegroom," he went on, "I have been pleased to honor my wife by releasing from the dungeon those loyal to her father, expecting that they will swear the oath of fealty to her, now that she sits in his stead."

At a nod, his men removed the fetters and herded the former prisoners to the fore.

"But before she accepts their loyalty, she will give her own pledge in and of her own free will."

He seated himself. The priest stepped forward. Sir Olyver seemed to scowl.

"Lady Meredyth?" Sir Garon, prompted her.

Dame Allison stepped back, and Meredyth was alone. Alone she must step across the Persian carpet to kneel at her husband's feet. Her soul cried out in a last moment of defiance, but she was mindful of the people at her back. She would do anything to protect their lives. And Glendire would remain, at least in part, Llewellyn.

As if in a dream, she crossed the space and knelt before him, her bridal gown spread out around her.

Sir Garon leaned forward. "Give me your hands."

She thought for one instant of refusing, of running away. But his dark eyes held hers, and she did his bidding.

The Wolf placed her hands, palms together, between his palms. The priest knelt beside them and put his own hands over theirs.

"Repeat after me," the Wolf said in a loud, clear voice. "I, Meredyth of Llewellyn, Glendire, and Saunders, enter into your homage and faith and become your man, by mouth and hand."

Her tongue clove to the roof of her mouth.

"Say it. I, Meredyth of Llewellyn, Glendire, and Saunders—' "

"I, Meredyth of Llewellyn, Glendire, and Saunders—"

"—enter into your homage and faith and become your man, by mouth and hand."

"—enter into your homage and faith and become your man, by mouth and hand."

"And I swear and promise to keep faith and loyalty to you against all others—"

"—and I swear and promise to keep faith and loyalty to you against all others—"

"—and to guard your rights with all my strength."

"—and to guard your rights with all my strength."

The priest took his hands away. The Wolf rose to his feet, raising her with him and turning her to face her people.

Someone raised a cheer of approval that Glendore was saved, a cheer soon taken up by the members of the castle household.

Gradually others took their cue, and the cheering increased. At last, the men freed from the dungeon joined in.

The rest of the ceremony passed without incident. Meredyth accepted the oaths of her people and heard their expressions of relief.

"Ye've saved us, my lady," her father's old captain and companion-at-arms murmured. "I'll not be forgettin' it. Ye can be sure."

The steward, too, looked at her with his forthright eyes swimming in gratitude. "Shall I continue with my duties, my lady?"

She looked to her husband. "Gethin is honest to a fault, my lord. He would serve you well. He knows every one of your subjects. He would assure that you get the rents you are entitled to. People might be tempted to hide things from a new man."

The Wolf chuckled. "I see the wisdom of your request. It is granted." As Gethin rose, his new lord leaned forward. "See you give the service that your lady has promised. For know you that you owe your life to her."

As the man bowed and backed away, the Wolf rose. "Good people, tonight there will be a feast, which even now is being prepared. Join us for the celebration of my wedded happiness and the peace that is herewith between Englishman and Welshman."

As another cheer went up, he took Meredyth's hand and led her into the castle.

From her new bedchamber, Meredyth could hear the preparations below. Once again the tables were being set up, cloths spread, the best plate polished and carried off to the kitchen to be filled with meat, bread, and fruit. Dame Allison would be bustling about among the minions, directing all with a firm, knowing hand, giving order to the elaborate proceedings.

Everyone was happy. At peace. And full of hope. And even Meredyth could not begrudge the extravagant feasting that but a day before would have had her fretting.

If only she did not feel the weight of guilt. Not that she had betrayed her people; she had done the best she could for them. Not that she had betrayed her father and brothers; she had even managed to save honor for the family name. When all was said and done, she could have done naught else but pledge fealty to the Wolf, her husband. Even the most courageous warrior would have done so in her position. It had been the wise thing to do. That she understood.

The guilt was within herself. Far from fighting him, she had literally leapt into her husband's arms, and, as if that were not bad enough, she had enjoyed it. And, worst of all, she feared she was falling desperately in love with him.

Desperately, she knew, because she could never tell him. He would make a slave of her. Doubtless, he would even despise her for losing her heart to the enemy. He had no such feelings for her. Of that she was certain. He was a warrior, a wolf, the cruelest and strongest of a powerful king's men. He would have no respect for such weakness.

She stared into her mirror. High color bloomed in her cheeks. Her body, apart from a few strained muscles, felt wonderful. Only her heart ached as if it would break in two. She sighed. She must be strong. She must keep her secret, if she would keep her self-respect.

"My lady?" A man's voice accompanied a knock on her door.

"Yes, Sir Olyver?" she called. She made a face at her reflection. She didn't trust the man. He was clearly jealous of Sir Garon. Her father had maintained that jealousy among troops was treacherous. A jealous man would turn against his friends if the temptation became too strong.

"Lord Garon bids you come," he announced.

She sighed. "I'm ready."

She opened the door.

"My lady." He bowed and offered her his arm.

She laid her own upon it, and they proceeded down the hall. At the top of the curving staircase, she hesitated. "Someone has forgotten to light the lanterns."

"Evidently," he agreed. "The servant responsible will be found and soundly whipped."

"I'm sure that's not necessary," she said firmly. "In all the confusion, he was probably set to another task and lost track of the time."

"You're very forgiving, my lady."

They came to the bend in the stairs by the garderobe. No light could filter up from below or down from above to reach the spot. They were temporarily in total darkness.

Suddenly, Meredyth was afraid, and she started down the remaining steps hurriedly.

Sir Olyver's hand tightened on her arm, and he crowded against her. "Watch your step, my lady."

She lost her balance, clutched at the wall.

"Look out!" he yelled, as something struck a smashing blow on the side of her head.

Watch for Chapter Seven by Sharon Schulze, of Lair of the Wolf, *appearing in June 2000 in* The Sword and the Flame *by Patricia Phillips.*

PRICKLY PEAR

RONDA THOMPSON

Daddy's little girl is no angel. Heck, she hasn't earned the nickname Prickly Pear by being a wallflower. Everyone on the Circle C knows that Camile Cordell can rope her way out of Hell itself—and most of the town thinks the willful beauty will end up there sooner or later. Now, Cam knows that her father is looking for a new foreman for their ranch—and the blond firebrand is pretty sure she knows where to find one. Wade Langtry has just arrived in Texas, but he seems darn sure of himself in trying to take a job that is hers. Cam has to admit, though, that he has what it takes to break stallions. In her braver moments, she even imagines what it might feel like to have the roughrider break her to the saddle—or she him. And she fears that in the days to follow, it won't much matter if she looses her father's ranch—she's already lost her heart.

___4624-5 $4.99 US/$5.99 CAN

Dorchester Publishing Co., Inc.
P.O. Box 6640
Wayne, PA 19087-8640

COUGAR'S WOMAN Ronda Thompson

On the journey to meet her fiancé in Santa Fe, Melissa Sheffield is captured by Apaches and given to a man known as Cougar. At first, she is relieved to learn that she's been given to a white man, but with one kiss he proves himself more dangerous than the whole tribe. Terrified of her savage captor, she pledges to escape at any price. But while there might be an escape from the Apaches, is there any escape from her heart? Clay Brodie—known as Cougar to the Apaches—is given the fiery Melissa by his chief. He is then ordered to turn the beauty into an obedient slave—or destroy her. But how can he slay a woman who evokes an emotion deeper than he's ever known? And when the time comes to fight, will it be for his tribe or for his woman?

___4524-9 $4.99 US/$5.99 CAN

Dorchester Publishing Co., Inc.
P.O. Box 6640
Wayne, PA 19087-8640

Please add $1.75 for shipping and handling for the first book and $.50 for each book thereafter. NY, NYC, and PA residents, please add appropriate sales tax. No cash, stamps, or C.O.D.s. All orders shipped within 6 weeks via postal service book rate. Canadian orders require $2.00 extra postage and must be paid in U.S. dollars through a U.S. banking facility.

Name_____

Address_____

City_____State_____Zip_____

I have enclosed $_____ in payment for the checked book(s).

Payment <u>must</u> accompany all orders. ❑ Please send a free catalog.

CHECK OUT OUR WEBSITE! www.dorchesterpub.com

Compulsion Elaine Fox

On the smoldering Virginia night when she first meets Ryan St. James, Catra Meredyth knows nothing can douse the fire that the infuriating Yankee has ignited within her. With one caress the handsome seducer has kindled a passion that threatens to turn the Southern belle's reputation to ashes—and with one torrid kiss she consigns herself to the flames. Ryan has supped at the table of sin, but on Catra's lips he has tasted heaven. A dedicated bachelor, Ryan finds that the feisty beauty tempts even his strongest resolve. In the heat of their love is a lesson to be learned: The needs of the flesh cannot be denied, but the call of the heart is stronger by far.

Lair of the Wolf

Also includes the first installment of *Lair of the Wolf*, a serialized romance set in medieval Wales. Be sure to look for future chapters of this exciting story featured in Leisure books and written by the industry's top authors.

___4648-2 $5.99 US/$6.99 CAN

Dorchester Publishing Co., Inc.
P.O. Box 6640
Wayne, PA 19087-8640

Please add $1.75 for shipping and handling for the first book and $.50 for each book thereafter. NY, NYC, and PA residents, please add appropriate sales tax. No cash, stamps, or C.O.D.s. All orders shipped within 6 weeks via postal service book rate. Canadian orders require $2.00 extra postage and must be paid in U.S. dollars through a U.S. banking facility.

Name_____
Address_____
City_____State_____Zip_____
I have enclosed $_____ in payment for the checked book(s).
Payment <u>must</u> accompany all orders. ❑ Please send a free catalog.
CHECK OUT OUR WEBSITE! www.dorchesterpub.com

Cinnamon and Roses — Heidi Betts

A hardworking seamstress, Rebecca has no business being attracted to a man like wealthy, arrogant Caleb Adams. Born fatherless in a brothel, Rebecca knows what males are made of. And Caleb is clearly as faithless as they come, scandalizing their Kansas cowtown with the fancy city women he casually uses and casts aside. Though he tempts innocent Rebecca beyond reason, she can't afford to love a man like Caleb, for the price might be another fatherless babe. What the devil is wrong with him, Caleb muses, that he's drawn to a calico-clad dressmaker when sirens in silk are his for the asking? Still, Rebecca unaccountably stirs him. Caleb vows no woman can be trusted with his heart. But he must sample sweet Rebecca.

Lair of the Wolf

Also includes the second installment of *Lair of the Wolf*, a serialized romance set in medieval Wales. Be sure to look for future chapters of this exciting story featured in Leisure books and written by the industry's top authors.

___4668-7 $4.99 US/$5.99 CAN

Dorchester Publishing Co., Inc.
P.O. Box 6640
Wayne, PA 19087-8640

Please add $1.75 for shipping and handling for the first book and $.50 for each book thereafter. NY, NYC, and PA residents, please add appropriate sales tax. No cash, stamps, or C.O.D.s. All orders shipped within 6 weeks via postal service book rate. Canadian orders require $2.00 extra postage and must be paid in U.S. dollars through a U.S. banking facility.

Name_____
Address_____
City_____ State_____ Zip_____
I have enclosed $_____ in payment for the checked book(s).
Payment <u>must</u> accompany all orders. ❏ Please send a free catalog.
      CHECK OUT OUR WEBSITE! www.dorchesterpub.com

SUPERSTITIONS

ANNIE McKNIGHT

Beautiful young Billie Bahill is determined. Despite what her father says, she knows her fiancé won't just leave her. So come hell or high water, she is going to go find him. So what if she rides off into the deadly Superstition Mountains? Billie is as good on a horse as any of the men on her father's ranch, and she won't let anybody stop her—especially not the Arizona Ranger with eyes that make her heart skip a beat.

___4405-6 $5.50 US/$6.50 CAN

And Gold Was Ours

Rebecca Brandewyne

In Spain the young Aurora's future is foretold—a long arduous journey, a dark, wild jungle, and a fierce, protective man. Now in the New World, on a plantation haunted by a tale of lost love and hidden gold, the dark-haired beauty wonders if the swordsman and warrior who haunts her dreams truly lived and if he can rescue her from the enemies who seek to destroy her. Together, will they be able to overcome the past and conquer the present to find the greatest treasure on this earth, a treasure that is even more precious than gold. . . .

___52314-0 $5.99 US/$6.99 CAN

Dorchester Publishing Co., Inc.
P.O. Box 6640
Wayne, PA 19087-8640

Please add $1.75 for shipping and handling for the first book and $.50 for each book thereafter. NY, NYC, and PA residents, please add appropriate sales tax. No cash, stamps, or C.O.D.s. All orders shipped within 6 weeks via postal service book rate. Canadian orders require $2.00 extra postage and must be paid in U.S. dollars through a U.S. banking facility.

Name_____
Address_____
City_____State_____Zip_____
I have enclosed $_____ in payment for the checked book(s).
Payment <u>must</u> accompany all orders. ❑ Please send a free catalog.
        CHECK OUT OUR WEBSITE! www.dorchesterpub.com

Marriage By Design

Jill Metcalf

Her sign proclaims it as one of a number of services procurable through Miss Coady Blake, but there is nothing illicit in what it offers. All a prospective husband has to do is obtain a bride—Coady will take care of the wedding details. But it is difficult to purchase luxuries in the Yukon Territory, 1898, and Coady charges accordingly. After hearing several suspicions about Coady's business ethics, Northwest Mounted Police officer Stone MacGregor takes it upon himself to search out the crafty huckster. Instead, the inspector finds a willful beauty who thinks she knows the worth of every item—and he finds himself thinking that the proprietress herself is far beyond price.

___4553-2 $4.99 US/$5.99 CAN

Lair of the Wolf

Constance O'Banyon, Bobbi Smith, Evelyn Rogers,
Emily Carmichael, Martha Hix, Deana James,
Sharon Schulze, June Lund Shiplett, Elizabeth
Mayne, Debra Dier, and Madeline George

Be sure not to miss a single installment of Leisure Books's star-studded new serialized romance, *Lair of the Wolf*! Preserving the fun and suspense of the month-by-month installments, Leisure presents one chapter a month of the entire on-line story, including some brand new material the authors have added to their existing chapters. Watch for a new installment of *Lair of the Wolf* every month in the back of select Leisure books!

Previous Chapters of *Lair of the Wolf* can be found in:

**To order call our special toll-free number 1-800-481-9191
or VISIT OUR WEB SITE AT: www.dorchesterpub.com**